THE LONESOME YOUNG

THE LONESOME YOUNG

LUCY CONNORS

razOr
bill

An Imprint of Penguin Group (USA) LLC

A division of Penguin Young Readers Group
Published by the Penguin Group
Penguin Group (USA) LLC
345 Hudson Street
New York, New York 10014

USA / Canada / UK / Ireland / Australia / New Zealand / India / South Africa / China
Penguin.com
A Penguin Random House Company

ISBN: 978-1-59514-709-7

Printed in the United States of America

1 3 5 7 9 10 8 6 4 2

This book is for Connor and Lauren (aka Lucy), who taught me everything.

CHAPTER 1

VICTORIA

Sometimes even other people's failures can taste like shame in the back of your throat.

I'd learned this the hard way over the past few days, and now the residue of that shame tangled my thoughts into knots as I watched the sun go down and the miles go by on the drive from the Louisville airport to the ranch.

"How is it? Having the entire family living at the ranch full-time?" I turned to look at Pete, Gran's foreman, noticing lines on his deeply tanned face that I didn't think had been there only a few months before during our annual summer visit. "Is my dad trying to tell you how to do your job, as usual?"

The shrill sound of fire truck sirens—*lots* of them—cut off whatever he'd been about to say. Pete finished rounding the curve around the side of the hill and then slowed and pulled off the road. Now that the view opened up, we could see the orange glow of a huge blaze in the distance and a black cloud of smoke silhouetted in the fading light of dusk.

"What the hell?" Pete switched on his emergency flashers and picked up his phone. "What could be burning like that out there? There's nothing on that hill but trees. Burning trees look different than that."

Four fire trucks zoomed past us, sirens screaming and lights blazing, chasing each other to the scene. Pete was firing questions at whoever he'd called, so I took the opportunity to step out and stretch my legs, which had been cramped in first the coach-class airplane seat and then the old truck.

The stench hit me first. The smoke was acrid and, even at this distance, burned my eyes and nostrils when I took a breath. There was something different about it from the scent of an ordinary forest fire; I'd smelled plenty of those. This one was metallic, somehow, and almost acidic—reminding me more of chemistry class than of a bonfire.

The roar of approaching motorcycle engines, which had been muffled by the hillside, blew around the curve of the road. I was well away from the edge of the pavement, but I took an involuntary step back. The lead rider, his long, lean body bent forward as if urging the bike to even greater speed, turned his helmeted face toward me, and a shiver danced down my spine—either to warn or to entice me.

The group of riders raced past me, and my momentary sense of danger vanished with them, leaving me feeling off-kilter and my stomach hollow. I shook my head, impatient with my uncharacteristically fanciful thoughts.

"Victoria! We've got to go."

I turned back toward the truck. Pete was waving his hand, beckoning me to "get a move on," as he liked to say.

I hurried back to my seat and buckled up. "What's going on?"

"Big fire over at the old Lightwater place. We need to get over there fast." His face was drawn in grim lines, and I knew it must be bad.

We headed toward the distant flames, following the path left by the speeding bikers. For the first time since Dad had called to tell me I had to leave boarding school, I felt a glimmer of light cut through the darkness of my mood as the memory of that boy on the motorcycle, turning to stare at me from behind the faceless anonymity of his helmet's dark visor, scratched at the edges of my awareness all the way down the road.

CHAPTER 2
MICKEY

I headed for the fire, my mind on the girl. She'd stood there on the side of the road, staring at me as I passed by, her lips parted and her white-blond hair whipping around her face in the breeze. Beautiful. Elegant, even in jeans and a sweater.

And I had no idea who she was, even though the truck had been vaguely familiar. In Whitfield County, we recognized our neighbors by their cars and trucks even before we saw their faces. The faded blue Ford Focus with the dent next to the left tail light was the guy with the drinking problem who always hung out at the Irish pub just a little too long. The red and white Chevy muscle car was the guy who used to like roughing up his girlfriends. The mint-green Escape was the woman who'd fought back one day. Chevy muscle guy's nose didn't look nearly as good these days as it once had.

But the girl? My brain didn't associate her with any car, but for sure she'd looked like money. Elegant. Understated. Probably rich, in spite of the beat-up farm truck. Almost certainly unattainable, at least for somebody like me. The thought pissed me off, and I took the next curve too fast and nearly went into a skid, forcing me to focus on the road instead of thinking about the girl who'd probably only been stretching her legs on a trip to someplace—*any* place—far away from Whitfield County.

When we arrived, having broken all speed limits, the fire was still raging. My half brother Ethan and his friends scattered around me, and we all parked on the open area of ground clear over by the trees and well out of the way. The firefighters on the scene, a mix of professionals and volunteers, were wearing masks, and the deputies who worked for my dad were making sure nobody else got anywhere close to the source of the fire, an old trailer that had seen better days even before the explosion.

Ethan stood next to his bike, arms folded over his chest. A picture of casual indifference to anybody who hadn't been at a "welcome home from jail, Ethan" barbecue with him an hour earlier, or hadn't seen him and his lowlife buddies take off like bats out of hell when he'd gotten a phone call. He'd shouted "fire" but nothing else before roaring out of there. I'd followed him with some idea that the fire might be at his mom's place, racing him for the lead in an echo of years-gone-by sibling rivalry, until I'd seen the girl on the side of the road.

But this wasn't his mom's place, and old trailers didn't blow up like that without a reason.

It was a meth lab, in spite of the fact that he'd told me not two hours earlier that he was out of the business.

"Going straight, little brother," he'd told me.

What a load of horse shit, and I was a fool for even thinking about believing him.

I walked over to him, forcing my hands to unclench. Ethan was older than me, bigger than me, and surrounded by his cold-eyed thugs, all of them covered with tattoos and most of them convicted criminals. But starting a fistfight in full view of my dad, the sheriff, who was pulling up now in his official car, was a bad idea, no matter how much I was itching to do it.

"One quart of ether has the exploding power of a stick of dynamite," Ethan said as I approached. "Did you know that, little bro?"

His face was all harsh angles in the reflected light of the fire, but his voice was quiet. Almost serene. As if he'd been talking about the weather instead of one of the main ingredients for cooking meth.

"I figure there were maybe sixty quarts in there, give or take," he continued, still in that dreamy voice.

"Give or take? Give or *take*? Are you insane?" I was shouting, but I didn't care. "Somebody could have been hurt, Ethan. You promised Pa—"

Ethan's harsh bark of laughter shut me up. He was still staring at the fire, still not meeting my eyes.

"Somebody could have been hurt? Look closer, Mickey. They've pulled at least five bodies out of that fire," Ethan said.

My gut clenched. "Five? You—are they yours?"

But he was shaking his head. "This isn't my place. At least four of them aren't from around here, but there's a rumor that a local was in there. Somebody took advantage of my vacation behind bars to move into my territory. Now we're going to find out who."

He stood up fast as a rattlesnake strike and grabbed my arm. "You won't want to mention any of it to Pa."

I yanked my arm out of his grasp. "Don't tell me what to do. You did this, didn't you? To destroy the competition. Only out of jail since yesterday—"

"And I'm not about to go back. So shut your damn mouth. Or are you planning to put me in the hospital like you did those boys at school?"

He waited a beat, as if judging whether he'd unleashed something darker than irritation, but I'd learned my lesson. I kept a white-knuckled hold on my self-control these days, because if I didn't, I was afraid I'd go too far. If I let the rage loose, I might hurt somebody beyond reason or understanding. Beyond repair or redemption.

They might not end up in the hospital this time—they might end up dead.

"Don't push me, Ethan," I finally said, with what I thought was admirable calm. "You might not like what happens."

"Welcome to my life. I don't know how to do anything else *but* push, baby brother," he said.

When I didn't reply, he shrugged, dismissing me, and headed off toward Pa.

I followed him, wondering why it had taken Pa so long to get here, when he'd been at the same barbecue as the rest of us. The answer became clear when another man stepped out of the passenger side of Pa's sheriff car.

This guy was no deputy. He stood ramrod straight like he had a stick shoved up his ass, and the suit he wore fit him perfectly and probably cost more than my bike. Nobody held themselves like that around here unless they were ex-military or blue-blood horse folk

who'd had lessons on posture fed to them on silver spoons along with
everything else in their lives.

Ethan stopped dead so abruptly I almost ran into him. "What the
hell is old lady Whitfield's son doing here?"

"That's Richard Whitfield? Are you sure?"

Ethan shot me a scornful look. "I've met him before, when Pa
used to drag me along to county fairs and crap like that before you
came along."

I caught the unspoken accusation. Ethan and Jeb blamed my mom
for taking Pa away from their mom, even though Pa hadn't even met
my mother until a year after he'd divorced theirs. They also blamed
me for taking Pa's attention away from them and their sister, and there
was probably some truth to that. In the early days, Pa had just wanted
to get as far away from Anna Mae as possible, although he'd tried to
stay in touch with the boys and his daughter, my half sister, Caroline.

Caro'd gone a little wild in her teens, though, and now she was
a single mom to two sweet, angelic little girls who looked like their
fathers. Their two *different* fathers, neither of whom had been seen
or heard from after knocking Caro up. We didn't see much of Caro,
either, these days. A twinge of guilt ran through me at the thought.

Pa must feel like a failure sometimes. He was the sheriff, but his
daughter was an unwed mother living on welfare, and his two oldest
boys were running drugs with their mother. No wonder he'd lost his
mind when I'd had my . . . *incident* . . . at school.

My steps slowed down as we got close. My father was not happy
to see us, if the scowl on his face was any clue.

"What are you two doing here? This is a crime scene," he snapped.
"Out of here, now."

He moved his stocky body as if to block us from Whitfield, but it was too late. The man's gaze flashed from Pa to Ethan to me, burning holes of contempt along the way. He pointed at me.

"Another Rhodale in the litter, Sheriff? When is this one going to end up in jail?" His voice was like a whiplash.

Ethan laughed in his face. "Louisville not work out for you? We heard you had to tuck your tail between your legs and run home to live with your *mommy*."

I had a moment to wonder why Ethan would be so knowledgeable about what the Whitfields were up to before Pa knocked him back with a hard shove to the shoulder.

"Why don't you get out of here? Mr. Whitfield is here to identify the body of one of his employees, not to get in a pissing match," Pa said, shooting a hard stare at me when neither of the other two were looking.

That stare was the "Mickey, I know you're the youngest, but please do something with your brothers" expression he'd given me since we were all kids rolling around in the dirt together. I hadn't seen it since the *incident*, so he must have been desperate.

Somehow, with Ethan, any ordinary conversation or disagreement could instantly turn into a dangerous brawl. He'd sent my brother Jeb and me to the hospital at least a half-dozen times between us. Finally, when Ethan was sixteen and attending my eleventh birthday party, I'd lost my temper and broken his nose after he'd smashed my cake. It had taken several minutes for them to calm me down and peel me off him, but he'd been too big for me to really hurt him after I'd gotten in that one good shot to his nose.

My mom had cried, drunk half a bottle of wine, and made me write an essay on the evils of violence. Then she'd called Anna Mae and told her Ethan was banned from our house.

Peculiarly enough, that also had been the first time Ethan had ever shown me any respect. And now? Now people painted me with the same brush they painted him:

Just another violent, dangerous, worthless Rhodale, in spite of our father's job as sheriff. Some reputations were harder to shed than others. And, after all, I *had* put two guys in the hospital not so long ago.

But I'd do it again.

There was a shout from one of the firefighters.

"Ethan, Mick, you should go. Let my guys and the firefighters do their jobs," Pa said, moving subtly so he was standing between Whitfield and my hot-tempered brother.

"I've heard about you," Whitfield said, pointing now at Ethan. "Your stellar rise in the criminal underworld. Your time in jail."

"I think you've been watching too many *Godfather* movies, Mr. Whitfield," Pa said. "This is Kentucky. We don't have a criminal underworld. Ethan had a spot of trouble, but—"

Ethan viciously shook off my restraining hand. "Don't apologize for me, Pa, especially not to this asshole. What was his *employee* doing at a known drug-cooking location? Are you turning to crystal after you bombed in Louisville, Whitfield?"

Whitfield's face contorted and I thought he was going to throw the first punch, but after a few tense moments he exhaled and backed down.

"Maybe you should keep a better grip on this lowlife son of yours before he ends up right back in the cage he weaseled his way out of," he told Pa. "Now, are you going to direct me to the body or not?"

He stalked off toward the fire trucks, where, I now saw, a row of plastic-sheet-covered bodies had been laid out, waiting for the ambulances or the medical examiner to pick them up. I swallowed, hard, past the lump that was suddenly lodged in my throat.

Ethan snarled something under his breath, but he headed the other way, toward his bike.

"Five dead bodies, and I'm pretty sure one of them was Caleb Stuart," Pa said grimly, as he watched his eldest son stalk off. "The other four I've never seen before, although one of them was too badly burned for me to be sure. We'll have to wait for ID."

"Caleb? One of the—the bodies?" Caleb had been a year ahead of me in school. He was a good guy. We'd played football . . . and now he was gone?

"He went to work for the Whitfields this summer on the ranch," I said after a moment, making the connection.

"Yeah. I'm not sure if Richard Whitfield even notices the faces of the hired hands, but their foreman had gone to the airport or something, so I got stuck asking that asshole to come out," Pa said. "Now get out of here. Make sure your brother goes too, and takes his idiot friends with him. Tell him that if I see a single civilian on this scene after the next three minutes, I'll have one of my deputies arrest him for obstruction."

He turned and took a long look at the fire. "That trailer is probably going to blow again, and the explosion could kill even more people if we're not careful. Who the hell knows what kind of chemicals are in the back where the flames are just reaching now?"

Without another glance at me or at Ethan, Pa took off after Whitfield, leaving me yet again to be the go-between in his weak-willed attempts to control Ethan. The anger caught in my throat dropped down and took up residence in my gut.

I wanted off this merry-go-round.

We'd had months of peace while Ethan had been locked up, especially after I'd finished my required hours of community service. I hadn't minded the community part of the gig—I'd always gone with Mom to her various causes and events, anyway—but the service part had been cleaning up the side of the highway. Long hours out in the fierce Kentucky summer sunshine hadn't done much for my mood or my patience, which had been the opposite of what the asshole judge had planned.

"Maybe this will wear you out, so you can stay out of trouble," he'd said, peering at me over his half-glasses and sneering. I'd heard later that his sister's nephew had been best friends with one of the guys I'd hurt. Nepotism was alive and well in Whitfield County, and it had jumped up and kicked me in the nuts.

In spite of that, it had been a fairly peaceful summer. While Ethan had been in jail, Jeb had played at being the big boss, but he didn't have the brains or the balls to take Ethan's place, and everybody, including Jeb, knew it. Pa had never been able to stand up to Anna Mae, either, but she'd been unusually quiet with Ethan away. Plotting, probably, like a spider in her hillbilly lair.

I headed toward Ethan, picturing his reaction to being threatened with arrest by his own father. Maybe he'd freak out completely, and I'd get to punch him after all, so the evening wouldn't be a *total* loss.

Just then, a Chevy rolled up and parked. The truck from the side of the road, I realized. A man I didn't know jumped out and ran past me toward the fire, and when I turned back toward the truck, the girl who'd silently stared at me before was doing it again.

All thoughts of Ethan and arrests scattered, and I stared stupidly back at her.

Beautiful.

Shouts from behind me snapped me out of it, as the emergency personnel kicked it up another notch in their efforts. The fire roared like a wild, living thing and the heat was intense now, even this far away. If county legend was true and Rhodales all did end up in hell, this was a damn good preview.

And yet there *she* was—looking like a lost angel with her blond hair whipping in the hot wind.

My brother and his goons fired up their bikes, and I ran toward her.

"We have to get out of here. That trailer is going to blow," I told her. "Get back in your truck and follow me out."

I was three strides past her when I glanced back and realized she hadn't moved. I turned around.

"Did you hear me?"

Her cool gaze was like ice shivering over the exposed surfaces of my skin as she studied me. Judged me, maybe.

Dismissed me.

She shrugged—the slightest of movement of her shoulders. Suddenly I wanted to shout at her, or shake her, or throw her in the truck and drive away with her.

I did none of those things.

"My father is the sheriff, and he said anybody who isn't out of here inside of three minutes will be arrested," I said, as calmly as I could. "That was two minutes ago."

She raised one delicate eyebrow. "Then I guess he'll have to arrest me, because Pete just headed toward the fire and I'm not leaving him."

CHAPTER 3
VICTORIA

He was gorgeous: tall, dark, and definitely dangerous. The gleam in his bright blue eyes told me he wasn't used to anybody defying him, and his sculpted cheekbones and long, lean body told me that most girls wouldn't want to even try. But I wasn't about to leave Pete there, so he'd have to get over it Waves of dark hair brushed the collar of his leather jacket when he turned his head, and suddenly I knew that this was the boy from the motorcycle. I started to say something—what, exactly, I didn't know—but then he grabbed my arm, and I instinctively shoved him away, pushing against a shoulder that was all hard muscle. He immediately let go of my arm and took a half-step back.

"I'm sorry, I didn't mean to scare you, but it's not safe here. You need to leave, *now*," he said, glancing at the fire and then at me.

"I'll leave when Pete is ready to go," I said.

I started to turn away, and the jerk had the nerve to pick me up by the waist and start walking toward the truck. I pushed at the steel band of an arm that was still holding me pinned to his body, but it was like trying to move a thousand-pound horse who'd decided to lean on me while I brushed him.

"Let. Me. Go," I gritted out from between clenched teeth.

"That trailer might blow up again, and you could get hurt, and then some of these folks would have to waste time taking care of you instead of stopping the fire," he said, and I could hear the exasperation in his voice. "Is that what you want?"

When he put it like that, it sounded reasonable. "Fine. Let me down."

He stopped and put me down, but stood staring at me as if he didn't really believe I meant what I'd said. Suspicion or confusion drew his eyebrows together, and I caught myself wanting to reach up and touch his face. Smooth out the lines of distrust in his forehead. What was the matter with me?

I started running for the truck, just as a group of motorcycles revving nearby roared toward us. One veered close, and the boy grabbed my hand and pulled me behind him. He flipped his middle finger at the guy who'd swerved toward, rather than away from, us.

"I'd rather you keep your hands to yourself," I said, hating that I sounded like a disapproving schoolgirl.

He laughed and shook his head and pointed to my truck. "After you, Princess."

I glanced over at the fire. "But Pete—"

"Can catch a ride when the fire is out. Let's go."

I finally nodded and ran for the truck and climbed in, and jumped a little in surprise when he appeared behind me and shut my door for me. I turned the key Pete had left hanging, and the truck fired to growling life.

"I don't even know your name," I said stupidly through the open window.

He grinned, and something rusty stuttered in my chest as the simple act of smiling took his face from stern to beautiful. I caught the gasp in my throat before it escaped, so it turned into a coughing fit, instead.

No doubt I was impressing him with my smoothness more and more every second.

I resisted the urge to pound my face on the steering wheel and instead turned to look in the rearview mirror so I could back up and get the heck out of there.

He stopped me with a hand on my arm, this time gently, as if afraid I'd bolt again. I stared down at his strong tanned fingers, stark against my too-pale skin.

"My name is Mickey Rhodale."

"Victoria Whitfield. It's nice to meet you," I said politely and completely inappropriately for the occasion, as years of conditioning rose up inside me to turn etiquette into farce, yet again. In Connecticut I'd once said "Bless you" to an indie rocker who'd just slammed too much cocaine up his nose, and I'd been famous around school for it for months.

But Mickey didn't laugh. Instead, he studied my face as if it held the answer to a question he needed to ask.

"It's nice to meet you, too, Victoria. Now get your pretty ass moving."

Furious once again, I gunned the gas and got out of there.

✷ ✷ ✷

By the time I pulled up the long, curving driveway to Gran's house—
which I guess was my house now, too—all thoughts of mysterious hot
guys scattered, because the sheriff department car parked in the driveway had its lights flashing and a deputy in the driver's seat.

I left the keys in the ignition and hit the door running. What
had Melinda done this time? The front of the house was empty, but I
heard voices coming from the room Gran called her parlor, and I ran
across the foyer to find out what was going on.

Gran, Mom, Melinda, and Buddy were all grouped on and around
the overly formal furniture, and their reactions ranged from surprise to
joy to disappointment, depending on the face and who was wearing it.

Buddy hurled his compact body at me and nearly knocked me flat
on my butt.

"You're home, Vivi! I missed you every day, and Mom won't let
me go out to the horses on my own, and Melinda is always grouchy,
and so is Dad, but I beat the Elite Four at Pokémon Black on my Nin-
tendo DS!" he rattled off in one long breathless sentence.

My sister walked slowly and carefully across the room to hug me.
Her eyes were glassy and unfocused.

"Hello, Victoria. We're having a tough night around here," she
said, enunciating very carefully in that way she had when she was high
or drunk. As if saying, "No. I'm. Not. Drunk," very precisely would
somehow convert wishful thinking—or defiant denial—into fact. I
hugged her warily. Some things hadn't changed.

"Call your sister Victoria, Timothy. We don't use nicknames," my
mother chided my brother, who'd only and always been called Buddy
by everyone else but her.

Buddy rolled his eyes up at me, careful that she wouldn't see. "Do you want some lemonade? Mrs. Kennedy makes it fresh. I'll get you some," he said as he escaped the room.

Mom held out her arms and, after a barely noticeable (I hoped) moment of hesitation, I walked over and hugged her. She'd gotten even thinner since August, but I only had a moment to worry about whether or not she'd been eating before Gran was there, gently nudging Mom to one side and throwing her arms around me.

"I missed you so much, girl," she said fiercely, and probably nobody but me noticed the shine in her eyes. "What took you so long? I thought your flight got in at four."

I started to explain about the fire, and Pete, but before I could get to the part about the amazingly bossy Mickey Rhodale, the tension in the room snaked its way past my exhaustion into my consciousness.

"What is it? What's going on? Why is there a cop out front in the sheriff's car?"

There was a confusion of voices telling me bits and pieces and rumors and truth. It took me a few minutes to get the story straight, especially because it seemed they were trying to hide what we were talking about from my little brother, who'd come back with a slightly sticky cup of lemonade for me.

The gist was that Caleb, one of our new ranch hands, whom I'd met last summer and remembered as a nice guy with tons of freckles and a big smile, might be a casualty of the same fire I'd been reluctant to leave. My dad had gone with the sheriff to see if he could identify the body, leaving a deputy here, which explained the cop and the car out front. In fact, Dad must have even been there when I was, and we just hadn't seen each other in the confusion, which wasn't surprising with all of those fire trucks and so many people running around.

The *body*.

I started to shiver, and a bone-deep chill settled into me, reminding me that I hadn't eaten since breakfast or slept much in days. Gran noticed. She scooped up a quilt from its cherrywood stand and wrapped it around my shoulders, urging me to sit down. Even Mom stepped up, heading to the kitchen to make tea and sandwiches—which was a wasted effort, since nobody seemed to be able to eat. And then we sat, waiting for more news about the fire.

Any news. News about Caleb, or why the sheriff wanted Dad, or whether anybody else was hurt . . . the room was shadowed by the threat of a tragedy we didn't yet know how to define.

Waiting for Dad or Pete to call. Minutes, quarter hours, and then an hour counted off on the incongruously curlicued art deco clock on the mantelpiece, and still we waited without word.

Finally, as much out of a desire to avoid the sight of Melinda's strained face as from exhaustion, I leaned my head back on the couch and closed my eyes. Unfortunately, the scene with Mickey immediately started to play itself out in my memory.

Now get your pretty ass moving.

Who *talked* like that? Especially to someone he'd only met a few minutes before?

"Do you want to play my game with me?"

Buddy, sprawled on the floor playing his video game, glanced up at me hopefully and then snuck a glance at the clock and my mother, clearly expecting her to send him to bed any minute. His mutinous expression said it all: Nine-year-old kids *never* got to have fun in this family.

I almost smiled, but the weight of the situation and the stern faces of past generations of Whitfields, staring disapprovingly down at me from their gilt-framed glory on the walls, quickly flattened the urge.

"Sure," I said, hoping to forestall the bedtime argument.

I sat down on the floor with him, and Buddy taught me the seriously complicated rules of one of his video games, while Melinda paced the room like a caged wild thing. My mother watched my sister stonily, pale with either nerves or rage. It was usually hard to tell with Mom.

"Ha!" Buddy grinned up at me and pointed to the screen. "You just got killed by the eighth-level wizard's apprentice, Gwork."

I pretended to be horrified. "You're the dork. I'm not a dork."

Buddy laughed. "Not *dork*. Gwork."

"Now it's definitely bedtime," my mother announced, crossing her arms and tapping her foot.

I felt an unwelcome flutter of familiarity at the gesture that had once cajoled and threatened my own nine-year-old self into bed. Buddy apparently knew enough not to argue, so he hugged me, hugged Gran, and trudged up the stairs toward his room.

"Brush your teeth," Mom called up after him, and he waved one hand in acknowledgment, a forlorn little figure marching to his certain doom.

Mom and I exchanged a grin at his resolute martyrdom, but it wasn't until she put her "perfect Mrs. Whitfield" mask on afterward that I even realized it. Her first unrehearsed smile in ages, probably, and I'd nearly missed it.

Melinda, oblivious to anything but whatever inner torment was clearly hurting her so much, whirled around and tripped over Gran's embroidered footstool. She nearly fell but managed to right herself at the last minute, while I watched her with a weirdly peculiar sensation of embarrassment and guilty contempt, as if I were a spectator at a really terrible play.

Mom finally lost it. She shot up out of her chair like a horse from the starting gate. "Sit down, Melinda. Just sit *down*, already. Haven't we got enough to deal with right now? Poor Calvin—"

"Caleb," my sister corrected, biting off the word. "You don't even know his *name*?"

Buddy appeared in the doorway, wearing his blue-and-white striped pajamas and looking freshly washed. He made a face at my mom before she could say anything.

"Yes, I brushed my teeth." Then he ran over and hugged me again.

"I missed you, Victoria," he whispered in my ear. "Nobody else makes them stop *fighting* all the time. I miss my friends from the city, too," he said, raising his voice, "but Gran says we can get a dog."

"I missed you, too, sweetie. I'm glad to be—"

"No pets in the house," my mother interrupted. "I know I've said that at least a hundred times. I have allergies. It's bad enough I have to live around all these horses. We're not bringing an animal inside the house, too."

Gran and I traded a glance over Buddy's head. Buddy ignored Mom, or at least didn't answer, instead running back out of the room. Seconds later, we heard his feet thumping up the stairs. A hot spike of guilt stabbed at me. I'd left him in the middle of Mom and Melinda's drama. Not that I'd had much choice. Mom was a proud alumna of the same boarding school she'd shipped me and, briefly, Melinda off to. I wondered how hard she was taking it now that neither of us had made it to the end.

She'd certainly become even more shrill since August, when I'd left for school. Life at our house had been really stressful all summer— we'd finally started to realize how far under Dad had gone with his business. For some stupid reason, though, he'd kept up the pretense that everything would be okay for long enough to send me off to school again. As he always said, the neighbors saw your outside, not your inside, and they judged you by it. So the surfaces in our family were as reflective as mirrors—hard, shiny, and with no depth at all.

"I didn't want you to have to leave that school you love so much," he'd said when he'd finally made the phone call that there was no more money for tuition.

Rick, my older brother, was already at college, but there was no talk of bringing him home. To be fair, his football scholarship paid for almost everything, but even if it hadn't, Dad would have found a way to keep him there. Rick was the heir apparent, of course. What Rick wanted, Rick got.

The truth was that I wouldn't really miss Connecticut; I preferred Kentucky autumns and winters. But I'd miss my friends. We'd promised to keep in touch, but Facebook and Skype were never quite the same as dropping into each other's rooms at any hour of the day or night. Maybe at least Simone and I would keep the promises we'd made to stay in touch; we'd been roommates for two years, after all.

Maybe.

Now I'd be spending my junior and senior years at Clark High School, home of the Clark County Wildcats.

Go, team.

"It *is* still my house, Priscilla," Gran said dryly, showing the hint of steel that came from growing up dirt poor and helping build a racing empire with my grandfather from two horses and a dream. "If I decide to get a dog, I'm sure you can take an allergy pill once in a while or something."

"Why are we talking about dogs when Caleb might be dead? None of you have one shred of human decency," Melinda said, and now she was crying, huddled around the ancient pillow that told us that *God Is the Light* in nine-year-old Gran's shaky embroidery.

"Hey. Calm down. Caleb might still be alive. He's probably still alive," I said.

"Lord willing, and the creek don't rise," Gran muttered. Her early years growing up in a very non-Whitfield family showed up at times of stress through old sayings and down-home cooking. Any minute now she'd be jumping up to make green bean casserole.

I crossed the room and put my arm around my sister's shoulder. At eighteen, she was a year older than me, but Melinda was fragile. I'd sometimes had to play the big-sister role, protecting her from my parents, bullies at school, and—pretty much—life itself.

Life and her own screwups, which usually involved really bad choices in guys. Caleb had just graduated from high school, and he was cute in that fresh-scrubbed, hard-muscled, farm-boy way. Even though I didn't want to make the connection between Caleb's being missing and Melinda's frenzied pacing, my relentless brain pushed it forward.

I waited to ask until Gran and Mom were arguing loudly about the dog.

"Were you involved with Caleb?" I whispered. I really didn't want to know the answer, but it felt like something I *should* know, in order to protect her from this. Whatever *this* was.

"He's my boyfriend," she whispered, grabbing my arm. "This is all my fault. If Caleb's dead, I killed him."

Somehow I managed to get Melinda upstairs to her room before she had a complete meltdown. She'd taken over the room I usually stayed in when we visited Gran's, the one with the view of the barn, but I didn't mind. I'd been at boarding school, after all, so it was only fair. Melinda's attempt at boarding school had lasted three weeks before they'd expelled her for underage drinking and fired the young assistant professor she'd been trying—fairly successfully—to seduce. She'd spent the past three years battling the addiction and depression that my parents both pretended she didn't have, so, even though she was eighteen, she was a junior like me. When she bothered to go to school at all.

I looked around the green and white ruffled decor and realized I'd outgrown the room, anyway. Melinda was more the ruffles type. She sank onto the bed and fought back tears. I hurriedly shut and locked her door and then grabbed a box of tissues, sat down next to her, and pulled her too-thin body into a hug. Although it had only been a couple of months, she felt unfamiliar, as if a sharp-edged stranger had taken her place, and the stench of alcohol was pretty obvious now that I was close enough to smell her. In spite of the camouflage of the open tin of breath mints I saw on her bedside table.

I was worried. Melinda had never gone along with the "Whitfields don't show emotion" crap, but she'd never been one for hysterics, either. Acid roiled around in my stomach.

"Honey, you have to stop. Melinda, honey, please," I said coaxingly.

I patted her back and then handed her more tissues, since I didn't really know how else to help. Discarded tissues littered the floor like abandoned good intentions, and I swallowed the accusations trying to escape my throat. Saying "but you promised" wasn't a good idea and—even worse—it sounded like something my mother would say.

Even though Melinda *had* promised.

She'd promised me that it would be different here. *She'd* be different. She'd said that I wouldn't have to worry about her in "Hicksville."

She would be *better*, away from the lure of Louisville's bright and shiny parties and drinks and drugs, and the bright and shiny people whose glittery surfaces reflected back all the lying promises that Melinda whispered to herself in the dark.

Saner. Safer.

Sober.

But, clearly, she was none of those things.

"Tell me," I said softly, but a small, horrible part of me really wanted to shake her until her teeth rattled. "You can't tell me something like 'I killed Caleb' without explaining."

She finally lifted her head from the pillow and looked at me. Her eyes were blank and so lifeless that it scared me.

"We're . . . dating. Sort of. You know," she said, her voice raspy from sobbing.

I nodded. I did know. There was no way Richard and Priscilla Whitfield would have let their daughter date a ranch hand, so what Melinda probably meant was that they'd been screwing around in the barn.

"He—I—we wanted to get high," she said, stumbling over her words. "He said he knew a place where they had quality weed, and he'd run out and be right back. Maybe he's okay, though. Maybe the sheriff was wrong, and he wasn't anywhere near that fire."

"Maybe," I said, wondering if she could hear the lie in my voice.

Over the summer, before he'd let me borrow the truck to do errands, Pete had warned me about the dangers of getting anywhere near certain parts of Whitfield County, which were known to be the central stomping grounds of a busy meth ring. I didn't have to be a chemistry whiz to know the basics about the drug that was destroying the state. The places where they created meth—"cooked" it—were explosions waiting to happen, because the ingredients were like toxic sludge.

For some reason, there were plenty of people who couldn't wait to put this deadly crap in their bodies. I'd never understood it, but then again, I'd never been forced to live with addiction issues like Melinda had. The immediate problem wasn't the national drug crisis though, but that if my sister's boyfriend had died in a meth explosion because he went to get pot for her, I wasn't sure she'd survive living with that knowledge.

"Let's wait until we get the facts, okay?"

I tucked her into bed, turned off her bedside lamp, and sat with her, holding her trembling hand, until she fell into an exhausted sleep. She'd lost more weight while I was gone, and a surge of anger swept through me, most of it aimed at my "you can never be too thin or too rich" mother. Maybe if she'd spent more time trying to be a mom and less time pretending none of us existed, she might have noticed that her eldest daughter was turning into a wraith. Of course, my dad was a self-absorbed jerk who ignored Melinda's problems just as much as Mom did, so there was enough blame to go around.

I'd abandoned her, too—I left for school without a second thought for how she'd survive.

Guilt and remorse joined anger and worry in the giant spinning hamster wheel of my brain, but I didn't even have the energy to defend myself from myself.

A little while later, a splash of light on the window from head-lights turning onto our driveway snapped me out of the half-doze I'd been falling into in spite of the situation. I hadn't slept well for the past few days, since Dad's phone call and the chaos of withdrawing and packing, and it was all finally catching up to me in the dark, quiet room.

I stood up, only to find Melinda staring at me with wide, terrified eyes.

"Will you find out what happened? If it really is . . . was . . ." Her voice trailed off, and I squeezed her hand in what I hoped was reassurance.

How do you comfort your sister when her boyfriend might be dead, and she believes it's her fault? Nothing in any of my advanced placement classes had prepared me for this.

"I'll find out, and then I'll be right back," I told her.

With one of Mom's sleeping pills, I promised myself. One way or the other, Melinda was going to need it.

I tucked the blanket more snugly around her thin shoulders and then went down to face the music. When I got to the door, Melinda called my name. The moonlight slanting in through the window highlighted the silvery tracks of the dried tears gleaming on her pale cheeks, and again I was struck by how wraithlike she'd become.

"Welcome home, baby sister."

CHAPTER 4
MICKEY

I parked my bike in the pothole-infested lot—and then thought about turning right back around and leaving. The last place I wanted to be was school, where nobody would want to talk about anything but yesterday's fire, but since escaping this rat hole of a town was high on my priority list, earning good enough grades to get into college was part of the plan. I played football, but I wasn't a superstar, so chances of a scholarship there were slim, and I had no intention of becoming just another uneducated, drunken, no-good Rhodale, with or without criminal tendencies. Having a teacher for a mom gave me some hope, but if anybody had been fool enough to make a scrapbook of my family tree, they'd see that the Rhodale genes always seemed to drown out whatever they mixed with.

Every Rhodale male had black hair, blue eyes, and a nose for trouble, no matter which side of the law he ended up on. One of my great-uncles had been a kingpin during Prohibition, running moonshine so good that people claimed Al Capone himself had special ordered it for his own table. Chicago was far enough from Kentucky that the story was probably pure bull, but rumor turned petty crooks into godlike myths in a place where there wasn't much hope for climbing out of poverty in any legal way.

On the other side of the law, another ancestor had been a Pinkerton man, riding trains to protect the railroad's payroll. His badge and gun were in a glass case at the Whitfield County Historical Museum, labeled with a neatly printed card that explained how Frank Rhodale of the National Pinkerton Detective Agency had been instrumental in the pursuit and capture of Jesse James and his gang. Again, probably overinflated bull, at least about the James Gang, but the badge was real enough. Like most legends, there was just enough truth in it to pay for a wagonload of maybe.

When Ethan got drunk enough, he liked to tell people that he would have been riding *with* Jesse James, not against him, and my brother Jeb was just gullible enough to go along with whatever Ethan said. Jeb was two years younger than Ethan and half as smart; he'd inherited both my dad's leanings toward drunkenness and Anna Mae's greed, which made for a really bad combination in a wannabe criminal. I'd heard whispers that it had been something Jeb had done (or failed to do) that had sent Ethan to jail, but the two of them had seemed amicable enough at the barbecue yesterday.

Then again, I'd seen Ethan smile and shake Junior Koslowski's hand just before he broke Junior's nose, so I didn't really believe Jeb was off the hook for whatever it was he'd done. I didn't know what it was, and I didn't want to know, not that anybody at this petri dish of a high school would believe it. Most of them probably figured I was involved. When Ethan went to jail, one of the senior girls had asked me in a breathless voice if I'd been the "wheel man."

She was a moron, but the gossip and speculation were at least partly my fault.

My brothers' reputations had always washed over me like an overflowing septic tank, and at first I'd been young and ignorant enough to like it. Nobody messed with a Rhodale boy, for fear of Ethan, and I'd swaggered through elementary school and junior high like a preening rooster until I'd discovered the dark side of borrowed infamy.

Maybe nobody messed with a Rhodale boy, but nobody let their daughters date a Rhodale boy, either. Nobody wanted their kids to be friends with a Rhodale. Parents who'd been afraid that Ethan would get riled up over some slight—whether actual or only in his overactive, quick-to-take-offense imagination—didn't even want their boys to play ball with me. Not that I could blame them after he'd gone after my Little League coach with a bat for yelling at me.

I'd tackled Ethan before he'd done any real damage except to put a dent in the batting cage, but I'd been banned from the league for life after that. Not a big deal, maybe, unless you were a ten-year-old kid who lived in a town where baseball was one of the only things to do all summer.

In a twisted kind of way, a lot of what he'd done had been because he'd been so protective of me. Of all of us, especially Caroline, even before . . . well. Before the incident. Not the drugs, but some of the violent stuff for sure stemmed from wanting to protect us. But nobody in town saw it that way, and everybody was always quick to think the worst of me, by association.

"Trouble always breeds true," they'd said.

"The Rhodale streak will show up in him sooner or later," they'd said.

My mother had told me to ignore them, but instead I'd proved them all right when I turned sixteen, saw two boys roughing up my half sister, and lost my mind.

"Mickey!" My buddy Derek angled his bicycle into the rack, but didn't lock it. It was a real POS and nobody would bother to steal it. Derek was one of the few kids whose parents weren't afraid of Ethan or of me—probably because they were preachers and believed God loves everybody. Or maybe because they didn't actually know who Ethan was or what I had done; they weren't exactly the type of folks to gossip. I'd never brought it up with them, so I wasn't sure which was true. I swung my leg over to dismount the Harley and headed toward him.

"I heard about the fire. Holy crap, was it really Caleb? I thought he was working for old lady Whitfield. What was he doing hanging out at a meth lab? Was he a drug dealer?" Derek's questions tumbled out so fast that he was making my brain hurt. He looked around and then lowered his voice.

"Was Ethan involved? Doesn't look good, with him just getting out of the big house."

I raised an eyebrow. "The big house? Have you been watching too much Netflix again?"

He punched me in the shoulder, and I pretended it hurt. When your best friend was short and skinny, sometimes it was good to make him feel like he was bigger than he really was. Especially when he'd been the only one from high school to visit me in juvie.

"Everybody's going to be talking about it," he continued, his smile fading. "If it was Caleb, the student council will need to arrange some kind of memorial service here at the school. He only graduated a few months ago."

Derek was on the student council. Also the yearbook staff, the school paper, and the wrestling team. He was a demon in his weight class.

"It was Caleb," I confirmed gruffly. Pa hadn't made it home till the middle of the night, but I'd still been awake long enough to get the details. When he'd headed for the bourbon, I'd headed for bed, not in the mood for another drunken round of "where did I go wrong."

The few hours of sleep I had managed to get had been restless. Over and over, I'd dreamed that Victoria had driven that old truck directly into the fire, instead of away from it. Every time I woke up, heart racing, my room seemed to echo to the sound of her screams.

The two cups of coffee I'd poured down my throat probably would be just enough to get me through to lunchtime.

"Whoa. *Whoa.* Who is that?" Derek's whistle cut through my glum mood, and I looked up to see a battered pickup truck with a WHITFIELD HORSES logo on the door pull into a parking space in the middle row, only a few spaces down from my bike. I shrugged and acted like I wasn't looking.

"Melinda Whitfield, probably. She's been going to school here since the beginning of the year. I'd have expected you to have noticed that, Mr. School Paper."

Derek rolled his eyes. "Melinda doesn't drive. She always catches a ride with somebody. Honestly, as spacey as she acts, she probably doesn't know how to drive. No, my friend, this is somebody else, and she's *hot.*"

He wasn't kidding. Victoria was gorgeous, yeah, but there was something else there that had caught at my imagination. A sense of sadness in her eyes. I hadn't been able to get the way she'd stood up to me out of my mind, either. She'd intrigued me, and I hadn't felt that sensation in a really long time.

Derek and I, and half the students in the damn high school, stopped and stared at her as she climbed out of the truck. Her silky blond hair swept down past her shoulders in a loose wave, and when she glanced my way I could see that her eyes were a startling green, which I hadn't been able to tell the night before in the fire-bright dark.

Her legs were a mile and a half long, and her curves under her hot little green dress were making me itch to walk over and throw my jacket over her, so none of the other guys currently checking her out could see the hint of cleavage on display. She looked elegant and untouchable, and I had the same feeling of hopelessness that I'd had driving by her on the road even before I'd known who she was.

A Whitfield. One of *them*. Horse folk. The family was the richest around. They employed a lot of people in town, and they were the people the whole damned county was named after. I might as well go after a *real* princess for all the chance I'd have at Victoria Whitfield.

She glanced around again, and when her gaze tangled with mine, she stumbled and then caught herself. Her cheeks blazed hot pink, and I grinned, unable to help myself. I didn't know many girls over the age of twelve who still blushed, especially on my side of the county.

Before I could stop myself, I was crossing the parking lot and heading straight for her.

She planted her feet, raised her chin, and stood her ground, unafraid of me, unlike every other person in the entire school except for Derek. *That* wouldn't last. By lunchtime, the gossips would have filled her in on the Rhodale myth—fact and fiction all jumbled together and presented as truth—and Victoria would stay far, far away from me.

My stomach twisted in a hard, angry knot at the realization. "Why are you here?"

She met my eyes coolly. "I'm registering for school. Why are *you* here?"

"I'm wondering that myself," I muttered. "I guess I just wanted to say hi before . . ."

"Before?" She tilted her head, gazing up at me, and her eyes flashed like emeralds in the morning sun. I caught myself moving closer to her, because she apparently was not only turning me into a damn poet, thinking about her jewel-like eyes, but she had actual magnetic powers.

Looking around, I noticed that every member of the Wildcat football team seemed to be converging on us, eyes glued to Victoria, so maybe I wasn't too far off on the magnetic powers.

Assholes.

"You should go," I said, clumsy and awkward and everything I usually wasn't, because something about this girl got to me in places she had no business reaching.

But she didn't leave. Instead, she started laughing. "Seriously? Is that what you do, hang around places waiting to tell people to leave?"

I could feel my face heat up, and I turned my head to avoid her, only to catch sight of Derek staring at me with his jaw hanging down somewhere around his ankles.

Damn.

"Or is it only me you're always trying to get rid of?" She tilted her head and smiled, equal parts beauty and defiance, and a fierce sense of longing swept through me. Longing that she would never find out about the real me. The monstrous me. The Rhodale who could beat two people nearly to death and—worse—not feel even a twinge of remorse.

"Most people are afraid of me," I blurted out like a complete moron.

"I'm not afraid of you, Mickey, but maybe you could work on your manners," she said lightly, but a finely controlled quiver of tension rolled across her shoulders. "This is the high school. I'm here to register. No fires or potential arrests or any other reason why I should leave this time, right?"

"Guess not," I returned. "So where are you headed? Need directions?"

She bit her lip; for a second I saw a hint of vulnerability beneath the self-assured surface. "I have to go to the office because my parents are too *busy* to bother with mundane things like finishing the registration process for their daughter for school," she said, and I heard a tinge of bitterness.

"Well, allow me to lead the way," I said. I took off, and she followed me—I felt her nearness pulling against my back. Again with the magnetic powers. If Victoria Whitfield didn't like me, that was for the best, right? She was out of my league. I should stay away, but I knew even as I thought it that I wouldn't.

I stopped outside the school office.

She paused with one hand on the door, lowered her head and took a long, deep breath, and then she turned to face me. "I'm sorry. I do appreciate you looking out for me last night, and this isn't how I wanted my first day to go. Maybe we could start over?"

I was too mesmerized by her green eyes to come up with any kind of coherent response. I stuck out my hand instead, and she shook it.

"Hi, I'm Victoria Whitfield. It's nice to meet you, Mickey Rhodale."

With that, she opened the door and slipped inside, leaving me speechless and staring after her like a fool.

Suddenly, for the first time in a very long time, I was glad to be at school.

CHAPTER 5
VICTORIA

Clark High wasn't hell. It was hell's trashy reality TV show.

I looked around the hallway after leaving the school office, schedule in hand, and expected to see Honey Boo Boo's cousin show up any minute. I was having an extreme case of culture shock, or culture jet lag, or something. My knees, already shaky from the first-day-of-school factor, had wobbled a little more after talking to Mickey. He was just so unbelievably gorgeous, in a broody, moody, dangerous way I'd never run into during my very sheltered time at Ashford-Hutchinson Academy. We'd had boys over for dances, sure, but they'd been from the nearest prep school and not one of them—ever—had been even a fraction as enticing and mysterious as Mickey Rhodale.

None of them had stood around parking lots trying to scare girls, either.

A perky redhead wearing jeans and a Wildcats T-shirt intercepted me in the hallway and took the schedule right out of my hand. She had a tan that was a little too dark and a little too orange to be natural, and her hair needed its own zip code, but her eyes were friendly, and I liked her on sight.

"I thought so. We have English together. Come on, you can walk with me," she said, flashing a warm smile. "I'm Denise. You can like me even though I'm a cheerleader, or maybe because I'm a cheerleader, because this is Small Town, USA, and high school football is king."

I blinked at this outpouring of words, which had the opposite effect of what she'd probably intended, because my shyness kicked in and my tongue got tangled up in my mouth. "Um, hi. I'm—"

"Victoria Whitfield. Yeah, I know. The whole county is kind of named after you." She rolled her eyes, but not in a mocking way. More like *duh*. "And you were talking to Mick Rhodale, in spite of everything!"

She stopped propelling me along the hallway by sheer force of personality and sucked in a breath. "Oh, no! It wasn't *because* of everything, was it? I'm just saying that if you have some weird kind of thing for violent guys, you need to move on, don't you think?"

It took me a second to process this, but by then she'd dragged me to English, and the ultimate cruel teacher sport of "stand at the front of the room and tell us about yourself, New Girl" blasted everything else out of my head.

During second period, French III, while Madame Thierry showed us a PowerPoint presentation of her summer trip to Paris, complete with soundtrack ("La Vie en Rose"), Denise filled me in on who was who in class, which guys were available, and why it would be dangerous to have anything to do with Mickey or any of the Rhodale boys. She was all too clear on details. Mickey's older brother Ethan evidently ranked somewhere between Satan and Osama bin Laden on the evil scale; Jeb, the middle boy, was stupid and horny, or maybe stupidly horny; and Mickey was a train wreck.

"He jumped five guys for no reason, I heard, and put four of them into the hospital," she whispered. "Or was it all five? I think one of them got away."

I turned my head to stare at her. The Mickey who'd picked me up last night was certainly strong enough to kick ass in a fight. But five guys? For no reason?

It didn't track.

By third period, and the third "Whitfield like the *county* Whitfield?" question, I was able to stand there with a straight face and say "no relation."

This earned me a laugh and maybe a little goodwill from the rest of the class, most of whom were now thoroughly sick of hearing me mutter a few basic facts about myself. It also earned me a slow clap from the direction of the doorway, where Mickey stood, leaning against the wall.

"Take your seat, Mr. Rhodale," Mr. Gerard said, waving toward the only empty seat in the room.

The seat next to mine.

Naturally.

A slow, sexy grin spread across Mickey's face as he sat down, sprawled his long legs out in the aisle, and stared up at me. "You were saying?"

My cheeks caught fire, and I stared right back at him, completely unable to remember what I'd been saying before he'd walked in.

"You were telling the *history* teacher that your family isn't related to the Whitfields who founded the county, I think," he drawled, and I wanted to punch him right in the middle of his perfectly straight nose.

"That's enough from you, Mr. Rhodale," Mr. Gerard said. "If you recall my class from last year, Miss Whitfield isn't the only one in this classroom whose family dates back to Kentucky statehood in 1792 and even prior to that, when we were still part of the great state of Virginia."

I glanced over at the teacher and noticed the University of Virginia flag hanging behind his desk. Ah. College loyalty was evidently as much of a cult in Virginia as it was in Kentucky. I'd seen friends almost come to blows and relationships die in shouting matches over basketball games between the University of Louisville and the University of Kentucky. When I looked back out at the class, I saw that Mickey was still watching me, and I could swear his grin was mocking me.

"You can return to your seat, Miss Whitfield," Mr. Gerard said. A trace of bitterness swept through me at the thought that Gran could have easily paid my boarding school tuition, but she'd flatly refused.

"Clark High School was good enough for me, and good enough for your father," she'd said. "I don't hold with this idea of shipping our kids off for other people to raise during the tumultuous teen years. God knows we don't want you to end up like your mother."

That had been a low blow, but true enough. Mom had gone into Ashford-Hutchinson in her freshman year as a normal kid, and she'd come out carrying only eighty-five pounds on her five feet, four inch frame. Yet she still held it up as the best school on the planet. But even she couldn't fight the combined power of my father, my grandmother, and the inescapable fact of her empty checkbook and maxed-out credit cards. And that, as they say, had been that. I was out of the school where I'd spent the last two years and knew who people were and how things worked, and into a school where the only boy I'd met so far had called my ass pretty and picked me up and carried me away from danger, like my own personal superhero.

And who, according to Denise, was a very violent drug dealer. Or at least the brother of one.

The teacher pointed at Mickey with his pen. "Mr. Rhodale, since you were so kind as to bring up Whitfield County history, you will do your midyear project on the history of your relative the Pinkerton man."

The pen swerved to aim its evil at me. "Miss Whitfield, you will take on the history of the Derby."

I relaxed. I'd been raised on the Kentucky Derby. This, at least, should be easy. I nodded, and he moved on to tell Denise that she'd be learning all about the history, good and bad, of the tobacco plant.

"I've never been to the Derby," Mickey said quietly, and his deep, husky voice caused a delicious shiver to race down my spine. Why was I reacting like this to him?

Okay, so yes, he was the hottest guy I'd ever seen and he'd carried me away from what clearly had been an explosion waiting to happen. There was *that*.

"How can you be from Kentucky and never have gone to the Derby?" I blurted it out in a whisper, mostly from a frantic need to say *something*.

"Are you kidding? Or are you really such a pampered princess that you wouldn't know the answer to that?" His voice had an edge to it, and I glanced over to see that his features had hardened. "The Derby experience isn't exactly cheap. Some of us have to save money for college."

"I don't . . . I didn't mean . . . It's just been part of my life forever," I said, realizing I'd put my foot in my mouth again. "You make me nervous."

He smiled, and the memory of the way his muscular body had felt against mine when he picked me up flashed into my mind. I had to clench my teeth against the shiver.

"You make me nervous too, Princess," he said, but his smile faded as he said it as if he, like me, had realized how much he'd given away with the admission. "And I know better than this."

"Better than what?"

But Gerard shot a dirty look our way, and I blushed and stared down at my desk. I'd never been on the receiving end of a teacher's annoyance before. I had the sudden, startled realization that perhaps more than my geography had changed; Whitfield County Victoria was morphing into a very different person than the Victoria I'd been before. Had the mere proximity of the town bad boy caused a ripple effect on my personality?

I shook off the absurd thought, but the tingle that raced down my spine told me that some part of me might just believe it.

During the rest of the class, while Mr. Gerard handed out project assignments and droned on and on, Mickey didn't try to talk to me again. When the bell rang, I was up out of my seat and on my way to find calculus before he could follow me.

Not that he even tried.

I couldn't figure out if the realization made me disappointed or relieved.

CHAPTER 6
MICKEY

Hypocrisy was always a featured side dish at the United Methodist Women's after-church potluck. The very people who gossiped with gleeful viciousness Monday through Saturday pretended that they gave a shit about their targeted victims on Sunday.

"Hypocrisy *salad*," I muttered.

"Excuse me?" Mom said, blinking at me.

"Why is it always called salad?" I pointed at the tables that were practically collapsing under the weight of the food. "Ham salad, potato salad, macaroni salad, even Jell-O salad. None of those have anything do with lettuce, so why do they call it salad?"

"I have no idea, but you'd think some of these people were allergic to vegetables, to look at their plates," Mom said disapprovingly, right on cue.

She was the Kentucky version of a health nut. We never had bean sprouts or tofurkey, or any of that crazy California stuff, but you'd never catch her within shouting distance of a deep-fried Twinkie, either, and there were always at least two veggies and a fruit with dinner. She'd almost passed out in shock the day in third grade that I'd come home with an empty Lunchables package in my lunch bag.

I'd traded my PB&J and apple to Lincoln Finn for it, I'd told her, proud of my bargaining abilities. She'd grounded me for a week, and I'd had to read a kids' book about the evils of junk food. To her. Out loud.

I grinned at her. "I'm going to get a piece of Mrs. Finn's store-bought cake."

Mom sighed and shook her head. "Chemicals and sugar, topped with frosting that's more of the same. Go ahead, rot your stomach. I'm off to rescue your father."

She headed over toward the far side of the room, where Pa and a few men stood near a window that had a group of partially deflated balloons taped to it, probably from a wedding reception the day before. The orange and green balloons made me feel a twinge of sympathy for the bridesmaids. I'd been to lots of weddings—Mom and Pa knew a ton of people, and they used to drag me along all the time, before I'd gotten old enough to put my foot down. It had always seemed to me like weddings were an excuse for brides to make their best friends look as ugly as possible, but I wasn't a girl, so I probably just didn't get it.

I headed for the desserts, since it would probably be a while before Mom could drag Pa away. As the sheriff, he always had plenty of people who wanted to talk to him about "important" business, even when he was off duty. We'd once been trapped at Dairy Queen for an hour and a half while some old guy complained about his neighbor's tree dropping branches on his lawn. On the bright side, Pa had let me have a second ice cream cone while we waited, after the familiar warning: "Don't tell your mother."

I smiled a little before the memory soured for me. Pa and I didn't go out for ice cream these days.

I worked my way through a slice of homemade apple pie and a cinnamon roll and was contemplating a plate of cookies when somebody poked me in the back.

"Hey, bro," Jeb said, staring past me at the dessert table. "How's it going?"

I automatically scanned the reception hall for Ethan, but my brothers had quit attending church several years before, when their mother had stormed out in a huff over an insult to her chocolate cake recipe or something like that.

"It's going. Surprised to see you here, though. Were you in church?"

He laughed, and a few girls in the vicinity looked over with interest. When Jeb laughed, he was one of the best-looking guys around, maybe because nobody noticed his shifty eyes.

"I don't believe in this shit, you know that," he said. "I'm just here to see you. You haven't been answering your phone or texts, so I thought I'd try to get you in person. It's not like your mom can kick us out of church, like she did with your house."

"Us?"

He nodded toward the door to the kitchen. "Ethan's in there, talking to one of the Orson girls."

"Which one?" The eldest, Rebecca, was engaged, so it was probably her. Ethan loved nothing more than to cause trouble.

"The pretty one," Jeb said, grinning at a group of girls who were too young and too nice for him.

"They're all pretty," I said grimly, weighing my options. I could go see what he wanted, or I could walk out the door and head home right now. Trouble might happen, but I wouldn't be anywhere near it.

My mom's laughter rang out from where she was chatting with one of her friends, and I sighed. She hadn't been able to laugh at much recently. I wasn't quite sure how or when I'd been elected family peacekeeper, but the last thing the Rhodales needed was another scene, especially at church. I headed for the kitchen.

Time to deflect trouble.

Ethan leaned against the stainless steel restaurant-sized refrigerator while he talked to—no surprise—Rebecca, the engaged Orson girl. He looked up when I walked in.

"That didn't take long."

"I like to get unpleasant chores out of the way first."

Rebecca cast an alarmed glance at me and left the room, walking fast. After the batwing half-doors had swung shut behind her, I curled my fingers and made a come-on gesture.

"Let's have it."

Amusement faded from Ethan's face. "I have a job for you."

I nodded. "Yeah. No 'hi, Mickey, nice to see you, kiss my ass' or anything. Just right to the point, as always."

"I don't have time to waste. I've got supply problems, and demand keeps going up, up, and up," he said.

"Supply problems because you stepped on somebody else's toes, burning down that trailer?"

He glanced over at the doors, and I could see the back of Jeb's head. Standing guard, no doubt.

"I don't know what you're talking about, little brother, but let's just say that I've learned that these aren't great toes to have stepped on." Ethan looked a little bit worried, and Ethan *never* looked worried. He'd had a half smile on his face even when the jury had found him guilty, so this was practically hysteria.

There was a commotion outside the kitchen, and then Reverend Dohonish entered the room. Mom had almost taken my head off the one time I'd said it out loud, but our minister was shaped like a bowling pin or a turkey vulture. I sometimes entertained myself during the most boring of his sermons by imagining that his long, skinny neck, undersized head, and enormous belly were covered with feathers and he was going to take flight any minute.

"You boys planning on doing the washing up?" His words were pleasant enough, but there was a hint of steel underneath them.

"Just having a simple conversation between brothers," Ethan drawled.

The minister's sharp gaze took in Ethan's carefully studied relaxed posture and my tenseness. "Maybe you can have it someplace else. The girls want to get in here and start doing the cleaning."

"Throwing me out, Reverend? I thought you'd at least preach a little bit about wages of sin at me," Ethan said, mocking the man and everything he stood for in two sentences.

I didn't want to be around when he snapped.

"I already gave two sermons today. You tell Anna Mae that we'd surely love to see her back here. Any Sunday. That goes for you, too," Reverend Dohonish said. He turned to me. "Mickey, you're finally right with the law and with God. Don't start this up."

I felt my spine stiffen at his words. The worst part of small-town life was the blithe way everybody stepped right into your business and felt entitled to offer opinions or advice. But I tried not to let any of it show on my face, for my mother's sake.

The reverend pointed at the doors to the hall. "Why don't you go help your mother rescue your pa? The mayor's talking to him, and that woman couldn't get to a point slower if she walked there backwards. City-council meetings would test Job himself these days."

"I will in a minute. I just need to finish up here," I said.

The minister hesitated, looking at me and then Ethan, but then he shook his head and left.

"Yes, *sir*, Reverend Dohonish, sir. Of course we want to be right with *God*," Ethan said, mocking again. He headed for the door to the parking lot. "I'll be in touch, little brother."

"Don't waste your time," I told him.

"Got nothing but time," he called after me.

Jeb grabbed my arm to stop me when I started to walk past him. "Did he ask you? Are you going to do it?"

I yanked my arm out of his grip and gave him a look. "Since when have I ever had anything to do with Ethan's business? Never have, never will."

Jeb bit his lip, and he looked scared. "Mickey, we need help. There's a problem, and it's bad. If you—"

"I can't, Jeb. I can't do it. I *won't* do it."

"But you're blood. Our *brother*," Jeb said fiercely. "You owe us."

I'd been starting to feel sorry for him, but "you owe us" put paid to that. "I don't owe you anything, but I'll give you some advice for free. *Because* you're my brother, I don't want anything to happen to you. Get out of Ethan's business before you end up in jail. Or worse."

I knew it was a waste of breath, but it somehow eased my conscience to say the words.

Jeb shook his head, his eyes bleak. "You don't understand. It's too late. I'm screwed. Leave, stay—it doesn't matter. It's six one way, half-dozen the other. They know who I am now, and they know I'm the one who messed up."

"Who's *they*?" It didn't sound like he was talking about Ethan.

He shook his head, misery plain on his face. "I can't. I'm already in deep enough."

"So you want to pull *me* in, too?" I'd known he was weak, but I'd never thought he was this selfish. A trace of guilt sliced through me at the expression in his eyes, though. Ethan played him like a fish on the line, and Jeb was clearly over his head in whatever this was. Whoever *they* were.

"Never mind. Ethan wants you, he'll get you. He always does." Jeb took off after delivering that parting shot, and I watched him all the way out the door as my flash of sympathy died.

Reverend Dohonish walked up next to me, and he was watching Jeb, too. "You in any trouble, son?"

"Not yet," I answered grimly.

I wondered how long it would be the truth.

CHAPTER 7
VICTORIA

Gran and I sat alone, the weight of hundreds of staring eyes practically boring into the back of my head, and I pretended to concentrate on Father Troy's sermon about redemption. Too bad my parents had refused to come. If anybody in the family needed any redemption, it was them.

The front pews of the Saint Francis Episcopal Church had wooden partitions in front of them, and when I was a little girl and Gran had taken me to Sunday services with her, I'd always wondered why. To keep the congregation herded back from the priest? To keep Father Troy from looking up our skirts as we sat there, all alone in the Whitfield pew?

Gran had shushed me when I'd asked, pretending to be scandalized, but I'd seen her lips quiver as she'd fought back a smile. She hadn't always been Episcopalian; I knew that much. She'd grown up in the Methodist church, but then she'd married my grandfather and been inexorably sucked into a new life, a new social class, and even a new religion—Whitfields *always* went to this church.

In fact, they'd built it. Back in 1890 or something, and it even had been known briefly as the Whitfield Episcopalian church, until the congregation had voted to change it in the mid-1950s. I wasn't sure why the name change had happened, either, but I was glad that it had. It was creepy enough being a Whitfield in Whitfield County and having our last name plastered all over everything, like we were the Donald Trumps of Kentucky. I couldn't imagine attending a church named after my family. A little too "pride goeth" and all.

"Don't make faces, Victoria," Gran whispered, and then it was time to stand up for the doxology and sit back down for the offering.

When I was little, I'd also wondered why, if we were praising "God from whom all blessings flow," we had to give the church our money, especially since Gran had always made me give up an entire quarter out of my one-dollar allowance.

If the blessings all flow from God, why does He need my quarter?

Be quiet and sit down.

When the service was over, we filed out, and I dutifully smiled and shook hands with everyone who wanted to say hello to the Whitfield granddaughter. Father Troy, standing at the door to say goodbye to everyone, smiled sympathetically.

"Are you starting to settle in, young lady?" He had a booming baritone voice that worked beautifully for singing hymns and preaching sermons, but not so much for private conversations. Everyone in a fifty-yard radius turned to look at me as they headed to their American-made cars and trucks—none of that foreign crap in God's

country—most of which had bumper stickers proclaiming their owners' personal beliefs and accomplishments:

JESUS IS IN MY DRIVER'S SEAT!

PROUD SUPPORTER: KENTUCKY HIGHWAY PATROL

MY CHILD IS AN HONOR STUDENT

Gran cleared her throat, and I realized that I was being rude.
Right. Father Troy had asked me about settling in. It was "tell us
about yourself" all over again, but this time even the parents of all
those honor students who supported the highway patrol were staring
at me.

"Yes, thank you," I mumbled.

"It's important to stand by your father through his career setbacks," he boomed, and my glance at Gran told me it wasn't just me
suffering the humiliation of his loud comments.

"Of course she's doing well. She's my granddaughter," Gran cut
in, and there was a hint of bite in her voice. I guess when you wrote
most of the checks that paid the church's bills, you were brave enough
to stand up to the nosy priest.

She waited until we were in the truck to say anything else.

"He means well, Victoria," she sighed. "People in small towns
can't help sticking their noses into everybody's business. It's what they
do for sport. Before there was TV or the Internet, gossip was the ultimate entertainment, and the people here are world champions."

"If lightning strikes the truck, it's your fault. God might not
appreciate your lumping Father Troy's priestly concern in with ordinary small-town gossip," I told her, not altogether joking.

"Forget that," she said, smiling. "Tell me about school."

"There's not much to tell," I said, concentrating on the road and
the American flag sticker pasted to the rear window of the Chevy

Silverado in front of me—bumper sticker: MY KID CAN BEAT UP YOUR HONOR STUDENT—all so I didn't think about Mickey. "I'm ahead in most classes, a little behind in one, I met a nice girl named Denise, and I think it will be okay."

There was a long silence, and then Gran started laughing. "Well, after that flood of information, I have to wonder if you're always such a blabbermouth."

"What about you?" I countered. "How are *you* adjusting?"

She didn't pretend not to know what I was talking about. "It's going to take some getting used to," she admitted. "Your father . . . he has a forceful personality, and he always thinks he should be in charge."

"But you've been running this place on your own for a long time," I said.

"Yes. Well, with Pete's help. I don't know what I'd do without him, and I'm afraid your father will drive him to drink. Or to leave."

It was one of the things I loved about Gran; she'd always been straightforward with me. Except now it was making me worry.

"You won't make *us* leave?"

I left the rest of it unspoken: We didn't have anywhere else to go.

She reached out and laid one thin, blue-veined hand on mine. "Never. You're my blood. My home is your home, for as long as you want it."

I squeezed her hand with the thanks that was stuck in my throat, and she nodded and squeezed back.

By the time we'd almost reached home, I thought of another question I wanted to ask somebody who would give me a straight answer.

"Gran, what do you know about the Rhodale family? I met this boy, Mickey, and heard a pretty ugly rumor about him." I didn't know how to finish up the question, but when Gran didn't immediately answer, I glanced over and saw that she was clenching her hands together so tightly that her knuckles had turned white.

"Gran?"

"Please don't *ever* speak that name to me again."

Surprised, I turned to look at her, but she wouldn't meet my gaze. Her clasped hands were shaking, her lips were pressed tightly together, and—for the first time in my entire life—she looked old to me.

"I'm sorry, Gran. I won't, I promise."

She nodded, a small, jerky movement. The conversation made me even more determined to get to the truth about Mickey Rhodale, but I'd leave her out of it.

By the time I pulled up next to the house and parked, Gran was looking more back to normal, and as we headed into the house we talked a little about what we'd make for lunch, since Mrs. Kennedy had Sundays off. But my mother met us at the door as if she'd been waiting for us. She pointed at me.

"You! You couldn't stay here and sleep in like a normal teenager, could you?"

"What? What did I do?" My stomach plummeted.

"Your sister is . . . sick, and she threw up in the kitchen," she said, looking even more pale and drawn than usual. "I had to *clean it up*. I don't know how to cope with this. Two daughters and neither of them is ever going to amount to anything. Melinda was getting better at home, and then we had to come here, and now—"

"Mom! She wasn't getting better. She was just hiding it from everyone better," I pointed out, as gently as I could.

"I liked it better when things were hidden," my mother said, her shoulders slumping. With that, she trudged up the stairs, shaking her head when I called after her.

"What was that about? Did she mean she'd have made you clean up, if you'd been here?" Gran asked, putting her hands on her hips and glaring after Mom. "That woman is as useless as tits on a boar hog."

I shook my head, miserable. "I don't want to talk about it. I'm not really hungry anymore, either."

"We'll figure this out, honey. I promise," she said, patting my back.

I shook my head. I didn't believe that even Gran would be able to keep that promise.

I wandered out to the barn after changing out of my church clothes, looking for a little peace in the one place I was almost always sure to find it. Pete was there, of course, one foot propped on the bottom of the doorway to Sylvan's Daughter's stall.

"How's she doing?" I walked up beside him and looked in at the pregnant mare. She tossed her glossy head and then reached her nose out to sniff me for treats.

"Good as can be expected. She's not due till Christmas, but we like to keep an eye on her after she miscarried last year," he said.

A miscarried foal was not only tragic for the mare but devastating for the people who'd raised her and cared for her—both emotionally and financially. Thoroughbred racehorses were, pound for pound, the most valuable creatures on the planet, and I knew well enough that the stud fee for Lucky Planet, who'd been the father of the lost foal, had been in the low six figures. Lucky Planet was racing royalty; three of his foals had been Derby contenders and at least another six had been great racers, here and overseas. His own career had been notable, but once a racing stallion retired and was set to breeding, his value was all about how many champions he sired.

Sylvan's Daughter had a pretty great pedigree herself. She was distantly related to Secretariat, one of the greatest race horses of all time. Of course, all thoroughbreds could trace their ancestry back to the same three horses, so in a way they were all cousins.

I winced as I remembered trying to explain some of this to my friends at school, and how they went straight for the Kentucky inbreeding jokes. We were more of a stereotype than a state to outsiders, I'd learned early on in my freshman year.

"How'd Keeneland go?"

The Keeneland Yearling Sale was one of racing's premier events. Each September, farms brought their horses and their hopes to central Kentucky, and buyers brought their checkbooks and their dreams of owning a champion. Maybe a Derby winner. Few dared to hope that a horse they owned might win the sport's highest honor—the Triple Crown—but it was the slight chance that they might that kept the buyers coming back and spending hundreds of thousands or even millions of dollars on unproven foals.

"We sold two to Ireland, one to Dubai, and one right here to that guy who owns too many car dealerships."

I glanced up at him, catching the hint of a grin. "The one whose wife wore the enormous hat with Hot Wheels cars on the brim to the Derby?"

He nodded. "Yeah, they're idiots, but they hired the best trainer around. He'll be sure that that foal out of Roseland's Promise gets the best care in racing."

I remembered watching the foal run, back in June. He'd raced around the paddock like he owned the place, and when he'd stretched out that long, elegant neck and really put his heart into it, he'd flown over the fields as if his hooves had been winged.

"He was really something," I said, sighing. "I wish we trained them, too."

Pete laughed, and Sylvan's Daughter briefly pinned her ears back, signaling her displeasure at the unexpected sound, and then went back to nosing around in her food.

"Training them to race is a specialized skill. I'm just the one who brings healthy babies into the world."

"We like healthy babies," I agreed, reaching out a hand to stroke the mare's silky nose.

She tossed her head again before allowing it, and I smiled at her. Life was a lot simpler for horses.

"What do you know about the Rhodale family? Mickey Rhodale, to be precise." Maybe a blunt question would finally get me some answers.

"Are you all right? Did he do something to you? Did he touch you?" Pete fired out the questions in a hard voice I'd never heard from him before, and I turned to look at him, raising my eyebrows.

"In the approximately seven seconds I've known him, did he touch me?"

Pete grimaced, and I saw something shift behind his eyes. "I'm sorry for jumping on you like that. The boy got into some trouble, and it was bad."

"How bad?"

"He put a couple of guys in the hospital. One of them will be in physical therapy for several months if he's going to regain full use of his hand ever again," he said flatly. "Stay away from him, Victoria. He's trouble."

"I have no plans to go anywhere near him. I just wondered, since I started hearing rumors—"

"Nasty rumors and cheap gossip. This county is perfect for both."

The bleak expression on his face made me wonder if he was thinking of something specific, but it also warned me not to ask. On impulse, I hugged him, something I hadn't done since I was twelve and Daddy had told me that Whitfields "don't hug the hired help."

"I'm fine, Pete. Don't worry about me. I have too much sense to fall for the town bad boy."

He hugged me back and then headed toward his office, clearing his throat in a manly "I wasn't all emotional over this" kind of way that made me grin at the back of his plaid shirt.

I gave the mare one last ear scratch and headed toward the door, but Pete's voice stopped me.

"About Mickey Rhodale, Victoria. All you need to know is that you'd better stay far away from him. Don't talk to your family about him, either, okay? We've had enough problems with Rhodales to last a lifetime."

"No, no, no, no, no!" I pulled the stuttering old truck over to the side of the road and used up my admittedly limited supply of swear words.

The gas tank needle showed the tank was half full. Now that I thought about it, the needle had been showing the tank as half full for more than a week, and I hadn't put any gas in it. Half full, half empty, all the way gone; the damn gas gauge must be broken.

There was a lesson in there somewhere about the global failure of optimism, but I was too annoyed to think about it.

I pulled out my phone and wondered who to call. Not Gran. I'd just dropped her off at her Sunday afternoon church group. Not my mother, who would shriek at me about personal responsibility and not know what to do. Not my father, who would expect me to handle it myself, if he even picked up a phone call from me in the middle of the day, which he probably wouldn't. Not Pete, because he was taking a rare day off today.

Okay, Victoria, think.

I dialed information for Clark, Kentucky, and asked for a gas station. Gas stations had gas, right? And also usually trucks that towed people. Maybe somebody could bring me some gas, and I could pay them, and nobody else needed to know about this.

The operator put me through to Howard's Gas Station, and I explained my dilemma to a cranky old man who sounded like he was approximately a hundred and ten.

"I'll send the boy."

"Thanks. But, ah, when do you expect—"

"He'll be there when he gets there. If you're in such an all-fired hurry, maybe you should have filled up your gas tank before you ran out."

Click.

I stared at the phone in my hand for second, thinking evil thoughts about small-town businesses that had monopolies and therefore no need to be pleasant. Then I pulled my book bag closer and grabbed *To Kill a Mockingbird*, hunched down in the driver's seat so nobody could see me, and prepared to wait.

An hour later, I was still waiting.

I sighed and started to call Pete after all, so he could send somebody after me, when a truck that was even older than mine pulled up behind me and a guy got out. My heart jumped into my throat when I realized it was Mickey.

His tight black T-shirt advertised some beer I'd never heard of, and the sleeves left his muscular, tanned arms bare so I could see the ink encircling the top of his left arm. Somehow, that glimpse of tattoo made him even more intriguing.

He smiled, sauntering up to my window, and I was toast.

Mickey Rhodale hooked his thumbs in his pockets and grinned down at me.

"You didn't have to pretend to run out of gas just to get me alone, Princess."

I started to sputter. "I didn't—you don't—*argh*. Just give me the gas so I can get out of here."

He tilted his head, saying nothing, but his smile faded. I couldn't see his eyes through the dark lenses of his sunglasses, but I couldn't miss the way his lips tightened.

"How about you get out of the truck and pour your own gas," he said. "I'm not one of your flunkies."

"I didn't mean—I just—"

But he turned and stalked back to his truck, so I jumped out of mine so fast that my book went flying. I bent down to get it and turned to see Mickey openly staring at my butt.

"Sorry, I couldn't help myself," he said. "You have a very nice ass, Princess. Why is that? Personal trainer? Thousand-dollar gym membership?"

"I ride horses," I snapped. "But thank you for the instant stereotyping."

He pulled his glasses off and stuffed them in his pocket, and those spectacular blue eyes danced with amusement. Yeah, he was laughing at me. Again. I was a little tired of it, and so I decided to turn the tables on him.

I checked *him* out. Slowly. From head to toe, I took my time staring at every glorious inch of that hard, toned, muscular body.

And it backfired on me—I almost choked when my mouth dried out completely, but no way was I letting him know that.

"On the other hand, you've got a nice ass, too," I said, trying for a slow drawl of my own.

"Oh, I'm nice all over," he said, and his gaze turned hot. "You have no idea."

I swallowed, hard, because I kind of *did* have an idea, and I was about an inch away from hyperventilating.

"Well, okay," I said, clearing my throat. "Now that we've established the relative niceness of our respective posteriors, maybe we can get on with the filling of my gas tank."

He blinked and then started laughing. "Oh, sweetheart. You are adorable."

Suddenly I'd had it. We kept dancing around this fierce attraction, and I had no idea what to do with it, but this tension was about to make my head explode, right here on the side of the road.

"Look, Mickey, either help me or go away. I'm not your sweetheart, and I'm not adorable. I'm tired and hungry and I'm getting a headache. Are you going to help me or what?"

He stared down at me, his eyes blazing with intent, as if he wanted to back me up against the truck and kiss me right then and there. Or maybe I was just projecting a whole boatload of wishful thinking on the moment because, up close, he was fiercely beautiful. His muscled arms were cut and carved like a sculptor's dream, and the silky waves of his hair made me want to throw my arms around him and run my fingers through it, over and over. I was caught in a bizarre spell created by pure *want*, and I'd never felt this way before in my life.

Naturally, it scared the crap out of me.

I took a step back.

"Mickey . . ." My voice was barely a whisper, a sound too fragile for the weight of the moment.

He took a step closer.

CHAPTER 8

MICKEY

I had to kiss her. Every instinct was telling me to pick her up so that hot little body was plastered against mine and kiss her until she didn't remember who she was, or that my last name was Rhodale. She made a tiny sound, almost like a gasp, and I stared down at those lush, parted lips, and wanted her so much my body actually ached with it.

I took a step back, and both of us let out shaky breaths at exactly the same time.

"I'm sorry. I don't know how to be myself around you," I muttered. A lame-ass confession that made me wince even as I said it. "You don't make sense. I barely know you, but I want to know everything about you. You're smart and gorgeous, and you make my skin too tight."

The more I rattled on with this stupid confession, the more bewildered she got. She tilted her head and stared at me, and by the time I got to the end, confusion was very apparent in her green, green eyes.

"What do you mean, *I* don't make sense?" She threw her hands in the air. "You're the one who doesn't make sense. You're always ordering me around, or calling me Princess like you know anything about my life at all. Maybe if you'd quit being such a . . . such a *dumb head*, you might *get* to know me."

I couldn't help it. I grinned. "Dumb head? I'm not sure I can recover from such a foul insult."

She actually growled. Clenched her delicate little hands into fists and growled at me.

It made me want to kiss her even more.

"You . . . you *asshole*!" she finally shouted, and all I could think was that she was even more freaking gorgeous when she was pissed off.

"Asshole. That's way better," I said, nodding as if contemplating the subject of insults.

And then I kissed her.

It wasn't a gentle kiss or a practiced kiss; I suddenly had no moves, no technique. No game. All I had was an overwhelming *want*—an all-consuming *need*. I needed to taste her lips more than I needed to think or breathe or exist on the planet.

So I kissed her.

And she kissed me back.

For one long, glorious moment, Victoria's arms wrapped around my neck and she kissed me with a heat and passion I'd never experienced. Never believed was possible.

When the kiss finally ended, I stumbled back a step or two and stared at her in disbelief while everything I thought I knew about girls and myself and, hell, life itself went up in flames.

Her eyes were a little unfocused, so at least it hadn't just been me whirling around in that tornado of feeling.

"Holy shit," I said reverently.

She inhaled sharply. "Really? 'Holy shit?' Evidently kissing a frog doesn't always turn him into a prince. Bad boys are called that for a reason, right? I'm the dumb one here."

"Victoria—"

"Nice, *Mickey*. Really lovely. You might work on your charming ways before you kiss the next girl you've lined up, though."

The warmth in my chest congealed and turned icy, becoming a rock in my gut.

"There's no next girl lined up, and you'd better not even be thinking about the next guy," I said flatly. "We need to figure this out. We need—"

"We need nothing. All I need from you is that gasoline," she snapped.

Over the next five minutes, while I poured the gas in her tank and then watched her drive away, she never said a single word.

Way to crash and burn, Rhodale.

I wasn't exactly sure how Victoria managed to sound sexy answering a question about carpetbaggers, but somehow she did. Maybe it was the little blue dress she was wearing.

Or maybe I was just losing it.

Two solid weeks of watching Victoria ignore me would be enough to drive the most reasonable person to distraction, and I was a Rhodale, which meant I wasn't on even a handshake acquaintance with reasonable. She didn't speak to me, didn't look at me, and didn't answer me when I tried to talk to her. To make things worse, while her campaign of studied indifference kept running longer, her skirts kept getting shorter.

Or maybe that part was just in my imagination, which had been working overtime trying to give me a mental picture of those long legs all the way up.

Everything else in my life felt like it was caught in the same stasis bubble, too. Ethan, for once, had been lying low. My mom was busy with her own students; she said this year's crop of fourth graders was the most challenging she'd ever had. Pa was around less and less in the evenings, which usually meant he was heading back down inside a bottle of bourbon.

Football practice was same old, same old, and even my job at the gas station had been slow.

"Do you plan to answer me sometime this class period, Mr. Rhodale, or shall I fax you a written request?" Mr. Gerard's dry voice cut through my mental meanderings, and I looked up from the drawing of a mule I'd been doodling to see that everyone was staring at me.

"Nobody faxes anymore," I said, not really trying to be a smart-ass but rather buying myself time to think back and see if I could figure out what he'd asked me.

Victoria glanced over at me, and I could almost see a hint of compassion in her eyes.

"Kentucky declared neutrality at the beginning of the Civil War, but it didn't last," she said.

He actually smiled. I thought I heard Derek gasp. Nobody had seen Gerard's teeth in years. There'd been bets as to whether he actually had real ones or if, like fireflies over the Kentucky hills, they only came out at night.

"Very nice, Miss Whitfield. Most people forget that. Perhaps you can manage to stay awake in my class from now on," he said, directing that last bit at me.

When he walked away, choosing his next victim, I leaned across the aisle. "Thanks. I owe you one."

She shrugged, but I noticed her cheeks turned pink. The beautiful and brilliant Victoria Whitfield wasn't as indifferent to me as she pretended.

"Remember outside the school office where you said we'd start over? What happened to that?" I persisted.

"That was before you were such a jerk when you kissed me. Now keep your voice down," she whispered.

"I will if you promise to talk to me after class."

"I can't."

"You can't?"

"I won't."

"Then I won't keep my voice down," I said loudly.

Mr. Gerard turned to peer at me over the top of his glasses. "Yes, Mr. Rhodale? You have something to add?"

"No, sorry. I just get so excited about the Civil War," I said, straight-faced.

When he turned around, I turned in my seat and faced Victoria. "Well?"

"Leave me alone," she demanded. Ice cubes would have been a few degrees warmer than her voice, and something inside me snapped.

"I don't think so, Princess," I drawled, being sure to put a lot of Kentucky-hills accent in there. "I need to talk to you, so I can quit wondering what in the hell I did to offend you."

She opened her mouth to say something, probably something really rude, and I deliberately cut her off.

"Or are you just afraid I'll Hulk out and beat you up?"

Heat turned her cheeks pink again. "I'm not afraid of you."

"Good. After class?"

The bell rang before she could reply, and I followed her out of the room. I was determined to figure out what was going on, and why the only girl I'd been interested in for a long time was shutting me down before I'd even had a chance to get to know her.

Usually it took me a while longer to piss people off.

I knew that at least a couple of the guys watching me in the hall were probably Ethan's thugs. The last thing I needed was for him to hear that I was chasing after a Whitfield down the school hallway. I realized I was clenching my fists at the thought, and I deliberately forced my fingers to relax. I would not impress Victoria by getting into a fight with these idiots.

As I watched Victoria disappear around the corner, though, the flash of blue skirt flaring out behind her was enough to make me realize that I didn't give a shit about Ethan and his flunkies, anyway.

I went after her.

I caught up to her and grabbed her arm just before she got to her math class. She looked down at my hand and then up at me, and slowly her eyebrows rose.

"I have to go to class," she said.

I glanced inside the room. "It's a substitute. Substitutes never know anything about calculus, or so Derek tells me, so you won't be missing anything."

"It doesn't matter. I need—"

"Please." I couldn't believe I'd said it, even as the word came out of my mouth. I was practically begging a girl to spend time with me. A *Whitfield* girl.

Great. Now I sounded like Ethan.

But apparently Mama hadn't called it the magic word for nothing, because Victoria was nodding. I froze, not wanting to act too eager or do anything else that would make her quit speaking to me again.

"Okay," she said, biting her lip. "I agree that we should talk. Let's go now, before the sub sees me."

Before she could change her mind, I grabbed her hand and practically dragged her down the hall toward the staircase that nobody was allowed to use until the cracked handrail was fixed. I had forty-eight minutes until lunch, and I intended to use them to get to know Victoria Whitfield.

CHAPTER 9
VICTORIA

I took long, slow yoga breaths as I followed Mickey down the hall, trying not to hyperventilate or stare at his wavy black hair or his muscular back and shoulders, and especially not at his butt in those well-worn jeans.

It's just . . . it was a really, *really* great butt.

He pulled me into the stairway through the door with the ABSOLUTELY NO ENTRANCE sign posted on it, and we sat on the steps and looked at each other. Now that we were here, I was chickening out and wanted to escape back to class.

"You wanted to talk, so talk," I said gracelessly. "Am I really so interesting, just because I'm the new girl, that you had to use all of your dubious charms to get me here? Wait—do I need to define the term 'dubious'?"

He scowled. "You think I'm stupid? Not quite up to your fancy Whitfield standards?"

"Unbelievable. I just skipped my first class *ever*, so I could talk to you, and you're giving me crap about 'fancy Whitfield standards'?" I stood up and brushed off my skirt. "You and your Rhodale prejudices can kiss my fancy Whitfield butt."

Unexpectedly, he flashed that killer grin that he used so rarely, the one that I'd seen melt freshman girls into swooning puddles in the cafeteria. It ticked me off just thinking about it.

"Your Whitfield butt? There are several parts of you that I'd like to kiss, Princess, but I wouldn't have started with your *butt*."

He stood up, too, and stared at my mouth. I suddenly felt way too hot, too confined—claustrophobic, almost—in the dusty stairwell, and I was finding it hard to breathe. I didn't know whether to kiss him or slap him. Maybe I should do both, like some swooning heroine in an Austen novel.

Mickey Rhodale was the most infuriating person I'd ever met.

"Let's try this again," I said, trying to be reasonable. "Why did you want to talk to me? Because you kissed me?"

"You kissed me back. Anyway, you're good at that, aren't you? Deflecting your anger?" He raised one eyebrow and grinned down at me, and my pulse went crazy. "Wait. Do I need to define the term 'deflecting'?"

I had to laugh at hearing him toss my words back at me. I deserved it; it had been a snotty thing to say.

"I happen to be the former third grade spelling bee champ, I'll have you know," I said loftily, still smiling. "At least until I was robbed at the district level. Just in case you ever wondered, rhinoceros does *not* end in o-u-s."

"You *were* robbed," he agreed, and a tingling sensation of warmth circled around inside me, trying to find a home.

Mickey Rhodale might be dangerous, but he had the most incredible blue eyes I'd ever seen, surrounded by long, dark lashes set in a deeply tanned face that was framed by those too-long waves of silky black hair. He was absolutely, stunningly gorgeous, and I didn't think he even realized it. Most hot guys acted like they were nature's gift to women. Mickey had the social graces of a clumsy foal.

The thought made me relax. I knew more about dealing with horses than boys and, as I'd told Pete, I had far too much sense to fall for the town bad boy.

Mickey pushed a strand of my hair behind my ear, and my breath caught in my throat.

Oh, crap, I'm falling for the town bad boy. That kiss . . .

"What's going on in that mind of yours?" he drawled, and it took me a few seconds to remember what we'd been talking about, because my attention kept getting distracted by the play of muscle in his arms when he shoved his hands in his pockets.

"I'm thinking that my family would fall over in a dead faint if they knew I'd skipped class to talk to the most dangerous boy in school," I admitted, glancing at the door while hiding my shaking hands behind my back.

Mickey threw back his head and laughed, and I stared stupidly at the column of his throat for a moment before remembering where we were.

"Will you be quiet? Somebody's going to catch us in here."

He pretended to shudder. "Oh, no, not that! We might get *detention*."

"I know you're mocking me, and I just want to point out that it's not really the best way to begin a friendship," I said, and I could hear how brittle I sounded, but I couldn't seem to stop myself.

A corner of his mouth quirked up. "As you wish. Is that what we're doing? Beginning a friendship?"

I sighed. "I don't know. Manhandle me at the fire, mock me in class, smile at me, bait me, kiss me—it's almost like you're two different people. Which Mickey is here with me? And everybody keeps telling me to stay away from you. I honestly don't know what to do."

"So why don't we sit and talk and figure it out?" He pulled off the flannel shirt he was wearing over his T-shirt and put it on the step. "A little late, maybe, but so you don't get your skirt dirty."

It was a nice gesture, but without the "as you wish" *Princess Bride* reference, I might have left him there alone in the stairwell anyway. It was hard to resist a good Westley quote.

I carefully sat down on his folded shirt.

"Sorry about coming on so strong. I was running out of ideas about how to get you to talk to me, especially after I kissed you like that," he admitted. "I just wanted a chance to get to know you—for you to get to know me—without the burden of everybody's judgment crashing into us."

I shrugged, not quite sure how to handle this new, sincere version of Mickey. "They won't tell me anything about you, you know," I finally said. "My family. Or at least my grandmother and our foreman. Pete warned me to stay away from you, and Gran won't even hear your name. What is that about?"

He laughed, but it was more bitter than amused. "The Rhodale line throws true, my grandpa used to say. We all look the same, and we all grow up to be lawmen or criminals. Hasn't everybody in school told you about us?"

"My grandfather sounds a lot like yours."

"Really? Did he have to leave the ranch to shoot possums and squirrels to make sure his family got enough to eat?" His sarcasm hung in the air between us, tangible as a slap in the face.

"No, what I meant was that my Gran told me he talked about how the Whitfield line were all born to be horse people, you jerk. You have to make up your mind, Mickey. Are we going to actually talk to each other like normal people or not? I'm kind of tired of the hot and cold running attitude," I snapped.

He narrowed his eyes, but then he nodded and sighed. "You're right. I'm sorry. I've heard about the horrible Whitfields for so long that I guess I've internalized it."

"Ooh, 'internalized.' Points for the SAT word," I said, smiling a little before what he'd said really registered. "Wait. The horrible Whitfields?"

He returned my smile and nudged my leg with his, and a little of the tension relaxed out of my shoulders. We might be able to have a civilized conversation after all, in spite of the almost painful sparks of sensation that snapped and pulsed along my nerve endings from his nearness.

"I don't actually know. I've heard Pa mention your father a few times. They never got along, apparently."

My head was starting to hurt. "What, like when they were kids? Dad hasn't lived here since high school. Who cares about that?"

"You really don't know?"

I sighed and closed my eyes. This circular conversation was getting us nowhere, fast.

"This is Kentucky, Princess. Everybody cares about everybody else's business and pasts and especially any misdeeds," he said, dropping his head into his hands.

The hint of vulnerability in the boy everybody else seemed to think was a monster tugged at me more than if he'd tried to charm me or seduce me.

"Mickey—"

"I'd like to get to know you," he said abruptly, raising his head. "I admit it, I'd like to kiss you again, too, but this is about more than that."

Time itself did a little hiccup as I stared into his blue eyes. He raised his hand and touched the side of my face so gently that it was more a whisper of a promise than an actual caress. My hands started to tremble, and I forgot how to breathe for a moment, as the connection between us flared into urgent, electric existence. I thought for a second that he'd kiss me, but instead he leaned back and stretched out his legs, shoving his hands back in his front pockets as if he had to forcibly keep himself from touching me again.

Or so I imagined. Hoped?

"But—"

"I know, I know. It's a bad idea. Your family told you to stay away from me. My family will probably tell me to stay away from you." He glared at the WILDCATS RULE, TROJANS DROOL graffiti that somebody had scrawled in purple marker on the wall, and I waited for him to continue. I wasn't going to ask about the rumors again.

I'd wait for him to volunteer the information. I wanted to explore the fragile beginning of whatever was between the two of us without being affected by what our families would or wouldn't say.

Finally, he quit staring at the wall and looked at me. "Well? Do you want to get to know me, too, or not?"

I started to laugh. "Has anybody ever told you that you're pushy and obnoxious?"

"Maybe a few times," he admitted. "Are you going to answer me?"

Talk about a loaded question. Did I want to get to know him? Of course I did. He was gorgeous and mysterious—every ounce of my teen-girl DNA was practically *programmed* to want to get to know him.

But there was more to it than that.

Mickey Rhodale, for all of his dangerous, bad-boy exterior, had a hint of damaged vulnerability about him that I was pretty sure he didn't let anybody else see, and he'd shown it to me.

Something inside me, in a very small voice, was saying, *Yes, of course. Finally. Here you are.*

And it scared me to death. But I had to face it head-on.

"Yes, I want to get to know you, too."

"So give me your phone," he said, holding out his hand.

I handed it to him and then watched as he added his name and number to my contacts. He smiled a little bit smugly when he handed it back.

"So *I* have to call *you*? Don't you want my number?"

"I have it from when you called the station," he said. "So now when I call you, my name will pop up, and you'll know it's me."

His admission that he'd deliberately kept my phone number almost made me forget what I'd been thinking about—that I needed to know more about him.

I tried again. "I do want to get to know you, Mickey. But— "

"But you need to know the truth."

I nodded.

"Okay, yeah, it's true. I beat the living shit out of three guys and put two of them in the hospital. I have anger management problems. I'm a nightmare waiting to eat your dreams and swallow you whole," he said bitterly.

I didn't know how to respond, so I just waited. There had to be more.

Finally, he sighed. "They were hurting my sister. She has—had—a bit of a reputation as a party girl. She has two kids by two different guys, and I guess they thought, like a lot of people thought, that she was easy."

His hands kept clenching and unclenching, as if some kinesthetic memory of the fight were controlling them, and I had to force myself not to flinch away.

"She's not. Easy, I mean. She just has a big heart and wants to be loved."

"I can understand that," I said quietly. "Don't we all want to be loved?"

He shot a sharp glance at me, but then he continued in a low, rough voice. "I was watching her girls one night, and these assholes waylaid her at the door to the apartment building. I guess they figured they'd bring her upstairs and rape her in front of her kids. Hell, I don't know. They were drunk. They probably weren't thinking at all."

Nausea rose in my throat in a hot rush, and I had to take a long, slow breath to force it back down.

"I can't—how—I'm so sorry." I put a hand on his arm, and he covered it with his own hand and squeezed my fingers tightly.

"Why were you the one who got in trouble for it? I mean, if that part is even true, if you, well ..." I stopped stumbling around the thing and just came out with it. "Did you really go to juvie? For this?"

"Yeah, I went to juvie. My family isn't rich, like the families of the guys who attacked Caro."

I recoiled at the bitterness in his voice, but it still didn't make sense to me. "But your dad—"

"Is only the sheriff, an elected official. Whose money do you think buys elections? It's sure as hell not ours."

"Mickey, I'm so sorry," I said. "For what happened and for judging you before I knew what really happened. You should let people know all this, so they quit thinking you're some kind of lunatic ready to explode into violence at any minute.

He still held my hand, and his fingers tightened on mine for an instant, but then he let go entirely.

"Yeah, well, I'd do it again in a heartbeat, so maybe they're not wrong."

The bell rang, and he stood up. "This was stupid. You should stay away from me. No matter how much I wish things were different, they never will be. This is *Whitfield* County, after all."

He shoved the door open so hard I thought it would crash off its hinges, and then he was gone, leaving me wondering what had just happened, and why I wanted so badly to rush after Mickey and comfort him.

Why it suddenly *mattered* to me so much.

I stood up and realized that he'd left his shirt behind, and I shook it out, folded it, and shoved it down inside my backpack. I'd give it to him later.

I'd *have* to see him to give him his shirt, right?

CHAPTER 10

MICKEY

I spent the rest of the day ignoring my teachers, ignoring Derek's questions, and thinking about Victoria. The powerful feeling of instant connection between us ran too deep to be pleasant, or even casual. But where I was mad at the world, she was compassionate as she confronted the demons of a guy she'd been told to avoid and even fear.

She deserved better than to get tainted with my reputation, however undeserved, so I tried to stop myself from studying her across the cafeteria as she laughed with Denise and some other girls. I tried to stop watching for her in the halls with a determination that bordered on obsession, like I'd done every school day for the past two weeks.

But fighting the compulsion meant that when I did catch a glimpse of her, the *feel* of seeing her was heavy and strange, and it ripped at my insides like a jagged-edged triangle being jammed into the unyielding square corners of my life's expectations. Something stronger than *want* waged a battle against my common sense and instinctive wariness; the pressure built up all afternoon until I finally escaped to my motorcycle, forcing myself not to look for her in the spill of students leaving school for the day.

I fired up my bike, but I didn't have a destination in mind, really. Coach had given us a rare day off practice, it was my day off work, and I wanted nothing more than a little solitude to try to figure out what was going on in my head over Victoria. I didn't feel like heading for home, though.

When I pulled to a stop at the light, my phone buzzed, and I answered it without thinking.

"Mickey. Ethan. Get your ass over here."

"I don't take orders from you." I deliberately revved the bike, so I missed what he said next. "Sorry. Didn't hear you."

"Get over here now, or else."

The phone clicked off, and I resisted the urge to smash it into the ground. I knew damn well that "or else" could be any of a number of highly unpleasant consequences, and we'd all learned over the years that it was generally easier just to give in a little bit sometimes when Ethan started up.

Choose your battles, Mom always said, with that tight-lipped expression she only got when the topic was Anna Mae or Ethan. Something told me I had bigger and tougher battles ahead of me, especially when he found out about my interest in Victoria Whitfield, so I turned left, past the flower shop, instead of right, past Junior's Pizza, and headed for Anna Mae's compound.

* * *

Everybody called it "the compound" instead of Anna Mae's place, or Ethan's place, or "that place where Sheriff Rhodale's discarded first family plots their criminal enterprises." I pulled up to the front gate and waited for the scuzzy-looking guy carrying the shiny new shotgun to open it for me. I'd been invited, and I was family—at least half of me was—but nobody went into the compound without getting past one of Ethan's guards.

The place consisted of several weathered, gray outbuildings loosely grouped around the main house, plus assorted scattered sheds and trailers. All told, Anna Mae owned thirty-five acres her pa had left her, and this had been the house she'd grown up in, raised her children in, and never left.

My pa had said once that living there as her husband had been like running into the angry ghosts of his wife's disappointments on a daily basis. It was the closest he'd ever come to saying anything poetic, and he'd been halfway through a bottle at the time, but I'd understood instantly what he'd meant. Anna Mae had worshipped the ground her daddy walked on, and nobody but Ethan, her firstborn son, had ever lived up to her ideal of what a real man was.

Whatever her ideal was, it involved guns and power.

"Ethan's up at the house," the guard said, taking time to spit a stream of tobacco juice on the ground next to him. He grinned, displaying a mouth full of stained, broken teeth. "Heard you got a little girlfriend."

I fought back the urge to punch him in the mouth. If he'd used her name, I probably would have. He was a flunky, and I shouldn't give a shit what he thought, but I'd had more than I could take today. Also, it was a sign that Ethan's rats had been busy. I'd always known that he kept eyes on me when I was at school, but I'd never cared about that before Victoria came to town.

I parked the bike in front of the house and took the steps two at a time. The hound under the porch lifted a sleepy head and then went back to dreaming about rabbits. One of Ethan's prized champion gun dogs growled at me from the corner of the porch, where she lay in the sun on a cushion with her pups.

I knocked once, then pushed open the door and entered the huge, homey kitchen where Ethan, as always, held court at the old farm table and Anna Mae, as always, stood at the stove, stirring something that smelled really great. In all the years I'd known her, she'd never once offered me anything to eat, but she was always cooking.

Pa's ex-wife was a sight to behold. She'd supposedly been the great beauty of the county once, before life, my father, and her father— him by dying—had all disappointed her. Now she was nearly three hundred pounds of manipulation and bitterness packed into a rat-gray housecoat. Today, she shot me a scowl that was so poisonous you'd think I'd killed her best friend.

"Heard you been consortin' with Whitfields, boy," she said before Ethan could speak. "You're gonna stop that right now, you hear me?"

I'd always tried to be courteous to her, especially in her own place, but her high-handed command set my blood to a slow boil.

Ethan stood up and patted her shoulder. "Shut the hell up, Ma," he said, but there was no real heat behind the words.

She smiled at him like he'd complimented her cooking, and I was struck for about the hundredth time by just how damn strange my entire family was. I bet Victoria didn't have to deal with weird relatives. The Whitfields probably all sat down together for tea and crumpets right about this time of day and complimented each other on their awesomeness. I grinned, imagining what Victoria would have to say to me about *that*, and unfortunately Ethan saw me.

"I don't think you have much to laugh about," he said, pointing a finger at me. "I heard about you and the Whitfield bitch. I want you to stay away from her."

I glanced down at the pistol tucked casually into his waistband, and wondered how many parole violations he committed on a daily basis.

"I don't actually give a damn what you want," I said flatly. "If we're going to talk *wants*, I want you to quit dealing drugs, and people in hell want iced fucking lattes, but we get what we get, right?"

I loosened my stance, ready for him to make a run at me. He'd done it before.

This time he laughed.

"Growing a pair of balls, little brother? She's not worth it. She's a high-priced piece of tail who'll use you and leave you crying, just like every Whitfield who has ever had anything to do with a Rhodale," he said, putting his gun on the table and slouching back down in his chair.

"Not every Rhodale," Anna Mae said, and her slow smile sent a shudder snaking down my spine. "If you ever get the chance, ask your girlfriend's daddy about me."

Ugh. I didn't want to know.

"She's not my girlfriend, and I don't even know her, so you can all quit worrying about it," I finally said, lying with a perfectly straight face. "Not that my personal life is any of your business."

"See that you keep it that way," Ethan advised darkly. "Rhodales and Whitfields don't mix."

"What the hell are you talking about, Ethan?" I was exasperated with the stupidity. "What did that family ever do to you?"

He narrowed his eyes, which were the exact same shade of blue as mine, Pa's, and Jeb's. Funny how the same color could look so different.

"It's more what did they do to all of us over the years, Mickey, and what they're trying to do now. Did your new little piece of ass tell you that no sooner did her loser father get back in town than he started making noises about getting his horse buddies to buy up land in the county? He's trying to turn our side of the county into some kind of suburban fucking paradise."

I deliberately looked around as if assessing the value of the tacky fake-wood-paneled walls. "So you'd get to sell this place for a fortune to the developers."

"Never," Anna Mae snarled.

"Big picture, Mick. If a bunch of rich assholes move in here, we're going to have a lot more law enforcement to worry about than dear old useless Pa."

I leaned against the door, nodding at Jeb when he clattered down the stairs from the second floor and walked into the kitchen.

"You're surprisingly well-informed for a twenty two-year-old who just got out of jail," I said. "Are you sure your facts are right?"

"When I get the wrong facts, people get hurt," Ethan said. The matter-of-factness in the way he said it got to me more than if he'd shouted and raged.

Whatever piece of the brain that governed compassion and morality was damaged in Ethan—or missing altogether. Jeb, laughing like a fool, wasn't much better.

"Maybe you need to grow a spine," I told Jeb. "Get away from Ethan and start thinking for yourself."

Ethan's eyes were cold and dead when he looked at Jeb, and I was suddenly very sorry for offering my opinion. I still didn't know what had happened between the two of them, but I didn't think it had been resolved, and I didn't want my big mouth to get Jeb shot.

"Have you seen Caro?" I asked, abruptly changing the subject.

Ethan knew exactly what I was doing, but for whatever reason, he decided to let it go. For now, at least.

"She's working at the Suds 'n Giggles," Jeb offered. "They let her use the apartment over the Laundromat in exchange for managing the place."

"And the girls?"

"School and daycare," Anna Mae muttered. "I don't know why that daughter of mine won't live here, where I could raise them babies right."

I figured that was exactly why Caroline refused to live at the compound. She'd seen first-hand how Jeb and Ethan had turned out under their mother's tender care, and she didn't want little Summer and Autumn anywhere near Anna Mae.

"I'm going to go visit her," I said, ready to end this encounter. "You want to send any message with me?"

Anna Mae loaded me down with an apple tart, a Tupperware dish filled with the stew she'd been stirring, and a loaf of fresh corn-bread. Then she started rummaging in the cupboards and refrigerator for more.

"This is all I can take in my saddlebags," I said. "I've got my books in there, too."

"You tell her I'm coming to visit those babies and get my dishes back," she said, and if it had been anybody else, I would have suspected the shine in her eyes was from a tear or two at being estranged from her only daughter.

But this was Anna Mae.

"You remember what I said," Ethan told me as I headed out the door. "I got a few days' grace period on certain things, but then we're going to talk about that job, too."

I turned around with my arms full of his mother's cooking and looked him straight in the eye. "No, we're not. I don't want to work for you."

"Want don't pay the same debt that *need* does, baby brother," Ethan said.

His cell phone rang, and a shadow crossed his face when he looked at it.

Jeb dropped the spoon he'd picked up to ladle out some stew, and gravy splattered across the white linoleum floor like arterial blood in a cop show. "More bad news?"

"Not in front of the boy," Anna Mae snapped.

Ethan nodded and pointed me to the door before answering his phone. All the way across the porch and down the steps, I imagined I could feel him aiming his pistol right between my shoulder blades. Rhodale brother had killed brother in Kentucky before, according to the tangled stories of our family history. Considering our violence-obsessed gene pool, it would probably happen again.

I didn't breathe easy until I was a good mile down the road.

CHAPTER 11

VICTORIA

I walked in on my mother arguing with Melinda but turned around before they saw me and walked right back out of the parlor, headed for the kitchen. Usually, I stood up for Melinda and tried to act as a buffer between the sharp edges she and mom used to slice and dice each other, but the day had already been exhausting. All I wanted to do was get a snack and retreat to my room.

Mrs. Kennedy was baking snickerdoodles, and I stopped at the entrance to the kitchen, enjoying the warmth and the scent of cinnamon and sugar goodness. Buddy, tucked up on a stool at the long granite counter doing his homework, flashed a grin at me, and I noticed another tooth was missing.

"Victoria, look!" He grabbed a pretzel stick off the fruit, cheese, and snacks plate in front of him and carefully pushed it through the gap in his smile. "Ta da! I can eat without opening my mouth!"

I dropped my backpack and applauded with real enthusiasm. "That's the best thing I've seen all day."

The best thing if I didn't count Mickey's deep blue eyes, his wickedly seductive smile, or the look on his face when he'd said he wanted to get to know me. But I didn't think Buddy would understand that.

"My teacher said I was very observant," he announced proudly.

Mrs. Kennedy smiled at him, waving me into the room. "I'm sure she did, sweetie," she said.

"And so you are," I said, kissing the top of his tousled head.

Buddy was Mom and Dad's miracle baby, born a good two years after the two of them had started sleeping in separate rooms, and I'd missed him like crazy when I'd been away at school.

Miracle baby, my ass. More like "too many mint juleps at the Derby" baby, Melinda had said once or twice, but I always told her to shut up. The last thing I ever, *ever* wanted to think about was my parents getting smashed and hooking up.

"I observed that almost everybody in Clark Elementary is a white person," he continued innocently. "Not like back home at all."

"Say goodbye to diversity, Buddy," I advised him, selecting a cookie.

The cook cast a disapproving glance at me, but she didn't disagree.

Buddy slapped his crayon down on the map of Kentucky he'd been coloring. "Hey, no fair! Mrs. Kennedy said no cookies before dinner."

I kind of envied him. I couldn't remember back to a time when a cookie had distracted me.

"You can share mine," I said in a stage whisper, breaking it in two pieces and giving him the bigger one. "But only if you let me color part of your map."

He happily agreed, and we sat there and ate our cookie and some fruit and colored Kentucky purple, green, and cornflower blue, while he quizzed me on the state bird (Cardinal), state flower (goldenrod), and state song.

"'My Old Kentucky Home'?" I guessed.

"Yes! But what about the state insect?" His entire face lit up, because he loved it when he stumped me, and we both knew insects were not my area of expertise.

"We have a state insect? That's gross," I said, stalling.

"Yes! And you have to guess what it is!"

"The horsefly?"

"It is around here," Mrs. Kennedy said, not looking up from her potato peeling.

"No!" Buddy swung around on his stool. "The honeybee!"

"You're a honeybee," I said, making my hands into claws and growling. "I'm going to tickle you!"

Buddy shrieked with laughter and ran out of the room, clomping down the hall, probably off to pester Pete just like I had at his age. We heard the front door bang shut and my mother yell at him not to slam doors. Mrs. Kennedy and I sighed at the same time.

"Can I do anything to help?"

She cooked a huge lunch for the ranch hands every day, but they got breakfast and dinner on their own. It wasn't like the old days, where everybody bunked in the barn and ate all their meals together. Half of the staff lived on the ranch in a series of small cottages, but the rest lived out in town, and they all wanted their own space during their time off. Then again, ranch hands hadn't had cable TV or the Internet in the old days, either.

Mrs. Kennedy had worked for Gran as long as I'd been alive, but I'd never known there to be a Mr. Kennedy, and she was kind but reserved, so I'd never felt comfortable asking her about him.

Before we'd moved in, she'd been used to relaxing in the evenings, since Gran never ate much, but now that we lived here, she had to do dinners, too. I felt like we'd added a burden to her day, so I usually asked if I could help, but she always said no.

Today she surprised me.

"Maybe you could slice up those carrots?"

"Sure."

We worked in silence for a while, and then she cleared her throat. "This is none of my business, and I know I'm overstepping, but I feel like somebody has to warn you—"

"About the Rhodales." I finished her sentence, setting my knife down on the cutting board with a little bit too much force.

"Well, yes." She dried her hands on her apron and turned to look me in the eyes. "They're trouble. That family has been no good since long before anybody can remember, and—"

"But the *sheriff* is a *Rhodale*," I said, knowing I was being rude to keep interrupting her, but I wasn't winning the rudeness sweepstakes in this conversation, after all. I wasn't the one butting into somebody else's private life. "So he turned out okay, didn't he?"

"Yes, but he's not . . . he's not . . ."

"He's not what?" I folded my arms.

"He's . . . not a good sheriff," she finished, almost triumphantly.

My mouth fell open, and all I could think was *poor Mickey*. Growing up under the cloud of past generations of "no-good Rhodales" must not be much of an incentive to turn out any better, especially when popular sentiment had already judged him and found him guilty. Guilty of being a Rhodale, at least.

Of course, we were the Whitfields, of Whitfield County. I wondered what people were telling him about us.

Melinda wandered in, only weaving a little, but I figured it was my cue to leave Mrs. Kennedy to her vegetables and her prejudices.

"Here are your carrots. I'm taking Melinda upstairs."

The kindness in Mrs. Kennedy's eyes made me feel vaguely ashamed for snapping at her, but after hearing the truth behind Mickey's story, I couldn't help but be outraged on his behalf.

I wondered what that said about me and my actual feelings for Mickey Rhodale.

I waited until Melinda turned off the shower to start my interrogation.

"How did you manage to get wasted when you stayed home sick from school?"

"I had a few pills left in one of my purses. The black sequined one," she admitted, opening the shower door.

I shook my head and handed her a towel, watching to make sure she didn't slip and fall. She'd done it before and had a small scar on her right temple. Showering while stoned wasn't a good idea.

Melinda had the same blond hair and green eyes as me and Mom, but while the combination looked stern and patrician on Mom, and not bad but fairly ordinary on me, on Melinda it looked ethereal, like she was an elf or a fairy changeling. Whenever I caught her watching the rest of us with a faintly confused expression, as if she didn't understand how she'd ended up in such a difficult family, it only enhanced the impression.

She dried off and started to get dressed, and I finally felt like she was steady enough to manage on her own, so I left the bathroom and headed for the chair next to her window. I had to move a pile of clean, folded laundry to the floor before I could sit on it. Melinda loved to fold laundry—sometimes she'd come into my room and fold all of mine, chattering away—but she never, ever put it away, so her room usually looked like a garage sale about to happen.

Not that a *Whitfield* would ever have a garage sale.

"You promised me no more pills," I said, knowing I was wasting my breath but unable to stop myself. Melinda's addiction was the carnival ride from hell; the rest of us whirled around and around, repeating our terrified reactions while never getting anywhere.

"What? You want me to take up meth, rural Kentucky's drug of choice? That stuff's poison, baby sister. One straight shot to selling my skanky, unwashed, toothless body on a street corner." Her voice was full of contempt, which struck me as unjustified.

Or perhaps there were class distinctions even among junkies.

"No," I said, trying not to grit my teeth. "That was not a multiple-choice question. it isn't check one for pills, two for alcohol, or three for meth. I want you to stop *all* of this stuff before you kill yourself."

"I don't know how to get through the day without something to make my brain shut down. I can't quit thinking about Caleb," she said, shivering in her oversized sweatshirt and baggy sweatpants. "It's my fault he's dead."

I couldn't figure out how to fix this for her, so I took refuge in practicalities. "Dry your hair, Melinda, you're going to freeze. You're dripping all over the place.

She toweled off her hair and then climbed into her bed and pulled a quilt around her shoulders, every slow, halting movement projecting misery and guilt, while I tried to think of what to say.

"Okay, first, it's all right to be sad," I began, but she violently shook her head.

"Not according to Mom. 'You barely knew that boy. We've had enough of your moaning and whining about him.'" She captured Mom's haughty impatience perfectly, and I had to fight back the urge to smile at the impersonation.

Instead, I tossed a stuffed dog that had been wedged in the corner of the chair at her.

"Since when do we ever use Mom as a barometer of emotional health? When Heather's Angel had such a hard time foaling, she told me 'horses die all the time, Victoria, deal with it.'"

Melinda shuddered. "She didn't!"

"Yes, she totally did, and I was only around Buddy's age," I said, getting angry all over again just thinking about it. "But that's not the point, here. You cared about Caleb, and now he's gone. There'd be something wrong with you if you didn't feel bad."

"Especially since I killed him," she said darkly.

"No. You didn't. He decided to go. Nobody twisted his arm. You haven't had time to figure out the drug scene around here, right? So it's not like you told him to go buy pot from the scary meth dealers in their dangerously explosive meth-cooking trailer," I pointed out.

It was hard to believe that it had only been a little more than two weeks since the night of the fire. The night I'd met Mickey. I'd spent most of that time trying to ignore him. *Two weeks*. How was that possible? I already felt like he'd been haunting my thoughts forever.

"You don't understand," Melinda said. She buried her head in her pillow. She wasn't ready to listen to reason, and I didn't have the patience or energy to try to force her to, when she just wanted to escape into sleep.

I met my mom in the hallway outside Melinda's room.

"She's napping."

"Good. She can sleep it off. I've locked up your father's liquor cabinet," Mom said, grimacing with distaste.

"That's not enough. She needs rehab, Mom. She's not going to get better on her own, especially after Caleb—"

My mother sliced a hand through the air in dismissal, as if I were an unruly child. "Whitfields don't go to rehab. It's trashy. Do you really want your sister exposed to that whole celebrity rehab mentality?"

"You haven't even been a Whitfield your whole life! How did you buy into their line of crap lock, stock, and barrel?"

"I've been a Whitfield long enough, Victoria," she said, sighing and showing me a rare glimpse of the real person under her mask as she pulled her sweater tight around her shrinking body.

"Are you eating, Mom? I'm serious." I suddenly wanted to hug her, even though part of me—the tiny, selfish corner of my soul I kept stuffed far down in the dark—wanted to run away from my family and their problems. I was so tired of playing the parts of dutiful daughter and responsible sister.

Her face stiffened and closed off, as if I'd crossed an invisible line labeled "Priscilla's Anorexia."

"I'm fine. There will be no rehab. We deal with our problems ourselves."

I threw my hands up in the air and headed down the hall toward Buddy's room, where I could hear him talking to his Xbox. I could always tell when I wasn't going to get any further with my mom. I'd try my dad later. I lobbed a parting shot, though.

"My sister needs to go to rehab, whether you think it's trashy or not, or you might have a Whitfield who winds up dead."

When I walked in his room, Buddy immediately grabbed my hand and pulled me down to sit next to him on the bed, handing me a controller for the game. Finally, the *one* relationship in my life that wasn't complicated. I settled in to fly dragons and defend the palace from evil trolls, wishing that I could identify the bad guys so easily in real life.

CHAPTER 12

MICKEY

"I don't get the 'giggles' part of Suds 'n Giggles," I told my sister. "What's funny about doing laundry?"

We sat in the tiny family room of her apartment. Caro was on the beat-up purple plaid couch, trying to hide her cigarettes between the worn cushions, probably so I didn't get on her case again about smoking in front of the girls. I was sitting cross-legged on the floor while my nieces brushed my hair, jumped on my lap, and told me the kind of long, rambling, incomprehensible stories that only four- and six-year-old girls could tell.

The apartment, like the Laundromat itself, had seen better days. The walls were painted a particularly nasty color of institutional green, the mud-brown dining table and chairs had probably come with the place, and the only splashes of color came from the secondhand red, white, and blue toy box and giant pink dollhouse that Caro had picked up at a garage sale.

Autumn, Caro's black-haired, blue-eyed eldest, had once spent an hour and a half at a barbecue telling me about the thirty-minute TV show she'd watched that morning. I'd walked around the rest of the day with my eyes glazed over and my brain stuffed full of pink sparkly unicorns. Summer, the brown-eyed, brown-haired youngest, was a little quieter until she got revved up. She was the budding hair stylist, who was clutching a fistful of my hair in a death grip while she whacked away at my head with the brush.

"I have no idea what's funny about it," Caroline said wearily. "It's a Laundromat. The sign should just say Laundromat. The owner thinks she's clever, I guess."

The place didn't close until nine, but Caro's part-time help ran the place during the afternoon and early evening while my sister took care of her kids. Then she'd put the girls in bed and run down to handle the closing, she'd told me. She looked tired, but I couldn't remember a time since she'd gotten pregnant with Autumn that she hadn't looked tired.

Autumn's loser of a father had hit the road as soon as he'd learned he was going to be a parent, and Caro had only been sixteen at the time. I remembered all the drama and shouting matches when she'd announced she was keeping the baby, and then two years later she'd turned around and done it all over again with a different loser. At least that had been my perspective as a smart-assed thirteen-year-old kid. Now I was old enough to understand how hard it was to be alone—and how far a person might go to be with someone he wanted, no matter the consequences.

Summer stood on the couch behind me and leaned over until she was staring at me upside down. "Would you like ponytails?"

I pretended to consider the question. "Only if you have purple ribbons," I said, spying the purple ribbons on the floor by the toy box.

She shrieked so loudly that my skull reverberated. "I do! And more in my room!"

She ran to get them, and Autumn tore off after her to find her latest doll to show me. Caroline smiled at me.

"You're always so good with them. I wish you could come around more often," she said.

Guilt washed over me. I hadn't even realized she'd moved in here, because it had been August since I'd seen her. The attack had lain between us, festering with guilt and shame, because I think Caro felt like it had been her fault I'd been sent to juvie. I'd been ashamed she'd seen me turn so violent—so Ethan-like. Instead of bringing us together, it had nearly driven us apart forever. But she was my sister—the only one I'd ever have—and she hadn't wanted to leave things between us like that, so she'd tried to reach out.

I hadn't been able to bring myself to respond at the time, but that she'd even tried had meant something, and here I was.

"I'm really sorry, Caro. School started, and—"

She waved a hand. "No, no. I wasn't trying to give you a guilt trip. God knows I understand being busy. Speaking of which, I need to feed the girls. Lucky for them that Ma sent food. It was going to be macaroni and cheese again."

"Hey, nothing beats a good mac and cheese," I said. "Can I help you set the table?"

Caro grinned as the girls shrieked their way back into the room. "I think you're going to be too busy getting beautiful, Uncle Mickey."

Twenty minutes later, I was beautiful, all right. I was wearing five or six tiny, purple-ribboned ponytails and eating Anna Mae's cooking for the first time, ever.

"She's a good cook," I had to admit.

"Her single maternal skill," Caro said dryly. "Speaking of cooking, did you hear anything else from Pa about Ethan's . . . kitchen fire?"

Autumn looked up, her eyes wide. "Uncle Ethan set fire to the kitchen?"

"We're not really sure, sweetheart," I told her. "We think it might actually have been an accident."

I didn't really think that at all, but that's what Ethan had convinced my Dad to believe, and I didn't want to worry Caro when I had no proof of my suspicions.

"I had an accident at daycare once," Summer confided, her tiny face solemn. "But that was back when I was little, and I had extra pants in my cubby. Did Uncle Ethan have extra pants?"

Autumn cracked up. "Not that kind of accident, dummy. Grown-ups don't wet their pants."

"My friend Nina's grandma does," Summer shouted. "They had to put her in a *home*. And don't you call me a dummy! I'm four!"

"Okay, bath time for overtired, overexcited little girls," Caro said. "Mickey, do you want to bring Summer?"

"Sure. Come with Uncle Mickey?" I didn't wait for her to answer before I scooped her up off her chair and into a hug.

Autumn promptly burst into tears. "I wanted to go with Uncle Mickey," she wailed, and then she ran off down the hall.

"I'm sorry, Caro. I'm not much help," I said, patting Summer's back when her little face crumpled and hoping she wouldn't melt down, too.

"It's not your fault, Mickey. They're kids, and sometimes kids get overstimulated this time of day."

"I'd better go," I said, feeling uncomfortably like my visit had made my sister's life more difficult. "Homework, and stuff. But could I maybe come back on a weekend and take them out for ice cream or a movie or something? Give you a break?"

For the first time that evening, Caro flashed a real smile as she took her sleepy daughter out of my arms. "That would be great. There's a new Pixar film coming up they're dying to see. I'll let you know when it releases, and maybe we can figure something out."

Impulsively, I leaned over and gave both of them a hug, and then I walked down to the bathroom and hugged Autumn, too. She'd been busy dumping all of the bath toys in the tub, apparently having forgotten her earlier tears.

"Have a nice bath, punkin."

"Bye, Uncle Mickey."

When I stood up, I caught sight of myself in the mirror and started laughing. "Maybe Uncle Mickey will leave these purple ribbons here at your house, for next time."

It was just getting dark when I made it home, but I noticed that Pa's car was nowhere in sight. The house was all lit up, though, which meant that Mom was home. I gave myself a mental smack for forgetting to call her and tell her I'd be late, but when I walked in she looked up from her papers and smiled.

"Is it dinner time already? I had a long chat after school with the neighbor about whether or not we should cut down that elm tree, and since then I've been sitting here daydreaming, I must confess," she said.

She did that a lot. Daydreamed. I wondered sometimes whether she was imagining a life lived in a different direction, one in which she hadn't moved to Clark, Kentucky, to take a job and wound up marrying my dad and taking on all of his problems when she'd said "I do." Ironically enough, they'd met when he, then Deputy Rhodale, had visited the elementary school to talk about Stranger Danger.

Should have paid attention, Mom.

"I already ate." I sat down at the table across from her and looked around, trying to see our house with new eyes.

Victoria's eyes.

Our whole house would probably fit inside the Whitfield guest bathroom. My folks had called this their "starter house," but I'd been the only baby that ever came along, and we'd wound up staying right here. It was a comfortable place, filled with warm colors and the Kentucky folk art Mom liked to collect. I wouldn't trade it for all the mansions in Kentucky.

"Victoria Whitfield is in my history class," I said abruptly, not sure why I was telling her.

"Her brother, Buddy, is in my class," she said, and we both sat and stared at each other for a while.

"I never understood why your father hates the family so much," she finally said. "It was a Rhodale who burned down the barn, after all."

She was right. Meredith Rhodale's husband had set the fire that had killed his wife and Larry Whitfield sixty years ago. Nobody had ever known whether he'd set it on purpose or not, just that he'd been carrying a lantern when he'd gone to the barn to check on his horse, and he'd found his wife in the act with a Whitfield.

Meredith and Larry had never made it out of the barn that night, but Rhodale's horse did, which fueled the speculation that he'd either killed them first and then set the fire to try to cover it up, or else he'd gotten his horse out of the barn and then blocked them in somehow so they'd burn to death together.

"The feud started a long time before that," I said. "It's strange, but Victoria doesn't know anything about it. How is that even possible? There have been Whitfields and Rhodales going at it for a couple of centuries."

She shook her head. "She grew up in a different life. This nonsense had nothing to do with her. The rest of the world is getting on with their lives."

"Mom, we looked this stuff up. Whitfields and Rhodales have been fighting each other since that first property dispute, way back when. It got worse, and then it got better. We're supposed to be more civilized these days, but I think we're only better at spackling a layer of polite over the surface of angry."

She sighed. "I know, but maybe it's only still alive on the Rhodale side—"

"No. You should have seen Richard Whitfield at the fire. He hated me on sight, just for being a Rhodale."

Mom's eyes narrowed as she went mama wolf on me. "What did he say to you? I'll have a talk with that man. Just because he's a Whitfield, he can't talk to my son like that. I'll—"

I grinned at her. "Mom. *Mom.* Stop. I'm seventeen, not seven. You can't fight my battles anymore."

She sighed. "I know. You're right. It's a hard habit to break. At least we don't have a Romeo and Juliet kind of thing going on—"

I met her gaze, and she faltered. "Oh, honey. No. Your father would hit the roof if he heard—"

I shrugged. "Ethan already has. He just called me to an 'or else' meeting at the compound, and Anna Mae suggested there'd been something between her and Victoria's dad."

"Did you ask what?"

I made a gagging face, trying to distract my mom from the subject of Victoria. "No. I was too busy trying not to puke. But I went to see Caroline and the girls afterward."

My mom's face softened at the mention of my nieces. "How are they doing? I need to get over there for a visit. I have Autumn's birthday present ready, and I bought a little something for Summer so she doesn't feel left out."

Mom and Caroline had struck up a surprising friendship over the years, and she'd been one of the few people to stand firmly on Caro's side and never try to talk her out of keeping the babies. It had been one of the only times she and Anna Mae had been on the same side of an issue.

"They're good. She looks tired, and the girls are a handful, but the apartment is way nicer than that dump she lived in over by the tracks this summer."

Mom froze, and I realized what I'd said. It was the first time I'd mentioned, even indirectly, the attack since it had happened.

Caro moved a lot, whether from a feeling of restlessness or in an attempt to improve her situation each time, but she hadn't realized that the bar down the block from her last apartment building had been so dangerous. After the . . . incident, while I was rotting in juvie and Ethan was in jail, one of Ethan's thugs had paid the bar owner, who also owned the apartments, a little visit. The landlord had quickly refunded Caro's security deposit and that month's rent, and the owner's sons had helped her move. I just hadn't known she'd moved into the upstairs of the Laundromat.

Mom stood up and headed for the kitchen, and I trailed after her, wondering why I hadn't kept my mouth shut. I grabbed an apple from the green glass bowl on the counter and bit into it, trying to figure out what to say, but she surprised me by leaving the subject of Caroline and going back to Victoria.

"You like this girl?" She had her back to me, but I could tell from the tension in her shoulders that she was worried.

" 'Like' isn't a strong enough word," I found myself admitting. "I don't know exactly what the word is, though. There's nothing between us yet, though, so quit worrying. I just want to get to know her. She's . . . different."

Mom turned around and leaned back against the sink. "You said *yet*, so I know you plan to go after her. Mickey, please be careful. I've always thought this feud was absolutely ridiculous, but it's deadly serious to your father. I don't know all the reasons why, either, but there has been quite a history of financial double-dealings and other problems between the two families over the years, too."

"Ethan's blaming Victoria's father for trying to get more law enforcement around here to protect his rich horse people. More cops means less freedom for his criminals."

Her eyes were troubled. "Ethan is more dangerous than ever. I've heard stories . . . just stay away from him for a while, okay? And Mickey, I think there was a problem between your dad and Richard Whitfield over Anna Mae, back in high school."

I choked on my apple. "Anna Mae? Are you kidding me?"

Mom got that pinched look on her face. "She was the beauty of the county back then, or so I hear."

"So her looks didn't always match her troll-like personality?" I grinned but then had to duck when Mom tried to thwack me in the head with a dish towel.

She smiled a little, too, but then she got serious again, fast. "I wish I could tell you to stay away from this girl, but since I know that won't work, maybe let's not mention Victoria Whitfield to your father just yet, Mick."

Probably a good idea, but I was getting awfully tired of hearing all the reasons why I should stay away from Victoria, especially when I knew I had no intention of doing it.

CHAPTER 13

VICTORIA

It was the high point of a small-town Kentucky week: the Friday afternoon of a home football game. I wouldn't be there, though. I'd be spending the evening at the ranch, instead, because Melinda had skipped school again, claiming a migraine, and spent her time figuring out how to pick the lock on Dad's booze cabinet. And she'd figured it out at least a few hours before I got home from school, according to the results of my personal Melinda Drunk-o-Meter.

Glassy eyes? Check. Too-careful pronunciation and increasingly devious attempts to hide both the bottles and her breath? Check. This time, though, I was rebelling. Instead of trying to sober her up and hide the evidence, I'd left the cabinet door swinging open, half off its hinges. I'd just smiled and nodded when Melinda snuck by me in the kitchen, hiding her stolen glass bottle under the crocheted throw from one of the chairs, while I prepped the chicken and put it in the oven.

We were finally going to have it out. It was the perfect storm of events: Melinda was drinking, Buddy was staying overnight with a friend, Gran was out to dinner with *her* friends, and Mrs. Kennedy had weekends off. Mom, Dad, Melinda, and I would be the only ones home, and this time my parents would have no excuse not to see how bad their daughter was becoming.

She needed rehab. At the very least, we needed not to have a *liquor cabinet* in the same house with a budding alcoholic.

Dad hit the door first, but went straight for the shower. I don't think he ever actually touched a horse, but he always wanted to wash off the day whenever he'd been anywhere near the barns. Or maybe it was another stench he was washing off every time he thought about the failure of his business in the city.

He wasn't good at losing, my dad. He didn't take it as a challenge—it didn't build his character. He was definitely not the type to pick himself up by his bootstraps. No, he raged and fought and kicked and screamed until the bitter end, and tried to take as many people down with him as he could.

Mom didn't get home until I was pulling the baked potatoes out of the oven, and she headed straight for the wine fridge and pulled out a bottle. I mentally smacked myself in the forehead. I'd forgotten about the wine fridge. Probably because Melinda hated the taste of wine, but if we took the other alcohol away, I bet she'd find a way to drink it.

"Why are you cooking?" Mom looked around vaguely, like she expected Mrs. Kennedy or Rachael Ray to pop up out of nowhere and produce a gourmet dinner.

"Nobody else was here." I started carrying everything out to the dining room table, knowing better than to ask for any help.

Dad came in when I was filling glasses with water, and he grinned at both of us and then took the pitcher out of my hands and finished the job. His great mood and uncharacteristic helpfulness probably meant that some poor rival had gone down in flames.

"Why don't you pour me a glass of that wine, Priscilla? I made a deal that smoked Emerald Farms today. Poor fool thought he could take advantage of me because I've been away from the horse business for a little while." His eyes were sparkling, and I wasted a futile moment wishing that once—just once—he could get that excited over something to do with his children.

Melinda sidled into the room and walked, very carefully, to the fridge for a bottle of water. Unfortunately, she knocked Mom's bottle of wine over. I rushed to grab it before it rolled onto the floor, and Melinda mopped at the puddle, making the mess worse. I finished the job for her and then started carrying the remaining dishes to the dining room table. Everybody helped carry, even Melinda. Setting the table was the one area in which my family could act like a team. *That* would be over by the time I asked for help with the dirty dishes.

Melinda wobbled a little—just the tiniest bit—as she put the salad bowl on the table. It slipped from her hands, but my dad, old Eagle Eyes himself, caught it. He probably recognized the fumble fingers from his own drunken teen years.

"What is going on here? Is she *drunk*?" He bit off the words in Mom's direction, so naturally she looked at me.

I sat down and starting scooping butter on my baked potato. Calm on the outside and shaking on the inside.

"Victoria? What is the meaning of this?"

I shrugged and reached for the salt. "Don't ask me. I came home from school and started cooking."

Melinda very carefully sat down on the exact center of the chair. "Why don't you two ever talk to *me*? I'm the one who's drunk," she admitted quietly. "I'm the screwup, not Victoria. Why do you always pretend I don't even exist?"

Mom, proving Melinda's point, ignored her and pointed at me. "You take your sister upstairs *right now*, and—"

"No," I said. I plunked a piece of chicken on my plate that my stomach was too messed up to eat.

Mom's mouth fell open. "What did you say?"

"I said no. She's not *my* daughter. Why don't you deal with her for once? Who handled all this when I was at school, anyway? Or didn't they give you directions for parenting your addict kid in the Ashford-Hutchinson Academy handbook?"

Mom gasped, and I almost felt bad for the low blow, but the ice in her expression put paid to *that*. "I don't know where this attitude is coming from, but—"

Melinda stood up, only shaking a little bit, and turned to face my parents.

"Am I invisible? That must be it," she said, but she never raised her voice. "I'm invisible to you! You don't see me at all. Well, that's great. That's fucking *great*. Because nobody misses invisible people when they're gone!"

With that, she reached for her glass of water and knocked over the bowl of buttered peas. Unbelievably, now both of my parents looked at *me*.

"Are you kidding with this?" Dad's face was red with not-very-well suppressed rage.

I shrugged again, almost shaking with the need to start fixing things. Drag Melinda out of the room, clean things up, smooth things over.

Not this time.

"I never liked peas much, anyway," I said, instead. I reached for the salad.

"My nerves can't take this," my mother said, and I finally snapped.

"This is not the eighteenth century. You do not have a *nerves* problem. You are not going to *swoon*. You have an addict daughter who needs rehab," I said.

"And you," I said, rounding on my father, who was still standing there, frozen, watching peas roll toward him. "You can't just check out on your family to play business tycoon. Can't you see that Melinda needs you?"

Melinda shot such a wounded look at me that I felt betrayed.

"What *now?*"

"You're doing it, too. Talking about me like I'm not even here," she said with such quiet dignity that I felt ashamed. "I thought at least *you* were on my side."

"I am on your side, Mel. But guess who else needs to take responsibility for your drinking problem? *You*. It's *not* your fault that Caleb died, but it *is* your fault that you're using his death as an excuse to act even worse than usual."

All three of them were staring at me. My mind flashed a visual of what we'd look like to anybody peeking in: a bizarre snapshot of American life, only one step away from our own trashy reality TV show.

Clark High: The Sequel—Watching the Wacky Whitfields.

I'd had enough of them, of the situation, of all of it.

"For once, somebody else can clean up the mess. I'm going to bed," I said, and then, slowly and calmly, I left the room and walked up the stairs.

Nobody said a word to stop me.

CHAPTER 14
MICKEY

The locker room smelled like stinky feet, overactive hormones, and smelly armpits—that distinct cloud of odor that only a crowd of teenage boys can generate. After the first five minutes, I couldn't even smell it anymore. After the first hour, the stench of nervous sweat joined the mix, and I yelled at somebody to prop open the door.

"Coach is late. He's never late," I said, adding to the Stupid Remark quota of the room, since probably every player on the team had said something similar during the past half hour. It was twenty minutes till kickoff, and we needed to be on the field, warming up.

Victoria hadn't so much as looked at me that day, which had put me in a foul mood. I knew it was contradictory of me to be ticked off that she'd done exactly what I'd asked her to do—leave me alone—but my head didn't seem to be talking sense to my gut much these days, especially where Victoria was concerned. Coach's no-show was making my mood even worse. I didn't like being worried that he'd been in a car accident or something. He'd been one of the few who'd been on my side after the incident.

Basically, I was no good at being worried, so it always turned into being pissed off.

Sam Oliver sat down on the bench across from me, and he looked as concerned as I felt. "There's something wrong. No way would he miss this game. And I hate to be a jerk, but there's a University of Kentucky scout stopping by, I heard. If I miss out on a chance to get noticed, that's a problem."

Sam's dad worked for the Whitfields, but I don't think he made a ton of money, and Sam had sisters. If any of them wanted to go to college, they were going to have to find their own money to do it, like me. Luckily Sam was a rock star on the field, so he had pretty good chances of getting noticed.

The U of K scouts loved us, since we were called the Wildcats, too. We suspected we got more than our share of attention from their scouts, and this was a fact that Coach took full advantage of. He always knew about their visits in advance, so if he wasn't here, it was bad.

Maybe really bad.

Just when I was trying to decide if we should move the team out to the field to start warm-ups, the door banged open and Coach stumbled into the room. His face was gray. I didn't know if he was having a heart attack or what, so I jumped up and grabbed my phone off the shelf to call 911.

"Rhodale!" His voice was wrong, too. Raspy and hoarse, as if he'd been already yelling at us for an hour or two, instead of just showing up. "Get your ass out of my locker room, you son of a bitch. Now."

All sound and motion stopped as everybody froze in place and stared back and forth between the two of us. Coach was a tough old goat, built like the retired Marine he was—all muscle and no fat. He didn't put up with any crap from anybody, but he'd never spoken to any of us in that vicious tone of voice before, and he'd sure as hell never called us any names worse than "lazy slackers" or "clumsy morons."

"What's going on, Coach?" I was proud of myself for sounding calm, because I wasn't even in the same ballpark as calm.

He stumbled forward, fists clenched. Sam and a couple of the other guys stood up, whether to help him or stop him, I wasn't sure.

"My sister is in the hospital, thanks to your lowlife brother. One time. That's all it took. One time she tried meth at a party, and now she might die. You tell Ethan that I'm coming for him, do you hear me?" He shoved me back with one meaty hand, and my back hit the metal front of my locker, hard.

Fury seared through me, burning restraint to ash, and I got right up in his face. "Tell him yourself. I'm not Ethan's messenger boy. In fact, I'm not his anything. I don't run drugs, and I don't have anything to do with them. How would you feel if people called you a druggie because your sister took some?"

His face contorted and turned from gray to a mottled shade of purplish red and choking noises and spittle came out of his mouth. "Get out! You're out of here. You're off the team. I never want to see your ugly Rhodale face again!"

I didn't bother to argue. I just grabbed my bag and walked out the door, still in uniform, still surrounded by complete silence. Nobody tried to stop me, and nobody stood up for me. It was Little League all over again.

I shoved my way through the crowds of people arriving for the game, trying to ignore the stares and comments from everyone watching me head the wrong way in my uniform.

"Isn't that the Rhodale kid?"

"Wonder what he did this time?"

I slammed the bike in gear and roared out of there, trying to drown out the whispered echoes of shame and humiliation in my brain. For some reason, all I wanted was to talk to Victoria about it, which would just add more humiliation when she hung up on me.

I had to get out of this damn town. I'd always known I had no future here, but now I was beginning to realize I had no present, either. My entire life was suffocating underneath the weight of the past.

CHAPTER 15
VICTORIA

I stared at my bedroom walls as they closed in on me, all but suffocating me with claustrophobia, and called myself a coward. It was true, and it made me mad. Then I said it out loud, and the rusty sound of my own voice, which I hadn't been using for much, made me even madder.

It had been a horrible week—ever since that horrible dinner. I'd hidden in my room, other than going to school. Nothing had changed, of course. Melinda was still a twitchy mess. Somebody had cleaned up the dining room and kitchen that night, but it was like they thought they'd swept the problem under the rug with the scraps.

Most of all I was aching to talk to Mickey. I had heard what happened—the whole school had been buzzing about how his football coach had gone insane and kicked Mickey off the team for something that Ethan had done. He'd told me we were a bad idea and I should stay away, but I didn't care. I figured he needed somebody on his side right now. He wasn't answering his phone, though, and he hadn't answered my text. So I wasn't going to be pathetic and keep trying to communicate when he'd obviously slammed a door between us.

I debated going to his job to find him, but the truck didn't need gas, so I didn't have a good enough excuse. Mostly, I sat around the house watching Melinda in case she went on another bender, or I escaped to the barn to spend time with the mares, particularly Heather's Angel, who'd been my special horse since I was a kid.

She was retired from breeding now, but she was so gentle that the other mares liked having her around. Since a stressed mare was more likely to have complications with her pregnancy, Pete kept Angel in the foaling barn and let her out into the paddock with the others. Some farms used donkeys or small ponies for what I thought of as "calming companions," but Angel did the job for us and it gave her a purpose in retirement. I'd always missed her so desperately when I was in Louisville or at school, and now we were both enjoying spending time together while I curried her and gave her special attention and treats.

Our relationship, like mine and Buddy's, was a simple, uncomplicated one that let me breathe and feel almost sane. Unlike how I felt about Mickey. Or, these days, Melinda.

I found Gran in her study, glasses perched on the end of her nose, going over paperwork. It was a job she hated, so my chances of pulling her away from it weren't too bad.

"Gran, can I talk to you?"

She glanced up at me, and her shrewd eyes took in my worried expression.

"Absolutely. I was getting tired of all this, anyway. Shall we head out to the barn?"

Gran felt like I did about the horses. She'd always loved them more than was practical, refusing to sell off the nonperformers until my grandfather had complained that she was putting them in financial jeopardy. The problem was that thoroughbreds that couldn't race weren't very valuable as breeders, either, unless they had very good bloodlines. Some owners would sell them off to poorer and poorer operations, until sometimes they weren't being treated right or fed enough, or maybe faced the worst fate of all—being sent to slaughter.

The thought of it made me sick and reminded me to renew my membership in the national group that was working on the issue.

We walked into the barn and down the springy rubber mats that were designed to be gentle for horses' hooves and legs, and Gran peeked into each stall. One of the grooms passed us, leading Temper's Folly's colt, and Gran automatically put an arm out to block me.

"Who are you more worried about, me or the colt?" I teased her, and she rewarded me with a grin.

"I'll take the Fifth. Remember to be extra careful around the colts' fronts and the fillies' backsides, because—"

"Colts usually rear, and fillies usually buck," I said, completing the instruction she'd given me since I was a toddler. "Because stallions in the wild fight to keep their territory and protect their herd by rearing and attacking, while the mares lash out with their hind legs. I know, Gran. You taught me well."

She touched a lucky horseshoe that was nailed to the wall near the first stall. She and my grandfather had built this place "with their own two hands," as she liked to tell us every summer. She missed him, still, I could tell, although he'd died so long ago that I couldn't really remember him, other than stories Dad told us of how his father had liked to talk about bloodlines—in people and in horses. Gran always said that he'd been the great love of her life, in a way that left no doubt it was true.

Watching the disaster that was my parents' marriage, I'd wondered what kind of relationship was in my future. Or relationships. Not everybody married her college sweetheart and then spent the rest of her life stuck with him, like my mother had done. For a second, my mind danced around the idea of Mickey Rhodale. What would his dark intensity become in five years? Ten?

Forget that. What would he be like in five *weeks*? And why did the prospect of finding out intrigue me so much?

I followed Gran down the aisle and watched her watch the horses. The intimacy of the quiet darkness, the only sound the soft snuffling of sleeping horses, helped me center my thoughts.

I took a deep breath. "Okay. I've already tried to talk to Mom and Dad about this, and they shut me down, so don't tell me to talk to them first. It's Melinda."

She nodded. "Her drinking problem."

I'd wondered if she'd known, although she'd have had to be in denial or stupid not to figure it out, and Gran was neither.

"It's drugs, too, Gran," I said quietly, almost whispering, although there was nobody around to hear me.

She made a little sound of distress. "Oh, no. That's—I don't know why, because drinking is equally bad, but drugs always feel worse to me. I guess it's my generation."

"We need to help her. We need to get her into rehab. This is not something she can kick at home on her own, or even with our help."

Gran slowly nodded. "I think you're right, but it's a matter of getting your parents to agree. I don't have any authority over you kids, you know."

"She's eighteen," I reminded her.

"There is that, but I can't imagine your sister having the strength to do this if your parents actively oppose her on it."

We headed back to the house in silence, looking up at the spill of stars in the night sky and listening to the sounds of nature that I'd never heard at night in the city. The cool autumn November air carried the faint scents of Gran's flower beds and the stronger one of horse, but then again, no matter where I went on the ranch, I could always smell that unmistakable aroma.

I'd always heard the pounding of hooves in the sounds of thunder, too. My childhood dreams, like those of so many little girls, had all been about horses, but unlike most of those girls, I'd had actual horses, riding lessons, and races in my life, whenever I'd been here at the ranch, and I'd been bereft when I'd had to leave.

"I'm glad you're my grandmother," I said suddenly.

Gran laughed, but I could tell she was surprised and pleased. "I'm glad you're my granddaughter."

I wasn't quite sure how to articulate the emotion that had been behind my words, but I tried. "You listen to me, and you actually hear what I'm saying. You gave us a safe place to land when Dad screwed everything up."

She sighed. "That's my son you're talking about, remember."

"Will you help me? With Melinda?"

"I promise I'll do my best, Victoria, but she has to want to get better, or it won't work," she warned.

"I think she does. I'm sure she does," I said, but it was more out of wishful thinking than any degree of certainty. I wasn't really sure *what* was in my sister's mind these days, other than sadness, guilt, and confusion.

Gran patted my hand. "We'll figure it out together. I wish you didn't always carry the weight of the world on your shoulders."

I didn't know how to respond to that. Who else in my family would do it?

Time to broach an even tougher subject, even though she'd warned me not to do it. "Gran, I know you don't want to talk about them, but I can't count on anybody else to tell me the truth. Will you please tell me about the Rhodales."

Gran inhaled sharply and sat down hard on the top porch step. "I told you that I don't want to hear that name."

"I know you told me that, but I'm tired of everybody warning me against them and nobody telling me why. I can't exactly Google 'what's wrong with the Rhodales,' and I don't know who else to ask. What's the big freaking deal?"

She gave me a look.

"It's a long, horrible story, and I don't care to go into it," she said, and the slight quaver in her voice suddenly made me remember that she was nearly seventy years old.

"Why can't you just let it go?" she asked.

I decided on the spot not to mention Mickey. I didn't want to cause her any more distress beyond what my family had already dumped on her shoulders.

"All I've heard since I got here is how I should stay away from the Rhodale family. If you were me, would you be able to let it go?"

When she didn't answer, I stood up and held out a hand to help her up. "Let's get inside before you get chilled, okay?"

"I'm not a fragile old lady," she snapped. "Sit down."

Her tone of voice startled me into sitting down, fast.

"It's not all that ancient. Sixty years ago, a Rhodale killed your great-grandfather. Burned him to death."

"*What?* How did I not know that?"

"It doesn't exactly come up in everyday conversation."

"What happened?"

She took a deep breath. "He caught his wife and your grandfather's father together. There was no proof he set the fire deliberately, so he never went to jail, but somehow his horse made it out of that barn alive, and they didn't." She stared off into the distance for several long seconds before continuing. "Your grandfather never got over his father's death, and he raised Richard on stories of hatred and vengeance. So your father grew up hating that family with a kind of violence that isn't normal—isn't healthy—and it's partially my fault for not stepping in to try to moderate all that feud talk. But the manure really hit the fan when that conniving bitch Anna Mae got between the boys—your dad and Jeremiah Rhodale— in high school."

I'd never heard Gran swear before.

"The murder started a feud between our families?"

"The problems date back long before that barn burned to the ground, but I'm definitely not going into all of that. It's stupid stuff, long since buried with the people who started it, and we're all the better for it. Maybe someday I'll pull out the trunks in the attic and let you see some clippings and things your grandfather kept after his grandfather died. Or maybe I'll just burn the damn things."

"Gran, I'm so sorry. We don't have to—"

"Oh, no, young lady. You asked about Rhodales, so you're going to listen to this. Your father was almost in a shootout with Jeremiah Rhodale over that horrible Anna Mae in high school. And now that awful man is the sheriff of Whitfield County, if you can believe it, even though his son Ethan is some kind of drug kingpin, freshly back from jail."

"I didn't know," I whispered.

"Of course you didn't," she said, her tone softening. "How would you, growing up in the city? But now you do."

She stood up and headed for the front door, but I stayed in the swing, stunned by what she'd told me.

Before going in, she paused and glanced back at me. "I know one of those Rhodale boys is in your high school. The one with the violence problem. Apparently he's even more dangerous than his brother. You have to promise me that you'll never, ever have anything to do with him."

"But what if—"

"No. This feud has never brought any of us anything but heartache and despair, and I'm afraid we have more of the same in front of us, especially now that your father has moved back to Whitfield County. Please, no matter what, don't do anything to start it up all over again."

With that, she disappeared inside, leaving me alone with my very troubling thoughts. It seemed like I'd stepped off that plane from Connecticut and into an old western. I was part of an actual, historical feud. If Gran's story was true, a Rhodale had murdered my great-grandfather.

I sat there for a long time with these new revelations spinning in my brain, and when my phone rang it startled me. I checked the display to see who was calling me so late.

Mickey Rhodale.

CHAPTER 16
MICKEY

My hand tightened on my phone as I silently willed Victoria to pick up. I'd told her she'd be better off without me, and I'd meant it at the time, but the past week had been hell, especially without the physical exertion of football to distract me. I was going a little bit crazy thinking about her all the time. Unable to talk to her. Having to watch other guys hitting on her at school. She'd called and texted after the catastrophe of the football game, but I hadn't been ready to talk to her, and now was probably too late.

Victoria finally answered her phone.

"Hi, Mickey," she whispered, and the sound of her quiet voice in my ear sent a shiver down my neck. How could a simple "hi" be more powerful than any seductive come-on that other girls had tried out on me?

"I need to see you. I mean, I'd like to see you," I said. I sounded like an idiot. She was going to dump my ass before we'd had our first date, and then she'd find some guy who had an actual, working brain.

"But you said—"

"I know what I said. I was a damn fool."

Silence for a few beats.

"I'd like to see you, too, but . . . I'm getting a lot of pushback about you—well, about your family," she said hesitantly. "I believe you, about protecting Caro. You know that I do. And it's not the thing with your coach's sister. I know you don't have anything to do with Ethan's drugs. But our dads hate each other from something in high school, and there's even a story about a burning barn, and a feud . . ."

Her voice trailed off, as if maybe she was waiting for me to jump in and deny it.

"I know. I meant to tell you what I know about it, but I didn't know how to find the right time to say 'Hey, our families despise each other, want to go see a movie?'"

I heard the door slam open downstairs, which meant Pa was home and he was drunk. He never slammed the door when he was sober. Between him, Ethan, and Anna Mae, I was getting tangled more and more in the sticky web of past dramas, and I was sick of it all.

Screw them. Why should I give a shit about what a drunk, a drug dealer, or the drug dealer's creepy mother thought about my friendships?

"Do you care about what a bunch of idiots on both sides of our families did in the past?" I asked. "Or are we going to live our own lives?"

Silence.

Just when I wondered if she'd hung up on me, her voice came back over the line. "We're going to live our own lives. But only if you quit blowing hot and cold. It's not worth risking a family upset if you're going to push me away again."

I realized I'd been holding my breath, and I let it out in a long, slow exhale. "I won't. You have my word on that. Meet me after school tomorrow? Maybe, say, at the Whitfield County museum . . . just to get away from the gawkers."

"Perfect. And, Mickey?"

"Yeah?"

"I'm glad you called."

The next day lasted forever, since I knew I'd be meeting Victoria after school. I was walking around in a fog, not paying attention to much, so when final bell rang I nearly ran Melinda Whitfield down when I turned the corner to my locker. It wouldn't have taken much to knock her over, so I was glad I'd managed to stop short. She'd wasted away to practically nothing since the first week of school.

She glanced around nervously, and I braced myself for a "leave my sister alone" lecture.

"So, hi. How are you? I think you have class with my sister," she said, looking anywhere but at me and biting her thumbnail.

"Yeah, that's right. I'm fine. How are you, Melinda?" It was the first time she'd ever spoken to me, and she was acting squirrelly.

Her eyes were wild, and she was biting her fingernails. *Damn*. So this was the "family stuff" Victoria had been dealing with. I was no Ethan, but I could tell she was some kind of user.

"I need to . . . I mean, I want to buy . . ." She trailed off. Looked at me with naked desperation.

"Look, I can't help you," I said, shoving my books in the locker with a little more force than necessary. "My pa is the sheriff. I don't do drugs, and I definitely don't sell them, no matter what Coach or anybody else says."

She blinked. "I don't understand. Everybody told me that your brothers—"

"Well, *everybody* can go to hell. Whatever my brothers are into has nothing to do with me, so you can go find somebody else to feed your habit."

Tears welled up in her eyes, and I suddenly felt like a monster. This was Victoria's sister, after all.

"Look. I'm sorry. I didn't mean to snap at you. You need to get help, Melinda. I know your sister is worried about you—"

"She told you? She told you that I killed Caleb?" She backed away from me and I stood very still, careful not to make any motions that she might perceive as threatening. She was maybe one stop away from Crazy Town, and I wasn't going to be the conductor who drove her to the station.

"I don't know what you're talking about. Caleb Stuart? He died in a fire," I said gently. "Melinda, let's go find Victoria, and we can figure this out."

"No! All I want is to get high, so I can forget his face, just for a little while," she shouted. I realized everybody in the hallway was staring at us. "If you can't help me, I'll find somebody who can!"

She ran off down the hall before I could stop her.

Great. I'd just added another nail to the coffin of my reputation. The only thing worse would be if Victoria showed up. And of course when I turned around, there she was.

"Was that my sister?" She looked horrified.

"Yes. I think she wanted me to find weed for her, but I said no. I think she's just embarrassed or something."

"Oh my God . . . We have to stop her. When she's embarrassed or ashamed, she gets self-destructive." Victoria started running, and I was right behind her. When we hit the front door and ran outside, I stumbled to a halt, because Ethan—the last person I'd expected to see here at school—was leaning on the hood of his truck, which was parked in one of the visitor's spaces.

Melinda was running down the sidewalk, and as she started to pass him, Ethan put out a hand to stop her. This was nothing but bad.

"What the hell is he doing here?" I groaned.

Victoria glanced back at me, wild-eyed. "Who is that guy?"

"That's my brother," I said grimly.

"What does your brother want with my sister?"

"Nothing good," I muttered, heading toward them to stop whatever trouble he might be planning before it could happen.

Victoria cried out behind me, and I whirled around fast enough to see her fall, probably from taking the stairs too fast. I leapt toward her and caught her before she hit the cement, but it cost us time we didn't have. When she got her feet underneath her again and we turned around, Melinda was already climbing in the passenger seat of Ethan's truck.

"Ethan, no," I shouted, but he laughed at me as he pulled out of the parking place, and then he paused and rolled his window down partway.

"I was actually here to talk to you, Mick, about that job. Isn't that funny? Came to find my brother, and now I've got me my own

Whitfield. Kind of hypocritical for you to argue with that, isn't it?"
He flashed a nasty grin at Victoria and took off.

"Let Melinda out. She's messed up," I yelled at him as he drove away, but Ethan just laughed at me again and sped up.

"We have to go after her," Victoria said urgently, digging in her purse, probably for keys.

"You're too upset to drive, and I know where he's going," I said grimly. "Give me the keys."

"What?"

"Do you want to ride on the back of my bike in that skirt?"

She looked dazed for a second, but then her eyes narrowed and she handed me the keys. "Let's go after them. Now."

I knew he'd head for the compound, if for no other reason than to piss me off, so I took off on back roads to try for a shortcut. Maybe I could get there before he'd taken Melinda into the place and I had to deal with the guards.

"That's your brother?" Victoria stared at the window, at her hands—anywhere but at me. "Nice guy."

"He's my half brother, and he's twenty-two years old. I don't have any control over what he does," I said tersely. "But if you want to lump me in with the rest of the Rhodale bad guys, go ahead. Everybody else does."

She sighed, and reached over to touch my arm. "I'm sorry. Of course you can't control him, any more than I can control Melinda."

My forearm burned where her fingers rested on my bare skin, and I wondered what would happen if I kissed her again. Spontaneous combustion?

"In some twisted way, he's doing this to get back at me, so I kind of do feel responsible," I admitted. "I refuse to follow orders, like my brother Jeb does, so Ethan gets back at me when he can."

"What was he talking about, a job?" She turned to face me, and her beautiful green eyes suddenly seemed huge in her face.

"I don't know. I've told him many times that I won't get involved in his criminal business, but he keeps coming at me. *Damn* it."

I wanted to punch the steering wheel or, better yet, Ethan's face, but I was trying to keep it under control. Victoria was already worried enough and she had good reason, though I wasn't going to tell her that and add to her fears. Ethan might pump Melinda full of drugs just for a sick, twisted joke. Meth wasn't like other drugs. It only took one use to become addicted.

I took a curve too fast, and Victoria clutched at the door.

"What are you doing? Trying to get us killed?"

"Sorry." I slowed down as we headed for a particularly tricky stretch of road. She was right.

"We'll get her back," I promised. "She's going to be okay. I'm taking a shortcut."

Victoria smiled a little, but she didn't look convinced. I didn't blame her. I wasn't even sure Ethan would be headed in this direction, but I had no place else to try.

CHAPTER 17
VICTORIA

By the time we reached the outskirts of the wooded hills ten miles outside of town, I was visualizing all the horrible things Ethan could be doing to my sister right at that very minute, and I felt like I was going to throw up if Mickey didn't slow down. Thankfully, he listened to me, and eased up on the gas at a hairpin turn.

We turned off the paved road onto a worn-out dirt track, and a couple of miles later, Mickey pulled up to a rickety looking metal gate. A man with a shotgun or rifle—I couldn't tell—sat in a chair next to a dilapidated shack that might have served as a guardhouse.

"What is this? Some kind of creepy militia headquarters?"

Mickey flipped his middle finger at the guard, who returned the gesture. "No, not quite, but he has enough guns in there to start his own private army, I think. That's why I wanted to catch him out here."

I wanted to reach over and hold his hand, but I stopped myself. This thing between us—this attraction, or electricity, or craziness, whatever it was—kept leading to problems and drama and strife. There was no way I was going to let Melinda pay the price for my stupidity and defiance.

Mickey put the truck in park and held out his hand for mine, almost as if he'd been listening in on my thoughts. I met his deep, blue gaze and had the crazy thought that if I took his hand, I'd be saying yes to more than momentary comfort.

I'd be saying yes to him.

I placed my hand in his, trying to block the involuntary shiver that happened every time he touched me, but I couldn't.

"It's not just me, then?" he asked, his fingers tightening around mine.

He watched me so intently that I suddenly felt like I was falling down the rabbit hole. He was no drug dealer, but Mickey was dangerous in his own way. He'd caused me to throw off my safe, sane existence for a wild ride I didn't have a clue how to handle.

"We're missing the museum," I said stupidly, and he grinned.

"I was really looking forward to the museum," he said. "Especially the chance to get you alone and kiss you."

My lips started tingling, and I found myself almost involuntarily leaning toward him.

The sound of Ethan's truck coming up behind us smashed into the moment, and I was saved from having to think of an answer.

"Here they come," Mickey said grimly. "Showtime."

CHAPTER 18

MICKEY

"Stay here. I don't want you in the middle of this," I said, and before Victoria could argue, I got out of the truck and walked into the road right in front of Ethan's truck.

I wasn't sure he'd stop. He stared at me through his windshield, grinning like a fiend, and I had a split second to wonder if I'd end up splattered all over his hood before he slammed on the brakes and jumped out of the truck.

"Melinda's coming with me," I told him. "No drugs, no messing with her."

"She wants what I've got, baby brother," Ethan said mockingly.

Behind me, I heard Victoria's door open. I should have known she wouldn't listen to me. She ran over to the passenger side of Ethan's truck and yelled at her sister to open the door. I didn't take my eyes off Ethan, though, just like I wouldn't take my eyes off a rattler in the road in front of me, either.

"Need any help, boss?" The thug at the gate had apparently finally figured out that something was going on.

"High-quality employees you've got there," I pointed out.

"I do like the dumb ones," Ethan said, still grinning at me.

"No, I don't need help," he called out to the guard. "This is my brother, you moron. Go tell Ma to put some coffee on."

"We won't be staying for coffee. We're taking Melinda home," I said evenly.

Ethan would either let us go without a fight, or he wouldn't. We stared each other down for a minute or two, until Melinda unlocked the door and fell into her sister's arms, crying. Victoria half dragged, half carried her across the road toward her truck, and I waited to see if Ethan would make a move on Melinda or shoot me first and then make a move.

"I just want to quit seeing his face," Melinda sobbed, and I could hear Victoria making shushing, soothing noises.

"She thinks she killed Caleb," Ethan said, his predatory gaze following the girls as they crossed the road back toward me. "I told her she was wrong. That fire was purely an accident. Bad ventilation in the trailer."

"Right. Bad ventilation. Whatever you say. The fact that they were moving into your territory had nothing to do with it."

"Accidents happen to people who get in my way. Doesn't mean it's my fault, but they still happen. You might remember that." He paused as if making a decision, and then his hand moved away from the gun in his waistband. "All right, little brother. You can have your Whitfield girl's sister, this time. But you're going to owe me one, and you might not like the favor I ask."

I nodded, glancing at the guard and knowing we weren't out of trouble yet. "Fine. I owe you one, but I won't run drugs in the high school for you. I won't run drugs at all."

He threw back his head and laughed. "I don't know what you're talking about. I'm a clean, upstanding citizen. I got rehabilitated in jail, didn't you know?"

I just stared at him, waiting for him to change his mind and try to take Melinda, but he climbed back in his truck, motioning to the guard to open the gate.

"Don't forget, Mickey. You owe me one. I fully intend to collect." He started to roll up his window but then stopped with the glass up halfway. "And you'd better stay away from these Whitfields. Consider this a friendly warning. The next one won't be so friendly."

Melinda sat silently, staring out the window, all the way to their house. Victoria sat between us, holding her sister's hand, and I wished that I could do something to relieve the terrible strain in her expression.

"You should take us to the school so you can get your bike," she said when we passed the road that would have taken us there.

"And leave you to drive home on your own with Melinda like this? Not a chance," I said quietly, not wanting Victoria's sister to hear me. "I can hitch a ride from your place."

She shook her head. "No, you can take my truck, and I'll get a ride to school in the morning."

"She needs help," I said finally, even though it felt wrong to talk about Melinda like that when she was sitting right there.

"You think I don't know that? My parents won't even let me talk to them about it, and Gran is worried that they'll block her from trying to get Melinda into rehab."

"Maybe this will make them open their eyes."

Victoria shifted restlessly. The long line of her leg came into contact with mine, and that sizzle of electricity sparked between us again. She glanced up at me, and then away.

"No, I'm not telling them about this. Can you imagine what Daddy would do? He'd call the FBI down on Ethan for kidnapping or some such nonsense. If the feud needs an excuse to flare up again, this would be it. And I don't think Melinda could handle the fallout."

Melinda, still crying, didn't say anything. I didn't even know if she'd heard us.

"You may be right. It's probably better to keep our parents out of this. And before you ask, I'm not saying that to protect my slimeball brother."

I turned onto the long, curving driveway marked with a sign that read WHITFIELD RANCH, PRIVATE PROPERTY, and realized I was entering enemy territory.

"I never thought that for a minute, Mickey," Victoria said. "Thank you for—for everything. We'll just tell anybody who's around that Melinda didn't feel well, so you drove us home because I was worried."

It wasn't a very good explanation, but it would probably work. As long as her dad wasn't around, nobody else would know who I was, after all.

But when we pulled up to the house, we discovered that it was too late for feeble cover-ups. Victoria's dad came storming down off the porch to greet us, and he was pissed. Melinda stumbled out of the car and ran past him up the stairs to the enormous house, and he didn't even pay attention to her.

"You," he shouted. "What the hell are you doing in Victoria's truck?"

Another man came running toward us from the direction of the huge barn, and he looked angry, too, but he headed for Victoria, not for me.

"Victoria, are you okay?"

Okay. At least *somebody* had his priorities straight around here. I waited for Victoria to answer, willing to take my cue from her about how much to say.

"I'm perfectly fine, Pete" she said, and her voice had a bite to it. "Mickey was nice enough to drive us home after Melinda got sick—"

"That's not how I heard it," her father broke in, glaring at me. "The principal called me. He said this Rhodale chased Melinda out of the school."

I forced my face into a perfectly blank expression. So he *had* heard that his daughter was in trouble, even though he'd gotten it all wrong, but he'd ignored her completely so he could get at me. What an asshole.

Victoria laughed. "Wow, gossip flies in small towns, doesn't it? And they always get it wrong. Melinda *voluntarily* went for a drive with Mickey's brother Ethan, and we picked her up and brought her home, because, as I said, she's *not feeling well.*"

The man she'd called Pete was giving me the once-over, his face skeptical, but at least he wasn't on the verge of hitting me, like her dad appeared to be.

"Now maybe, instead of yelling at Mickey, Dad, you could thank him for—"

He spat on the ground. I hadn't even known Whitfields knew how to spit. From the expression on her face, neither had Victoria.

"It will be a cold day in hell before I ever thank a Rhodale for anything. Now get the hell off my property."

With that, he grabbed Victoria and headed for the house, dragging her after him. Every instinct I had was urging me to go after him and teach him a lesson about how to treat his daughter, but I fought it back and stared blandly at Pete.

"So."

"So," he echoed me. He was staring after Victoria and her father, and I had the odd feeling that he wanted to punch Whitfield as much as I did. "You need a ride?"

"Victoria said I could take her truck back to school to get my bike, and she'd get a ride to school in the morning."

Pete gave me a long, measured stare. "How about I drive you back now, instead? That way we'll have a chance to talk."

I couldn't think of a good way to refuse, so I just nodded and held out the key ring and then climbed into the passenger side of the truck.

Pete started the ignition and then shot me a look. "You want to explain what the Rhodales are doing messing with the Whitfield girls? Your pa will have your hide when he hears about this, and you know he will. It's Clark, after all. Everything that happens around here during the day is practically plastered on the front page of the *Clark Gazette* by dinnertime."

He had a lot of fucking nerve. I wanted to laugh in his face, but couldn't quite bring myself to do it. He'd been worried about Victoria, after all.

"I don't know you, and I don't feel any obligation to discuss what my father will or will not do. Respectfully."

He laughed, which I hadn't expected. "Oh, I doubt that you're feeling respectful at all, or in the mood to listen to me, but I'm going to warn you, anyway. Nothing good can come of your having anything to do with Victoria. There are plenty of girls out there. Pick one of them."

"There aren't any girls like Victoria. Also, if you care so much about them, why aren't you helping Victoria get Melinda into rehab?" I fired back.

He shot me a look that, if he had been anybody else, I might have thought held a measure of respect. "It's not quite that simple."

"Nothing ever is," I said, and after that we drove the rest of the way to the school in silence.

CHAPTER 19
VICTORIA

"Don't even think about leaving this room, young lady." Dad pointed to the couch. "Sit."

"I'm not a dog," I snapped.

"No, but you're hanging out with one. Stinking Rhodale dogs." He tried to open his liquor cabinet, found out it was locked, and slammed a fist on the wooden top so hard the bottles inside rattled. "Why is this locked?"

I stared at him in disbelief. "Are you freaking kidding me? It's *locked* because your daughter has a problem with alcohol. How can you not know that? Now she's trying to work her way up to a serious problem with drugs, which is how she ended up climbing—voluntarily, I repeat—into Ethan Rhodale's truck."

He whirled around and glared at me, and his face was turning red, which was a prime indicator that we were about to have a patented Richard Whitfield Big Damn Blowup.

"So what's your excuse? Why was the other Rhodale in *your* truck? If you think I'm going to let you have anything to do with any of Anna Mae's whelps—"

"What are you talking about?" I was confused. "I thought this was about the stupid feud. The sheriff and Anna Mae got divorced a long time ago, and his new wife is Mickey's mom."

"She's also Buddy's teacher," my mom said from the archway to the dining room.

I hadn't heard her walk in, and apparently neither had my father, who took a deep breath and started yelling at *her*.

"What the hell are you talking about? And where is the key to my booze cabinet?"

My mother narrowed her eyes, but her voice was calm and steady when she answered him. "If you yell at me again, I'll bury your key in a pile of the most reeking horse manure I can find on this ranch."

I was stunned. *Go, Mom.*

"We should have never moved back here, Richard," she continued, producing the key out of a pocket and unlocking the cabinet. "I still have some of the money that Daddy left me. We can move back to the city and start over. It would be a smaller house, but—"

"No. Are you out of your mind? Let the Rhodales drive us out of our own place?" Dad pulled out a bottle of bourbon and sloshed a lot of it into a cut-crystal glass. He took a long drink and then glared at Mom and then me.

"Are we going to have to battle Rhodales at every turn because of some blowup you and Jeremiah had in high school? How can this be a healthy place to raise the kids? And with Melinda's little problem . . ."

Mom's voice trailed off, and then she glanced at me with a warning expression, as if telling me to keep quiet. Too bad.

"Two things," I said, holding up the first finger. "One, I'm glad you finally realize she has a problem. Two, there's nothing little about it."

"Melinda just needs to have some willpower," my dad muttered as he put his glass down, apparently conscious of the bitter irony of saying this with a drink in his hand.

"Willpower isn't enough, and you know it. There has been a lot of drinking in this family, right? Your father, his father, and even you . . . She needs help," I said. "Look, I'll do all the research. We can find a nice, discreet rehab facility, and—"

His face hardened when I mentioned his own drinking, but then he sighed. "Yeah. Maybe. Do the research. Let's see what's out there. I can't—we can't—let Melinda fall into the pit because we were too proud or stupid to do anything about it."

My mom's eyes widened. "But *rehab*. It's so—well. Forget that. What about moving?"

Dad snatched up his drink and downed it in one long gulp. "No. No moving. This is Whitfield County, not *Rhodale* County. I'll be damned if I'll let a bunch of petty criminals and a crooked sheriff with delusions of godhood run us out of our family estate."

Now the ranch he'd avoided for most of his adult life, since he'd never liked horses anyway, was our *family estate*? Hypocrite. But his agreeing to let me search out rehab facilities was a huge victory, so I kept my mouth shut.

"I'm going to fire anybody who has even the slightest association with those damn Rhodales, that's what I'm going to do," he continued with that icy calm that meant he'd irrevocably made up his mind. "The last thing we need is another Caleb problem, one of our hands getting mixed up in Rhodale drugs, especially when I plan to host a major party for the Kentucky thoroughbred racing association."

"And you planned to tell me about this *when?*" my mother interjected coldly.

I didn't give a crap about upcoming parties, and I couldn't believe they were cold-hearted enough even to be talking about it right now.

"Caleb problem? Right," I said bitterly, unable to help myself. "We wouldn't want to tarnish our reputation with another dead ranch hand, would we? Is everything about image with you? Don't you have one shred of compassion?"

"Your mother is going to have something to say about this plan," Mom said. "New hands around the horses are going to spook them, especially if there are a lot of them, and you know as well as I do that everybody's related to everybody around here, so there are bound to be a lot of distant cousins to the Rhodales working in our barns."

"Not to mention that people will *lose their jobs,*" I told my cold-hearted mother. "In this economy, we're going to put people out of work just because of who they're related to?"

"If it avoids stress, it's good for the horses," Dad said flatly, and I knew he'd go through with it. When he got that tone of voice, a dirty deed was as good as done.

"Your mother—" my mom began, but he cut her off.

"She'll do what I tell her to do," my dad said, refilling his glass and taking another gulp of bourbon.

Right then, I almost hated him.

He pointed at me. "You. Stay away from Rhodales. Do your damn homework. Go buy a party dress for the Founders' Day Dance. And, if you must, research rehab facilities. We'll figure the Rhodale thing out by ourselves."

I stood up, shaking my head in disgust. "Since when were we ever able to figure *anything* out by ourselves?"

Before he could change his mind about Melinda's rehab, I ran out of the room. One win at a time: it was all I could manage.

CHAPTER 20

MICKEY

Dusk spread her vivid colors across the sky as I pointed the Harley down the pavement, trying to find some clarity in the open road and the roar of the wind in my ears.

I was riding around aimlessly, trying to ignore the urge to go back to Victoria's, pound on the door of the damn mansion, and find out if she was okay. I'd tried calling, but her phone went straight to voice mail every time, and I didn't want to call the house phone, because it would probably get her into even more trouble with that jerk of a father of hers.

Asshole fathers, problem siblings—we were turning out to have a lot more in common that I'd ever thought possible.

When I got hungry, I stopped for a burger that I couldn't even taste, and then I gave in to the impulse that had been riding me all

afternoon and evening. Within half an hour, I found myself on the
road that bordered the Whitfield ranch, and I called myself six kinds
of fool. There was no way Victoria would want to talk to me now, after
everything that had happened today. I should head for home.

A shimmer of movement in the darkness off to the right caught
my attention, and somebody came into view, riding one of the glossy,
expensive horses that probably had cost more than my entire house.
Somehow, I *felt* it was her before I could even really see her. Victoria
was racing across the field like a wild thing, like she was part of the
horse, not just riding it.

I pulled my bike to the side of the road and parked it in the deep
shadows cast by the trees, where the moonlight didn't penetrate. I
walked over to the fence, content simply to watch her.

She was beautiful. Her hair shimmered like silver in the moonlight, streaming out behind her as she rode. She was like a princess in
a fairy tale.

But I sure as hell was no Prince Charming.

I'd been kidding myself to think that I'd ever have a chance with
Victoria Whitfield. I took one long, last look at her and steeled myself
to go, but then the horse stumbled. Victoria flew through the air, and
I started running. By the time I reached her, she was sitting up, and
the stupid horse was ambling along, munching on grass, completely
unconcerned that she'd nearly given me a heart attack.

"Mickey? Where did you come from?" I couldn't ignore the way
her face lit up, and something wild inside me settled, calmed.

I dropped to my knees next to her, looking for blood or broken
bones.

"I was riding my bike, and then I saw you, but I was leaving, and
you fell—forget that. Are you okay?"

I tilted her head up with one hand under her chin, examining her face for bruises or signs of injury.

She smiled. "I'm okay, I think. I didn't hit my head, and I've taken enough spills over the years to know how to fall. I think I might have twisted my ankle, though. I'm more worried about Heather's Angel."

I bared my teeth at the horse, who was clearly fine. "You *ought* to be worried about her. She could have hurt you. There would have been a glue factory in her future if she had."

Victoria shuddered. "Don't even joke about that. Anyway, she's walking fine, so I'm not too worried. I'll be able to check her out thoroughly when we get back to the barn. Can you help me up?"

I put my hands on her waist and lifted her up off the ground, holding tightly and supporting her weight in case her ankle was bad. Or at least that was the reason I gave myself for not wanting to let go. It was nothing at all to do with the way she smelled like sugar and sunshine, or the way I'd spent the past week with a perpetual hard-on, wondering what her lips would taste like in the moonlight. What her body would feel like underneath mine.

"You're kind of my own personal hero," she said, laughing a little. "Rescuing me the night I met you, rescuing Melinda, rescuing me from this fall—how are you even possible?"

"I'm no hero. I'm just somebody in the wrong place at the right time," I said.

Her smile faded. "Is near me always going to be the wrong place?"

I wanted to kiss her. I *needed* to kiss her, more than I needed to think or talk or breathe. I leaned closer, but she stumbled a little, wincing when she put weight on her injured ankle.

"Ouch. Yeah, I wrenched it. Not too bad, though. I'll be able to get home on my own. It would be better—"

"If the big, bad Rhodale didn't take you home twice in one day," I said bitterly. "Yeah. I know. The best thing for both of us would be if we forgot we'd ever met, wouldn't it?"

She looked up at me, and I fell, drowning, into her wide green eyes, which were almost silvery in the moonlight.

"You promised not to do this. Is that what you really want?" Her voice was a whisper, and I couldn't tell which answer she wanted to hear, so I just told her the truth.

"No, that's not what I want, but what I want isn't sane or reasonable. I want to spend all my time with you. I want to know why I can't sleep without dreaming about you. I want to kiss you until you can't remember a time before you met me."

She took a deep, shaky breath, and then she put her arms around my neck. "Then kiss me again. Because even though I'm hardly brave enough to admit it, that's all I want, too."

CHAPTER 21
VICTORIA

"**Y**ou are brave, you know. You stood up for me, today. With your father," he said softly, staring into my eyes. "Nobody ever did that for me before. Don't think I'll forget it."

I couldn't help it. The expression of pain that flashed over his face caught at something inside me, and I was powerless to resist him, so I kissed him—the gentlest touch of my lips to his.

Before I could retreat, he put an arm around my waist and pulled me closer to him. He angled his head and deepened the kiss, and suddenly it wasn't gentle anymore. Summer lightning storms had burned through hayfields with less heat and power.

I didn't even try to resist. I let myself sink into the moment, surrendering to his demand. Somehow I felt safer with his strength surrounding me than I'd felt in so long. I couldn't breathe—couldn't think—couldn't run away and, for once, I didn't even want to try.

My entire body was trembling by the time he raised his head from mine. Stunned, I looked up at Mickey, wondering how one kiss could have shifted the entire world. As if suddenly Whitfield County, Kentucky, had turned into fairy-tale land, and a nerdy, smart girl had turned into a princess.

He was breathing hard, and his eyes were wild, reminding me of nothing so much as a racehorse that had been completely and utterly spooked.

"I think we're in trouble," he said, his voice rough. "There's no way I'm going to stop wanting to kiss you now, after that."

I touched shaky fingers to my lips. "This is moving way too fast, and both our families are against it, and there are so many problems—"

He kissed me again, and I stopped thinking, stopped breathing, and stopped feeling anything but him. I was pressed up so close to him that I could almost feel his heartbeat. When he finally raised his head, I didn't even try to offer any more protests.

"This is going to be dangerous," I said, conceding my surrender.

"You're worth it. And I'll make sure that any danger doesn't come anywhere near you," he said, his dark eyes gleaming.

Angel suddenly lifted her head and nickered, and I realized I could hear Pete yelling my name in the distance. He was probably riding out toward us.

"You have to go," I said, panicking. "We'll talk tomorrow."

He kissed me again, and then he lifted me up onto Angel. "You can count on it."

I headed back toward the barn, my lips tingling and my head

spinning so much I could hardly feel any pain in my ankle. Dangerous had probably been an understatement, but Mickey was worth it, too.

By the time Pete reached me, I was able to pretend to be completely calm. I told him Angel had stumbled, and concern for the horse outweighed any suspicions he might have had about why I was dawdling out in the fields so late.

I talked to him, focusing on the conversation with one part of my mind, while the rest plotted out how I'd find ways to spend time with Mickey. I must have missed something Pete had asked me, though, because I realized he was giving me a strange look.

"Long day?"

"The longest," I said, smiling so brightly I think it made him nervous. "But tomorrow will be *wonderful.*"

I hoped.

CHAPTER 22

MICKEY

I smelled like sweat, gas, Cheetos, and fried pig skins. It wasn't an appetizing aroma.

The bell over the door rang, but it was only my boss.

"You leaving already?" He glared at me, holding his arm in its cast protectively close to his chest. He'd broken it trying to find something in the hoarded-out nightmare he called a storage shed.

"I was supposed to clock out an hour ago. You need to find us more help," I said, wiping my face with the bottom of my shirt.

"I'm trying, but nobody wants to do an honest day's work," he grumbled.

"Nobody wants to work for *you*, you mean," I countered.

"Aw, get out of here. And don't be late next time." He stomped off, but I knew he secretly liked it that somebody actually stood up to him. Or, at least, he'd never fired me for it, even on the days that I wished he would, which were usually inventory days, like today.

I washed my hands and headed home. All I wanted was a hot shower, a big dinner, and a chance to call Victoria in case her idiot father had finally given her phone back after taking it away for her "bad judgment" of letting me drive her home.

If he ever found out I'd kissed her, he'd probably ship her off to boarding school in Switzerland.

But as I pulled up to my house, my mood plummeted straight down past zero, because Pa's sheriff car was parked at a careless angle behind Ethan's truck. As far as I knew, Ethan hadn't been back to my house for six years, so something big must be going on. With Ethan, something big always meant something bad, and my first instinct was to turn around and avoid the situation altogether. Let him and Pa shout it out.

Then I saw that my mother's car was there, too. I couldn't leave her to deal with the two of them, especially if Pa had been drinking again.

I heard the shouting when I was only halfway across the yard, so I started running.

They were in the living room, and Ethan was up in Pa's face. "And don't you think he's going to come after your job next? You're up for election next year. Don't you think Whitfield is going to throw his money behind your opponent?"

"He doesn't have any money," Pa shouted at him. "Why do you think he had to move back here in the first place?"

"Whitfields always have money. You think he doesn't get to take over the ranch when his mother kicks it? Maybe he'll push her along toward her casket a little quicker. I wouldn't put anything past a Whitfield."

Mom came out of the kitchen to intercept me when I started toward them.

"No, Mickey, please stay out of this," she pleaded, but I didn't stop.

"What is it about this time? Why can't you just leave the Whitfields alone, Ethan? That old feud is ancient history—what did they ever do to you?" I grabbed his arm to pull him away from Pa, and Ethan whipped around and shoved me, hard.

"Are you fucking kidding me? Didn't your girlfriend tell you about their newest asshole move?" He advanced on me, fists clenched, but I stood my ground.

"What are you talking about? And why are you even here? I figured you'd be too busy selling drugs to the rest of Coach's family to make social calls," I said bitterly.

"Yeah, I heard about that. Want me to pay him a little visit and get you back on the team?" Ethan's eyes gleamed, and I wanted to punch him in the face.

"No, you psychopath, I don't. That shit didn't work when I was a kid, and it's not going to work now. Just stay the hell away from me."

"I'm not here about your football problems, asshole. You couldn't listen to me, could you? I told you to stay away from that little bitch, but you had to play the knight in shining armor," Ethan said. "Well, *Dick* Whitfield retaliated. He talked to his employees today and went down a list of everybody he'd found out was in any related to a Rhodale and fired their asses. Every single one of them. Said this would teach the Rhodales to mess with his daughters."

I looked at Pa. "Is that even legal?"

He sighed, and he suddenly looked about ten years older. "It's legal. You can fire your employees for any reason you want in Kentucky, unless they're part of a protected class. So, you can't fire somebody on account of their race or gender or for being pregnant, that kind of thing."

"Being a Rhodale is in no way a *protected class*, is it? Never has been. We've always been the ones who have to protect ourselves," Ethan said bitterly. "So now we've got to explain to eleven people who just lost their jobs why it is that my little brother had to ruin their lives chasing Whitfield tail."

I was stunned by the news of such vicious retaliation, but there was still no way I was taking the blame for Victoria's dad's actions. "This isn't all on me. Let me refresh your memory. You know, about how you took off with Melinda Whitfield in your damn truck?"

Ethan and Pa both started yelling at the same time, with me in the middle, until a tremendous crash shut us all up. Mom stood in front of the kitchen, the shards of the glass fruit bowl she'd just smashed all over the floor around her.

"That's enough," she said quietly. "Ethan, please leave my house. You are not welcome here until you can behave in a civilized fashion."

Pa started to speak, but she held up a hand for silence. "I've had enough from you, too. We are going to talk, about your sons, and your ex-wife, and your drinking, but that's between the two of us. For now, you will please escort Ethan out of the house while I have a conversation with Mickey."

Ethan sneered at her, then turned his contempt on Pa. "That's always been your problem, hasn't it? You let the women wear the pants in your marriages."

"And you let your mommy tell you what to do," Pa shot back,

and we all looked at him with shock. He rarely stood up to Ethan, or Jeb for that matter, but this thing with Ethan taking off with Melinda must have sparked something in him.

Pa followed Ethan outside, and I turned to look at my mom. Now that the crisis was past, she leaned against the table and started shaking. I rushed over to pull out a chair for her and made her sit down while I cleaned up the mess.

"I always liked that bowl, too," she said quietly, and then she put her head down on her folded arms and started crying.

I didn't know what to do, so I finished cleaning up the glass and then sat down beside her and patted her back until Pa came back in. He gave me a helpless look. The one thing that always brought a Rhodale man to his knees was a woman's tears.

Mom probably realized that, too, because she sat up and wiped her face with the backs of her hands. I jumped up to get her a box of tissues, and she nodded her thanks. She pointed to a chair and my father joined us at the table.

"Ethan is right, you know," she said, surprising us. "If this is true and not just rumors getting out of hand, as happens so often around here, then Richard Whitfield's vindictive action is going to cause a lot of trouble."

Pa nodded wearily. "And you know where some of those unemployed Rhodales will go? Into the drug business with Ethan. Some will be willing to uproot to move to wherever they have to go to stay in the horse business, but others won't want to move their families. Not much work around here now, and there's big money in drugs. *Huge* money. That's why it's so damn hard to fight."

"It's so hard to fight because you don't want to stand up to Ethan,"

I said, figuring what the hell, we might as well get it all out on the table. "He's your son, but he's also a criminal. You're the sheriff. You need to shut him down."

Pa shook his head. "You don't understand. We can't root it out. Meth labs are all over the state, and the big drug cartels are taking over the sales and distribution. If Ethan magically gets out of the business or—more likely—goes back to jail, then somebody worse takes over, and the whole damn county becomes a hellhole. At least Ethan keeps it away from the schools and the kids."

"You're both fools if you don't realize that Anna Mae is behind most of this," my mother said.

"Of course I realize that," Pa said wearily. "Do you think I'm an idiot? But we can't prove anything, because we'd need a warrant to search the compound, and she's very careful to cover her tracks."

Mom reached over and took his hand. "I didn't know, because every time I tried to bring up Anna Mae, you shied away from the issue."

"Ethan had better not go after the Whitfields," I inserted. "I will put everything I have into stopping him if he tries to hurt Victoria's family."

Pa switched his gaze to me, and a muscle jumped in his jaw. "Victoria, huh? So it's true? You have feelings for this girl? In spite of everything we've told you?"

I looked Pa dead in the eyes and lied to his face. "No. There's nothing between me and Victoria Whitfield, but I'm not going to let Ethan start up any crap and turn this county into a war zone, either."

"Mick, I want you to stay out of this," Pa said. "It's too dangerous to get in Ethan's way. Let me handle it."

He'd never handled Ethan before, I thought. But I shrugged anyway and pretended to give in. "Sure. Fine. Whatever you say. I need a shower, and then I have homework to do."

"Dinner's keeping warm in the oven for you, honey," Mom said.

She still looked kind of shaky, so I patted her shoulder and then headed upstairs. If my father handled this problem as poorly as he'd handled Ethan in the past, Rhodales and Whitfields would be shooting it out in the streets within a week.

I showered the day's grime off and then took a minute to plug in my phone, which had died sometime during the afternoon. The display lit up with text messages I'd missed.

4:16 PM: *Mickey, big trouble. My dad has gone insane. He's firing anybody related to you. It's the feud all over again. I stole my phone back from his office. Call me after 8.*

6:12 PM: *It's worse. He's blaming this all on Melinda for going off with Ethan. She got into a hidden stash of whiskey she found in the barn and is passed out. Fights are breaking out in the yard. The poor horses*

The poor horses? She was worried about horses when so many people had just lost their jobs? Maybe she was more like her father than I'd thought.

6:15 PM: *Sorry, had to hide my phone so that last message got cut off. The poor horses are in a state from the turmoil they don't understand and I am not much better. It is devastating that good, hardworking ppl lost their jobs because of this insanity.*

Guilt nudged me that I'd thought, even for a minute, that Victoria was the type to care more about horses than people. I kept misjudging her, based on her last name. I was no better than Ethan.

6:58 PM: *Have screamed myself hoarse, but he refuses to change his mind.*

Gran argued with him all day, but she'd signed over control of so much to him that she can't stop him. Mickey, I'm so sorry. I feel guilty by association.

7:18 PM: *Do you hate me now so much that you won't text me back?*

Damn it. I needed to call her, now. It was 8:30.

She picked up on the first ring.

"Mickey?" Her voice was so tentative and somehow broken that I damned myself for a fool for not charging my phone earlier.

"My phone was dead. I wasn't ignoring you. Don't worry. We'll get through this."

On the other end of the line, she took a deep breath, and I sat on the edge of my bed, feeling sick that I was unable to comfort her.

"I had to tell him that I will never have anything to do with you, Mickey," she said. "He was kind of nuts. I've never seen him like that—so cold. Completely emotionless about firing people. This hatred between our families . . . it's not even normal how it takes over everything else."

"I told my family the same thing, basically," I admitted. "Ethan was here. The news about the firing is out, and it's enough to start up the whole damn feud all over again. Pa thinks half the folks who got fired will end up working for Ethan and Anna Mae."

"Anna Mae?'"

"She's the real mastermind behind the drug running," I said, wondering what in the world Victoria would think about all this.

"What are we going to do? I don't know how to fix this; it's too big for us." She took another shaky breath, and I slammed my fist against the wall in frustration.

"What was that noise?"

"Nothing. Hey, how's your ankle?"

"It's fine. A little ice and it was better the next morning."

"Good to hear. Listen to me. Get some sleep, I'll see you in school tomorrow, and then we'll try to meet at the museum again. Nobody ever goes there, so we'll be able to talk in peace. We'll hash this all out then."

Silence.

"Mickey, should we do what they all want? Just forget—just stay away from each other?"

No.

"I can't make that decision for you, Victoria. I can't tell you what to do, and I wouldn't even try. But I can tell you that the only thing in the world that makes sense to me right now is you and me."

CHAPTER 23
VICTORIA

I can tell you that the only thing in the world that makes sense to me right now is you and me.

My heart wrenched in my chest at his words; I actually felt a physical pain. I'd lived a life of reserved solitude—playing peacekeeper and sanity arbiter in my family had required a high level of calm to buffer me from all the crazy. Every year when they shipped me off to school, I'd added a layer of distance to the wall between me and the rest of the world, and I hadn't even noticed when my hard-won serenity had turned into isolation.

Or when solitude had turned into loneliness.

But now, the first and only person I'd ever met who saw me for me was willing to defy everyone and everything to be with me. I could almost hear the cracking noise as the walls I'd spent years carefully building around my emotions began to crumble into dust.

"I feel the same way. It doesn't make sense, and I can't understand it, but maybe emotions aren't supposed to make sense," I finally said.

On the other end of the line, Mickey blew out a deep breath. "Tomorrow, then."

"Tomorrow," I agreed.

Just when I thought he'd hung up, I heard his voice again. "Victoria? Take care of yourself, until I'm with you to do it."

After that, I sat and stared at nothing, holding tightly to my phone, for a really long time. Mickey Rhodale wanted to take care of me.

Nobody else ever had.

By the time history class rolled around, my nerves were jangling underneath my skin. Everybody in my classes had been staring at me with varying degrees of hostility. The whispers had been bad, but the actual taunts hurled my way had been worse.

"Rich bitch, what kind of family does that to people?"

"Bet she thinks her shit don't stink. Maybe we should teach her a lesson."

And, worst of all:

"This will start up the feud again, for sure. Better watch out for Ethan Rhodale."

Denise stomped down the hall next to me, practically daring anybody to get in our way, but she wasn't all that happy with me, either.

"What the hell, Victoria? My friend Leila's dad lost his job yesterday because your dad went nuts."

"I know," I said miserably, wishing I were anywhere else but in school today. "We tried to stop him, but he'd already hired new people. It was a nightmare last night."

She shot me a look. "Well, probably more of a nightmare for the families who are wondering how they're going to put food on the table, or pay their bills now, don't you think?"

"I didn't mean—"

But she was already dashing forward into class, leaving me behind to face the waves of anger and contempt from everybody in sight.

I breathed my first unconstricted breath all day when I walked into class and saw that Mickey was already there, but he was having a heated discussion with Derek just inside the door.

"Why would you defend that family? They're going after yours," Derek said hotly, but he broke off when he caught sight of me.

Mickey took a step toward me, but then he stopped when he realized everybody in the room was staring at us.

"Later," he said fiercely, and his eyes gave me the message that the single word hadn't. He was still on my side. We just needed to keep everyone else from knowing it, or this might explode into an inferno that could burn down the entire county.

Denise, eyes wide, reached out to touch my arm when I walked past her.

"Omigod, did Mickey just threaten you with retaliation? We have to figure out a way to keep him away from you," she said. Amazing how a perceived threat from a Rhodale could win her back to my side. I appreciated the support even as I resented it, on Mickey's behalf.

"Thanks," I said automatically, even though I winced a little at the thought that everyone would naturally have taken Mickey's terse "later" as a threat. The realization of what it must feel like to be a Rhodale, trapped under the expectation of bad intentions, suddenly added a crushing weight to the anxiety I'd been carrying around since the night before.

Would we ever be able to find a way out of this? I didn't want to end up as a player in a Shakespearean tragedy I'd had no part in creating.

Mr. Gerard, either oblivious to, or ignoring, the tension in the room, droned on about Reconstruction and gave us a pop quiz. By the time I handed mine in, I realized I had no memory of what answers I'd written down. My stomach was churning so much I had no idea how I was going to face the cafeteria, either the smell of the food or the anger of everybody there.

Mickey brushed by me on the way out of class.

"Hang in there," he said quietly. "Only a few more hours."

His words gave me the strength to square my shoulders and follow Denise to lunch, but we'd only made it a few steps inside the cafeteria doors when the trouble started, in the shape of a large, scowling guy wearing a Wildcats letter jacket covered with football pins.

"Who the fuck do you people think you are?" He pushed Denise aside and got so close to me I could smell his morning breath. "My dad has worked for your family for twelve years, and now he's out on his ass because my mom's cousin is a Rhodale?"

He shoved my shoulder, and I stumbled back. Then suddenly someone lifted me clear up off the floor and to the side, and it was Mickey. I leaned back against him for a moment, breathing in his unique scent of fresh air, spring grass, and leather, and then he moved in front of me and confronted the guy who'd pushed me.

"Picking on girls now, Oliver? What's the matter, Coach make you run too hard in practice, so now you have to beat up on a girl to feel like a man?"

I could see Oliver's face twist in confusion. "What the hell, Mick? This chick's family just fired my dad and a boatload of other people for the big crime of being related to Rhodales and now *you're* defending *her*? Are you nuts?"

"I don't care what her father did. That doesn't make it right to take it out on Victoria, does it? No more than it's right to blame me for Ethan's crimes or for defending my sister from those animals, but you didn't bother to stick up for me either, did you?"

I realized that several other guys had started crowding around, and their mood was dangerous. All I wanted was to get out of there and take Mickey with me. I put my hand on his arm. "Mickey, let's just go. We don't—"

"Why would he want to go anywhere with you, bitch? Maybe we'll take you out in the woods and teach you a lesson about fucking with people," one of them taunted, leering at me so viciously I started shivering.

"Yeah," Oliver said, his eyes lighting up. "Maybe we'll take our turn to be the ones doing the fucking."

"Over my dead body," Mickey said, his voice low and razor-edged. "I don't need you to fight Rhodale battles for me, Oliver. You want to go after her, you're going to have to get through me first."

"It's not your battle, dickhead. It was *my* father he fired," Oliver roared, bunching his hands into fists.

No. Not again. I wasn't letting Mickey take the heat with everybody at school over this, like he had with my father over driving us home. I pushed forward and put myself in between them.

"No. Listen, I'm so sorry. I tried to stop my dad—"

I don't think Oliver heard a word I said, or even noticed that I was there, because his gaze was locked on Mickey as he threw the first punch. Mickey shoved me out of the way, but Oliver's fist was moving too fast. If the full force of the blow had struck me, it probably would have broken my jaw or cheekbone. As it was, even partially deflected, it sent me flying back and crashing into a table of freshmen girls.

Before I could move, or think, or even breathe, Mickey went after Oliver. He wasn't as tall or as broad as Oliver, but it was like watching a panther tear into a sheep. Mickey knocked him to the floor in two blows and then yanked the bigger boy up off the floor and hit him again. When Mickey tried to pick him up again, some of Oliver's friends got between them, but Mickey was fighting like a wild thing, his eyes blind with rage, and suddenly I knew exactly what had happened when those monsters had attacked his sister.

"Jesus, Mickey, I give up," Oliver panted.

His mouth was bleeding, and one of his eyes was already swelling up, but I didn't have a lot of sympathy for him, because I could feel my own right eye trying to do the same. I ran up to them anyway and threw my arms around Mickey.

"I'm here. I'm okay. You have to calm down," I told him over and over, feeling his big body shake in my arms like a tree caught in a tornado. He finally took a deep, shuddering breath and his eyes cleared, and I knew he'd come back from wherever he'd gone when Oliver hit me.

"Touch her again and I'll finish this," Mickey told Oliver, deadly calm.

I was quietly trying to keep from puking or having my head spin off my shoulders, so when Mickey tightened his arms around me, I gasped. I'd never been struck in anger before, and I fervently hoped it would never happen again.

Mickey caught my chin with one suddenly gentle hand and tilted my head, staring at the side of my face that had taken the blow. His eyes narrowed, and I could almost feel the heat of the rage pouring off his body.

"That son of a bitch. I'm going to *kill* him."

I caught his arm before he could turn away.

"Please, no. I need—will you help me get out of here?"

The principal ran into the cafeteria—where had *he* been all this time?—and started yelling.

"Rhodale! Oliver! My office, now. You're both going to be suspended for this, and I—"

He broke off when he caught sight of my face and winced, which didn't make me feel any better. "Victoria, are you okay? Do you want to press charges?"

"No. I'm fine. It was all a misunderstanding," I said, glancing at Oliver, who'd gotten up and was wiping blood off his mouth with a napkin.

"I don't think so," Principal Scott fired back. "The lunch monitor ran into my office yelling that you were all trying to kill each other."

"She was a little off base," Mickey drawled. "It was the food. Lunch is so bad today that you nearly had a riot on your hands."

The principal narrowed his eyes. "Don't give me any of your lip, young man. And let me tell you something. We will not tolerate this kind of violence on school grounds, do you understand me?"

The unfairness of it scorched through me. "He was only defending me!"

Principal Scott rounded on me. "Really? Why did you need to be defended from a misunderstanding?"

"She's telling the truth. It was a misunderstanding all the way around," Oliver said, backing my story, but he trained his hard gaze on Mickey the whole time, promising retaliation.

"Well, this kind of misunderstanding is going to result in a two-day suspension for both of you," Scott said. "And you, young lady, are going to the nurse to get checked out."

"I need to go home," I said. I couldn't face the rest of the day, and I wanted ice and Tylenol more than anything else in the world right at that moment.

Denise, who'd been hovering at the edges of the fight, handed me my backpack and volunteered to take me home. Before the principal could answer, Mickey scooped his backpack off the floor and took mine out of my hands.

"No. I'm driving her home," he said flatly.

Principal Scott folded his arms. "You're going nowhere, young man. We have—"

"You're suspending me anyway, so it can start now. I'm taking Victoria to make sure she gets home safely," Mickey said, sweeping his hard gaze over the guys who'd crowded around me earlier and were now pretending they'd had nothing to do with any of it. "You can take it up with my pa. You will, anyway."

With that, he swung both backpacks over one shoulder and put his other arm around me and led me to the door. The crowd in front of us shrank back, nobody wanting to get in his way.

The principal called out after us. "Victoria, do you want me to call the police?"

I took a deep breath and turned around, facing him but speaking to the whole room.

"No, I just want to go home. I'm sorry for the trouble my father caused. I fought him on this, and I'm still fighting him. I don't know what else to say."

A surge of pain stabbed through my cheek and made me flinch, and Mickey pulled me back around and held the door open. As we walked out, I was already having second thoughts.

"This is a bad idea. When our families find out we left school together—"

"They can go to hell. They got us into this mess to begin with," Mickey said.

I dug in my bag for my keys and handed them over, and then I leaned my poor bruised and swelling cheek against the cool glass of the window as we drove away from the school and all the unresolved conflict still seething inside.

"I'll have to face them again tomorrow," I said.

"Tomorrow's Friday. Skip school. Your face is going to get worse before it gets better," he said grimly.

I made a sound—of denial or protest, I didn't know which—and he glanced over at me.

"I'm sorry. Hell, I'm not good at words of comfort, am I? It's the truth, though. I've been on the receiving end of a fist often enough to know that you're likely going to have a black eye from this."

"I can't imagine that," I whispered, closing my eyes.

"Having a shiner?"

"No. Having enough experience with being punched to diagnose what's going to happen next. Your life has been so different from mine, in some ways. And so similar, in others."

He put a hand on mine, and I closed my fingers around his almost convulsively, taking comfort from the same hand that had beaten Oliver so savagely and thoroughly such a short time ago. I didn't know how to reconcile the two Mickeys, and I was hurting too much to even try, but I knew he was only violent when he was protecting somebody he cared about.

We drove along in silence for a while, and when he pulled off the road and stopped the truck, I opened my eyes to see we were in the parking lot of a small restaurant called the Buckeye Diner.

"Buckeye? Really? Here in the heart of Kentucky?"

Mickey grinned. "He's an old ex-Navy guy, and his burgers are so good that everybody puts up with his Ohio State origins."

"I don't think I can eat anything." My stomach was tied in six different kinds of knots.

"Well, let's at least get you some ice for your face and some Tylenol, and then see how you feel," he said.

He unbuckled his seat belt and then leaned across to unfasten mine, and his breath feathered across my cheek and made me shiver. He stilled, and then he moved back and stared into my eyes.

"I won't let anybody hurt you again, but I can't stay away from you, Victoria. Please don't ask me to," he whispered, and then he kissed me, a gentle caress of his lips on mine, and I shivered again as an almost too-powerful sensation raced through me.

"I won't," I promised, and his beautiful blue eyes lit up with triumph, or joy, or simply intense satisfaction, and I had to force myself not to hurl myself into his arms right there in the truck, in a public parking lot, in broad daylight. It didn't make sense, this fierce connection between us, but it was so intensely real that I didn't even try to deny it.

"I—ice," I finally stammered, and he grinned.

"Ice."

CHAPTER 24
MICKEY

Mr. Judson's thick eyebrows came together when he saw me walk in. "Little early on a school day, isn't it, Mick?"

"We got early dismissal, so I thought I'd bring Victoria by to try the best burgers in the state," I told him.

She was hiding her cheek under the fall of her hair and staring at the floor, and I thought I'd wait till we got to the table to ask about ice so as not to attract any more attention than we already had.

"Well, at least the best burgers in the county," he said, grinning at both of us. He started polishing his spotless counter again, and I led Victoria toward the last booth in the row, so we could have a little privacy to talk.

Nora, the diner's only waitress, pointed at the rack of plastic-covered menus, and I took two as I passed by. Nora preferred to work hard only on days of the week that didn't end in "Y," but she was always cheerful about it, so nobody ever complained much.

"Drinks?"

"Water, please," Victoria said.

I waited until I got closer and nobody but Nora and Victoria would hear me. "A Coke for me, Nora, and can I get an extra cup of ice, please, and a clean cloth?"

Nora's sharp eyes scanned Victoria's face, but she just nodded and headed toward the drink dispenser.

I gestured to Victoria to take the seat with its back toward the rest of the diner, and I slid into the seat facing her.

"Is it really bad?" She looked up at me, lifting her hair up out of the way so I could see, and rage flooded me. I wanted to go back in time and knock Sam Oliver down all over again.

"It's bad," I admitted. "Your skin is so fair that the bruising really shows up. I'm so sorry."

"It was my fault." She attempted a smile, and my gut clenched at her courage.

I doubted many girls—hell, many guys, either—who'd been clocked by one of the biggest guys on the Clark High football team would be brave enough to smile about it.

"If I hadn't tried to get in his way, my face wouldn't have punched him in the fist so hard," she said, but then she flinched and put a hand over her face. "Okay, smiling actually hurts quite a bit. No more smiling."

Nora showed back up at the table with our drinks, the ice, Tylenol, and a furious expression.

"Who did this to you, young lady? Mickey, I hope you beat the shit out of him, whoever it was," she said fiercely, and warmth spiraled up through me at the complete sincerity in her voice.

She obviously hadn't thought for a second that I'd been the one who hit Victoria, and it was almost pathetic how grateful I was for someone who didn't condemn me on the spot—guilty of nothing more than being born a Rhodale.

Victoria studied the menu while she took a couple of Tylenol and put some ice in the cloth Nora handed her and then against her cheek. She ordered a chocolate milkshake and I asked for a shake, too, and a double burger and fries to go with it.

"Extra pickles," Nora said, and I nodded my thanks.

She rested her hand briefly on Victoria's shoulder. "Honey, if you want to call the cops on whoever did this, or you need a place to crash for a few nights while you get away, you let me know. Any friend of Mickey's and all that."

Victoria's beautiful green eyes shimmered, but she didn't let the tears spill over. "I can't tell you how much I appreciate that, Nora, but it really was an accident. I got in between two stubborn guys—"

"No need to say anything else, honey. Mickey, you make sure she doesn't do it again, you hear me?"

I nodded and waited until Nora headed off with our order before I spoke. "She's right. I need to make sure it doesn't happen again, but first you have to tell me how to keep a stubborn girl from standing up for me whenever she thinks I need it."

Victoria's cheeks turned pink, and she shrugged. "You keep trying to take the blame for things that are my fault. What else can I do?"

"You can let me sink or swim on my own efforts, like everybody else in my life. Except my mother," I said.

"Now you're comparing me to your mother? I'm not sure how to take that," she teased, and I could tell she was trying to distract me.

It was my turn to shrug. "My mom is smart and kind, and so are you. I think you two would like each other."

Victoria blinked, moving the ice away from her cheek for a minute. "Most guys I know never talk about their mothers except to complain, like they think it's not cool or something."

"I'm not most guys." I leaned forward and gently lifted her hand so the ice pressed to her cheek again. "The more you keep ice on this, the less it will swell. We can stop at the drugstore and get you some arnica gel, too. That really helps."

Nora headed back toward us with our milkshakes, and she pulled a tube of the very stuff out of her pocket. "This will help a lot, honey. Apply some a few times a day, until the bruising goes away completely."

"Oh, I couldn't—"

"Take it. I have extra," Nora advised, her lips tightening.

"Thank you," Victoria whispered. "You're very kind."

"Humph." Nora marched off, but I could tell she was pleased.

"What's the story? Why does she have Tylenol and arnica gel?" Victoria questioned, looking grim, and I nodded.

The story was grim.

"Nora's ex beat her nearly to death with her own furniture when she asked for a divorce. After she recovered from that, she made it her mission in life to make sure that any woman who needs to get away from an abuser has a safe place to land. She works at the women's shelter several days a week."

"How do you know all this?"

"Small town, small county. Also, Mom does a donation drive for clothes for the shelter a couple of times a year. Some of her students wind up living there with their mothers for a while, sometimes."

A dark shadow crossed over Victoria's face, and she dropped her gaze to stare blindly down at her milkshake. "Those boys . . . they were threatening to take me in the woods and . . . do you think they— that they—"

"Would have raped you if I hadn't been there to stop them?" I was blunt, but she deserved an honest answer.

She nodded.

"I don't know. I don't think so. I know Sam Oliver and the rest of them, and none of them have been the type to hurt girls in the past. I also think that somebody would have called 911. Sam wasn't think-ing straight because of his dad getting fired, and the rest was just mob mentality kicking in."

"Mob mentality, though—that's led to rapes and worse," Victoria pointed out, and I didn't disagree.

She put the ice down on the table, and I saw that her hands were shaking. "This is going to get worse before it gets better, isn't it?"

I grinned and took her hands in mine, both to warm them up and to stop the trembling. "Hey, at least you're optimistic."

She blinked. "What are you talking about?"

"You think things are going to get better."

CHAPTER 25
VICTORIA

I started to laugh; it was that or cry, but my face hurt too much to laugh. The Tylenol would probably start to kick in soon, so I tried to sip the milkshake. It was thick and good, and the icy smoothness actually helped my jaw feel a little better. Or maybe it was just my inner chocolate fiend telling me that. Either way, it made me happy.

Nora brought Mickey's enormous platter of food, and I stole a few French fries while he demolished the rest of the plate, and we talked about anything other than the feud. He told me about growing up with his family and a half, and I told him about the pressure to always maintain the Whitfield image. He thought I'd like his half sister, Caroline. I told him Buddy would adore him, especially when he heard that Mickey knew how to play ball.

"There's a great league he can be part of this summer," he said, before downing the rest of his milkshake.

"I mean this in the nicest possible way, but do you have a hollow leg? How do you eat like that and stay in such great shape?"

He flashed one of those unfair sexy smiles of his, so hot it almost melted the ice I was still holding to my cheek. "You think I'm in great shape?"

"You know you are." I rolled my eyes. "Don't ask me to stroke your ego when I look like an escapee from the World Wrestling Federation."

His smile faded. "You look like the bravest and most beautiful girl I've ever met. I spend half of my time wanting to be with you and the other half knowing I should stay away from you, for your sake."

"Don't say that," I said, my breath suddenly catching in my throat. "Not now, not after all this. I don't think I could take it."

We stared at each other for a long time, trapped in the moment, the other diners' voices fading to a distant buzz in my ears, and finally he nodded.

"Okay. Tell me about riding and races and horses. Why don't you ride sidesaddle, like the rich girls in those movies?"

I started to laugh. "Ouch. Okay, I don't ride sidesaddle because I'm not a delicate flower living a couple of hundred years ago, or somebody who takes part in the very specialized niche of sidesaddle riding and competition."

"Tell me about thoroughbreds, then."

I told him about the ranch and the horses and about how I'd always lived for the time we spent at the ranch with Gran. I'd never felt at home in the city, not really, and it was only when I was out on the ranch, working in the barn or riding, that I felt like I could finally take a deep breath.

"Riding is the closest a person can come to flying without an airplane, Mickey. It's incredible. And yet so many things can go wrong; the balance is so delicate—it's dangerous, too, but the risk is worth the reward, a hundred times over."

Was I still talking about riding? Or the chance at a relationship with Mickey? I realized I didn't even know.

"I wouldn't have agreed the other night, watching you fall," he said dryly.

He paused. "Was the horse okay, by the way?"

His concern made me smile. I couldn't have cared about anybody who treated my beloved horses callously.

"She's fine, thank goodness. Anyway, it wasn't her fault. Horses are the most amazing creatures. So powerful and so incredibly beautiful, Mickey, and even when I'm mucking out the stalls or cleaning hooves, I can't help but be struck by the wonder of nature and feel privileged to be around them."

I stopped, suddenly aware that I was rambling like an idiot, but he was nodding seriously.

"It's like Kentucky," he said. "Or how I feel about it, anyway. There are so many parts of this state that are suffering crushing poverty, but when you drive by and see a little kid digging in the dirt of a barren yard in front of the backdrop of the Kentucky hills, there's a kind of stark beauty in it. Almost as if God is saying, poor folks can be beautiful, too."

The words reverberated in my mind, catching at my emotions.

"Who *are* you?" I whispered, leaning forward and reaching across the table to touch his sternly gorgeous face, almost afraid he'd disappear beneath my fingertips. "The face of an angel, the soul of a poet, and the fists of a fighter. I don't know how to understand you, Mickey."

Mickey caught my hand with his and then turned his head and pressed a soft kiss in my palm. "I'm not the only poet at this table."

"So which of you two poets wants a piece of our excellent pecan pie?" Nora asked. I jumped, almost knocking over my glass of water.

"You move quietly," I said, smiling at her.

"Nah, I clomp around pretty loudly. You were both too busy staring soulfully into each other's eyes to notice." Her eyes were twinkling when she said it, so I couldn't take offense or even be too embarrassed, although my cheeks flamed hot anyway.

"I'll have pie," Mickey said, and I groaned.

"Where does he put it?"

Nora laughed. "Been wondering that about teenage boys for nearly forty years, hon. That and how is it fair that they get the best eyelashes?" She grabbed Mickey's face and tilted it up, so I could fully admire the long dark sweep of his lashes.

"Okay, okay," Mickey muttered, pulling his face away and grinning sheepishly. "Enough. I'd better get Victoria home. Why don't I take that pie to go?"

Nora nodded, scribbled something on our check, left it on the table, and headed off.

My face started to hurt again at the mention of home. I wasn't ready for that.

"Mickey, I don't know if I can."

"I know, but Principal Scott will have called your house. They're going to be wondering where you are, and probably calling the National Guard any minute."

My eyes widened. "Crap. I left my phone in the truck. I wasn't even thinking about that."

He sighed, closing his eyes. "Yeah, and my Pa will have half his deputies out looking for me. This was a wonderful bubble of escape, but it's time to face the music."

I cautiously tried moving my face. It still hurt, but the Tylenol had kicked in and given me a little relief.

"I don't—wait. Tomorrow night I have to go to some stupid Founders' Day dance downtown. Are you going?"

He shook his head. "Not a chance. When Pa hears I've been suspended, he'll hit the roof. My mother won't be happy either; she's a teacher. Buddy's teacher, actually. Anyway, they won't let me show my face at the dance."

"Buddy loves his teacher. She told him he was very observant." I grinned when he looked confused, but then my stomach sank again. "Well, I should probably stay home anyway, since I'll look like Frankenstein's monster by tomorrow."

"Wait a minute," Mickey said slowly. "You tell them you want to stay home. I'll stay home. Then I'll come get you and we'll get out of town and have an actual date, someplace where nobody knows either of us. No Rhodale crap, no Whitfield crap—just me and you. What do you say?"

I *should* say no.

There was no way I was saying no.

"*Yes.*"

We picked up the pie, paid the check, and left Nora a great tip.

She pulled me aside before we left and pressed a piece of paper in my hand.

"Just in case, honey. You stick with Mickey, you hear? He's good people." She smiled, and I impulsively leaned forward and hugged her. My mother would have been horrified.

When we got outside, I saw that she'd given me her phone number. I held it tight, feeling her kindness permeating the paper as if it were a tiny scrap of magical protection.

Mickey drove again, holding my hand all the way. We pulled into the now-empty school parking lot, and he kissed me very gently before he got out of the truck, careful not to hurt my poor wounded face.

When I pulled away to breathe, the slow, sexy smile that spread across Mickey's face scattered my thoughts even further.

"You have to quit biting your lip, Victoria." He wrapped a strand of my hair around his fingers. "Every time you do, it makes me want to kiss you again."

I smiled and deliberately bit my lip, and he groaned.

"Sure, use my own pitiful confessions against me. One of these days, I'll get you completely alone for longer than five minutes, and then we'll have this discussion again," he said—either a warning or a promise—and a thrill of anticipation zinged through me.

"Maybe tomorrow," I said, trying not to sound too eager.

"I really hope so," he said fervently, making me laugh.

"There. That's the smile I wanted to see before I let you go face the dragon," he said, stepping back from the truck. "Call me later if you can."

"I will," I promised. "Good luck with your parents."

He nodded. "I'm going to need it."

CHAPTER 26
MICKEY

The principal *had* called my parents. There was plenty of yelling from Pa and disappointed looks from Mom, until I explained the whole thing, and then my sweet, kind, peace-loving mother told me she hoped I'd broken Sam's nose.

That took the wind out of me and Pa, and we kind of tiptoed around after that, doing chores and eventually making dinner on the grill out back so she didn't have to cook, while trying not to talk too loudly.

"Do you think she's going through the change?" Pa looked anywhere but at me when he asked it, and I turned and started studying the rain gutters to see if they needed cleaning. The Rhodale man's way to handle female stuff. Any minute now, one of us would head off to club a woolly mammoth or something.

Mom's voice came floating through the kitchen window. "I heard that. I am *not* going through the *change*. I can be proud of my son for being chivalrous and standing up to bullies who were trying to harm an innocent girl without it having been caused by hormonal imbalance."

Her face appeared in the window, and she stared out at us, waving a spatula around. "Maybe this can be the first small step in resolving this nonsense, once and for all. A Rhodale protecting a Whitfield! A Whitfield and a Rhodale getting along! Film at eleven!"

She moved away from the window, and Pa and I stared at each other, dumbfounded.

"Film at eleven? Is that like 'catch it on YouTube'?"

Pa shook his head. "I have no idea. Maybe I need a beer."

I reached into the ice bucket Mom had put out on the back porch. "Here's a Coke. Learn to love it. I think your drinking days are over for a while," I advised.

After that, we had the most pleasant family dinner we'd had in weeks. I kept looking back and forth between them, wondering when the other shoe was going to drop—hard—probably on my head.

None of this made any sense. I do my best to toe the line, and Pa's always got something up his ass about me. I punch a kid and get suspended, and everything is peachy.

Parents. Who could understand them?

I went and got the double-sized piece of pie that Nora had packed for me from the fridge and shared it out between the three of us.

"Nora says hi," I said.

Mom paused, holding a forkful of pie in front of her. "Yes, I know. She called me. Said you were eating a good lunch, and you were a good boy."

I held my breath, waiting for the rest of it, but thankfully my mother did not share with Pa that my lunch date had been Victoria Whitfield. It was better that way. When he wasn't looking, she actually winked at me, and I breathed a sigh of relief.

"Tomorrow is the Founders' Day gig," I began tentatively.

"You can forget that, son," Pa said, pointing a finger at me. He shot a look at my mother. "I guess we've decided that you were in the right, defending a girl from a bully, no matter what her last name is, but I'm not about to let you flaunt yourself around the town celebration when you've been suspended from school."

"Melvin Scott is a wussy little bureaucrat who doesn't know his butt from a hole in the ground," Mom said sharply. "He should have given Mickey an award, not suspended him."

I looked at the level of wine in the freshly opened bottle and wondered if she'd had a little bit too much. An award?

"Hey, Mom, I love that you're sticking up for me like this, but I should have just taken Victoria away from the situation instead of wading in, fists flying," I said, because even if I would have done the same damn thing if it came up again, she'd raised me better than that.

Pa, shockingly, was grinning at Mom.

"You've always been a mama wolf about that boy," he said admiringly. "Remember how you stood up to Anna Mae when she tried to give him a whiskey-soaked rag to teethe on?"

She shuddered. "That woman. Just because we had to interact for the sake of your children was no reason I was about to let her get her evil clutches on my son."

Pa put his hand on hers. "You're a tough woman, Julia Rhodale."

She smiled at him and actually batted her eyelashes. "Don't you forget it, Jeremiah Rhodale."

Okay.

"This is getting too lovey-dovey for me, so I'll stack these in the kitchen and do the cleanup after homework," I told them.

Pa waved a hand at me. "No worries. Do your work and get an early night. We'll clean up here. You'll need your strength to clean out the garage tomorrow."

I froze. "The garage? Pa, that'll take days."

He grinned at me, and it was an evil, evil grin. "Yep. I figure the two days of the weekend plus the two days of your suspension ought to do it. Might make you think twice the next time you decide to get in a fistfight at school. Be sure to wear really old clothes. It's filthy in there."

I groaned all the way up the stairs, but then my phone rang and I forgot about tyrannical fathers who used their sons for slave labor. It was Victoria.

She gave me the bare bones of what had probably been a pretty ugly blowup at her house, so I took my cue from her and didn't press her on it. Instead, I told her about Pa and the garage, and she told me about Sisyphus and his boulder, and I watched through my window as night fell and the stars came out to the quiet music of her voice.

CHAPTER 27
VICTORIA

Gran came downstairs slowly, holding tightly to the handrail. She seemed to have aged dramatically since the uproar with Dad over the firing. I smiled brightly to hide any sign of what I was thinking.

"You look beautiful," I told her.

That much was true, anyway. She wore a lavender suit with brocaded accents of deep purple that was gorgeous with her snow-white hair and blue eyes.

She smiled at me.

"There hasn't been a Founders' Day party in Whitfield County without Lucinda Whitfield in attendance since I first married your grandfather," she said, straightening her spine and suddenly looking like the belle of the ball again.

Dad rushed into the room, muttering.

"Where is your mother? It's bad enough you're not coming, but she has to be late, too," he snapped at me, looking anywhere but at my bruised and swollen face.

This morning, nobody had even tried to make me go to school. The ice and arnica gel had helped, but anybody looking could tell I'd taken a punch. Even without the visual evidence, the blistering headache would have kept me home.

I'd run into my mother at breakfast, when she'd headed straight for the espresso machine before catching sight of me and flinching.

"What happened to you?"

"I ran into a door," I'd said calmly, knowing that Dad wouldn't have told her about the incident at school and wondering when I'd become such a good liar. Wondering how many lies were in my future. Wondering why the prospect of continuing deception didn't bother me more than it did.

The day had dragged by, but now they were all getting ready to go to the big party, leaving me with a study date with Denise to go to—yet another lie—and Melinda in charge of Buddy. Pete would be escorting Gran, and Mrs. Kennedy had gone to her sister's for the weekend, so Melinda would be alone with Buddy. Which scared me.

A lot.

But the liquor cabinet had magically disappeared, and the wine fridge had been emptied out, so though I was still waiting on Dad to sort through the rehab options I'd researched and presented him with, there'd been some progress since the dinner from hell. Not enough, though, for me to feel happy about leaving Buddy with Melinda. She was an alcoholic. She wasn't going to magically get better without some serious help.

For about the tenth time, I considered postponing my date with

Mickey. For about the eleventh time, I decided against it. We'd been through a lot. We deserved this date. How much trouble could Melinda and Buddy get into with popcorn, sodas, and the *Pirates of the Caribbean* movie collection?

"I'm here," Mom said, appearing at the head of the stairs.

She looked too glamorous for a county festival; more like she was heading to a cocktail party in the city, but I really couldn't fault the black sheath dress she wore. It was more the way she wore it than the dress itself. Priscilla Whitfield had a patrician elegance she wore like a second skin, and she somehow always managed to outshine everyone around her.

I had the uncomfortable epiphany that maybe that's why her two daughters always tried to escape the pressure of living up to the Whitfield image—me through worrying more about being smart than pretty, and Melinda through partying. We'd grown up with a mother who was coldly perfect; we could have looked to her as either a role model or a terrible warning—and we'd both seen her as the warning. Melinda wanted to escape everything, especially her own emotions. I worried again that maybe this wasn't the best time to leave her alone with Buddy, but he was nine, not four, and pretty self-sufficient these days.

"Victoria, you look hideous," Mom said sharply.

"Gee, thanks. It's so great to always have you on my side." I rolled my eyes, but she was kind of right. I'd spent the day in sweats, my hair was a mess, and I wasn't wearing any makeup. That plus the bruising, and I probably looked like an escapee from juvenile detention to my fashion-conscious mother.

"Who cares what she looks like? She's going to study with a

girlfriend. They'll probably paint each other's nails and eat junk food," Gran said, grinning conspiratorially at me.

I felt a pang of guilt for lying to her. She was the one person who always told me the truth. I didn't want to hurt her, though, or involve her in my plotting. She'd just get caught in the middle later or—almost as bad—feel compelled to say something to my parents.

Pete showed up to escort Gran, Mom and Dad followed them out, and I watched the two cars head down the driveway before I allowed myself to believe they were really gone. For the first time all day I felt like smiling. I ran up the stairs to my room and headed straight for the shower.

My door banged open, and Melinda walked in, her face set in stormy lines.

"I can't do this," she said. "I'm flying apart, Victoria, I can't do this."

I took a deep breath and put the mascara wand down so I didn't stab myself in the eye with it—or turn around and stab Melinda. My patience with her had been running thin, which made me feel even guiltier. I knew she was going through a lot, but sometimes I wished that, just once, she'd wake up and realize that other people had problems, too.

"I want to go to the party," Melinda said, her eyes darting around the room. "I need to get out of here, Victoria. Are you sure you have to go out? Maybe you could stay here with us."

"I really need to go. It'll just be for a few hours," I said, closing my eyes and sending up a little prayer that she wouldn't have a meltdown. Not tonight.

Please.

She drifted over to my bed and picked up the green dress I'd been planning to wear.

"You're wearing this to a study date with Denise?" She stared from the dress to me and back. "Does Denise have a hot brother I don't know about?"

"No, of course not. I thought if I wore something pretty, I wouldn't feel so hideous with my face like this," I said, which was actually the truth. Mickey had seen me yesterday, if not quite as black and blue, but this was our first real date. I might not be as image-conscious as my mother, but I certainly had enough feminine vanity that I wanted to look pretty.

I wanted to see admiration in his eyes instead of pity.

Melinda forgot her pouting and rushed over to me. "Oh, I'm so sorry. Of course you do. Sit down and I'll do your makeup."

"Melinda—" More guilt washed over me—this time for thinking she was entirely self-absorbed—and I realized I'd been spending an awful lot of my time feeling guilty lately.

Maybe I wasn't cut out for a life of crime, or even deceit. Maybe this was a bad idea.

She took the mascara wand and swirled it around in the tube. "*Sit.* I'm not taking no for an answer."

I sat.

"Just remember that moderate is key with me, please? Last time you did my makeup you made me look like Cleopatra-gone-wild."

We cracked up at the memory, and it was the closest moment to normal that we'd had between us in a while.

"I love you," she said unexpectedly, and I had to blink back tears.

"Stop that, you'll mess up the makeup I'm getting ready to put on you," she said, laughing. "We can't have Cleopatra with raccoon eyes."

When she was done, I was beautiful. I almost couldn't believe it. Not only had the bruising disappeared, but the swelling was camouflaged, and she'd used some trick of eye shadow magic to make my eyes look huge and almost exotic.

It was so not me, and yet it was— it was the me I'd like to be.

A girl beautiful enough to belong inside a fairy tale, instead of on the outside looking in. I'd always secretly thought that if all those stories had been real, I would have been cast as the supporting player— the girl who came in later and fixed things. Somebody would have had to hire a new cleaning staff after Cinderella headed for the castle, find a gardening book to figure out what to do with the beanstalk, and organize new housing for all those dwarfs.

Practical, smart Victoria would have stepped in and saved the day; she would have been quite happy to get a glimpse of the handsome prince from afar, thank you very much. Handsome princes were way more trouble than they were worth.

But now there was Mickey. He was larger than life—he'd never have been content to take on a supporting role in any story. He wasn't Prince Charming, though.

He was Prince Dangerous.

I shook my head, smiling at my own silliness, and Melinda grinned at me.

"Now I'll do your hair."

By the time she was done with me, I looked amazing, and I held my breath, almost unable to believe the version of me I was seeing in the mirror. The dress looked better on me than it ever had before, and I slipped on a pair of ballet flats, glad that I'd hidden my heels in my bag earlier.

Melinda would believe a lot of things, but that I'd wear high heels when I had any chance to avoid it was not one of them.

By the time I'd dressed, pulled on a nondescript cardigan to tone down the effect a little, at least until I got out of the house, and stuffed my cover-story books in my bag, she was flaking out on me again.

"Victoria. Vivi," she began, using the name she hadn't called me since I was maybe in first grade. Mother didn't approve of nicknames.

"What is it, Melinda? I told Denise I'd be there by eight, and I still want to stop and buy some snacks to bring with me," I said, glancing at the clock and feeling my stomach twist. More lies.

Mickey would be waiting for me in the side parking lot at the school in approximately thirty-three minutes. A thrill of anticipation winged through me, but I was careful not to let it show. Nobody in the history of the world had ever been this excited about a study date. Even Melinda would figure that out, eventually.

"I just don't feel . . . right," she said softly. "I wish you could call this off and stay here with me tonight. With us. My insides are churning, and I—"

I seized on that. "Of course they are! You haven't had anything to eat since lunch. Mom said to order pizza. Do you remember the phone number? It's on the list on the fridge."

"I don't think it's hunger," she said, twisting her hands. "It's just—"

I whirled around and put my hands on my hips. "It's just *what*? Please tell me, so tonight can be about you, just like every other night, Melinda. I've only lived here a short while, and already everybody hates me. I'm not going to stand up the one friend I've made because your hunger pangs are making you anxious."

When her face started to crumple, I immediately regretted every word. I was the worst sister in the world.

"I'm sorry," she whispered, and I hugged her.

"No, honey, I'm so sorry. I think I'm hungry, too, and low blood sugar is making me cranky." I dropped my bag, feeling my hopes for the evening hit the floor with it, and tried to smile.

I couldn't quite manage it.

"If you really feel like you need me to be here, I'll stay. Give me a few minutes to call Denise."

Melinda blinked away the tears and raised her head. "No. Of course you shouldn't do that. We'll be fine. We have pizza, popcorn, and pirates. It's going to be great."

"Are you sure?"

She nodded, and I decided to take her at her word. I hugged her again, afraid to stay any longer in case she changed her mind. I called out a good-bye to Buddy and hit the stairs running. It almost felt like I should have a carriage, or at least a convertible, but I'd have to make do with the old farm truck I'd been driving.

I glanced at the clock on the dashboard. Fifteen minutes. I kept my lips clamped shut, almost superstitious, until I'd pulled out onto the main road, but then I couldn't keep it in anymore.

"Yes!"

There may even have been happy seat dancing involved.

CHAPTER 28
MICKEY

I'd had to scrub beneath my fingernails three times to get all of the grime that had built up in there during ten solid hours of cleaning out the garage. We were either going to have a yard sale or I was taking a truckload to the dump, because there was no way I'd hauled all of that crap out of there only to turn around and put it back. Broken equipment and tools, rusty parts, half-used bags of lawn fertilizer and potting soil—it was a nightmare, and I'd only made it through about a quarter of the job, so Pa hadn't been kidding about the four days.

Damn it.

I grabbed a shirt out of the closet and did a smell check to be sure it was clean—usually, the ones on hangers were—and threw on a newish pair of jeans and my boots. I'd heard my folks heading out for the party just before I got in the shower, so nobody was around to wonder why I was getting all dressed up. Usually I'd be wearing one of the dozens of free T-shirts vendors left us at the gas station and my oldest jeans to kick back on a Friday night, but I didn't think a motor oil shirt would impress Victoria.

I froze, suddenly realizing I'd been about to *comb my hair*. I was trying to *impress Victoria*. I dropped the comb and watched as it seemed to fall to the floor in slow motion.

I was out of my league with this girl. League, hell. I was out of my fucking mind. Any day now, she was going to wake up and realize that she could do a hell of a lot better than me. Her folks probably had a bunch of rich horse-people friends with sons named Biff and Chad and what-the-hell-ever who'd make a lot more sense for her. Guys without the baggage I carried around with me from my family and my name.

"Fuck *that*," I said viciously, and I kicked the comb across the room. "They're not getting anywhere near her, and I'm not trying to turn myself into somebody that I'm not. She'll have to take me as she finds me."

I closed my eyes and groaned. Talking to myself in an empty room. Yeah, I was losing it.

The sound of motorcycles roaring up the street knocked me out of my crazy thoughts, and I walked over to the window to see that Ethan, Jeb, and a few of their flunkies had pulled up to my house. Worse, Ethan was getting off his bike and looking up at my window.

Pretending I wasn't home wouldn't work, or at best would only delay the confrontation, so I headed downstairs and met him at the front door.

"Pa's not here. I'm on my way out." I stepped out on the porch, because there was no way I was inviting him inside. "What do you want?"

He'd been drinking, or sampling his own product, or something.

His eyes were wild and aggressive, and his body was bunched up and twitchy all at once.

"I want you, little brother. Got a party going on tonight."

I pointed at Jeb, who was drinking a beer right there on his bike. "If you're thinking of crashing the Founders' Day party, I'd think again. Pa won't like it if you guys show up wasted."

"Wouldn't be crashing, would it, since the party is for everybody?" He started laughing before I could answer that. "Hey, no worries. We have a different party to go to, and I wanted to stop by and bring you along. Do you good to get out of your head a little bit. Quit being the perfect son and let loose."

"Perfect son, my ass. I got kicked off the football team, suspended from school, and ordered to spend four days cleaning out the garage." I swept an arm toward the evidence, all neatly stacked on the lawn next to the garage and covered in tarps.

Ethan whistled. "He never got rid of that busted riding mower? Hell, he had that when I was a baby." A flash of some indefinable emotion crossed his face.

Anyway, I had plans, and Victoria must be almost to the school by now. It was on the other side of town from the town hall and town square, where the night's festivities were taking place, which was why we'd picked it as a meeting place.

"I need to get going."

Ethan raised an eyebrow and gave me the once-over. "New jeans? Nice shirt that actually buttons? You got yourself a hot date, little brother? I know it's not with Paula, because she already told us she'd be waiting for you at the party, and I told her she was nuts."

"It's not with Paula. We were over a long time ago," I said evenly. "You made sure of that."

Ethan had warned me that Paula wasn't faithful, but I hadn't believed him, too full of myself to believe she'd cheat on me. He'd made sure I walked in on the two of them in her living room one evening. She'd been sitting on his lap. I might not have minded so much if either of them had been wearing shirts.

I let myself enjoy the memory of punching him in the face.

"I let you hit me, didn't I? And all I was doing was trying to protect you from a cheating slut."

I pushed past Ethan and headed for my bike. "Right, Ethan. Funny how I've never had anybody to protect me from you."

He stopped me with a hand on my arm. "We need to talk. I have a job that would be perfect for you."

"I won't deal drugs for you, Ethan." I shook off his hand. "I don't know how many ways to say the same thing, over and over. I won't do it—not now, not ever. I'm going to college, which will be hard to do if I'm in jail or dead."

"I don't want you to deal drugs. I want you to be a kind of procurement manager," he drawled.

"What? What the hell is that? A pimp? You gonna run girls now, too?" This was more than I had time or patience for right then, but hearing the words "procurement manager" come out of my brother's mouth had definitely caught my attention.

"No, idiot," he said, but a speculative gleam came to his eyes. "Although that might be a great idea for the future. Anna Mae has all those empty trailers. . . . No. Forget that. I need somebody fresh-faced and criminal-record-free to manage my supply chain. Everybody's cracking down hard on the sale of pseudoephedrine."

"What?"

He grinned, trying to play it casual, but I could see the fear skittering behind his eyes. Something or someone had him running scared.

"I just need you to round up a chain of kids to buy cold medicine."

Now I got it. Cold medicines contained the main ingredient necessary to cook meth, and there were limits on how much you could buy at one time or in one place. Mom had complained that she'd had to give her drivers' license at Wal-Mart to get some cold medicine one day, and Pa had filled us in on the reasoning behind the new rules. The stricter the regulations governing buying the cold meds, the smaller the state's problem with meth labs, he'd said.

Now my brother was offering me a way to get my name on a rap sheet and my fingerprints in state and federal police records.

I was touched.

"Not a chance in hell," I said.

"You owe me," he said calmly. "I could have let your girlfriend's sister get really and truly fucked up that day. I let her go for you."

"Fine. I owe you one. Tell me when you want me to clean out *your* garage," I said impatiently. "I'm not turning into a criminal because you didn't assault Melinda Whitfield."

Jeb, apparently bored, smashed his bottle on the sidewalk in front of the garage and wandered over.

"I just cleaned that sidewalk, asshole," I told him.

He wobbled a little—I guess that hadn't been his first beer of the evening—and glared at me. "We heard you stood up for that Whitfield girl at school after her pa fired all the Rhodales, and we're here to tell you that you're on your last fucking chance with us."

I looked at Ethan. "What's with all this 'we' and 'us' shit? Does the drunken idiot speak for you now?"

Before Ethan could answer, Jeb took a swing at me that didn't come close to hitting me. "I've had enough of your holier-than-thou bullshit, Mickey," he shouted.

"Whatever, Jeb. Why don't you go climb inside another bottle?" I turned away, but Ethan's warning sound stopped me.

"Jeb, put the gun down," Ethan said calmly.

I slowly turned around, no sudden movements, and discovered that Ethan and Pa weren't the only Rhodales going around strapped. Jeb had a Glock in his shaking hands, and he was pointing it right at my stomach.

"Say you're sorry," he demanded.

"I'm sorry," I said instantly. Only a damned fool would argue with a drunk with a gun.

"You better be sorry," he blustered. "You better—"

"He said he was sorry, Jeb," Ethan said. "Give me the gun."

Jeb moved the gun so now it was pointing at Ethan. Since Ethan was standing only two feet away from me, this didn't reassure me at all.

"You shut up, too! I'm tired of taking orders from you, like you're the big damn king of the world," Jeb shouted.

"You're right," Ethan said reasonably, and Jeb faltered in his tirade.

"What?"

"You're right. Screw it, we're brothers. We should be nicer to each other. Let's go get drunk and leave Mickey up to whatever junior high bullshit he's into tonight." Ethan said. He took a couple of slow steps as he talked, so Jeb had to turn a little to the right to keep an eye on him, and then Ethan moved three fingers against the side of his leg in a signal we'd worked out when we were kids playing pickup games of football in the neighborhood.

Go for the interception.

Ethan started talking about how Paula's older sister had the hots for Jeb, which distracted him enough that he lowered his arm a little, and I tackled his ass, making sure I got the gun before it hit the ground and accidentally discharged.

"Good job," Ethan said, but when I tried to hand him the gun, he wouldn't take it.

"You keep it. Consider it an advance on salary."

Jeb moaned and slowly worked his way up off the ground, and I tensed for a fight. Ethan knocked Jeb out with a fast, powerful, right hook, and then gestured to his flunkies to pick our unconscious brother up and put him on one of the old lawn chairs I'd cleaned and set out to dry.

"He can sleep it off," Ethan said grimly. "If he's lucky, I won't kick his ass later for this."

"Take this gun, Ethan, or I'll give it to Pa," I warned him. "You'll be out hundreds of dollars and in a world of hurt, because we both know this is not registered."

"Do what you need to do, Mickey. We'll talk more later," Ethan said, glancing at his watch. "I'm outta here."

He and his thugs took off, leaving me standing there holding the gun. I hid it in a dark corner of the still-untouched part of the garage, stared at it for a while, thinking, and then changed my mind and took it with me. No time to change my now grass-stained and ripped-at-the-knees jeans for my date. Victoria would have to take me for who I was, and it was sure as hell no squeaky-clean, country club Biff.

If she hadn't already given up on me because I was late.

When she didn't answer her phone, I broke the speed limit all the way to the school.

CHAPTER 29
VICTORIA

He was fifteen minutes late. No, seventeen.

    He wasn't coming.

After everything it had taken for me to get out of the house, I couldn't believe it. I started the truck, because neither my wounded dignity nor my pride would let me wait for him to be twenty minutes late.

Mickey roared into the parking lot before I could put the truck in drive, taking the turn at a breakneck speed that left me gasping. Before I could even turn the ignition back off, he hopped off his bike, strode over, threw the truck door open, and pulled me to him. Then he kissed me until I melted against him and had to cling to his shoulders just so I didn't fall out of the truck.

"I—what was that?" I was feeling as dazed and breathless as I sounded, and I looked up into those beautiful blue eyes for some kind of explanation.

"You waited for me," he said. "Thank you."

"You're welcome."

"Would you like for me to drive, since I know where we're going?"

I liked that he didn't automatically think he was driving my truck, just because he was a guy and I was a girl, but I was happy to have him drive. I slid over to the passenger seat, and I caught his gaze on the top of my thighs, bared almost up to my panties when I scooted.

I yanked my skirt down, and he closed his eyes and muttered something under his breath that sounded oddly like "forget it, Biff," but I didn't ask. I didn't want to know. I was having a hard enough time breathing after those kisses, and every time I stole a glance at him, so darkly delicious in his navy blue shirt, my pulse raced, and I realized again that I might be in over my head with this boy.

We headed out, and he kept turning to look at me.

"You're not even bruised?"

I touched my cheek. "I am, but the arnica and ice helped, and Melinda—well, she's a genius with the magic of makeup. I think all the times she had to hide a hangover made her an expert."

He looked at me again, this time for so long that I started to worry.

"Hey! Watch the road, or I'm going to drive."

"How do you expect me to watch the road when you're the most beautiful thing I've ever seen?"

In anybody else, it would have been a line, but from Mickey, the words had such fervent sincerity that I melted a little bit more.

"Thank you," I whispered. "I feel beautiful tonight—I love this dress."

"It's a great dress. I'm trying really hard not to stop the truck and take it off you," he said bluntly.

"Mickey!" My face felt like it was on fire.

His hands tightened on the steering wheel. "I'm sorry, Victoria. I'm not smooth, or much of a gentleman. You make me crazy, and just looking at you in that little dress makes me want you more than I've ever wanted any girl in my life. I'll try to be more delicate about saying stuff to you, but I'm not sure how much success I'll have."

I didn't know what to say. I'd tried very hard not to think about what sexual experience he'd probably had, with pretty much any girl he wanted, especially since I hadn't had any. This was definitely not a conversation I'd thought we'd be having in the first ten minutes of our first date.

"I don't—"

"Maybe you'd be better off with Biff," he said savagely, and I blinked.

"Who the heck is Biff?"

By the time he explained about Biff and Chad, his imaginary rivals, we were both laughing, and the tension level in the truck had ratcheted down about a hundred degrees. He flipped on the radio to a station I never listened to, but I recognized the singer.

"That's Blake Shelton. I like him," I said.

Mickey gave me a skeptical look. "I wouldn't have pegged you as a country music fan."

"I'm not, really, but I used to watch *The Voice* with my roommate, and Blake's cute and funny."

Mickey drummed his fingers on the steering wheel for a while. "I can be funny, but I'm definitely not *cute*," he said, sounding disgruntled.

"Maybe you should tell me what happened to put you in this state," I said.

He'd taken us back out to the Buckeye Diner. I sighed a little and prepared to climb down out of the truck, but he stopped me.

"No. I just have to pick something up."

He was back in a few minutes with a large, heavy-looking picnic basket.

"I couldn't think of any place that would let us take up a table on a Friday night for as many hours as I'm going to want to be with you, so I paid the diner to pack us a picnic."

My heart fluttered. Bad boy Mickey was intriguing, but sweet, thoughtful Mickey was charming me beyond anything I'd ever expected.

"That's a great idea. Where are we going?"

He laughed. "Well, it might be a great idea, or I might be an idiot. It's warm enough now, but Mr. Judson just told me that rain is forecasted for later this evening."

"I hope not," I said, my mood dimming. "My family went to the Founders' Day party. I hope it doesn't get rained out for everyone. I think Gran was going to be giving a speech, and she looked happy for the first time since . . ."

Mickey glanced at me as he backed out of the parking spot. "It's okay. If we try to avoid every land mine in the conversation, we'll be dancing around subjects all night. Why don't we agree that we can be completely honest with each other?"

"I think that's a great idea," I admitted. "I can't really talk to anybody else about all of this."

"Okay, I'll start. Your pa fucked up," he said flatly. "That mass layoff really fired things up again."

I felt my face getting hot as I instinctively wanted to defend my father. "Well, he had provocation. The truth is—"

Mickey made a sound like a buzzer, and I broke off. He was right. Why was I denying it?

I sighed. "You're right. He messed up."

"Score one for honesty," he said. "But don't worry, we have enough fuckups to go around in our families. My brother Ethan wants me to run a ring of high school kids to buy ingredients for his meth business, my brother Jeb almost shot me tonight, I hid Jeb's almost certainly stolen Glock in my garage, but then . . ."

"But then what?"

He hesitated. "Nothing. Oh, and Jeb is lying unconscious in a chair on my lawn."

"*What?* Are you joking?"

Mickey signaled a turn and pulled off one back road onto another, this one a dirt road that looked like it headed straight up a massive hill.

"No, I'm not kidding. Would I make up something like that?"

Blake ended his song, and Carrie Underwood started singing about how she'd let a tornado carry her scumbag father away, and I experienced a moment of total empathy. Carrie wasn't the only one who wanted horrible family members to disappear.

I stared out the window into the thick trees bordering the uneven road as we climbed up and up, trying to process.

"Ephedrine?"

"Yeah. It's hard to buy at stores these days," Mickey said. "He's nuts. I'm not doing it."

He told me what had happened at his house, and even what I suspected was the very abbreviated and toned-down version he gave me was enough to scare me to death.

"Interception? Are you crazy? You could have been shot!"

"Calm down. I'm fine."

"Calm down? Calm *down*? What kind of life do you live, where people calm down after their brothers—"

"Half brothers."

"—after their half brothers almost shoot them and ask them to run the procurement part of their drug rings?" I could hear my voice getting hysterical.

"At least it wasn't hookers." He laughed, but I didn't find any of it funny. At all.

I forced myself to take a deep breath, and then I twisted in my seat and turned to stare at him. "This is crazy, Mickey. All of it. It's completely out of control. It's like we're living out the plot of a really horrible movie, where the bad guys are always going to win."

He slowly and carefully drove the truck over a small bump and then around a final corner, and pulled to a stop. I looked out the windshield and actually gasped. We'd reached the top of the hill, and a panoramic vista of the entire county lay spread out in front of us. The glittering lights of Clark shone like a diamond pendant centered in velvety darkness and surrounded by the scattered jewels of other homes and businesses.

"Oh my gosh, that's beautiful," I whispered.

"Yeah. Beautiful." Mickey's voice was husky, and I turned my head and saw that he wasn't looking at the scenery at all.

He was looking at me.

CHAPTER 30
MICKEY

"Hey," I said as my blood and probably my brain cells drained out of my skull and down into a more painful part of my body. "If we stay in the truck, I'm going to kiss you again. If I kiss you again, I might have a hard time stopping. So maybe we should walk around outside and have our picnic."

She studied my face, biting her luscious pink lip, and I had to clench my jaw against the urge to offer to bite it for her.

"I want to walk around and eat and I want to kiss you, too, but I think we have to talk first," she said.

I groaned and let my head drop back against the headrest. "Nothing good ever came out of those four words."

"I want to kiss you? Wait. That was five."

I grinned at her so she'd know I was joking. "No. 'We have to talk.'"

She folded her arms in front of her, drawing my eye to the scooped-out neckline of her dress.

"Mickey. I don't have much experience."

I dragged my gaze away from her chest and gave myself a stern warning to quit being a horndog. Just because, blue blood or not, the girl had spectacular tits, legs that went on forever, and the fierce heart of a mama badger, there was no reason to lose control and jump her.

And just because she seemed to care about me—she *stood up for me*—was no reason to lose control and fall for her.

I wasn't sure which scared me more.

"Did you hear me?"

I shoved my hair back out of my eyes and tried to remember what she'd been talking about before my brain fizzled at the sight of her breasts. "Yes. Sorry. Experience with feuds? Trust me, I don't think that's going to be a problem."

She turned away from me, and suddenly I was looking at the back of her head.

"No. *Experience* experience. I've never done it before. I've never even, um, done anything beyond kissed a boy. So if you thought we were going to have sex, well, we're not," she said in a very small voice.

First, I irrationally wanted to find every guy she'd ever kissed and beat them to a pulp. Then, I irrationally wanted to jump up and down and cheer that she hadn't done anything else with them.

It was Crazy Town in my brain.

"Ever?" I finally said, trying for lighthearted.

She glanced at me reproachfully over her shoulder, and I felt like a jerk.

"I'm sorry, Victoria. I'm an idiot. Look, I should never have made that stupid comment about taking your dress off. Guys my age are a mass of boiling hormones, it's not personal—"

"It's not personal? So, any girl would do?" She bit off the words, and I realized I'd put my size-ten boot firmly in my mouth.

"No! That's not—I'm not good at talking to girls," I muttered. "What I meant was that I'm not going to attack you like some crazed beast or something, just because I want you so bad I can taste it. No matter what everyone says, I'm not violent or a dangerous animal."

Except when I was beating the shit out of Sam Oliver, a little voice in my head nagged at me.

Unexpectedly, Victoria turned to me and smiled. "Mickey, of course I know that. Do you think I would have come here with you if I thought you were dangerous? I just wanted to put it right out there on the table that I'm not the type of girl to jump in bed with every boy who says romantic things to me in the moonlight."

"You thought I said something romantic?" I thought back, trying to figure out what it had been, but she laughed at me and opened her door.

"There's a blanket behind the seat. Let's get this picnic started, okay?"

CHAPTER 31
VICTORIA

"It's incredible. If I could, I'd build a house right here so I could have this view all day long," I said.

We walked over to the edge of the grass, where there was a steep drop-off. I'd put my flats back on, because the heels would have been stupid, but I still stumbled a little. Mickey caught me and pulled me away from the edge, and then he leaned back against a large boulder, still holding me.

I gradually relaxed against him, resting my arms on his where they circled my waist. I could feel the warm hardness of his chest against my back, and I felt completely safe but also a little breathless, like I was poised on the brink of something hugely wonderful.

Or maybe, like Melinda, I was just hungry.

Thinking of Melinda and Buddy made me feel restless and a little

guilty, but I'd only been gone an hour and a half or so, not even the
length of the first movie they'd been planning to watch.

"Does it have a name? This place?"

"People call it Lonesome Ridge," Mickey said. "I never thought of
it that way, though. To me, it's not lonely at all, but peaceful. We can
see the whole of Whitfield County up here in all its glorious potential,
but we're too far removed to be part of any petty troubles."

"It feels peaceful to me, too. We're not like everybody else,
though," I said. "We're both alone in the middle of large families.
Except for your mom and my Gran, but nobody else really."

"The young and the lonely. Sounds like a soap opera," he said,
and I could feel his chest vibrate with his quiet laughter.

"This is Lonesome Ridge, so we'd be the lonesome young," I
pointed out. "Sounds like a song."

"Sounds like a heartache," he said, tightening his arms around me
and resting his cheek on the top of my head. "I don't want to be lonesome. I want to be with you."

"I want to be with you, too, but nobody wants to let us. Mickey,
are we ever going to be normal?"

"Who knows? Is anybody really normal?"

"Biff probably is," I said lightly, because he'd started to sound
depressed, and I didn't like the idea of him hurting.

Mickey's stomach growled loudly, and I jumped, and then started
to laugh.

"Even my stomach hates Biff. Or else I'm really hungry," he said.

"Me, too," I confessed. "Should we find out what's in the basket?"

"It's fried chicken, or Nora's in big trouble."

I turned to go back to the truck, but he stopped me with one
hand on my shoulder and bent down and kissed me. It was gentle and

undemanding, a whisper of a promise, but without any pressure to take it further right now.

"I don't want to be with you so I can have sex with you," he said quietly, but then a corner of his mouth quirked up in a smile. "Okay, we said total honesty. I absolutely want to have sex with you. I have dreams about getting you naked. But we can talk about all of that way in the future at some point, on *your* timetable, okay? For now, just the chance to spend time with you is enough."

"With kissing," I said, trying not to hyperventilate at the idea of Mickey making love to me.

"Definitely with kissing."

There was, in fact, fried chicken in the basket, and potato salad, baked beans, and chocolate cake. I ate way more than I should have and then lay back on the blanket in a carbohydrate haze and stared up at the stars, because what else was I going to do on a romantic picnic with the hottest guy in the known universe?

The sound of crickets whispering secrets to each other was the only thing we could hear for miles, and I realized that it was the first time in my life that I'd been surrounded by true silence. The silence and the stars blanketed the world and wrapped me in a sudden feeling of being part of eternity's very own horse race. What did petty hatreds matter to the stars that circled the universe?

Mickey moved the basket out of the way and then lay down next to me.

"Do you ever think about what you'll do after this? After high school?"

"I think I want to be a large-animal vet," I said, surprising myself. I hadn't admitted that to anybody except my old boarding school room-mate, Simone.

"Horses?"

"Always horses. Other farm animals, too, and the usual cats and dogs that come with a farm and ranch practice, I guess," I said. "I don't know how practical that is in today's world of veterinary specialization, but I grew up with horses and with James Herriot's books, and I've always wanted to be part of that world. Except with modern medicines."

"*All Creatures Great and Small*? I loved those books," Mickey said, surprising me. "My favorite story was the little old lady who healed that abused golden retriever with her special magic powders. She sounded like somebody who could live here in Kentucky, you know?"

"I felt that way about all his stories," I said. "I think that's what was so great about his books. Growing up in Kentucky, or Ireland—it didn't matter. The characters were so real, they felt like people we could meet anytime."

"Except for Siegfried," Mickey said, laughing. "Nobody is like him."

"What about you?" I turned to face him, propping myself up on an elbow. "What's in your future?"

His smile faded, but he reached out and twirled a strand of my hair in his fingers.

"What's my future? I don't know. When I was little, I wanted to be a cop like my dad. When I got older, I just wanted *not* to be a criminal like my brothers. These days, I actually think I might want to write."

"Write what? Books, movies, comics, plays, blogs, news?"

He shrugged, looking uncomfortable. "Books, I guess, but that sounds presumptuous, doesn't it? What could I have to say that anybody would want to read? I'm just some hick kid from a backwater town in Kentucky that nobody's ever heard of."

"Don't do that. Don't put yourself down. There are enough people around here who want to do it for you. Don't help them."

His eyes widened, and then a beautiful smile spread across his incredibly gorgeous face. "You always do that."

"Do what?"

"Stand up for me. Even when it's myself you're defending me from. I don't know how to take it. It causes a funny feeling in my gut."

I considered that for a moment, and the butterflies dancing in my own stomach. "That funny feeling might be the potato salad," I said, teasing. "Mayonnaise can go bad fast."

He pounced on me and tickled me, and then he was kissing me, long, slow kisses that made the stars overhead swirl crazily around in the night sky. His tongue touched my lips, and when I opened my mouth to his unspoken demand, he angled his head and deepened the kiss until I was trembling beneath him with the sensation of too much, too much, *too much*.

Or maybe not enough.

He pulled away from me, breathing hard, and then sat up, and I realized I wasn't the only one shaking.

"We need to take it slow," he said. I nodded, and he groaned.

"Help me out, here, Victoria, because I'm trying to say what I *should* say, not what I actually want to say."

"We need to take it slow," I parroted, trying to believe it.

He looked down at me and then closed his eyes. "I need a cold shower."

The first crack of thunder sounded, and a fat raindrop smacked me on the nose exactly then, in a feat of spectacular timing, and I started to laugh.

"I think you're going to get your wish."

We raced to pack everything up and get back to the truck before the rain became a deluge. Mickey carefully backed up the truck, turned it around, and headed back down the hill.

"The last thing we need is to get stuck up here if the road washes out," he said, shaking his head so that drops of rainwater from his hair sprayed all over. "We'd never be able to explain that one."

I checked my phone to see if Melinda had texted me that our folks were back yet.

"Crap. My phone must have died."

Mickey glanced over. "Yeah, I think it died way earlier, unless you were deliberately ignoring my call when I left my house."

A shiver of unease snaked through me, and I plugged my phone into the car charger and it immediately lit up with a listing of six missed calls. I pressed the speakerphone button, and the first voice mail message shrieked out at me.

It was Buddy, and he was nearly incoherent.

"Victoria where are you? They took Melinda, they came to the house on motorcycles and took her, and I'm all alone and nobody is answering their phones, you have to come home *right now*."

I dropped the phone out of suddenly numb fingers and stared at Mickey in horror.

"Oh, my God, what happened? What is he talking about?"

I retrieved the phone and called the house, but there was no answer. Then I tried my parents, who also weren't answering. Gran didn't own a cell phone, and Pete wasn't answering his. Finally, I tried Melinda's phone, knowing she probably hadn't charged it in weeks.

No answer.

I hit play on the rest of the messages, and they were all increasingly worried and then hysterical messages from my little brother, who had been *all alone in the house* and afraid, while I was stealing kisses with Mickey.

I was going to hell for this.

I was *already* in hell for this.

My hands wouldn't quit shaking. "Take me home. No, to the school for your bike. No, it's raining too hard. To your place, and then I'll go to my house by myself, and—"

Mickey's phone rang, cutting off my frantic chatter, and his face hardened when he read the display.

"Hello, Anna Mae. I should have known you'd be involved in this."

He listened for a minute. "And the boy?"

When he shut off the phone and put it back in his pocket, I wanted to strangle him. "Well? What was that? Does she know something? Where is Buddy?"

He finally reached the road and pulled out, headed toward Ethan's place if I had my directions straight.

"She doesn't know anything about Buddy. Maybe he wore himself out and fell asleep, Victoria," he said, taking my icy hand in his. "Isn't there anybody in the barn you can call? I know you must have staff who work the night shift with the horses, right?"

I hadn't even thought about that. I dialed the barn number but got the answering machine. I left a message and then looked at Mickey.

"What about the police? Can I call your dad's office to have somebody go out to the house to check? I know it sounds extreme, but he's only nine—"

My phone rang again. Pete's number, but when I answered, it was Gran.

"Your parents are on the way to the Rhodale compound, Victoria, and I'm on the way home. They took Melinda, or maybe she went with them on her own, we don't quite know yet. Either way, you need to get home right now, do you hear me?" Her voice was shrill and quavering, and I had the desperate thought that if my family didn't drive her to a heart attack or a stroke soon, it would be a miracle.

"Gran, I'm on the way," I said. I could hear Pete trying to get her to calm down and then she hung up. So he must be driving her home, and my parents were on the way to Anna Mae's.

I related to Mickey the part of the phone conversation that he hadn't heard, but he shook his head. "We're heading to Anna Mae's. She said if we don't show up, she won't let anybody in the gate to get Melinda."

"Mickey, we've got to find a way to end this," I said, throwing it out as a challenge—or maybe a prayer.

Or a death wish.

He held out his hand, and I took it, holding tight in the darkness as we sped toward the most terrifying encounter I could imagine.

After several long minutes of silence, he squeezed my hand. "I agree. Let's end this. We'll make it our goal. They can't keep acting this way, and they can't keep us apart. Pact?"

I took a deep breath and slowly let it out, centering myself, trying not to panic—either at the situation or the thought of trying to accomplish something so enormous in the future.

"Pact."

And then we raced through the night to the compound, hoping the entire world wasn't about to explode in flames.

CHAPTER 32

MICKEY

The gun. I had the gun.

The words ran through my head continuously, like a mantra or a curse, as we drove through pounding rain toward my brother, his mother, and whatever the hell they had in store for us.

I have the gun, I have the gun, I have the gun.

I'd changed my mind back at the house. Staring at it, I knew I couldn't take the chance that Jeb would wake up and somehow find it. I hadn't known what to do with it, so I'd carried it with me and slid it under Victoria's seat when I took my jacket off.

Problem: Ethan knew I had the gun.

I'd worry about that later.

Would I be able to use it? Would I be able to take such a dark and final step toward a wasted future like Ethan's, even if Melinda was in danger? I didn't know.

If *Victoria* was in danger?

No question.

So what did that make *me*?

I didn't know that, either.

"I'm scared," Victoria whispered.

She tightened her grip on my hand, and I squeezed back, but then let go to put both hands on the wheel. If we were going to get hurt tonight, it damn sure wasn't going to be because of reckless driving.

"Would it make you feel better or worse to know that I'm scared, too?"

"I don't know," she said. "Worse."

"Nothing scares me," I shot back with a straight face, and she rewarded me with a ghost of a smile.

She put her phone on speaker and kept compulsively calling her parents, but both of their phones were going straight to voice mail. I gritted my teeth against pointing out that her dad sounded like an asshole even on his voice mail greeting, ordering people to leave a message in a tone that implied he didn't particularly give a shit if they did or not.

"Why would he take her? Is it revenge for last time? Do you think she went voluntarily?"

Her teeth were chattering, and I pushed my jacket across the seat toward her. She wrapped it around herself, and I turned on the heat in the truck and pushed it up a notch. Taylor Swift started to sing something cheerful and up-tempo, and Victoria viciously stabbed the off button with her finger.

"This is my fault, you know. I had to be so clever and stage a showdown at my house to try to get my parents to pay attention to Melinda. She said we all treated her like she was invisible, and I researched the rehab but didn't push hard enough. She probably thought I was abandoning her, too, and when I left her tonight . . . It's my fault."

Victoria told me the long, painful story of the "dinner from hell." It wasn't her fault—not even a little—but I could see why she thought so. Her asshole parents had really done a number on her over the years.

"I would have paid money to see your dad watching those peas roll down the table," I told her, but she didn't even blink; she just started speed-dialing her house again to see if her brother would pick up.

"Drive faster, Mickey. Please, just drive faster."

The lights at the compound were all blazing. We were the last ones to the stage, and the other players were shouting at each other in front of the gate, standing in the rain. I pulled up behind Mom's car and the Whitfields' fancy car. Victoria and I stared at the nightmare in front of us. Her eyes were dry, though. She wasn't going to break down. She blew me away with her courage.

"Full of sound and fury," she murmured, and I glanced over at her. We'd read *Macbeth* at Clark High, too.

"So which idiot's going to be telling this tale that signifies nothing?"

"I am," she said grimly.

She unfastened her seat belt and shrugged my jacket off, and then she stepped out of the truck. The shouting stopped, and everybody turned around and stared at her. I reached under the seat and retrieved Jeb's pistol and then put my jacket back on to hide it, so when I climbed out of the truck, I wasn't Mickey anymore.

I was just another dumbass Rhodale carrying a gun.

Guess I'd have something to write about, now.

CHAPTER 33

VICTORIA

It was complete and utter chaos. The rain had died down some, but it was still more than a drizzle. My parents were both standing out in it, dressed up from the dance, bedraggled in their soggy finery. Dad was right up in the sheriff's face, shouting at him and being shouted at in return.

Mom and the woman who must be Mickey's mom both stood silently, looking bewildered and very unhappy.

Ethan stood behind the gate with more of his thugs, who were all armed, and in the distance a large, squat figure dressed all in black stood on the porch of the house. My sister was nowhere to be seen.

When Ethan saw me get out of the truck, he started laughing and opened the gate.

"Nice job, baby brother," he yelled at Mickey, who'd come around to join me. "Banging the Whitfield princess. Is she as cold as she looks or did she warm up when she got up close and personal with a Rhodale man?"

I flinched at such crude language coming out of a face that was so like Mickey's, but I didn't answer him. I had more important things to worry about than defending my honor to a criminal.

My father, though, apparently didn't have the same sense of priorities. He went after Ethan, screaming obscenities I hadn't even known he knew, and one of the guards blocked his way. My mother stumbled and almost fell down in the muddy road, but Mickey's mom caught her arm and helped her up.

Mickey ignored all of this and took my hand, staring steadily across the muddy road at his brother. The rain turned Mickey's hair to a deeper, glistening shade of black, and rivulets of water ran down his face and shirt.

"Where's Melinda, Ethan?"

"She's warm and safe and happy. More than I can say for the rest of you fools. Why don't we all go inside and have a little chat?"

The sheriff shouted at Ethan to bring the girl out right now, but Ethan flipped a middle finger in the air and kept walking, leaving the rest of us with no choice but to follow. He surprised me and turned right, into a large outbuilding, instead of heading up to the house. The large wooden doors opened into a huge space that looked like a hollowed-out barn, but in addition to bales of hay, this place had crates and boxes stacked along all of the walls.

I so did not want to know what was in those boxes.

Melinda sat curled up in the middle of the place on an old

cloth-upholstered recliner that was pulled up next to a space heater. The guard was still blocking my father, so Mom ran to Melinda and even tried to pull her into an awkward hug, but Melinda pushed her away.

"You're getting me wet," Melinda complained.

When I got close enough to see her eyes, I could tell she was stoned out of her stupid little mind.

"You did this on purpose?" I asked her. "You left Buddy alone so you could get *high*?"

Mickey tightened his grip on my hand, like he was afraid I'd go after my sister. It was true that I wanted to shake some sense into her, but I also wanted to rescue her from this situation.

My dad pointed at me. "You shut up right now, Victoria. What the hell are you doing with *him*? You're supposed to be at Denise's house studying. You're as much of a worthless liar as your sister."

"Don't talk to her like that," Mickey said, and his voice was low and dangerous.

Without thinking, I tried to step between the two of them, but Mickey pulled me back. Ethan, standing across the barn from us, started laughing. "Problems?"

Mickey whirled to face him. "Let Melinda go."

Ethan shrugged. "Sure. Anna Mae wants to have a little chat with everybody first, though."

"Can't you control your own kid in your own town, *Sheriff*?" My dad advanced on the sheriff and his wife, and she stumbled backward and fell, hitting her head on the edge of one of the crates. Blood started to run down the side of her face, and my mother cried out. She'd never been able to take the sight of blood, and I was afraid she'd pass out and I'd have two family members to rescue.

Mickey yanked his hand free of mine and ran to help his mom, getting between my dad and his parents. "Step away from my mother."

My dad sneered at Mickey. "That's your mother? How does she feel about getting leftovers from Anna Mae's table?"

I gasped. I'd never heard my dad say such vile things, and I'd heard a lot over the years. Something about the feud had driven him to such poisonous depths of anger that I was afraid he'd never come back.

Mickey's face went dark, like it had in the cafeteria, but before I could say anything to stop him, he shoved my dad and knocked him back a step.

Dad almost fell down. I gasped and Mom screamed, a high, piercing sound that completely blocked the small, hurt noise I'd made when I saw the boy I'd just been kissing shove my father.

Mickey ripped his shirt off, balled it up, and held it to his mother's face to stop the bleeding. I walked over to my dad in what felt like slow motion. He looked at Mickey with murder in his eyes, and I watched my future implode with devastating clarity. There could never be a hope of a relationship between me and Mickey now.

"Richard!" My mother pulled Melinda with her. "Are you okay?"

"Oh, shut the hell up," Dad said, glaring at her as he stood up. He started to go after Mickey, but then thought better of it as we all heard the ratcheting noise of a shotgun from behind us.

"Maybe you should stay away from my brother, *Dick*," Ethan said, waving the gun in the air.

"We need to get out of here," Mom moaned, but Dad didn't even look at her.

He was too busy staring at Mickey.

"Did you touch my daughter?"

Mickey glanced at me, but I was frozen, shaking. Unable to think. I slowly shook my head.

"Maybe you should ask yourself if she touched *him*," Ethan said, laughing.

"Shut up, Ethan," Mickey snapped. "I'm taking Mom out of here. Move or we're going to have this out right now."

"I don't think so," Ethan drawled. "You're not the only one who wants to have something out."

Dad swung around and stared at me before pointing at Mickey, who was still next to his parents. "Did this Rhodale shit lay a hand on you? I'll kill him if he did."

I was cold, wet, and maybe even starting to go into shock, because I realized that while my father and everybody else waited for me to answer, I was looking at my hand. The hand that Mickey had dropped so readily to go stand with his family—and attack mine.

Nobody was standing with *me*. Nobody at all.

"Well? Did he touch you?"

"No, he didn't. Let's go home," I said, suddenly more exhausted than I'd ever been in my life.

"Not just yet," a new voice said, and I turned to see the woman who must be Anna Mae Rhodale standing just behind me, all in black like a spider from a children's story.

"Hello, Richard," she purred. "Glad to see me?"

Two things happened simultaneously: All the blood drained out of my father's face, and Melinda passed out.

CHAPTER 34

MICKEY

I've noticed, looking back at moments of extreme stress in my life, that I tend to fixate on something trivial and unimportant and let it occupy the entirety of my consciousness like a Holy Grail. For example, when I was six and smashed my thumb with a hammer, I focused so intently on the spreading snowflake pattern of the blood on the wood grain beneath my hand that it took way longer than it should have for me to feel the screaming pain.

Right now, I was focused on Anna Mae Rhodale's shoes.

Pink and high-heeled, with bows on the tops, they were like a caricature of women's shoes, purchased by someone who had no idea what fashion was. She wore them with a giant black sweep of a cape, a black dress, and a string of pearls that hung halfway down the jutting prow of her front. The entire effect was hideous beyond the sum of its parts, and we all stared at her for several long moments.

"Hello, Anna Mae," my mom finally said. "Isn't this a little bit over the top, even for you? If I'd known you were hosting a costume party and a kidnapping, I'd have dressed differently."

The Whitfields stared at Mom in shock, and I felt a burst of pride shoot through me. Mom had been dealing with Anna Mae and her crap for a long time. She might be the only person here who could manage her now.

And I'd rather think about anything else—even women's shoes—instead of the look on Victoria's face after I'd pushed her father.

Anna Mae sneered at her. "Shut up, Julia. Let the grownups talk."

I started toward her, but Ethan raised the shotgun. "Let it be, little brother. She has a thing to say, and then you can all go home."

"First, your girl there called my boy for drugs. Weren't no kidnapping involved at all," Anna Mae said.

Victoria's dad rolled his eyes. "Since when did you sound like a character out of a hillbilly comic strip? What happened to you? You were headed for college."

"*You* happened to me, you son of a bitch," she snarled. "And yes, I know your mother, so the expression holds doubly true. She paid me off to leave you alone. There, is that grammar appropriate enough for you?"

"What is this all about? You need to leave the Whitfields alone. Both of you," Pa said, looking back and forth between her and Ethan. "We've got enough trouble since they moved back without you starting up the feud again."

Anna Mae laughed. "Me? I didn't start anything, but I'm going to end it. My way."

She turned to Whitfield. "We took your poor, addled girl there to teach you a lesson about firing our kin. Maybe next time you want to pull shit like that you'll remember we can get to those pretty little girls of yours anytime we want."

"You're going to keep your lowlife sons away from my daughters, Sheriff, or I'll have the FBI and the U.S. Marshals in here, and anybody else I can find with a badge that can't be bought," Whitfield said, and he stared a hole in Victoria. "*Both* of my daughters."

"You'd better shut up, Whitfield," Pa said hotly. "Who the hell do you think you are, that you can come back here and stir things up like you did? Firing a bunch of good people who did nothing to deserve it. You ought to be shot."

"So now we get to it," Whitfield shouted. "You're as gun-happy as your loser kid the drug dealer. Go ahead. Shoot me. Your aim is probably as bad as everything else you do."

I'd had enough. "Mom, I need to get you out of here."

"I'm not going anywhere without your father," she said stubbornly. "It was just a scratch."

She lowered my shirt, and I could see that it was true. There was only a graze on the side of her forehead, but scalp wounds bled a lot, so I wanted to take her to the hospital.

She put a hand on my arm. "Don't think we're not going to talk about you shoving Mr. Whitfield," she warned.

"Dick Whitfield can kiss my ass," I said flatly.

Mom flinched, and I felt a momentary twinge of guilt, but I needed to salvage the other relationship in my life I'd ruined before I could deal with this.

"Well if you won't come, I'm taking Victoria out of here," I told her, and I headed across the barn toward Victoria, who was standing alone, so pale I was almost afraid that she'd pass out like her sister had.

I ignored our fathers, who were shouting at each other, and took Victoria's hand. It was icy and almost limp, and she stared at me through dull eyes.

"Go back to your family," she said, almost indifferently, and my gut clenched.

"Victoria—"

"No." She pulled away, and her eyes were still so lifeless and distant that I wanted to howl. "You left me standing here alone, after you promised we'd face this together. That's fine. I understand. She's your mom. But you *attacked* my *father*. I can't forget that."

"Victoria, I—"

"No. You pushed my father. We're done. I can't keep pretending I can count on anybody else when it's never true."

Everybody else was shouting at each other, stuff about way back when Pa was in high school with Whitfield and Anna Mae, but I didn't care about any of it. I wanted my mom out of danger, and I wanted to get Victoria away from here and someplace alone with me, so I could find a way to fix what I'd broken between us.

Suddenly, a shotgun blast tore through the noise, and everybody flinched or ducked until we realized that Anna Mae had fired a warning shot into the air over our heads.

I had Jeb's gun in my hands before I even realized I'd grabbed it from my waistband, but only Victoria saw it before I hid it again. Her eyes widened, and she took a shaky step away from me.

"Here are my terms," Anna Mae said calmly, as if we were sitting around a negotiating table instead of in the middle of an old barn.

"First, my boys will run their business without interference from you," she said, pointing at Pa.

"Second, you will quit trying to turn our half of this county into a damn suburban country club estate," she said, pointing at Whitfield.

Victoria's mom finally spoke up, and she had the iciest voice I'd ever heard in my life. "I don't know who you think you are, but we are taking my daughters and leaving. If you try to stop us, you will be very sorry. If you think you have any say at all over how we live our lives, you are very mistaken."

With that, she and Whitfield lifted Melinda between them and headed for the door.

Anna Mae stopped them with a voice like a whiplash. "Who do I think I am? Well, I'll tell you, sweetheart. I'm the woman who loaned your husband the cash to start up his finance business in the city, with my *illegal drug money*. And he's the man who never paid me back."

CHAPTER 35
VICTORIA

Anna Mae had loaned money to my father? No. It wasn't possible. I felt like I'd fallen through some kind of hillbilly looking glass, where toothless men with shotguns determined my freedom, and a boy who'd promised we'd find a way to end a feud—together—abandoned me at the first sign of a problem.

I looked at Melinda hanging unconscious between my parents, and I kind of envied her.

"I paid you back every cent of that money," my dad told Anna Mae, clenching his fists.

His face was turning an ugly purple color, and I was suddenly terrified that this evening was going to go from awful to fatal if we didn't get out of there. Dad's colleague, who'd been the same age as Dad, had died of a heart attack in the spring.

"You didn't pay me the interest," Anna Mae said silkily. Apparently she was trying to be seductive, given her history with both my dad and Mickey's dad.

I suddenly wanted to throw up. Mickey moved closer to me and reached for my hand, but I yanked it away. I couldn't risk my heart with this person who resorted to violence so casually—against my own father, no matter that Dad had been acting like an ass.

"I paid you a fair rate of interest," Dad shouted.

My mom was looking at him like he was something she'd scraped off the bottom of her high-heeled pumps.

Mickey's dad broke into the conversation. "I don't give a damn what the two of you have going between you, but I'm the sheriff here, Anna Mae, and you will not pull this crap on me. You definitely will not dictate terms about what I will or will not do, and if you think Ethan is going to run a drug ring in my county, unhampered, you're out of your tiny little mind."

She swung her reptilian gaze to him. "Do you know whose trailer that was that blew up? There was skinhead cartel money backing that operation. Founders' Brotherhood. It wasn't a cooking lab; it was distribution. The skinheads have a better product, and they can sell it cheaper. We were at two hundred fifty dollars a gram, and they're distributing for ninety bucks a gram. What do you think that means?"

"It sounds like you're finally admitting that you're the brains behind the operation," Mickey's mom said, throwing a glance at her son and husband that I didn't understand.

Mickey took my hand in his and wouldn't let me pull away this time, and I didn't have the energy to make a scene. I knew he was trouble, but my heart didn't always listen to my head, and so the touch of his hand comforted me a little bit in spite of everything. I was shaking a little bit, and Mickey must have realized it, because he pulled me closer, against the warmth of his body. It felt so good, and maybe I was being weak, but I let him do it, though I swore to myself that it would be for the last time.

Anna Mae started laughing. "Brains? Yeah, I've always been the brains around here. It's not like anybody else could volunteer for the job."

Ethan, standing just outside the loose circle of people in the barn, shot his mother a look of such fierce hatred I was surprised she didn't burn up on the spot—but I didn't think anyone but me saw it. I was suddenly glad that he hadn't looked at me like that—it was an expression that promised very bad things.

And she was his *mother*.

I almost laughed at myself. Considering my own mother, Ethan and I were zero for two on the maternal excellence scale. The thought made me realize why Mickey had been so quick to leave me to go protect *his* mom. I guess if I had a mom like that, I'd do the same thing.

But I wouldn't push his father in the process. I wrenched away from Mickey. Just then Ethan glanced over and caught me looking his way, and his face changed. Anger turned to something harder to define. The moment caught and held between us, and I had to struggle to escape his hypnotic gaze.

A sardonic smile crossed his face when I turned away, as if he'd won a point in some kind of battle between us—a battle I hadn't agreed to take part in, one in which I didn't know the rules of engagement. But I damn sure wasn't going to surrender, either. Not to him, his horrible mother, or even to Mickey.

I was done.

"We need to go, Anna Mae," Mrs. Rhodale said.

"You need to shut up and listen to me. Do you think that a gang of murderous skinheads is going to hear the rumors that Ethan's idiots blew up their trailer and do *nothing about it*? Or do you think we're going to have a war?" Anna Mae stared around the room at each of us, her chin thrust out like she was ready to strap on her guns and lead the first charge.

"It won't be a war," the sheriff said. "It will be a massacre."

Ethan hooked his thumbs through his belt loops in a pretty good imitation of somebody who didn't give a damn. "It won't be a massacre, because I'm not afraid of them."

"Then you're a damn fool," the sheriff said.

"He might be, but I'm not," Anna Mae said. "We're getting into bed with the cartel, so you'd better back off. These people like to make examples of local law enforcement. I want you to keep your sheriff's department flunkies off our asses, and I want you, Richie dear, to keep your grubby fingers out of my side of the county."

Mickey's mom gasped and turned dead white. I thought she was going to faint, but she was tougher than that. "You devious bitch. I hope you know what happens to people who play with really bad guys. They always end up dead."

Mickey bent his head and whispered in my ear. "Anna Mae just wants an audience. She'd never actually shoot anybody, especially not with all these witnesses."

I didn't know how to take that. It sounded like he thought she might actually shoot someone if people weren't around.

I had never wanted so badly to be back in my tiny dorm room in Connecticut.

"We're leaving," Mickey called out, loud enough to break through the intense arguments that had broken out from all sides. "All of us."

"You don't speak for my family," Dad snarled at him, and I had suddenly had enough.

Way more than enough.

"Dad, why are you going along with this crazy woman? We need to go home and see if Gran is all right—"

Gran. *Buddy.*

"Oh, my God," Mom said. "Buddy. We haven't heard from your mother, Richard."

"Did you take him, Ethan?" Mickey's voice was a whiplash of anger that sliced through the room. "If you hurt that little boy—"

"I didn't take him," Ethan snapped, and then he turned those dark eyes on me and continued in a low, urgent tone. "I don't hurt kids, Victoria."

I froze—trapped again in his stark, bleak gaze and almost helpless to avoid believing in his sincerity. It didn't make sense; I couldn't figure out why he'd care what the "Whitfield princess" thought about him, but somehow I knew he did.

Even more bizarrely, I believed him.

My phone rang. It was the house number. I snatched at it to answer.

"Gran?"

"Buddy's gone, Victoria."

"What?" I stared up at Mickey, and he put an arm around me.

"He left a note and said that he took Heather's Angel and went to find you." I could tell from her voice that she was crying. "We're short-staffed now, but Pete and the few left here who know their way around the ranch are out looking, and we called the police," she said. "Get back here right now and bring your parents. I need all of you with me."

"On our way," I promised, my heart icing over, and then I looked up at Anna Mae. "Shoot me if you have to, but I'm leaving. My baby brother is out alone on a horse, in the rain, and he didn't grow up here. He doesn't know the ranch."

"Or the ravine," my mother cried out, and my dad started swearing.

I only nodded, so terrified I was almost numb.

"I'll drive you," Mickey said.

"I'm coming, too," Ethan said.

"We don't want you," Mickey told him.

I ignored them both and started running for the truck.

"This isn't over," Anna Mae called out. "But I hope you find that boy and he's all right."

"You can go straight to hell," I said.

Please, God, whatever you do, let Buddy be all right. I'm so sorry.

"You get in the car with us, young lady," Dad shouted, but he was helping Mom carry Melinda, so he couldn't come after me.

"You can go to hell, too," I yelled back at him.

I climbed in the truck and started it up, but Mickey jumped in the passenger's side before I could get away, and I didn't take the time to argue with him. I reversed out of there in a squeal of tires and a splash of mud, and I could hear the cars starting up behind us.

"We'll find him," Mickey promised, trying to take my hand.

"Don't touch me," I snapped, starting to shake as the terror and the cold and the pain crashed through me. A landslide of guilt was crushing me under its weight. I didn't deserve to be comforted. I'd kissed Mickey Rhodale, who'd shoved my father, and now my brother was missing and maybe worse.

This was all on me.

"If he's hurt . . ." I couldn't finish that sentence. There was no sane place to go at the end of a sentence that started with my baby brother being hurt. I pushed the accelerator a little bit further toward the floor and went back to praying.

"Victoria—"

"I saw how fast you reached for that gun, Mickey."

He started to answer me, but then just shook his head. "I know. I'm as bad as the rest of them."

I think he was waiting for me to deny it. He'd be waiting a long, long time.

CHAPTER 36
MICKEY

The rain started up again, harder, and Victoria sped down the road to her place in half the time it should have taken, only glancing at me once when she was unsure of which way to go at a turn.

"Our families . . . all this hatred . . . it's too much. Too much history, too much violence," she said, and her voice was so empty and hollow that I knew she'd already pulled away from me, possibly beyond my reach or hope of reconciliation.

The violence inside me, hunched over like a rough, crouching beast, had ruined the possibility of something precious between us, probably forever.

Maybe it was better that way. Every time we were together, something bad happened, as if our feelings for each other were the catalyst that would power the worst kind of chemical reaction. I didn't want Victoria to get caught in the explosion.

"If he presses charges, he'll make sure you're tried as an adult this time," she said, and then she didn't say anything else until we got to her house.

She slowed for the turn to her driveway, tense and leaning forward in the seat, hands clenched together, every muscle straining toward the ranch and her missing brother. She yanked off her seatbelt and was out the door almost before she'd even pulled the truck to a stop outside the barn. It was blazing with lights, probably set up as search headquarters. She ran inside and I stuffed the gun under the seat, triple checking that the safety was on, before I followed.

Warmth and the unmistakable smell of horse met me at the door. Victoria was talking urgently to a couple of guys who were leaning over a map that was spread out on a wooden table, but most of the people seemed to be congregating near a stall that was farther down. I walked across the thick rubber matting that lined the entire corridor to get to the group at the table.

"What's going on down there?"

Victoria glanced up from the map, her face set in tight lines. "Wanderer's Quest picked tonight to foal, naturally. She's not having an easy time."

One of the guys put a hand on Victoria's arm, and I had the irrational urge to shove him away.

"We're going to find your brother. Pete's already out there, and nobody knows this place like he does," he told her.

"I'm taking one of the three-wheelers," Victoria announced. "None of the horses need to be out in this. No *more* of the horses."

"Hey, Heather's Angel might be old but she's sure-footed," the other guy said briskly. "I should go. You stay here to man the phone; everybody's calling to check in when they've cleared a section."

I studied the map and saw that the circled sections had been marked with names. Only two of the smallest circles had been checked off so far.

"No way. He's my brother, and I'm going after him," Victoria said. She headed out, grabbing a set of keys off a corkboard as she went, and I followed, taking a minute to grab a couple of rain jackets that were hanging on pegs.

By the time I got outside, Victoria had already opened a shed attached to the end of the barn and was inside, sitting on the floor, pulling on some long socks. A pair of old boots lay on the floor next to her.

"I don't need you, Mickey. Go home," she said, not looking at me.

"Like hell I will." I tossed her one of the jackets. "I'm going with you and we're finding your brother."

She hesitated, but I could almost see the desire for extra help with the search win out over the need to get away from me. "Fine."

She finished pulling on the boots and jacket, and climbed onto the three-wheeler. It started right away, and I swung up behind her, wishing she'd been able to find some pants wherever she'd gotten the boots. Her bare legs would soon be freezing in the cold rain.

"You need to put on some jeans," I said, knowing it would be futile. She was already driving out of the shed.

"Later. Now we find Buddy."

"Do you even know where to look?" I had to shout to be heard over the motor.

"I know exactly where to look. The worst possible place. Because if he's not there, then everything gets better," she shouted.

I understood instantly. We were headed for the ravine.

She put the pedal to the floor, and I wrapped my arms around her waist to hold on.

Please, let the kid be safe and all right.

A roar of sound swept up behind us and then passed by. I barely had the chance to register that it was Ethan on his motorcycle before he was gone, riding helmetless at a breakneck speed in the rain, heading God only knew where.

"If he hurt your brother—"

Victoria cut me off with words I didn't expect and sure as hell didn't understand. "He didn't."

CHAPTER 37

VICTORIA

I didn't know why Ethan was there, and I didn't care. Another body to help in the search. Mickey tightened his arms around my waist and leaned into me, and I knew I should be grateful for the little bit of warmth and protection from the rain that he offered, but mostly I just wanted him gone. Even allowing him to touch me felt like a betrayal—of Buddy, of Dad, of all my family. If I'd stayed home, none of this would have happened.

The perfect daughter had screwed up again. I was blasting through a lifetime's worth of mistakes in the space of a few weeks, and now maybe my sweet baby brother would pay the price.

I swerved the ATV to miss a fallen tree limb and instead hit a big rock that had been half-hidden in dirt and mud. I barely had time to scream before the bike was flipping over and Mickey and I were flying off the back. Cartwheels of stars cascaded through my vision as I tumbled through the air, and I had a moment to think, *so this is how I'm going to be punished*, before I hit the ground, hard. I landed on soft grass, though, so I only had the breath knocked out of me. By the time I could suck in enough air to be able to sit up, Mickey still hadn't come to find me or even made a sound, and I was terrified that he'd been hurt badly.

I made it over to the upside-down three-wheeler and turned off the ignition to keep it from catching fire. But the left front tire was shredded. So we were walking. I scanned the area for Mickey, and saw a dark shape lying against another rock—this one more like a small boulder—and I started toward him, fighting the mud sucking at my boots with every step.

He was crumpled against the side of the rock, unconscious, and I didn't know whether to shake him or leave him where he was—what if he had a neck or spine injury? I saw a trail of dark blood running down the side of his face from a gash on his forehead, and the world suddenly swirled around me at the thought he might be dead.

"Mickey," I screamed, as if my voice could pull him back or wake him up or I don't even know what. I was an idiot, but I didn't care because I didn't want the last thing between us to have been anger and regret.

I pulled my phone out of my jacket pocket with shaking fingers and started to call the barn phone, but then Mickey opened his eyes and blinked a couple of times.

He said something I couldn't quite make out, and I leaned closer. "What?"

"Next time, I'm driving."

I didn't know what to do with the tangled-up emotions threatening to tear me apart, so I punched him in the shoulder, and then I put my hands on the sides of his face and kissed him.

"I'm willing to fall off any number of three-wheelers if you'll kiss me like that every time," he said when I pulled away.

"Idiot. Are you okay? Your head's bleeding. You might have a concussion," I said, but then I forced myself to stop babbling. I had no idea what I was talking about, anyway. "I'll call the barn and we'll get somebody out here to take you to the doctor."

"Screw *that*. We're going to go find your brother," he said.

He shoved rain and blood off his face with one sleeve, and then he held out a hand for me to help him up. I hesitated, not knowing what to do. What if he had a concussion? Would walking around make it worse?

Mickey didn't wait for me to decide. He pushed up off the ground, wobbled a little, and then braced himself. "Let's go find Buddy."

"We're not that far from the ravine," I said, making up my mind. Mickey could see a doctor later, but Buddy might be in serious danger now. "This way. We're walking. The tire on the ATV is blown."

We were covered with mud, but I figured the pounding rain would wash some of that off. If only it could wash away some of my guilt and worry, too, I'd be happy to walk around in freezing rain and mud all night long.

"Buddy," I shouted. "Buddy, can you hear me?"

Mickey's deeper voice echoed beside me. "Buddy!"

We trudged on in the freezing rain, slowed down by mud and fallen debris from the storm, screaming for my brother until I thought I'd never be warm again. Deep shudders kept working their way through me, stronger and stronger, until I thought they might knock me over from the inside out, and all I could think was my baby brother was out in this somewhere.

Freezing. Wet. Maybe hurt.

Determination surged through me, substituting for warmth and strength and courage. I would find him.

I would.

"Buddy!" I glanced at my phone to check the time. It had been almost two hours since Gran's call, and Buddy had been gone even longer than that. How long did it take for a little boy to go into shock from being cold and wet?

I tripped over an uneven spot on the ground and went down face first, but Mickey caught me before I hit the ground. He pulled me back up and toward him, holding me tightly for a moment before he let go.

"He's going to be all right," he said again, for maybe the tenth time since we'd started walking. "We'll find him."

"If we don't . . ." I couldn't finish the thought. Pain ripped through me, and I doubled over, holding my arms over my stomach, trying to contain the terror.

"We will," he said, so firmly that I almost believed him.

He took my hand, and I let him in spite of everything between us, and we started walking again. Another few minutes should get us to the trees bordering the ravine.

"Buddy," I shouted, over and over and over, while Mickey did the same, but the only response was the echo of our own voices.

CHAPTER 38
MICKEY

I was freezing, soaked, and losing hope, so I almost missed it when it finally happened. But then I heard it again. The thin sound of a horse nickering in the distance.

"That's Angel," Victoria said, and she let go of my hand and started running straight toward the thick grouping of trees that she'd said bordered the ravine.

I caught up to her and passed her, scanning the ground for anything that might trip her again and for any small bundle or shape that might turn out to be a little boy. She pushed me aside at the ravine's edge and then pointed.

"There she is!"

The horse was standing so close to the edge that any misstep would cause her to fall over, and her reins were tangled tightly in a bush. I started forward, but Victoria grabbed my arm.

"No. She's scared, and she doesn't know you. I'll do it. You look for Buddy." She walked forward, calling out to the horse, which recognized her and started to whinny in earnest.

While I tried to keep one eye on Victoria in case the horse fell and took her over with it, I scanned the area for Buddy. A dark lump next to the creek below looked oddly bent but suspiciously boy-shaped and, while I stared at it, it moved.

I shouted down to him. "Buddy?"

"Help!"

I took off, scrambling down the side of the ravine, and when I got to Buddy I saw why his shape had seemed odd. His leg was clearly broken, and it was tangled up in a coil of weeds, as if he'd fallen into the creek and then climbed back out.

"Hi, Buddy, I'm Mickey," I said, using the same tone of voice Victoria had used to calm the horse. "I'm going to help you. Your sister Victoria is here, too, okay?"

"Okay, but it really hurts," he said, whimpering. "I tried to be brave, but it's so dark and wet, and it hurts really, really bad. It really hurts."

He was repeating himself, and I tried to figure out whether that was from shock or just normal for a scared little boy in pain, but then I realized it didn't matter. We needed to get him out of there. I yanked my jacket off—the inside was still dry and held some warmth from my body—and wrapped it around him.

"Call my pa to get the search and rescue helicopter," I shouted up at Victoria, who'd evidently secured the horse, and was starting down the ravine. "Cell reception won't work down here."

She must have heard me, because she stopped and made the call. Seconds later, she began scrambling toward us again, slipping and sliding on the muddy slope. She pushed me out of her way and ran to Buddy.

"Where were you? I was so scared," he said accusingly, and she wrapped her arms around him and held tight.

"I'm here now, shh, it's okay, Buddy," she said over and over, and I started wondering if she was going into shock, too.

We'd been walking around in the rain for hours, after all, and the rain jacket over her dress and boots wasn't nearly enough.

"Did you reach my pa?"

She nodded. "I called Gus at the barn, too. He called everyone in from the search, and your father already had a helicopter in the air. It's on the way to take Buddy out of here and to the hospital. Some of the staff who were in on the search are on their way out here on the other three-wheelers. When they get here you should go, so you can see a doctor, too. We're fine now."

I stared at her in disbelief. "I should go? I'm not leaving you alone."

She raised her head, and I could see the pain and exhaustion stamped in her face. "You did it before. Remember, when you pushed my father? I'm glad you're alive, Mickey, and not seriously injured from our fall, but my brother is hurt, *because of us*."

My head, which had been throbbing like a thousand bass drums going off at once since I'd hit that rock, felt like it was going to explode, and I suddenly didn't know how to be calm anymore.

"Your father looked like he was going to hit my mother," I shouted, clenching my hands into fists so I didn't rip my hair out in frustration. "I didn't *abandon* you. I went to stop a situation, and I came *right back*."

"No, you didn't," she shouted back. "You pushed my dad, even knowing that doing it would mean the end to any chance between us. He might send you to *jail*, you idiot! And then what about your future?"

A noise alerted me just before Pete, the Whitfield ranch foreman, punched me in the same side of the head that had hit the rock. I fell hard, hitting the ground right next to Victoria, who put one hand on my cheek and then stared up at Pete.

"What are you doing? He might already have a concussion, and now you hit him? Has everybody in the world gone insane?"

"He was yelling, and I was worried he would attack you," Pete said, shaking out his hand like it hurt.

Good. I hoped he'd broken some bones. My damn head certainly felt broken.

"So what? I was yelling at *him*, too. Mickey would never hurt me. You all can't go around hitting people," she shouted, and I was glad not to be on the receiving end of it this time.

The roar of the helicopter finally sounded, and I pulled myself up off the ground to a sitting position and put my arm around Victoria's shoulders, hoping she'd allow it.

"Sorry," Pete muttered.

I started to nod, but stopped when the motion split my head and made me feel like I was going to puke. "No problem. But the kid's leg is stuck in those weeds. Do you have a knife?"

Pete pulled a knife from the sheath at his belt, and as he turned it, the moonlight glinted off the silver blade. He leaned down across me, toward Buddy, and then his entire body jerked almost simultaneously with the sound of a loud *crack*.

Victoria flinched. Buddy started to cry. I looked around for the source of the sound, hoping against hope that it hadn't been what I'd thought, but I knew better.

That had been a pistol.

Then Pete stumbled back, clutching his shoulder, and even in the rainy night we could see clearly enough the dark, spreading stain pouring out from between and around his fingers.

"Shot me," he said almost wonderingly, and then he fell.

I looked up. There was Ethan, kneeling at the top of the other side of the ravine, pointing his gun at us.

Victoria screamed, and I realized she'd seen him, too.

The confusion of lights and sounds; the urgent pace of medical personnel as they realized they had *two* patients, one of them critical; the arrival of what seemed like dozens of people all at once—I watched every bit of it through a hazy filter, as if from a distance. I realized that, ironically enough, I was finally the one in shock. The chopper lifted Pete and Buddy out of the ravine, and I stood back up, swaying as the world tilted around me. Victoria may have been right about that concussion; maybe not at first, but it certainly felt like I had one now after Pete hit me with that right hook to my head.

Pete. *Ethan.*

People were helping me and Victoria back up the side of the ravine, everyone chattering on about the shooting, and still I hadn't said a single word, and neither had she. At least not to me. Once we were back on solid ground, she pushed past everyone trying to help her and headed for her horse.

"I'm riding Heather's Angel back to the barn. Somebody take Mickey. He probably has a concussion, and he needs to see a doctor," she said, swinging up on the horse's bare back.

"Victoria," I called out, not sure exactly what I wanted—*needed*—to say to her, but it didn't matter anyway, because she was in no mood to listen. She started to turn the horse back toward the ranch, and I ran over to her.

"Victoria," I said again, touching her leg as if to stop her, but she looked down at me with flat eyes in a hard face.

"No," she said in a low voice. No one else could hear us. "I don't want to listen to anything you have to say. I *saw* him. Ethan shot Pete. And Buddy never would have been hurt, or Melinda taken, if you and I had stayed away from each other. I never want to see you again."

CHAPTER 39
VICTORIA

Emotional torment played games with me all night. Cruel, evil games in which I was the pawn, and pain, guilt, anger, and emptiness were my adversaries and tormentors. It didn't let me sleep, didn't let me eat, almost didn't let me breathe while we paced the floors and stared at our phones, willing them to ring.

Gran finally fell asleep on the couch at around three in the morning, which was when Melinda managed to rouse herself from her drunken or drug-addled state. I couldn't talk to her—I couldn't even look at her—so I didn't even try. This might be on me, but she owned her share of the blame, too. Anger at my sister warred in my mind with guilt over blaming her for something her addiction drove her to do.

Anger kept winning out.

Anna Mae, Ethan, even Mickey's dad, who seemed pretty useless as a sheriff—I hated them all. But most of all, I hated myself for allowing my heart to get tangled up with someone who would shove my dad—someone who was related to a . . . a . . . *murderer*.

But Dad scared his mom into falling and hurting herself, and you didn't really see that shooter's face, a little voice in my head tried to insist. I ignored it. After all, Dad didn't lay a finger on Mickey's mom, so the retaliation was way overdone, and Ethan—I couldn't even think about him right now.

Mickey hurts people. He told you about those guys he put in the hospital, and you saw the way he went after Sam Oliver in the cafeteria. What makes you think you'll be safe?

"Shut. Up," I muttered to the stupid voice, but it gleefully went on and on, pointing out all the reasons I was a fool for having even thought about getting more involved with Mickey.

I spent the next two hours alternately trying to sleep and trying not to cry, and when the phone finally rang at five-thirty, I pounced on it. "Mom?"

"They're going to be fine, Victoria," my mother said. "Honey, they're both going to be fine."

My knees buckled with relief, and I fell onto the couch. A gasp alerted me to Melinda's entrance, and as I watched, the glass of water she'd been holding tumbled down out of her hand and she cried out.

I instantly realized she'd interpreted my reaction totally wrong. "No, Melinda! They're okay. Mom says they're both going to be fine."

Melinda fell to the floor and started to cry, but for once I wouldn't be the one comforting her.

"Tell me everything, Mom."

My mother took a long, deep breath. "They're very efficient here, of course. You know your father plays golf with the administrator, and—"

"I don't care about the good old boys network right now," I said impatiently. "Tell me about Buddy and Pete."

Her voice softened. "It's just been so crazy here—well. Buddy's leg is broken, but it's a clean fracture, and they expect him to heal quickly and completely and be playing ball just fine by spring."

"That's so great. Oh, wow, that's so great," I said, clutching the phone tight like a lifeline. "And Pete?"

"His injury was serious. They had to rush him into surgery, and apparently it was rough going, but the EMTs on the helicopter did exactly the right thing, and the surgeons here were spectacular. It all came together in the perfect confluence of medical excellence."

"He's going to be fine?"

"He's going to be fine," Mom confirmed, and the relief and joy in her voice reminded me of the mother I'd had when I'd been Buddy's age or a little younger. The one who'd bandaged up my hurts and made owies better with kisses. It had been a very long time since I'd heard from that side of my mother.

"I love you, Mom," I said impulsively. After all, Whitfields didn't do emotion, she always told me.

"I love you, too, honey," she said in almost a whisper.

Apparently it was a night for miracles.

CHAPTER 40
MICKEY

Five a.m. at my house. Nobody could sleep, but at least we were all clean and dry for the first time all night. I was slumped on the couch, and Pa sprawled in his recliner. Mom handed me a mug of coffee and then did something she hadn't done in a few years—she leaned over and kissed the top of my head.

"Thanks for the coffee. Been a while since you kissed my head," I said, trying to smile at her.

"I usually can't reach it, since you grew taller than me when you were twelve and got that big growth spurt," she said. "It's hard to be five-four in a house full of six-foot-tall men."

"Where's Ethan?" I finally asked the question that had been squatting in the middle of the room like an unwanted guest.

"Nobody can find him," Pa said, staring at his phone. "He was never there."

I put the coffee cup down so I didn't throw it at him. "You can't cover this one up, Pa. Victoria saw him, too."

He glared at me through reddened eyes. "Victoria was tired and distraught over her brother and her employee. She did *not* see Ethan from clear across the ravine, on a dark, rainy night."

"Maybe she didn't. But I did. He's not getting away with this one."

"You don't understand. If he goes away for this, he'll be gone for years. A lot of hard time," Pa said. "There won't be anything left of your brother if and when he gets back from that."

"What's left of him now?"

I stomped up the stairs, figuring I'd at least get a little sleep, because sitting around waiting for news was driving me insane. After the EMTs at the barn checked me out—no concussion—I'd managed to retrieve the gun, unnoticed in the chaos of people milling about. Dad had driven me home and told me that they'd Life-Flighted Pete and Buddy to Louisville, and we had put calls in to find out any news, but nobody was saying anything except that Pete was in surgery.

When I reached my room, I tried to call Victoria, and the call went straight to voice mail again. Same with the next five times in five minutes.

On the sixth, she picked up.

"How are they?" I got the question out before she could start shouting or, worse, tell me to go to hell.

Silence.

"Victoria, please, I'm going crazy here. At least tell me they're going to be okay—that *you're* going to be okay."

More silence as my consciousness telescoped down into a pinpoint of focus that centered on the sound of her breathing. Finally, she sighed.

"Buddy's going to be fine. Simple fracture. He has a cast but didn't have to have any pins or anything. They're keeping him there for the weekend in an excess of caution and probably because my dad is being an ass," she finally said.

"That's terrific! I'm so glad—"

"Pete just got out of surgery."

Shit.

"Do you know anything—progress, or?"

"They expect him to pull through," she said, and I wanted to start cheering.

"Thank God," I said fervently.

"If he'd died, your brother would be a murderer." Her voice was precise, and so very icy. "I will testify against him, Mickey, no matter what you say, so if this is about—"

"So will I."

Silence.

Finally, I heard her breathe in a deep, shuddery breath. "I thought—"

"You thought I was calling you to get you to protect Ethan? *Fuck* him," I said viciously. "I'm calling because I'm so worried about you I think my scalp is going to fly off my skull. I'm calling you because I want to be with you, and hold you, and comfort you."

"Oh, Mickey," she whispered, and her voice held so much sadness that I knew she'd made up her mind against me. Against us.

"Victoria, if you still want me to stay away from you, I will. But I need you to know something first. I need to tell you that I'm falling in love with you."

She inhaled sharply, and then the phone went dead.

I guess that gave me my answer.

I went to bed and stared at the ceiling for the next three hours, and then I went outside and cleaned the hell out of the garage. Luckily for Jeb, he was gone, because if I'd found him there, I might very well have let loose of the anger and loss churning around in my gut and tried to beat some sense into his sorry ass.

CHAPTER 41

VICTORIA

Funny the difference a weekend made. I was actually glad to go back to school after two solid days of Melinda's hysteria, Gran's migraines, my own aching anxiety and guilt, and my parents' long-distance interference and vague reports.

Only Heather's Angel and Buddy hadn't been angry with me. I'd spoken to my little brother on the phone, and he'd been chattering happily about the comic books one of the nurses had brought for him. Angel was recuperating from her adventure, immensely enjoying the extra attention she was getting from everyone.

And Mickey—*Mickey*.

I'd picked up my phone to call him a hundred times after he'd told me that he was falling in love with me.

Falling in love with me.

I hadn't been able to admit I felt the same way—that I'd maybe passed "falling" and gone straight to "already fallen"—because it was wrong. I'd told him I never wanted to see him again, and I meant it.

We were cursed. Every time we were together, terrible things happened. How could that ever be worth it? And the violence simmering inside him, just under the surface—I didn't know how to deal with it, and he certainly didn't know how to control it. What if he could *never* learn how to control it? What if something set him off around Buddy? Was I willing to risk everything for what might only be a crush?

I dismissed *that* thought immediately. No. Whatever my feelings for Mickey, they went way, *way* beyond a crush. I'd never felt like this before—might never feel this way again. So I could refuse to see him, but I couldn't lie to myself about what it would cost me to do it.

Mom had talked Dad out of pressing charges against anybody for the fiasco at Anna Mae's—not that we could really figure out who to blame for what—but she'd told me he'd been on the phone to an old college frat buddy who'd joined the FBI. So I couldn't stop worrying.

I wandered school in a daze all Monday morning, ignoring the speculative stares and whispers, until Denise finally caught up to me in the hallway just before lunch.

"I hear you had a busy weekend," she said, giving me a look that was somewhere between curious and pissed off.

"Trust me, you don't even want to know."

"Actually, I do. The next time you use me for a cover story, at least do me the courtesy of telling me," she fired off. "I had the unique experience of hearing that the matriarch of the Whitfield family was at my front door, demanding I tell her where to find her granddaughter."

I stopped fumbling with my locker and turned to her. "Oh, no. Denise, I'm so sorry. You said you were going out of town, or I would have told you—would have *asked* you—and I never gave them your last name, and—"

"Do you really think anybody in this town would have had a hard time figuring out who the Denise in your classes was?" She gave me a look. "Just because you're blond doesn't mean you're stupid."

I banged my head against the locker. "Yeah. I kind of am. And I need a friend. A real friend. Can you forgive me, and we can go somewhere to talk?"

She stared at me for a long, silent beat before the look in her eyes softened. "Oh, come on, then. It's not like I've never screwed up."

We bailed on school—I was turning into a truant officer's nightmare—and went to Dairy Queen. The twenty-something behind the counter gave us our Blizzards and burger combos, nodded to a table around the edge of the counter, out of sight of the front door, and waved off our thanks.

"Emergency carbs have no calories, right?" Denise stared down at her red plastic tray.

"You think I'm going to eat salad after a weekend like I've had?" I poured extra salt on my fries.

"I hope Pete and your brother are okay," she said, reinforcing my belief that everybody knew everything in small towns.

"Buddy is doing great. And the doctors tell us Pete is doing well in recovery. Thanks," I said.

I sat there at the Formica-topped table, surrounded by mint-green walls and posters of ice-cream sundaes, and told Denise everything. Well, almost everything. I left big chunks of it out, actually—anything too private between Mickey and me, and anything that sounded like an accusation of criminal conduct. Oh, and the part about Anna Mae and my dad.

Okay, actually, I didn't tell her a whole lot.

Enough to blow her mind, though.

"How is it you even want to be my friend?" I took a sip of my soda and stared down at the sandwich and fries I felt too nauseous to eat. "Why aren't you hanging around with the other cheerleaders in a flock or something?"

"It's a pom pom," she said, grinning. "A flock of geese, a murder of crows, a pom pom of cheerleaders."

"A touchdown of football players?"

She considered that. "No, more like a jockstrap, I think. A jockstrap of football players."

I laughed out loud for the first time in days. "I like that. Denise, I'm really sorry. You're really the only person who has tried to get to know me and, like a jerk, I used your friendship. Please forgive me. I just . . . I'm just caught up in something that's way over my head."

Instead of instantly accepting my apology, Denise stared at me over her Blizzard for a long minute. Finally, she nodded. "Accepted. But don't ever do that again."

"I promise," I said miserably, feeling about two inches tall. Then she smiled—a warm smile—and I felt better.

"And to answer your question, I never quite fit in here, either," she admitted. "I'm too smart for the jocks, too dumb for the brains, not nerdy enough for the geeks, etc. etc. They all kind of tolerate me, but I'm not swimming in BFFs, if you know what I mean."

"Oh, yeah. I understand completely." I'd blown just enough curves on exams with my grades; I'd dressed up okay but never been ruled by clothes and makeup. Simone, who'd been the indie-rock goddess of Ashford-Hutchinson, had always told me I'd figure out who I wanted to be one day.

Somehow, *this* didn't feel like what she'd had in mind.

"Speaking of jockstraps, Sam didn't mean it," Denise said, her face troubled. "He's really a good guy, but he was worried sick. His mom lost her job last year, and they've been having hard times as it is, so now with his dad . . ."

My soda turned to acid in my stomach.

"I know," I said. "I'm so sorry. I did hear one piece of good news about that, at least. A friend of my grandmother said she's in a big hiring push on her ranch because a bunch of her staff retired and a couple quit to have babies—a lot of things like that all happened at once. And it's just the next county over. If I give you the information, can you find a way to get it to Sam and anybody else you know who needs it?"

"That's pretty nice of you, considering what he did," she said, and her gaze lingered on the side of my face, where there was still a little bruising and swelling.

I shrugged, uncomfortable with the attention. "He didn't mean to hit me, and the rest was just talk. Gran and her staff are calling everybody with the information, but some people aren't picking up their phones when they see the call is coming from us."

"Are you okay?"

I didn't know how to answer that, so I evaded the question. "Well, Buddy is doing well, charming all the nurses, and—"

She put a hand on my arm. "I don't mean Buddy. He'll be fine. Little boys are resilient. Are *you* okay?"

I very carefully put my cup down on the table and looked up at her. I couldn't hide the misery that was threatening to crack me open any longer.

"Mickey Rhodale told me he's falling in love with me, and I think I'm falling in love with him, too."

"Holy shit," she whispered.

"But we don't have a chance at a relationship, because there's something so dark inside him that I don't know if he can ever control."

"Holy shit," she whispered again.

I couldn't have agreed with her more.

We devoured our Blizzards and fries, ignored the burgers, and talked. She told me about cheerleading, and I told her about boarding school. She told me about the miniature golf course her family owned, and I told her about racehorses.

"I never got the appeal," she said, almost apologetically, as she reached over to snag my last fry. "I mean, all that money and all that training for the Kentucky Derby, and it lasts, what, two minutes? Why don't they at least run a long race, like the Indy 500 or something, so you guys can get your money's worth?"

I blinked at the idea of a horse running five hundred miles and tried to frame a reply, but then I realized she was joking.

"Ha! Got you!"

I laughed and realized I'd been doing that a lot with her while we ate and chatted. The entire interlude had been like a shiny bubble of escape from the misery and drama of my life.

"You could come out and ride with me sometime," I ventured.

Her entire face glowed with excitement. "I'd love that! Can I ride a racehorse?"

"Not a chance," I said cheerfully. "Pete won't even let me ride them, but we do have other horses you can ride."

"Probably better, anyway. Knowing my luck, I'd break a

million-dollar horse and have to spend my life mucking out stalls to
pay for it." She chuckled, and I joined in.

"That's a lot of horse poop," I advised her, and she started to howl.

"Mount Horse Poop, the h-h-highest hill in K-K-Kentucky," she
said, barely able to breathe for laughing.

The mother who'd sat at the table behind Denise with her two
little boys glared at me, and for some reason I found that hysterically
funny. I put my head down on my arms and laughed until I couldn't
catch my breath, while Denise made more and more outrageous poop
jokes.

Finally the clerk walked over.

"Shut up or I'm kicking you out," she said, grinning at us both.
"And have a nice day."

By the time we pulled into the school parking lot, the bell was
about to ring so I decided not to bother going back in. Denise did the
same, and we sat in the truck for a minute, comfortable with our budding friendship but not quite sure where to go next.

"You realize you need to come over for a *real* study date now, right?
To balance the karmic scales?" Denise shot me a sideways glance.

"I'd like that. And maybe you could come for a sleepover or something," I said hesitantly, before I immediately felt like a fool. "Do we
still do that? Sleepovers at our age?"

She whistled. "You really are a special, sheltered snowflake, aren't
you?"

I hung my head. "Two years of boarding school in Connecticut.
I can teach you how to make a school uniform look slutty, but I can't
figure out the social norms of conventional high schools just yet."

Denise burst out laughing, but I could feel that it wasn't directed
at me. It was more just *near* me. "You? Slutty? I doubt it. Also, 'social

norms of conventional high schools'? Oh, honey. You are flying your nerd flag high."

My cheeks heated up a little and I sighed. "Yes, I confess. I'm a closet nerd. Geek. Whatever you want to call it. I can tell you the details of every show that's been on the Syfy channel for the past four years, and I read Jane Austen for fun."

She was gasping for air now. "Syfy? I knew it! Those hot alien dudes just get you, don't they?" We both cracked up simultaneously.

"I can tell this is going to be a wonderful friendship," Denise said. "I have to go now, or I'll get stuck digging out the balls under the Sleepytime Palace."

I blinked. "I'm sure that makes sense in your world, but—"

"Mini golf, remember? Someday I'll write a book about the seamy underbelly of mini golf," she said darkly, and then she waved and climbed out of my truck.

I watched her bounce over to a smallish green Chevy (bumper sticker: A WOMAN'S PLACE IS IN THE HOUSE—AND THE SENATE) and a tiny tendril of warmth unfurled inside me. I'd just made my first real friend in Clark, Kentucky.

Maybe friendship would help me get over the dangerous boy I couldn't stop thinking about, no matter that I was so angry with him and almost his entire family. Friendship and Dairy Queen.

All this ice cream and I was going to need some bigger jeans.

CHAPTER 42
MICKEY

By mid-afternoon, the scent of cleaning liquid and Windex was gradually winning over the smell of dust, grime, and my own sweat, and the place was looking more like a garage and less like the setting for a horror story about chainsaw-wielding psychopaths.

Derek, my spy at school, had been texting me periodic updates.

Victoria showed up but then she and Denise ditched.

They're still not back.

They're still not back.

Quit nagging me, they're still not back.

And, finally:

They're back, but only in the parking lot. Denise looks hot today.

I rolled my eyes at the corkboard I'd just finished installing on one wall of the garage and then texted him back.

Just ask her out already. Quit being a pussy.

Seconds later, I had a response.

Why would I ask Victoria out?

Denise, idiot.

Yeah, like I'm taking love life advice from you, loser.

I turned off my phone after that, because he was right. I *was* a loser. Victoria had dumped me, Coach had kicked me off the team, the principal had suspended me, my brother had committed attempted murder, and I was one step away from a life of crime. I already had the gun to go with my future mug shot.

College, hell. I'd be lucky to get into the prison library and learn how to make license plates. Did prisoners still make license plates? I didn't even know—more evidence of my headlong rush toward mediocrity.

Mom called my name, and I left the garage, blinking at the bright sunlight like Edmond Dantès emerging from the Château d'If. Maybe that was the trick. I'd vanish for a few years and then return to Whitfield County triumphant and with a different name, like some kind of redneck Count of Monte Cristo.

"I brought you some lemonade," Mom said, holding out a tall glass that sparkled from the crystalline drops of condensation running down the sides.

I drank most of it in one long swallow. "Thanks. I needed it. I'm beginning to have hallucinations about Dumas novels."

Mom, who'd read *The Count of Monte Cristo* and *The Three Musketeers* to me when I'd been around five, when most moms were reading picture books to their kids, laughed. Tales of sword fights, corruption, and revenge had been the lyrics to the melodies of my childhood, and I'd loved every bit of it. I remembered how I'd talked Ethan and Jeb into playing musketeers instead of cowboys and Indians sometimes, and Jeb had always run around the neighborhood brandishing his plastic sword and yelling "On garden!" instead of *en garde*.

I grinned at the memory. "On garden, Mom."

She laughed again. "Poor Jeb. He was always a brick shy of a full wheelbarrow, wasn't he? Bless his heart."

"Any news?"

She sobered and shook her head. "No word of Ethan, but he could be sitting pretty in the middle of Anna Mae's kitchen and we'd never know. Last I heard, Pete is still recuperating slowly but steadily, and Mr. and Mrs. Whitfield will be bringing Buddy home from the hospital in Louisville in a few days."

"Leaving Victoria to deal with the mess they left here. Typical," I said, kicking the riding lawn mower. Hard.

Ouch.

"That'll teach that mower a lesson," Mom said.

"She hates me, Mom," I said quietly. "She never wants to see me again."

My mom sighed and then hugged me. "Are you sure? Right now, she might be hating herself."

She stepped back and looked up at me. Then she flinched, so evidently the raw pain that was ripping through me must be clear in my expression.

"I need a better poker face."

"You already have a pretty good poker face, Mickey. But I'm your mother. Mothers know these things. That's why I want to tell you to stay away from her."

"That's what she wants, too," I said bleakly, and then I drained the glass. "Thanks, Mom. I'd better get back to it."

"Dinner's on your own tonight, kid. I'm forcing your father to take me to see a movie over at the mall. I need a little escapism, and if he spends another evening staring at his phone, waiting for word about Ethan, I'm going to go mad."

"Wouldn't be a long trip," I told her, grinning a little.

She shot me a mock glare, but then she sighed. "I said I *want* to tell you to stay away from her, not that I will. Try again with Victoria, Mickey. I saw the way that girl looked at you. The last thing in the world she wants is to push you away, no matter what she thinks."

Hope blazed through me. "I love you, Mom."

She walked off, nodding. "I know, I know. I *am* very lovable."

Maybe it was true—maybe I did have another chance.

But did I deserve one?

I thought back to the way Victoria had responded to my kisses on our picnic with such innocent eagerness that I'd had a hard time putting the brakes on, and the sound of her voice in the dark, telling me about her dreams of being a vet. The look in her brilliantly green eyes when I'd told her she was beautiful.

The way she kept standing up for me, over and over.

Please, let it be the truth.

CHAPTER 43

VICTORIA

I arrived home after school to a flurry of movement. Gran was stuffing things in an oversized tote bag, and Melinda was carrying a suitcase down the stairs.

"What's going on?" I dropped my backpack and tried not to freak out. "Is it Pete? Is he worse?"

"Calm down, everything's fine," Melinda said, and I realized that she sounded almost like her old self. Calm, confident—I hadn't heard this Melinda in a couple of years.

"Are you drinking again?" I stepped closer and sniffed, but I didn't smell any alcohol.

She rolled her eyes. "No. I'm not drinking, Inspector Whitfield, but thanks for asking. In fact, I hope never to drink again. That's what this trip is about."

"Trip? What trip?"

Gran walked in from the direction of the kitchen. "We're going to check out that rehab facility you found before Richard changes his mind or Priscilla tries to stop us."

I looked from one to the other, but they both appeared to be completely serious. "I'll run and throw some stuff in a bag. Give me five minutes."

"No," Gran said. "You've got school and, with Pete gone, there has to be at least one Whitfield here on the property. What if the new staff has questions?"

"We both know that I'm not the person to answer any staff questions, and that Pete's second-in-charge will be on top of everything," I said impatiently. "I've lived here for five minutes, in relative terms, anyway, and I don't know anything. Why don't you stay, and I'll drive Melinda to rehab?"

"I want Gran," Melinda said, and her voice held a trace of shakiness—just enough for me to back down, fast. "I'm sorry, Victoria, but I'll feel a little better about this if Gran goes with me to hold my hand."

"And you have to learn this stuff, anyway. Who do you think is going to run this place after I'm gone?" Gran picked up the enormous saddle-brown leather purse that she still insisted on calling her "pocketbook" and started rummaging through it, completely unaware that she'd just knocked me on my figurative butt with that statement. "Also, I trust you to block any inquiries from the Louisville contingent until I can get back."

Melinda took a deep breath. "If I like this facility, I'm going to check in. Today. There's no time like the present, right?"

I hugged her. "I'm so proud of you, Mel. So proud. I hope it's a great place."

"I'm so sorry about leaving Buddy," she said, meeting my gaze for the first time all weekend. Her eyes were tormented. "He fell asleep, so I was sure it would be fine. Well—just another example of my screwed-up addiction thinking. It needs to end. I finally figured that out. I have to fix this before someone else gets hurt."

"You need to get better," I said, and I hugged her again. "Buddy's going to be fine. It's time to take care of you."

After they left in Gran's little sedan, I wandered around the empty house for a while, too restless to settle down anywhere. I wanted something that I couldn't quite put my finger on; a formless feeling of anxiety pushed and pulled at my insides, dragging me here and there. After a half hour or so, I found myself in Gran's study, contemplating the bookshelves.

Maybe I could read. Something like *The Complete Book of Equine Anatomy* might help me avoid yet another sleepless night spent thinking about Mickey. I slowly walked over to look at the book titles, trying to avoid thinking about Rhodales. Any Rhodales.

Denise had made a very good point just before we'd left Dairy Queen to head back to school. If Mickey really cared about me, he wouldn't have given up so easily. He would have tried to fight for me.

A wave of bleakness swept over me, and I shoved it all away, concentrating on the books. Maybe *Techniques for Success in the Kentucky Derby and Other Races.* That ought to be a nail-biter.

A large, cloth-covered binder wedged in between a couple of equine medicine texts up on the top shelf caught my attention, and I worked it out from where it had been jammed in pretty tightly. When I got it down, I realized it was a photo album, and it was really old.

I flipped it open, and my dad, at around age ten or eleven, smiled out at me from a horse that was way too big for him.

I took the book with me out to the kitchen and made a sandwich. Mrs. Kennedy wouldn't be back for another week, so I was on my own for meals, pretty much as I had been for most of my life. I enjoyed the sound of perfect silence in the kitchen—nobody talking or working; the phone wasn't even ringing—so I sat right there with my food and a glass of milk and started to walk down memory lane, feeling vaguely like a trespasser or a thief. Stealing somebody else's memories, trespassing on somebody else's lane.

My grandfather was in a lot of the photos. He was almost always smiling when Gran was in the shot with him, but in the other photos he had a hard-edged wariness, as if he'd been waiting for an unknown opponent to try to take what was his. Or maybe I was reading far too much into an unsmiling face in an old photo album. I turned the pages, watching the years go by, watching my dad grow from boy to teen. Wondering when the obvious joy he had for riding and the ranch had turned to disdain.

When I got to the final page, I saw that someone had tucked a loose photo into the corner of the binding, and I stopped and stared at it, feeling like I was going to throw up.

She'd been so much younger and thinner and prettier, but her identity was unmistakable. It was a prom photo of my dad with his arm around Anna Mae Rhodale.

CHAPTER 44
MICKEY

After I demolished the pizza, I flipped through channels until I couldn't stand it any longer.

I had to see her. Not being near her was torture, and I couldn't take it anymore.

I was on the road five minutes later, calling myself a fool the entire ride to her place. Hoping that she wouldn't turn me down.

I didn't call until I'd parked my bike in a stand of trees next to the main road near her driveway, because I didn't want to be discouraged. She had to talk to me this time—especially if I showed up on her doorstep. I knew her parents were still in the city, and her grandmother probably went to bed ridiculously early, like most old people, so hopefully Melinda was occupied, and Victoria and I could have this out.

Whatever *this* was.

If she told me to leave, I'd never bother her again, but I needed to hear the words. Needed to see her face.

Before I could change my mind, I called her. She answered on the second ring.

"Mickey?"

"I need to see you," I said, digging my fingers into the fence rail so hard it hurt. "I have to apologize. Beg. Grovel. Whatever you want me to do that might make this right, but I need to see your face and convince myself that us being apart is really the best thing. Because it doesn't feel like it."

Silence.

"Victoria—"

"Where are you?"

It wasn't "yes," but it hadn't been "no," either.

"Practically on your front porch."

Another, longer silence.

"Come to the back porch, instead," she whispered.

I left thousands of dollars' worth of motorcycle without a second thought and ran the half mile to her house in under four minutes.

The back door was open just wide enough that I could see the long sliver of light from the kitchen and Victoria's shadow standing behind it. I knocked quietly anyway, and she opened the door all the way and motioned me inside.

Now that I was here, I didn't know what to say first. I watched as she closed and locked the door, and I tried to frame my arguments for why we should ignore everything our families wanted and everything that made sane, logical sense, just so we could be together.

"Victoria, I—"

She stepped forward into my arms and kissed me.

CHAPTER 45

VICTORIA

All the carefully planned-out reasons I had for why we should stay away from each other evaporated like mist over the fields at sunrise when I saw his face. I threw myself at him, desperate to touch him—to hold him—to kiss him.

Everything I'd believed I'd never have the chance to do again.

He felt like sanity in a world that had gone crazy. I clung to his strong shoulders, and he stroked my back and my hair, kissing me and murmuring gentle, calming things that didn't make any sense at all. None of it made any sense.

I didn't care.

The house phone rang, and I didn't care about that, either, until the answering machine clicked on and I heard Gran's voice.

"Victoria, in case you're there ignoring the phone, we checked

out the place and Melinda loves it, so we're signing her up. I'm staying overnight in the guest room, and I'll head back tomorrow around
lunchtime, so I'll be home when you get back from school. It's going to
be okay, sweetheart. Get some rest." The machine clicked off.

"What was that? Signing Melinda up for what?" Mickey asked.

"Rehab," I whispered. "Finally, *finally*, rehab. They were on the
way out the door when I got home today. Gran said that she wanted
to get Melinda out of here before my parents got home to try to stop
them."

Mickey looked puzzled. "Why would they stop her? That's the
best place for her."

I struck a haughty pose. "Rehab is trashy, Mr. Rhodale, don't you
know that? A Whitfield would never be caught dead in rehab."

He laughed, but I stopped—stricken. Talking about anybody
being "caught dead" was a terrible idea in our situation.

"Don't," he said.

"Don't what?"

"Don't get the second-thoughts look on your face. It's too late.
You can't kiss me like that and then throw me out again," Mickey said,
looking grim. "We need to talk."

"There they are again."

"What?"

"Those four horrible words."

"I don't care. I need to apologize. I never should have pushed
your dad; I was out of my mind when it looked like he was threatening my mother, and he said those awful things to her. She was bleeding." He stopped and shook his head, shoving a hand through his
hair. "It was so damn stupid, and reactive, and all the things I know
better than to do, but hell, Victoria, it was my *mom*. She's the one

innocent, truly good person in my entire shitty family drama, and I just went kind of nuts."

"I understand, but I don't know how to be with you if you can't figure out a way to control your temper, Mickey," I said, clasping my hands in front of me.

"I know. I know. And I also know it was a half-assed apology, but it was the truth. There's something in me that explodes when I see somebody hurting or threatening the people I care about."

I remembered his face in the cafeteria, before he'd laid into Sam. I imagined that his sister had seen the same face, only a dozen times more intense.

"You don't have to grovel," I whispered. "But maybe therapy, or anger management classes?"

"Yes. Anything. Definitely," he said, taking a step closer to me with each word, until he had me backed up against the kitchen counter.

"Anything for you," he murmured, and then he kissed me, and it felt like my world had righted itself again.

When he let me catch my breath several minutes later, I took his hand and showed him around the house, and he laughed when I pointed out the downstairs guest bathroom, but he wouldn't tell me why. None of the rooms downstairs felt right as someplace for us to sit and talk, so we ended up in the upstairs rec room, where the *Pirates* movies were still scattered all over the place.

"Interesting choice," Mickey said, picking up one DVD case. "There are some strange tides around here, that's for sure."

I sank down on the sectional sofa. "What are we going to do?"

"I'm hoping by that you mean that you don't want to never see me again. Wow. How was that for a tangled-up sentence? I've been

cleaning the garage for four straight days, so my brain might be rusty."
He smiled but his face was tense, as if he was waiting for me to shut
him down or throw him out.

I couldn't blame him, either, since I'd been up and down with
him from the beginning. Changing my mind with the tides of family
opinion, in a way, even after I'd made him promise he wouldn't do that
to me.

I looked down at my hands. "You know I want to see you. I *always*
want to see you. But look what happened. Buddy got hurt, Melinda
could have been hurt, and Pete got *shot*."

"I know." He sat down next to me, and I curled up against his
side, unable to resist his warmth. "But none of that is our fault. Well,
my shoving your dad is totally my fault, but I swear to you that nothing like that will happen again."

I glared at him. "It better not. If anybody gets to shove my dad
when he's acting like a jerk, it's going to be me."

He smiled, and then he kissed me, and I had to push him away so
I could think.

"You were right, Victoria. We need to find a way to end this
hatred between our families. Things are going to keep deteriorating
if we don't."

"I don't know where we'd even begin. Most of this is way over our
heads. Anna Mae said she loaned Daddy money he never paid back. I
asked him about that on the phone, and when he got done blustering,
he admitted to borrowing the money, but claims he did pay it back, at
least at the original interest rate. Evidently when she found out about
my mom—that Dad was dating her—Anna Mae tried to retroac-
tively jack up the interest."

Mickey took my hand and rubbed his thumb in circles on my palm, contemplating what I'd said, and I tried to keep from shivering at his touch.

"I'm surprised he told you that much."

"I doubt he would have, except he was in full-on defensive mode. This was when we weren't sure that Pete—that he—" I fought back tears, trying to hide my face, but Mickey pulled me across his body and onto his lap and held me, rubbing my back, until I'd calmed down.

"I'm sorry," I said. "I'm tougher than that."

"You're one of the toughest people I've ever known, but you can't cry," he said, a little desperately. "I can't handle it."

He stared down at me as if hypnotized by the sight of my pale face and swollen eyes. I started to jump up so I could go wash my face or find makeup or something, but he tightened his arms around me and kissed me.

Sensation shivered through me, and I pulled Mickey closer, almost trying to climb inside his skin, or at least inside his courage and confidence, so I could be as brave as he was about the challenges we were facing.

"I don't know how to let you go, Victoria. So let's figure out a way that we can be together."

"I think I'd better sit over here, then." I moved to the other side of the couch, far enough away that I couldn't feel the heat of his body against mine and be tempted to do something from which there would be no turning back.

Also, I knew I had to ask the question that had been weighing on me ever since Friday night.

"Was it really Ethan who shot Pete?"

CHAPTER 46
MICKEY

"You didn't see him?" I had to take this carefully, because I wasn't sure what I wanted her to say, and I didn't want to unconsciously influence her.

"I don't know. I saw somebody, but to swear it was Ethan? I can't be sure. It was too dark and rainy, and I was at the wrong angle—your dad's deputies were here on and off all weekend, but I couldn't name a name, because I didn't see his face."

I suddenly realized that Pa had protected me from any interrogation about the shooting, and I wondered, not for the first time, how many rules he broke doing his job and trying to protect Ethan and Jeb—and now me—all at the same time.

"I'm pretty sure it was Ethan," I admitted slowly. "I guess a good defense attorney could crack me in two, considering the weather conditions, but who else could it have been? He saw Pete hit me, and he went ballistic."

"So he does care about you," she said slowly.

"Yeah, in his twisted way. He's always been crazy protective of me and Caro, and even Jeb. *He* might give me or Jeb a black eye, but nobody *else* better so much as lay a finger on us."

"I don't think 'who else could it have been' is going to stand up in court," Victoria pointed out, and I nodded.

She wasn't wrong.

"What if . . . what if we weren't sure at all? Pete is going to be fine. What if we kept Ethan out of it? If we accuse him when we can't prove it, we will have accomplished nothing but turning him and Anna Mae against us even more than they already are," she said.

She had a very good point, but we were talking about obstruction of justice. Also, my gut rebelled at the idea of Ethan getting away with something else, and this time he'd almost killed a man.

"My pa would be pleased as moonshine-spiked punch," I said bitterly.

Victoria shook her head. "Your father has a somewhat . . . *complicated* relationship with the law, doesn't he?"

"You have no idea."

She jumped up and started putting DVDs away and straightening the room, more out of an excess of nervous energy than anything else, probably. I didn't mind, because I was content to watch her move, her hair flying around her delicate face, the long lines of her body, the rounded curves just where curves ought to be. I was getting hot just from watching her, and I had to casually pull a pillow over my lap so as not to shock her.

If I got this turned on just from watching her clean up, I was in trouble if she ever did anything purposely sexy, like dance.

She put a CD in its case and turned to me. "What do you think?"

Shit. She could tell?

She bit her lip. "About Ethan?"

Oh.

"I can barely stomach him getting out of this so easily, but you might be right. Maybe we could use this as our trump card, though," I suggested. "Like, we could say, 'Ethan, we won't rat you out, but you have to promise to end this crap right here and now.'"

"Is that even possible? It seemed to me like Anna Mae was the one holding the reins. Or at least the shotgun." Victoria shivered, and I didn't think it was from the cold.

"She wants money, right? And for everybody to leave her alone so she can live her life of crime. Maybe we can find a way—"

Victoria was shaking her head. "Maybe. Or maybe she wants revenge. A woman scorned and all that. Or both."

"Well, she's going to have to agree to let it go. Ethan is her favorite. If the threat of him going to prison for a really long time is hanging over her evil head, she'll have to go along."

Victoria looked doubtful, but I was on a roll.

"On your side of things, you have to convince your dad to quit being such an—" I started to say "asshole" but reconsidered, in light of how tactful she'd been about Pa. "So *complicated*."

She started laughing, but she didn't look like she found it funny.

"I can try. I can tell him we got Anna Mae off his back, but he has to stop going after Rhodales. I don't know how to face Pete if we do this, though. He's the one who got shot."

"It was his shoulder, not his chest," I reminded her, and got what I deserved when she glared at me.

"Really? Are we in the Wild West now? Getting shot in the shoulder is 'just a bitty thing' and a real man should suck it up?"

I scanned the room, as if the racks of DVDs and CDs or the pinball machine in the corner might hold some answers.

"No, of course not. But I'm kind of out of options here, and the truth is, even if we decided right this minute to never see each other again, our families would both be better off if we found a way to stop the fighting."

"Pete doesn't know who shot him," Victoria said, her face troubled. "The police interviewed him, Gran told me, and he said he didn't see anything; he just heard the shot and then he was down. He's more worried about the horses than he is about catching whoever shot him, I think."

"So we use Ethan's guilt as a bargaining chip, and everybody will be better off," I said slowly.

"You'll have to convince them that you can identify him as the perpetrator, for sure," Victoria said.

"Perpetrator?"

She grinned shyly. "I like police shows on TV."

I pointed at the enormous flat screen. "Should we watch one? Solve somebody else's problems for a while?"

"I'll make popcorn."

The bowl sat untouched, though, while we watched the show's crime scene investigators wrap everything up neatly in the space of forty-three minutes or so. Or, at least, Victoria watched it. I mostly watched her, captivated by the way the strands of her hair caught the light. Enjoying the feel of her body next to mine on the couch, my arm around her shoulders and her head leaning back against my chest. I forced myself to keep from touching her, other than holding her hand, because I didn't want to push anything on her that she wasn't ready for.

During the final ten minutes or so, Victoria kept glancing at me and then down at our clasped hands, and I got the feeling she was trying to work up to something. When she switched off the TV, she took a deep breath and turned to me.

"I'm here alone tonight. Is there any chance you could stay?"

CHAPTER 47
VICTORIA

Mickey's eyes flared hot, and I'd never seen blue eyes burn like that before. I suddenly had a hard time breathing.

"Are you asking me—"

"No! No, I'm not—I can't. Not yet." My cheeks were burning. "I just want you to hold me for a while. Is that asking something unreasonable? I completely understand if it is."

He looked down for a moment, and adjusted the pillow over his lap, and I suddenly understood. For a girl who grew up around horses, I was being pretty stupid. "Never mind, I'm an idiot. What was I thinking—"

"Victoria, I'd love to stay with you for a while. I can sneak in my window when I get home. I've done it before, when I stayed out too late with the guys."

"I'll just . . . I'll give you a minute, and I'll be back." I ran down the hall to my bedroom, my heart pounding in time with my feet. What had I been thinking? Mickey wouldn't want to hold me platonically. He'd been with girls before. He'd think I was stupid. . . .

I stopped and stared at myself in the mirror.

No.

I wasn't an insecure little girl. Mickey wanted to be with me. He'd said he was falling in love with me. He'd risked everything to be with me. He wasn't going to change his mind because I didn't take my clothes off for him.

He wouldn't have been worth my time if he did.

I washed my face and put on a nightgown, then threw it off and changed into old sweatpants and a faded T-shirt, and then I went to get Mickey. He met me in the hallway, as if he'd been afraid that I'd disappear.

"Are you sure you're okay with this?" His voice was as gentle as his touch as he moved a strand of my hair behind my ear. "I can tuck you in and get out of here. Just say the word."

"I want you to hold me," I said, and he smiled.

I took his hand and led him to my room, but I didn't give him much time to look around at the mess before I turned out the light, so only the soft light from the hall illuminated the room.

"Looks kinda girly," he teased.

"You should see Melinda's room, the one that used to be mine. It's all ruffles."

"I'm allergic to ruffles," he said solemnly.

I laughed and climbed onto my bed, on top of the covers, and pulled a thick spare quilt over me. Then I held out my arms and, after hesitating for a few seconds, he sat on the edge of the bed and kicked off his boots, and then lay down on his back next to me.

I curled up next to him, with my head on his shoulder, and shivered a little. I felt daring and delightful and dangerous all at the same time. He curved his arm underneath my shoulders and shifted around a little to get comfortable, and I reached across his hard stomach to take his other hand in mine.

"I've never been in bed with a girl before," he admitted, and I snorted.

"Really? You expect me to believe that?"

"It's true. Backseat of a car, front seat of a truck, in a barn once, but never in a bed."

I stiffened and tried to pull away, but he pulled me closer.

"You knew I wasn't a virgin, Princess. I can't rewrite history just because I finally found you."

"I wish you could." I hated every one of those girls.

He laughed, and his chest rumbled beneath my cheek. "Yeah, well, when you told me you'd kissed boys before, I wanted to track them all down and punch them."

I smiled. "That's more like it. Except for the punching part."

"I'm done with punching. I swear it."

"Are you going back to school tomorrow?"

"I'm going to try. I'd rather be there than at home doing any new horrible chores Pa can come up with."

"Is the garage finally clean?"

"Sparkling. I hope never to see the inside of that building again," he said fervently, and I started laughing.

"You sound like me when Pete first taught me how to muck out stalls. Do you have any idea how much a horse can poop?" I shuddered.

"Just when I think you're a delicate, fragile princess, you say something like that and I get an image of you shoveling out mounds of horse shit," he said.

"Makes you hot, doesn't it?"

When we stopped laughing, the irrepressible tidal wave of an enormous yawn swept me under, and I realized how little sleep I'd actually had since Friday's ordeal.

"This is going to sound unbelievable, but I think I'm going to fall asleep," I whispered, hardly believing it myself. I'd expected to be so awkward and overly excited about having him in my bed, even on top of the covers, that I'd never fall asleep.

Instead, I was already halfway there, surrounded by the safety and comfort of his strong arms.

He groaned. "It is a little bit unbelievable, kind of like how old sweats can be so sexy when you're the one wearing them."

I smiled a private smile and reached up to kiss him softly on the cheek.

"Does the back door lock automatically?"

"Yes."

"Then get some rest, Victoria. I'll let myself out once you're asleep."

He kissed me on the forehead, and then he stared up at the ceiling and started to tell me a long, complicated story about a man who loses the woman he loves, finds a treasure, and is later finally reunited with her again. Slowly, bit by bit, I relaxed and drifted off, content in the sure knowledge that we were going to figure this all out.

It wasn't until I was almost asleep that I realized he'd been telling me the story of *The Count of Monte Cristo*. Lots of people had died in that book. I hoped he wasn't drawing a parallel.

When I woke up in the morning, with the sun streaming into the room like a promise, Mickey was gone, and Gran was yelling my name from downstairs. I swung my feet out of bed and kicked over a pair of boots.

Big boots.

Mickey's boots.

Oh, crap.

CHAPTER 48
MICKEY

"Mickey, wake up!"

Victoria's scent, that unique mix of sunshine and sugar that was all her, surrounded me, and I pulled her close before I ever opened my eyes, knowing it was a dream but wanting to kiss her, anyway.

Dream Victoria had morning breath.

Shit. That meant I had morning breath, too—which meant it was morning, this was not a dream, and I was still at her house, on the couch in her TV room where I must have fallen asleep sometime after I'd sat down with the lame-brained idea of keeping watch for a while.

I sat up fast, and our foreheads knocked together.

She sat back, rubbing her head and wincing. "Just like a fairy tale."

A new voice sounded from the doorway. "So what does that make me? The evil witch or the big bad wolf?"

"Gran!" Victoria fell back on the other side of the couch. "Look! Fully dressed. We were talking, and we just fell asleep. I mean, I fell asleep in my room, and Mickey fell asleep here. Nothing happened, I promise."

I jumped up off the couch and tripped over the coffee table but—just barely—managed not to fall on my ass. "Ma'am. I'm really sorry to be here, but Victoria's telling the truth. We were talking, and she started to fall asleep, and I must have been so tired from cleaning out the garage for four days straight—"

"Enough! You're dressed. I can see this was no den of sin. Meet me in the kitchen in ten minutes for coffee."

I started to sit back down, and she pointed at me. "Not *you*, Sunshine. You get your butt downstairs right this minute."

"Yes, ma'am. I'll—"

"You'll make a pot of coffee, if you know what's good for you, *Mickey Rhodale*," she ordered, and I knew enough to get moving.

The matriarch of the Whitfield clan was a tiny thing, and kind of sweetly grumpy looking in her purple jogging suit, but I had no doubt she employed plenty of people who could kick my ass physically when she was done kicking it verbally, so I'd have to try my best to be charming and throw myself on her mercy.

She glared at me when I walked past her.

Yeah. I was doomed.

By the time the two of them came downstairs ten minutes later, Victoria's grandmother still in her track suit and Victoria in clean clothes and wet hair, holding my boots; I had coffee ready and had set out the cream and sugar. Mrs. Whitfield narrowed her eyes at me, but then nodded.

"So, let's have a little chat," she said.

"How is Melinda?"

She stared at me, but she must have seen that I was sincere, because her shoulders lost a little of their aggressive readiness and relaxed.

"She's ready. She wanted this, and they tell me that's the first step," she said.

"I thought you were staying later," Victoria said, and then she seemed to realize what she'd said, and she winced. "Not that I was plotting anything. I only meant—"

"They told me that they like for the clients to get started on the program without long, drawn-out good-byes, so I hit the road when I woke up. And trust me, I'd know if you were plotting anything, because everything you feel shows up on your face."

I realized it was true; it was why Mom had known I had good reason to hope, and it had been one of the reasons I'd been drawn to Victoria from the first time I'd met her. She didn't have a single artificial or deceptive bone in her body.

"I hate that, you know," Victoria grumbled. "I could never get away with anything, growing up."

"We had enough trouble with Melinda," her grandmother said tartly, pouring herself a cup of black coffee.

Victoria, on the other hand, used three spoonfuls of sugar and half a cup of cream in her coffee. I watched as she prepared this hideous concoction, and then I looked up and met Mrs. Whitfield's eyes and realized we were both grimacing.

"Little coffee with your cream?" I poured my own. Black.

Victoria shrugged and smiled. "Mock me if you like. I'm used to it. I don't like the taste of coffee much on its own."

Mrs. Whitfield cleared her throat and put her cup down. "We'd better talk about this, and then I never want to hear about it again."

"The coffee?" Victoria smiled, but it was shaky. "We can talk about coffee as often as you want to."

"It's entirely my fault," I said. "I was supposed to go home as soon as Victoria fell asleep, but I—"

"No, it's my fault," Victoria broke in, giving me a frantic look. "We were talking, and one thing led to another—no. No! Nothing led to nothing. I mean, just talking things. Not naked things. I mean, oh, *crap*, I'm saying this all wrong."

"I think I get it," Mrs. Whitfield said dryly. "Amazing as it might seem to the two of you, I was a teenager once. However, I might be the only adult Whitfield who *would* understand, or at least the only one who would let Mickey leave without stringing him up."

I wanted to hug the old lady. I settled for grinning at her. "I bet you were a beautiful teenager, just like your granddaughter."

"Shut up now, Mickey," she advised.

"Shutting up now."

Victoria drank some of her coffee, looking from me to her grand-mother, before she finally spoke again. "I don't really understand. I mean, I'm thrilled you're being reasonable, but what you said—about your father-in-law. And you know Mickey is a Rhodale, so . . ."

"You're wondering why I'm not getting the shotgun, like I heard Anna Mae did?"

"Something like that."

Mrs. Whitfield sighed. "I probably would have done it, just last week. But Pete getting shot was a scary wake-up call. We can't con-tinue on like this, and maybe you two will be the ones to help us all get past this insanity."

I almost couldn't believe what I was hearing. All my life, Pa had told me that old lady Whitfield blamed a Rhodale for killing her husband's father. Now she was prepared to accept me in her granddaughter's life?

Or maybe I was pushing it. Not stringing me up was still a far shout from accepting me.

"You have your grandmother's eyes," she said suddenly.

Victoria tilted her head. "You knew Mickey's grandmother?"

"Samantha Rhodale and I were best friends, before the tragedy pulled us apart," Mrs. Whitfield said, her gaze turned inward, probably to a sixty-year-old memory.

Then she turned those sharp blue eyes on me. "Let's all hope the mistakes of the past won't taint the future, but I have to admit I don't think much of the chances."

"Oh, Gran! That's exactly what we were hoping. If you were on our side, it would help."

"I'm on nobody's side but my horses," Mrs. Whitfield said sternly, but she patted Victoria's hand. "All I can do is pray that this thing between you doesn't destroy the whole family."

"Maybe you can explain what your son is doing in his new real estate venture?" I knew I wasn't helping my cause, but I needed to understand what the hell was going on. "Ethan and Anna Mae seem to think he's buying up all the property he can get his hands on in order to bring more horse people and other rich folks in, and drive property taxes up so high it will run ordinary people out of the county."

"I wouldn't put it past him," Victoria said darkly.

"He might be trying, but he doesn't have enough money to buy much right now, not that my son's business dealings are any of your concern, young man," Mrs. Whitfield said.

I started to back down, but I couldn't leave it like that. "They're my business if it's starting the feud sh—, uh, *stuff*, all over again, ma'am."

"I promise to keep an eye on it. I won't discuss it any further, but I won't let this leftover anger from the past destroy our family."

I started to answer her, but she shut me up with a look.

"Either of our families, young man. I hope it doesn't destroy *either* of our families."

CHAPTER 49

VICTORIA

When we went out to the truck, Gus and a few of the ranch hands were out in front of the barn, and I practically felt the virtual scarlet *A* painted on my chest blaze so fiercely that it was a wonder it didn't set the entire ranch on fire. On her very first night alone, the perfect Whitfield princess had invited a boy to sleep over. They must all think I was a slut.

I glanced over at them again but, other than Gus lifting a hand in a wave, none of them seemed to be paying any attention to me at all. This was small-town Kentucky, though—we'd probably be the talk of the Dairy Queen by lunch and the VFW lodge by nightfall.

I suddenly realized that it really didn't matter if everybody gossiped, because those people had nothing to do with my life. Sure, they'd talk about me for a while, but then they'd move on to someone more interesting. I was behaving as if I were Melinda when her addiction had her by the throat, believing that the universe revolved around me, when in fact I was only hanging on to the spinning earth by my fingertips like everybody else.

Perhaps humiliation bred clarity. I'd certainly never forget looking up and seeing Gran standing in that doorway.

On my way to school I dropped Mickey off where he'd left his bike.

"Are your parents going to be really angry?"

"They probably don't know I was gone. They leave for work before I get up, so they usually don't come in my room." He flashed a smile. "I'm seventeen, not seven, in spite of the way your grandmother made me feel."

"I'm so sorry."

"I'm the one who fell asleep." He leaned across the seat and kissed me. "You're beautiful when you sleep, by the way."

I blushed. "So are you."

"Guys aren't beautiful. We're . . . rugged or something."

"Well, you're especially rugged when you sleep, then."

He grinned and opened the door, but then looked back at me. "We will figure this out. I promise. I'll call Ethan this morning, and if he's still not answering his phone, I'll call Anna Mae."

"Phase one?" The whole plan sounded idiotic and futile in the cold light of day, but it was the only plan we had.

"Phase one."

I spent the entire drive to school worrying myself sick.

CHAPTER 50
MICKEY

It took me until Friday to reach Ethan. Neither he nor Jeb would answer their phones. I didn't have Anna Mae's number, and when I drove out to the compound, the guards at the gate turned me away.

Finally, Friday morning when I was getting ready for school, my phone rang. It was Ethan.

"Where the hell have you been?"

"Seemed like a good time for me to get out of town, little brother. Why? Do you miss me?"

"Yeah, right. I only want to talk to you long enough to offer you a deal. You leave the Whitfields alone, and Victoria and I won't tell anybody that it was you who shot their foreman."

Silence, and then mocking laughter.

"Why, Mickey Rhodale, are you recording this phone call? Trying to trap me into confessing something I did not do?"

"Of course not," I said, surprised. "This is a legitimate offer. If you want to meet in person, we can do that, too."

His voice turned low and deadly. "Shut up. The only offer between us is the one I'm getting ready to make to *you*. Meet me at the old Henderson place in half an hour."

"I have school—"

"Suit yourself, baby brother. This is a one-time-only offer."

He hung up. I headed for the Henderson place.

When old man Henderson had died, neither of his two sons had wanted to come back to Kentucky for long enough to make anything of the small farm they'd grown up on. Instead they spent a lot of time fighting over the provisions of their father's will. Or so I'd heard. I'd also heard the place was haunted and the old man stalked around with his ghostly hunting rifle every night at midnight, looking for "varmints"—animal or human, he didn't care which.

Mostly, though, it was just an old, falling-down wreck of a place.

It looked like nobody had set foot on the property in years when I drove up. Weeds had aggressively devoured the front lawn. Shingles were missing from the roof, and one of the porch support beams had collapsed, causing the porch roof to droop drunkenly over the front door. I parked the bike, ready to wait for my brother, but a darker shadow separated itself from the doorway, and Ethan stepped out on the porch.

"You came alone?"

I waved a hand at all the nothing surrounding me. "As you see. You weren't afraid that the house would come crashing down on your head?"

He threw back his head and laughed. "Like I don't have worse things to worry about."

Ethan looked rougher than I'd ever seen him. He hadn't shaved in days, and his face looked thinner. Almost haunted.

"How is he? The man I—the man who got shot?"

"What? Your spies aren't keeping you in the loop?"

Ethan stepped down off the porch and then leaned back against the railing. "They are, but I figured you get better intel. From your *girlfriend*."

"She's not my girlfriend, and even if she had been, you would have put paid to that," I fired back. "You need to leave her family alone."

"Or what?" he said tiredly. "You forgot the melodramatic 'or else' at the end of that sentence, bro."

Time to play our trump card and see what hand it captured. "Or else we'll both tell Pa that you were the one who shot Pete."

He smiled sardonically. "Oh, so now it's 'we.' You just got done telling me she's not your girlfriend."

"She's not, but she wants to see this feud ended as much as I do, and this is our price."

He studied my face for a long moment, making me glad I had more of a poker face than Victoria did. Finally, he shrugged. "If you want me to stay away from your girlfriend and her family, you can come join the family cupcake business. Otherwise, we'll have cupcakes for all your friends."

"What the hell are you talking about? What cupcakes?"

He laughed again. "You've always been the straight-laced one of the bunch, haven't you?"

"Listen, Ethan—"

"No, you listen, shit-for-brains. Anna Mae is planning to send a message to *Dick* Whitfield. The only way I can put her off is if you agree to work for me. Otherwise, you can tell your pretty little girl-friend that we hope she isn't all that fond of her horses."

"If you think for one minute—"

"I don't think," he said bitterly. "Didn't you hear my loving mother say just that at our place? That she was the only brains in the place? Well, here's one that you'll enjoy. If I don't go along with it, she'll use Jeb, and the last time she tried that, she nearly got him killed and I ended up in jail. How long do you think he'd survive Anna Mae's tender loving care if she puts him in charge? Especially now that she's climbing into bed, so to speak, with the skinheads?"

I thought about that. Ethan, in his own peculiarly twisted way, was trying to protect Jeb. Yeah, it fit. He'd always done the same for me and Caro, and now her girls.

I figured I'd come right out and ask him. "Were you trying to protect me when you shot Pete?"

"He *hit* you. He knocked you down and then he pulled that knife, and I thought he was going to stab you," Ethan snarled. "Nobody hurts my brother."

Before I could say anything, he closed his eyes and inhaled deeply.

"Not that I was there to see it," he finally said, opening his eyes and staring at me. "If that's what happened, then somebody would have been right to shoot, wouldn't he?"

I didn't know how to answer that. I didn't know how to even try.

"We can't keep going like this, with the feud and the drugs and the guns," I finally said. "Somebody is going to die, and I'm afraid that would only be the beginning of all hell breaking loose."

"It's too late," he said. "Pick a side, baby brother. And choose it now, before one gets chosen for you."

We stood there, just staring at each other. I knew that Ethan and Anna Mae had to be stopped. I just wished I knew someone with the power and the balls to do it. Since Pa never would step up, and nobody else was volunteering, I guessed it was up to me.

"You win. I'll come work for you. If you stay away from Victoria and her family."

"I'm not sure if I can get Anna Mae to go along with that," he said.

"You tell her that either she agrees, or you're going to jail for attempted murder."

I expected him to yell at me or hit me, but he just nodded. "Done."

Great. Now I just needed a plan.

"Good timing, too," Ethan said tersely, putting his sunglasses on and staring down the road.

The roar of what sounded like a hundred approaching motorcycles, and the cloud of dust that accompanied them as they tore up the dirt road toward us, ate up the world.

Ethan moved closer to me. "My new *partner* wants to meet you. Remember that you're on my side, all right? These guys do not play around."

I stared at the massive, heavily tattooed men—not one hundred, maybe, but at least fifty of them—who were parking their Harleys, calling out to each other, and coldly assessing us.

"I'm sure as hell not on their side," I muttered. I moved slightly so I was side by side with my brother, two Rhodales facing maybe fifty members of what looked like the devil's own biker gang.

I wasn't a fan of the odds.

The biggest man there stepped off his bike and looked around, and then he nodded to a smaller, wiry kind of guy I hadn't really even noticed. The smaller guy pulled a bandanna off his head to reveal the

word BARON tattooed on his bald skull. He also had teardrop tats raining down his left cheekbone, down his neck, and disappearing into the
black T-shirt he wore underneath his leather jacket.

"I thought those signified people a banger has killed?" I said
softly, so only Ethan could hear me.

"It does. Now keep your mouth shut."

Ice dripped down my spine. I was actually afraid for my life—and
for my brother's.

"So, now there are two pretty boys to work with us," the man with
the skull tattoo called out. "How did we get so lucky, eh?"

His people, lined up behind him and straddling their bikes,
cheered and hooted. A few whistled at us. Wolf whistles. Seemed
appropriate, considering I was feeling a lot like a sacrificial lamb at the
moment.

"You have a deal in mind, Baron, or are you going to spend all
day flirting with me?" Ethan drawled, sounding for all the world like
he was bored.

I glanced at him out of the corner of my eye and realized he looked
bored, too. Damn, my brother was either a seriously talented actor or
he really did have iced moonshine running through his veins.

Baron slapped his leg with his bandanna and laughed heartily,
but his amusement didn't spread to his eyes, which were cold and
dead. Nobody was home behind those eyes—nobody with a shred of
humanity. This man would kill us as easily as I'd cleared out spider
webs in the garage.

"This must be your brother," Baron said. "Is he in on the plan?"

"He's my right-hand man," Ethan said, not giving away by so
much as an eyelid twitch that he was anything but calm.

"Right-hand man," Baron said, walking up to us, his dead gaze fixed on me. "We use our right hands to jerk off with, my friend. Is this boy going to jerk us off?"

"I back my brother," I said, looking Baron in the eye. Instinctively I knew this man would pounce on any show of weakness. "How you jerk off is up to you."

Baron laughed again, but this time there seemed to be at least a glimmer of real amusement in it. "Feisty son of a bitch, aren't you?"

"Leave my mother out of this."

"I met your mother, punk. She's a world-class bitch," he said.

Ethan shook his head. "You met *my* mother. Mick has a different mother."

Baron's gaze shifted back and forth between the two of us. "Doesn't seem possible that you don't share all the same DNA. You look too much alike."

"The Rhodale genes," Ethan said lightly. "They always throw true. Now, can we move on from this fascinating discussion of genetics and get to the specifics? When we met in jail, you mentioned that you'd like to team up on distribution."

Baron pointed to the edge of the warped and rotting front porch. "We might as well get comfortable. This chat might take a while. We've got the FBI on our ass, so we're going to be operating with a little bit of heat chasing us for a while."

When Baron walked past me, I could finally see the back of his jacket. The words RED BARONS blazed across the top in a semicircle, and a vividly red WWI fighter plane flew across the center.

"Von Richthofen," I said, pulling up the memory of lazy afternoons spent in front of the History Channel with Pa when I was a kid.

Baron swung around and looked at me with some interest. "You know your history."

"Top flying ace of World War I, some say of all time," I said automatically, and then it hit me that I was discussing world history with a meth-dealing gangbanger.

"He scored the most kills in the war," Baron said proudly, as if describing his own accomplishments.

"Yeah, but he was at *war*," I said slowly. "Flying in air battles."

"We're always at war," Baron said. "History is written by the victors. I don't plan to have anybody else write my history."

He tried to stare me down, but I'd be damned if I'd drop my eyes first.

Ethan laughed, breaking the intensity of the moment.

"German flying ace?" Ethan asked. "Famed adversary to Snoopy in *Peanuts* cartoons? I always wanted a flying doghouse when I was a kid."

Baron aimed one long, last icy stare at me. "It's good to have balls, kid. Be careful nobody cuts them off for you."

Then he and Ethan sat down and started discussing specifics of their plan to take over all drug distribution in Kentucky, or on the planet for all I knew. I stood at attention, as if there was a damn thing I could do if fifty skinhead bikers decided to pull out their guns and start shooting. The bear of a man who was clearly Baron's second-in-command gave me a flat stare over the top of his shades, but other than that he ignored me.

Which was fine with me. I wasn't sure what I'd have to say to him. "Hey, killed anybody lately?" seemed a little presumptuous.

When they finished talking details, they shook hands, and I figured it had gone okay.

"We'll be calling. Weekly meetings at first, and then we'll see how it goes," Baron said.

Ethan nodded. "I'll be in touch."

"I know you will," Baron said. He walked over to his bike, mounted it, and then smiled at us. His teeth, oddly enough, were perfectly straight and Hollywood white. It was a weird detail to notice, but it ran so counter to my expectations that it stood out.

"Bear here will be paying a visit to your sister—Caroline, isn't it?—and those two cute little ones if you fuck this up. So don't fuck this up."

A wave of red washed over my vision and I started for him. Ethan's hand shot out to grab my arm in a steel vise grip.

"Feisty," Baron said, and then he laughed. He waved an arm and the thunder of all those bikes filled the air again, and then they were gone in a cloud of dust.

Ethan dropped my arm and I rounded on him.

"You son of a bitch."

"Mickey—"

I punched him in the face as hard as I could. He staggered back and then came up swinging, but he stopped before his fist connected with my head even though I'd done nothing to deflect the punch. I was too busy seeing the disappointment on Victoria's face—and maybe the fear—if she knew that I was breaking my word to her so soon.

But I doubted any of the anger management classes in the world had a section on dealing with your brother's meth operation in a violence-free way. I was screwed.

"Why kill each other when we have them handy to do it for us?" His shoulders slumped, and he shook his head. "Anna Mae got us into this, and I'm trying to get us out, but we have to go along to get along for a little while."

"Ethan, he threatened *Caroline* and the *girls*," I said hotly. "What the hell are you planning to do about that?"

"I'm putting guards on them, twenty-four seven. We'll figure this out, baby brother. We'll figure it out, but I'm going to need your help. Two Rhodale brains are better than one, especially when one of them is yours."

The bleakness in his voice convinced me where no amount of bluster would have. Ethan was trapped in a situation that was out of his control, and now I was in it with him.

"We'll figure it out," I said slowly, echoing him.

A trace of relief crossed his face. "Thank you."

"Don't thank me yet. I still might kill you when this is over."

CHAPTER 51
VICTORIA

"So what do you think?"

I looked at Denise. "Um, about what?"

She sighed. "Have you heard anything I've said in the past five minutes?"

I thought back and glanced down at her untouched tray. "You hate fish Friday at the cafeteria?"

I was living a double life and not doing a very good job of it. Part of me had spent the week going through the motions of being a student, but most of me had been dreaming of Mickey and a life free of dangerous plots.

"The movies, Victoria," Denise said with exaggerated patience. "Do you want to go see a movie tonight with me and Derek?"

I perked up. "He finally asked you out?"

She grinned and glanced over at where he was sitting with the school paper staff by the vending machines. "Yeah. Apparently he grew a pair. So we're going to a movie tonight. Wanna come?"

I rolled my eyes. "The poor guy finally gets brave enough to ask you out, and you're inviting me along? Don't you see a problem with this?"

"Not really. If I get him alone so soon, he'll get all tongue-tied and nervous, and we'll have a crappy time. Or he'll get all handsy, just to prove to himself that he's *not* nervous, and we'll have a crappy time. If we ease into the situation slowly, we might have fun."

I was impressed. I wasn't really sure how to handle a relationship with one guy, and Denise always seemed to be juggling two or three, and doing it with a strategic flair that would have impressed an army general.

I made sure nobody was within hearing distance. "Is it okay if I bring Mickey?"

"Sure, as long as we don't let him sit near Derek, or they'll talk to each other all night."

Denise picked me up, and we met the guys at the theater in the next town over, where Mickey was parking an actual car. It looked old, and it was ugly, but I hadn't even known he had a car.

We made a game out of pretending we'd all met by accident and then Mickey walked away from us, but I doubt we fooled any of Ethan's spies who might be watching. Now that I was living in Paranoid City, I expected all the other residents to be actively out to get me.

As soon as the lights dimmed, Mickey made his way to the seat next to me and took my hand, and he didn't let go of it for the next hour and a half. His thumb kept stroking my hand, and just the feel of his body so close to mine sent shivers through me. I sank into a lust-fueled and popcorn-scented haze that made me jittery and nervous and excited all at once. I wanted to be alone with him so I could touch his hair, so I could kiss him. I had no idea at all what drama was playing out on the screen, because I was too focused on our own.

He apparently felt the same way. "Is this movie ever going to end?" he whispered.

"Let's bail," I said, feeling daring. Plus, if we snuck out now, while the lights were still down, we were just another faceless couple stealing time to be alone, instead of a Rhodale and a Whitfield who dared to be seen in public together.

I whispered our plans to Denise, and I noticed she was also holding Derek's hand. She nodded, but looked worried.

"Be careful," she whispered, but I didn't even know what that word meant anymore.

"Happy birthday," Derek said as I turned to go. I grimaced, and he grinned at me. "The office gives me all the birthdays to print in the school paper."

I groaned. I hated my birthday and always tried to avoid letting anyone know.

We barely made it into the car before I was in Mickey's arms, kissing him frantically, rediscovering the shape of his mouth and the feel of his lips. He pulled back, breathing hard, and jammed the key in the ignition.

"Let's drive somewhere," he said roughly.

I fastened my seat belt and nodded, afraid to say anything and break the moment.

We were at least five miles down the road before he spoke again. "Happy birthday? Why didn't you tell me?"

"I never tell anybody."

"I'm not just anybody, I hope, or I want to find all those other guys whose tongues have been in your mouth lately and have a little chat with them."

I think he meant it as a joke, but it came out just a little too rough for me to think he really thought it was funny.

I laughed anyway. "No other guys. Just you."

"Good. Now, about your birthday?"

He took the turn to head out of town, and I realized he was heading to Lonesome Ridge.

"It's a yardstick," I explained reluctantly.

"What?"

I sighed. "A yardstick. Every year, my parents take the opportunity of my birthday to tell me how I'm not measuring up. I got a B. I don't dress properly. I have bad penmanship. For the past few years, they've called me at boarding school to have the yardstick talk. Before that, we'd have it before they allowed me to have any cake."

There was a little silence, but I caught him glancing over at me.

"That's seriously fucked up," he finally said.

"I know. That's why I'm happy not to remind anybody that it's my birthday."

"Your parents kind of know when your birthday is," he pointed out.

I shrugged. "Once in a while, if I'm very lucky, they forget."

He held out his hand for mine and then squeezed my fingers in a tactile and unspoken display of support.

"My mom once made me a dinosaur cake. Actually, two of them," he said. "We had half the neighborhood over for a barbecue and cake and ice cream. I was crazy about those dinosaurs, and I cried when we had to cut into them."

"How old were you?"

He grinned a little. "Oh, this was last year."

I groaned and laughed all at once.

"I was four, I think. No, three, because I remember the spots on the dinosaurs' backs were each in the shape of the number three."

"Your mom sounds wonderful," I said wistfully. "My mother never made a cake in her life. She buys them from the bakery and asks for the sugar substitute frosting."

"That's pretty terrible."

I nodded. "Honestly? It tastes like paste. But she's more worried about the calories than about the flavor."

"So let her get the sugar-free crap on her own birthday!"

I loved that he sounded so outraged on my behalf. Maybe this would finally be a birthday that I wanted to remember.

CHAPTER 52

MICKEY

Victoria was out the door almost before I'd turned off the car, but I sat there for a minute watching her. She was so beautiful in the moonlight. She shone, almost lit up from within, and her hair gleamed in a pale waterfall around her shoulders.

I wanted her so bad it hurt.

She glanced back at me, serious now, and I climbed out of the car, as helpless to stop myself as a drunk following the smell of moonshine, or as almost any Rhodale man in history chasing the lure of a life of crime. We knew it was wrong, but we justified it to ourselves.

I looked at Victoria shining in the darkness and didn't have to justify anything. Being with her could never be wrong.

"Happy birthday." I leaned back on the hood of the car, content to wait for her to come to me.

"I'm seventeen," she said, and I nodded.

"I figured."

"I'll be eighteen in a year."

"That's usually how it works."

"When I'm eighteen, I can leave town," she said, and my brain finally kicked on.

"You want to leave? Where would you go without a high school degree and with no money?" My voice sounded harsh, but the thought of her leaving me made me a little crazy.

"We could both leave," she said quietly. "If the feud shows no sign of stopping. Gran would help us out with money, and we could finish school somewhere else. What chance do we have here? We can get out, or we can end up dead. Neither is a good choice, but I know which I'd prefer."

The idea suddenly appealed to me more than anything I'd ever heard. Get out. Go someplace where being a Rhodale or Whitfield wasn't any more or less desirable or newsworthy than being a Smith or Jones. I'd always thought college would offer that escape for me, but maybe this was it instead.

"We could take off down the highway in the old farm truck. I have some money saved up," she said almost wistfully. "We could be free. We could support ourselves, and live our lives away from all this violence and hatred."

"The wind in your hair, looking for adventure," I said, almost smiling. I tugged on a strand of her hair. "The American dream of hitting the open road with the most beautiful girl in the world sitting next to me in an old, rusty farm truck."

For a moment, I could almost picture it. The image was so strong that I leaned into it, wrapped myself in its deceptive promise.

Then reality intruded, knocking me back down to earth.

"But we can't. I told Ethan I'd work for him if he'd leave you and your family alone."

Victoria gasped. "You can't do that. You'll go to jail. Your entire future—down the toilet with a huge flushing noise. No. Absolutely not. I won't let you."

"It's bigger than me and my future now, Victoria. There's a new player involved, and he's dangerous. He threatened Caro and her kids if we don't cooperate. I'm sorry, but you can't stop me on this." I wasn't defiant or loud; I was matter-of-fact. I'd do what I had to do to protect Victoria from my half brother and his crazy mother, and now it was even more crucial, since Baron had made an overt threat against my sister and the girls.

And if Baron found out about Victoria . . . Ice closed over my mind, and I almost stopped breathing.

"Well I can at least stop you from thinking about it," she said, and she stepped closer. "At least for tonight."

She started to unbutton her shirt.

CHAPTER 53
VICTORIA

I was trembling like a racehorse caught in a thunderstorm, but I felt braver than I'd ever been before. It was my birthday, and—just this once—I wanted something all for me. No sugar substitute, no educational toys when all my friends got Little Miss Sparkle Doll.

I wanted Mickey. And if I could help him focus on something—*anything*—but the horrible dilemma he was facing with his brother's criminal empire, then that was all for the better. But mostly, this was about me. Just for once, I wanted this moment to be about me, about *us*, and for the rest of the world to disappear.

He put his hands on me to stop me from unbuttoning any further.

"Are you sure? I don't want this unless it's because you want me, not over some screwed-up idea about giving me your body to keep me from helping Ethan." His voice was hoarse, and he was staring at me like I was a threat to his composure or his sanity.

I knew he wanted me, and the knowledge gave me a feeling of confidence like I'd never known before.

"Forget him. All of them. I want tonight to be only about you and me," I whispered, and he nodded, and then he was kissing me.

It was an unseasonably warm evening, but the winds up on the ridge were cool, and I was shaking with nerves, reaction, and cold. He pulled his jacket off and draped it around me, on top of my sweater, and I started laughing even though my teeth were chattering.

"After how you started off our first date, I would have thought you'd be more eager to get me undressed, instead of covering me up."

He grinned.

"Trust me to do everything backward. Believe me, though, I have never wanted anything more in my life than to get you undressed," he said so sincerely that I blushed. "I just want to be absolutely, one thousand percent sure that this is what you want, too."

"Mickey, shut up and kiss me."

He did.

When he kissed me, it was like poetry exploding inside my head. Everything else vanished—the feud, our families, our problems— and my world kaleidoscoped down into a swirl of color and sensation. Mickey never stopped touching me, stroking my back and sides and hair, and I touched him, too, daring to explore the hard planes of his chest through his shirt and then reaching up to put my hands in his hair and combing the silky mass with my fingers.

He shuddered, his body shaking, hard, and I was glad it wasn't just me reacting like that. No matter what experience he'd had before, this was now, and we were here together, and it was more than everything I'd ever wanted.

So much more.

I wanted to give myself to him—I wanted him to give himself to me. For us to explore this emotion between us and to be part of each other, to forget the world, even for just a little while.

"Mickey," I whispered, and he pulled me even closer.

"Yes," he said. "Oh, please, yes."

CHAPTER 54

MICKEY

Suddenly, with Victoria, something that had been fast and furious and all about hormones transformed completely. I wanted to linger, savor, enjoy. I wanted to make sure that she felt every moment and never forgot any of it. I found a couple of emergency blankets in the trunk, neatly folded in the small plastic bin that held roadside flares from Pa and bottled water and power bars from Mom. The tangible proof of how much they cared about me brought me up short, and I pulled Victoria closer and held her so tightly she probably couldn't breathe.

I couldn't imagine what it must have been like to grow up with parents who used her birthday as a *yardstick*. I'd been so wrong with my stupid stereotypes and preconceived notions about the happy, rich Whitfields.

"Stop," she said, her voice husky. "Whatever you're thinking about, it's making you sad, so you have to stop. Kiss me again."

"Yes."

I kissed her and somehow managed to unroll the blankets without ever letting her go. I kissed her and tried to pour every ounce of my feelings for her into my lips and hands, because I knew I'd never find the words. She touched me with shaking fingers, and I touched her. I caressed her silken skin with kisses and suddenly, wildly, wondered if I'd hit my head harder than I thought when I flew off that three-wheeler and this was all a concussion-induced fever dream.

Victoria shivered, and that was too real to be a dream. I covered her body with mine, and looked down into eyes that were so like liquid starlight.

"Please," she whispered.

I found the condom that had been riding around in my wallet for a while and fumbled it on with hands that weren't very steady, and then I kissed her again.

"I don't want to hurt you."

"Then don't," she said, and I knew she wasn't talking about now, or physically, because my heart was afraid of the same thing. I did my best to convince her with kisses instead of words that I'd die before I'd hurt her, until one of us or both of us were gasping to take a breath that wasn't intermingled with the other's.

She pulled me to her, and I tried my best to be slow and gentle, and for a little while the world started spinning backward, and then the stars collided above us as she said my name, over and over, and I said hers. When we were done, she curled closer to me, and I wrapped my arms and legs around her, protecting her from the wind and the future.

"I thought I'd feel different," she whispered.

"Do you?" I knew I did. Something indefinable in my life had changed, maybe for all time.

"I do, but not how I expected. I feel . . . so close to you, like you've climbed inside my heart."

"You climbed inside mine a long time ago, Victoria. I love you."

She hid her face against my chest. "I can't say it right now—the emotion is too huge. I can't—"

"It's okay. I understand." I wasn't sure if I did, but I instinctively knew that I didn't have to understand everything about this moment. It was enough to be part of it.

We got dressed and went to sit in the car and out of the wind, still holding hands, content to look out at the view.

Eventually, she looked at her phone. "It's nearly midnight, Mickey. I need to get home. I can't cause Gran to worry."

I nodded and then kissed her again, giving her the goodbye kiss I'd never feel comfortable giving her in her driveway.

We headed back down the hill forever changed, forever marked by what we'd shared.

"Maybe we should rename it," she said.

"Rename what?"

"The ridge. It doesn't feel lonesome anymore."

We spent the drive to her place trying out sillier and sillier names while we held hands against the cold reality waiting for us, but when I drove up her driveway, Victoria turned serious.

"Everyone will be back tomorrow. My parents, Buddy—everyone but Pete and Melinda. Her rehab will be at least ninety days, total."

I understood what she was saying. "Things will be different."

"Everything will be different."

I rounded the gentle curve in her driveway and had to slam on the brakes to avoid hitting the truck some idiot had parked in the middle of the road.

"What the hell?"

"Mickey, look!" She pointed, and I saw shadows darting around the corner of the barn.

My stomach dropped into my boots. If this was Ethan causing problems for the Whitfields, I was going to hurt him for real this time. He'd promised me he'd take care of this, and like a fool I'd believed him.

I slammed the car in park and opened the door.

"Mickey, no! We need to call 911!"

"Stay here. I mean it this time, okay? We don't know who that is or how dangerous they are."

"Which is why you shouldn't go over there, either," she said, clutching at my arm.

But I didn't have a choice. If this was about Anna Mae "sending a message," the authorities would never get here in time. I couldn't sit by and let my family cause Victoria more heartache, especially not if they were going to hurt her beloved horses. Not ever, but especially not tonight of all nights.

"Stay here," I repeated. "Lock the door after me."

I headed toward the barn running.

I ran into the dark barn and almost tripped over the unconscious man in the aisle between the horse stalls. That was my first clue that something was really wrong. He didn't seem to be bleeding, and when I checked, he was still breathing, so they must have just knocked him out. Up close, he looked familiar. He'd been in on the search. His name was Gus, maybe?

I reached for my phone, but decided against it. Victoria was calling 911; I was better off focusing on the situation at hand.

"What the hell are *you* doing here?" It was Jeb's voice, but all I could see was his shadow.

He moved into the aisle from one of the stalls, and he was holding a gun, but at least it was pointed down and not up at me. I realized I'd left Jeb's other gun in the car, because I'd never even thought about the fact that I had it. Some criminal mastermind. And I'd thought I'd beat *Ethan* at his own game? I wasn't even smarter than Jeb.

"I could ask you the same question." My eyes were adjusting to the dark. I watched as probably a half-dozen thugs moved around, tying lead ropes on horses. Oh, no. They were stealing Victoria's horses. She was going to lose her mind. "Ethan gave me his word."

"Ethan isn't here, and he doesn't know about this. Anyway, he doesn't get to make choices like that, and his word isn't worth much when it goes up against what Anna Mae wants," he said, and though I could barely see his face, I could hear the sullenness in his voice. "She wanted to set fire to the barn. I convinced her we'd take a couple of horses instead."

"So his word is worthless, and you're just the flunky."

Jeb laughed bitterly. "You're just figuring that out?"

I wanted to shake some sense into his thick skull. "You can't keep dancing to their fiddles, Jeb. They're going to get you killed."

"Yeah, maybe. But I'm all out of options. Now get the hell out of my way."

CHAPTER 55
VICTORIA

I called 911 and stammered out the details they asked for, but I couldn't stay on the line. I had to go after Mickey. He'd been gone too long. If the intruders weren't his brothers and their thugs, then he was in big trouble. Of course, if it *was* Ethan and Jeb, he might be in bigger trouble.

This damn feud. Would Ethan mess with our horses out of Rhodale-Whitfield spite? Even after Mickey had agreed to work with him? Maybe he wouldn't. Maybe this was a random coincidence.

Except I'd never believed in random coincidences.

I looked around for something to use to defend myself, but there were no handy baseball bats in the backseat. I reached under the seat, almost on a whim, and my hand felt cold, hard metal. Jeb's pistol. Mickey still had it.

I yanked my hand away. I didn't want to escalate whatever was going on in there, but what if Mickey was in danger? What if Angel might be harmed?

I took the gun.

Pete had taught me the basics the summer I was fourteen, so I checked that it was loaded and clicked the safety off. Then I put my phone on the seat and took off toward the barn.

Our security system should have been going off by now. Sure, this was the older of the barns and none of the current crop of yearlings or pregnant mares were in it, but several of the older horses were stabled there along with tens of thousands of dollars' worth of equipment and tack. Not a lot of it was easily portable, so I was surprised thieves would be interested. . . .

Unless they weren't intent on stealing but vandalism.

Heather's Angel. Pete had moved her into this, the quieter of the barns, for a while so she could recuperate in peace from her ordeal with Buddy.

I started to run across the slick, wet bluegrass toward the barn, praying I wasn't too late.

CHAPTER 56

MICKEY

I didn't move. "How do you think you're going to get horses out of here? In the backseat of your truck?"

"Smart-ass. We have a horse trailer that should be here by now," Jeb said.

"This is way over the line, Jeb. I'm going to stop you."

"You and who else? I've got five good men with me. Oh, and Cooter," he said, snickering.

"Hey! I heard that," a moose of a man called out. The horse he was trying to lead balked at the sound of his loud, drunken voice.

"Stupid damn horse," he snarled, and he pulled out his gun—and shot it in the side. The world itself seemed to freeze, and everyone held their breath for a few seconds that lasted an eternity. Then I heard a sound I never, ever want to hear again in my life, when the horse started to scream. She staggered drunkenly to the side for a step, and then another, and then she fell over, thrashing her legs.

Her unrelenting screams shattered the silence in the barn and everyone jumped into frantic motion at once. Men ran out of horse stalls and toward the door, and my brother swore a blue streak beside me.

"No," I shouted. "No, no, *no!* Are you insane?"

I started for the horse but then stopped. She was thrashing around in pain, and I realized helplessly that I didn't have the first clue of how to help her. She twisted her long neck, almost as if she wanted to see me, and there was something so familiar about her—oh, please, God, no.

It was Victoria's horse. Angel.

Jeb turned on Cooter. "What the hell did you do that for?" he shouted.

"It wouldn't listen to me," the man said sullenly.

"We've got to get help," I said, turning to run for a phone, but behind me, the barn door crashed open, and it was too late. Victoria ran in, waving Jeb's gun around. I put out a hand to try to stop her before she could see, but it was useless.

She flinched away from me when she saw the fallen horse and then she screamed too—loud, long, and nearly as high-pitched as the horse's scream had been—and shoved me out of her way, dropping something that I realized was Jeb's gun as she ran by me. She clenched her hand into a fist and slammed it against the wall. It wasn't until the alarm started to shriek, piercing the night with its strident warning, that I realized she'd activated a security panel.

"No! Not Angel! No, no, no, no!" Victoria ran to her horse, either oblivious to the guns or not giving a damn. She hurled herself down to the floor next to Angel and started stroking her neck over and over, and then she threw an anguished look over her shoulder at me.

"How could you let them do this?"

"Victoria, I didn't—I tried—I'm so sorry." I took a step toward her, but Jeb grabbed my arm and yanked me back.

Victoria, tears streaming down her face, turned back to Angel. "My baby. My poor baby. It's going to be okay."

But I stared down at her golden head in despair. I knew there was no way it could be.

"I'll get help. I promise. She's going to be okay," I told her anyway, yanking my arm out of Jeb's grip and fumbling in my pocket for my phone.

"I don't think so," Jeb said, and he picked up the gun Victoria had dropped.

CHAPTER 57
VICTORIA

They shot my horse.

They *shot* my *horse*.

The world started to slide sideways. I threw myself on Angel's neck to keep her from struggling to stand up. The alarms were distressing the other horses, but it couldn't be helped. Right now we needed the entire cavalry or the Coast Guard or something big and powerful and deadly. Somebody who could get these monsters out of my barn, help Angel, and stop this nightmare.

"It's going to be okay, baby," I said, using my calmest, most soothing voice. "You're going to be okay. Mickey and I will get help, and we'll get you fixed up. Dr. Arnold will make you as good as new, and I'll bring you sugar cubes and apples, and all the things you like."

A hitch in my breath stopped me for a second, but then I kept at it, still soothing. "All the things. Everything's going to be okay."

But when I turned around, I saw one of the shadowy figures hit Mickey in the back of the head with something, probably a gun, and then a couple of the thugs picked him up and ran out of the barn. Another of them pointed his gun at me.

"I'll be watching you. Stay right here for ten minutes, or I'll shoot your pretty boy for you," he snarled. I had no choice but to stay where I was, putting pressure on Angel's wound and screaming for help while the thug disappeared out the barn door.

Moments later, staff from the racing barn ran in and flipped on the lights. That's when I saw that Gus was down, possibly dead.

"Help him," I shouted. "And get me pressure bandaging for Angel until Dr. Arnold gets here."

One of the grooms flipped open his phone; I knew they all had our vet on speed dial.

The petite woman trainer—Rachel? I should know all their names, but so many were new—knelt down next to Gus and felt for a pulse and then looked up at me and smiled with no little relief. "Looks like he just got knocked out. Hopefully there's no concussion."

The sirens, Gran, and more of our staff from the racing barn all arrived at about the same time, and they headed for Gus. Seconds later, the alarm stopped sounding, and Gran and the grooms spread out to calm the frantic horses.

Suddenly Dr. Arnold was there, wearing scrubs and a very tired face. She ran up to us carrying her vet bag and eased me back and away from Angel. The faintly spicy aroma of the vet's shampoo—her hair was wet, and there was still a trace of soap behind her ear; she must have been in the shower when we called—contrasted with the sharp, rusty smell of Angel's blood.

Dr. Arnold examined my beloved horse, but it only took a few seconds before she shook her head. When she looked up at me, her eyes were kind, but brimming with sadness.

"There's nothing I can do, Victoria, I'm so sorry. She only has a few moments left."

I wanted to shriek and fight and howl out my rage, but the truth beat against my brain like a summer downpour hitting the barn roof: screaming and fighting wouldn't help Angel. It would only scare her more and make her last few moments on earth terrifying and horrible.

Instead, I reached down deep and pulled up every ounce of strength I had left and tried to channel Gran.

"It's going to be all right, my beautiful girl. They have rich, green fields of sweet clover in heaven, and angels will brush you and pet you and spoil you every day," I crooned as Angel tracked me with her eyes, her breathing harsh and rasping, but slowing with every beat. "Cherubs will bring you apples, and you will learn to love harp music, and one day I will join you and we will go on long rides through clouds so soft that your hooves will never be sore."

She shuddered once, her fallen body trembling with the force of it, and then my beautiful Heather's Angel died with her head in my lap.

CHAPTER 58
MICKEY

I woke up in a familiar place, and placed it immediately as Anna Mae's barn, although a strange smell that I didn't recognize was chokingly strong and somehow metallic. The back of my head throbbed so hard that the pain, combined with the smell, made me feel like I was going to throw up, but when I moved, I didn't get far.

I was tied to a post that somebody had driven into the dirt floor.

"Not so high and mighty now, are you?" Jeb spat in the dirt next to my foot.

I slitted my eyes against the early morning sun slanting in through the windows and made a croaking noise, which was all my dried-out throat could manage. "Where's Victoria? If you hurt her—"

"Oh, I hurt her, all right." He snickered, and my blood ran icy.

"You should have seen her crying and carrying on over that stupid horse. *Heather's Angel, Heather's Angel*. It was pathetic."

"I'm going to kill you. You're going to be so sorry you ever stepped foot on Whitfield property," I vowed, yanking at the ropes binding my wrists.

"Good luck with that."

He laughed and wandered off, leaving me alone with an uncontainable rage to match my uncontrollable headache. I thought I might have a concussion; it wouldn't be the first time I'd had one of those after tangling with my brothers. I planned to repay the favor in full. I went to work on the ropes, sending up fervent prayers to any angels who might be generous enough to listen to prayers from a Rhodale. Angels. *Angel.*

Please, let Victoria and her horse be all right.

After about twenty minutes, Ethan walked in, carrying a bottle of water, and he put it down next to me and then untied the rope, swearing under his breath the entire time.

"Sorry about that. Jeb's an idiot, and he gets carried away trying to be a hard-ass sometimes. What in the hell happened?"

"You don't know? You didn't plan this?"

He shook his head. "I didn't know anything about it. You saw what I'm dealing with out there with the Red Barons. Do you really think I'd lie to you about the Whitfields when I need you so much right now?"

I could tell he wasn't lying to me. Jeb had claimed he was acting on his own, or maybe this had been at Anna Mae's direction. Either way, somebody was going to pay for this. When he got the ropes off, I took a step and promptly fell down because my stiff muscles didn't want to work right.

"What time?" I managed, and he helped me up and handed me the water bottle.

"Morning. I had to meet . . . someone, or I would have been here to realize what was going on. I'll kick Jeb's ass for tying you up and leaving you all night. He was probably passed out in a corner, again."

"He was just here and left me like this," I said grimly. "He is going to be so very sorry."

"From you and me both," Ethan replied.

"Victoria?" I waited for his answer before drinking.

"She's fine. They didn't touch her," he said, his face darkening. "You were supposed to be leaving her alone, too, remember? She's not your girlfriend, you said. So why were you driving her home at midnight? If she'd been safely home in her virginal little bed, the two of you at least wouldn't have been here and maybe this wouldn't have escalated."

I drained the water bottle and then threw it on the floor. "You're blaming *her*? Are you freaking kidding me? For Jeb's crazy bullshit?"

"No, little brother," Ethan said flatly. "I'm blaming you."

CHAPTER 59

VICTORIA

When I woke up on the couch, the first thing I realized was that the night before had been neither a dream—the part with Mickey—nor a nightmare—the part with Angel.

My heart clenched with pain, but my eyes stayed dry. I was done with tears, maybe forever.

It was time for me to grow up and take charge of this situation before everything got worse . . . worse made me think about Mickey and the guy I'd seen hitting him, knocking him out.

Mickey.

"We have to call the sheriff," I shouted, and Gran, walking into the room with two coffee cups in her hands, froze.

"What now?"

"Mickey! They took him. Knocked him out and kidnapped him. I saw them carry him—"

"Victoria. You told us that last night. Don't you remember?"

I thought back, but the night had been a confusion of voices and questions and pain, all punctuated by the sound of the gunshot, Heather's Angel's scream, and the harsh blare of the sirens.

"No," I finally admitted. "I don't remember much after Angel . . ."

Gran's eyes brightened with tears she'd never shed in front of me. "I loved that horse too, honey. Doc took her. She'll take good care of her, you know that."

She would. We weren't able to bury our horses out in the fields anymore, the way they had in the old days. Now the vets had to take charge, but Dr. Arnold was one of the best Gran had ever known, and I'd seen for myself how careful she was with the mares and foals.

Now there'd be another urn to line the shelves in the racing barn.

I fought back the pain. For now, I needed to find out what had happened to Mickey.

Gran handed me a cup of coffee, full of cream and sugar the way I liked it, and she carefully lowered herself into her chair. I noticed that she was moving really slowly this morning, and I realized that all this drama and tragedy must be hardest on her.

"Are you okay? Gran, do you need to see the doctor?"

"I'm fine, young lady, other than understandably upset. Don't be putting me in the old folks' home just yet," she retorted, and, underneath her exhaustion and distress, I saw a glimmer of the tough woman who'd run this place on her own since my grandfather had died.

I wished I had a little of that toughness right about then. My hands were shaking so badly that I had to put the mug down on the coffee table.

"Gran, what if they hurt Mickey? Anybody who could shoot a horse like that . . ."

"I understand how you feel about Angel, sweetheart, but these are not horse people. They probably didn't care about shooting an animal, but that in no way leads to the conclusion that they'll harm Mickey, who is, more than likely, their brother."

I inhaled sharply as she put into words what I'd been thinking—during the short spurts of time when I'd been capable of rational thought—since I woke up.

"You think it was Ethan?"

"Who else? Him or that idiot brother Jeb of his. Didn't you see any of them well enough to identify them?"

"I wish I had, but it was too dark, and I was focused on Angel, and then they hit Mickey and took him. I didn't recognize the voice of the guy who threatened me—"

"He threatened you?" Her voice rose, and I hastened to reassure her.

"No, just to stay put, but he said . . ."

"He said what?"

"He said he'd shoot Mickey if I didn't listen."

I wondered how I'd be able to cope with this impossible situation. Mickey was gone, maybe hurt—or worse—and my skin still held the scent of him. I could still feel his touch. I hadn't even had a chance to live with and process what we'd shared when those criminals had shattered the night.

Now he might be lying dead? Shot? All because Anna Mae hated my father for picking another woman over her, or because sixty years ago two people had committed adultery, or because of who knew what else?

Like everything else related to the modern translation of the feud's bitter history, it was too big—too much—overwhelming me with the hopelessness of trying to fight it or end it, as if crushing reality had painted a stark modern caption on a very old, sepia-toned portrait:

Hopeless.

I clenched my hands into fists and forced them to stop shaking as I took long, slow breaths to calm down. Hyperventilating never solved anything, and I was damn sure not going to admit that fighting back was hopeless.

"Your parents will be back in less than an hour with Buddy and Pete," Gran said.

Then again, hyperventilating might be underrated.

"So we need to find Mickey now," I told her.

I found my phone and called him, not expecting him to answer and getting exactly what I expected. Then I called the sheriff's office.

"I need to talk to Sheriff Rhodale," I told the nasal-voiced person who answered.

"He's gone to pick up his son Mickey and take him out to break-fast," she said.

I had a second to think, good old small towns, telling the sheriff's business to any random person who calls, before the impact from her words really hit me.

"He's taking *Mickey* out to breakfast? You're sure it was Mickey, and not one of his other sons?"

"Well, I've worked here for eighteen years," she said, sounding annoyed. "I guess I know which Rhodale boy is which."

"Thank you. Thank you *so much*," I said.

I hung up and looked at Gran, a smile stretching my face. "He must be okay. His dad went to get him for breakfast."

"Thank God for answered prayers," she said, relaxing back into her chair. Her eyes drooped a little, and I realized she must be as tired as I was, or even more, since it didn't look like she'd slept at all.

We sat there in an exhausted silence and sipped coffee for a little while, and then Gran smiled at me. "I do have a little bit of good news to balance out all this bad. I talked to Melinda's doctor at that rehab this morning. He said she's doing really well, and she'll be allowed to call home Monday."

I groaned. "I'm glad she's doing well, but how are we going to talk to her? We have more to hide than we have to talk about."

"We'll find a way. She deserves that from us. We won't mention any of this, either. I don't want to cause her any setbacks."

"Of course we won't mention any of this but, speaking of Melinda, did you ever tell Mom and Dad that she'd gone to rehab?"

Gran looked nervous. "Not yet. I thought we'd tell them when they got back."

"Well. We're going to have a lot to talk about."

CHAPTER 60
MICKEY

Pa arrived at the compound hollering for me. He put his arm around me as he helped me up, and I was grateful because I was a little worried I'd fall down again. My legs were still stiff from spending the night tied up.

"Don't you ever hurt Mickey again," he told Ethan, who watched us both with hard eyes.

"It was Jeb this time, but go ahead and keep on jumping to conclusions. One of these days you're gonna fall and break your neck," Ethan said grimly. Ethan then walked over to one of the wooden crates, picked up a crowbar, and opened it. "While you're here, let's have a little show and tell."

Pa made a weird sound of disbelief, and I somewhat stiffly walked over so I could see. Rows of guns lay packed in straw, gleaming with the metallic sheen of the gun oil I'd been smelling all morning.

"Are you insane?" Pa snatched up one of the shotguns. "This is big time, Ethan. I can't protect you from this kind of heat."

"I don't need your protection," Ethan said, and his voice was flat and dead. "Thanks to dear old Mom, I've got a gang of the highest-quality skinheads backing me now. They've got access to massive labs, so I won't have to waste time and resources on the one- or two-person drug operations anymore, and we keep the toxic side effects mostly out of Kentucky altogether."

I stared at my half brother in disbelief. "Then what do they need you for?"

"Distribution. You should be happy, little brother. I don't need you to find me a ring of epi buyers now."

"You won't need much for very long, because you're going to be dead," Pa shouted. "Have you ever read a newspaper or watched the news? Don't you know how this kind of thing ends up? You get crushed under the boot of your so-called business partner, and then they betray you and kill you. There's no honor among meth-dealing gangbangers."

"No, I'll get rich and out from under the thumb of my bitch of a mother," Ethan said, shoving his too-long hair out of his face in a gesture that reminded me painfully of when we'd been kids together, playing ball in the hot sun. How could the big brother who'd taught me how to throw a curve ball have turned out like this?

How could he have gotten me mixed up in the very heart of it?

"You leave Mickey and those Whitfields alone," Pa warned him, but his warnings rarely carried any bite when it came to Ethan, so we both ignored our father and stared at each other, instead.

I started toward Ethan, but my legs cramped and I staggered. I threw my hands in the air instead. "Why? Why do you even need me? There are no shortage of idiots who will be happy to be part of your gang."

For a second, something dark flashed across Ethan's face, and he looked almost trapped. Almost scared. But it was gone so fast I convinced myself I hadn't seen it.

"I need you because you're *not* an idiot. You met Baron. I can't guarantee I'll come out on top without help. I need family I can trust. Jeb is a buffoon."

Ethan walked over to a cabinet and pulled out another bottle of water and tossed it to me. I drained the entire thing and immediately felt a little better.

"It's an easy choice. You hold up your end of the deal, and you agree to stay away from Victoria Whitfield—and you mean it this time—and you get rich. Plus, I can guarantee that Jeb and Anna Mae stay away from her and her family," Ethan said, staring at me speculatively.

"Why would I trust you on that? Where the hell were you last night?"

"I didn't know about last night," Ethan said, his voice troubled. "But you can trust me this time. I have something on Anna Mae that she really, *really* doesn't want to get out. Plus this new gang—she made a mistake there. They don't negotiate with women. I'll be taking lead on this new deal."

A goose walked over my grave at the casual way he mentioned blackmailing his own mother. His own crazycakes, criminal mastermind, psychopath of a mother. On the other hand, I didn't mind the blackmail at all.

"What does he mean about Victoria? About you meaning it this time?" Pa asked me, but I ignored him again, my gaze trained on Ethan.

"I need your help, and you know why," Ethan told me. "Or you can continue to be stubborn, we'll drive the Whitfields out of their own damn county, and I won't necessarily be able to protect Caro, the girls, or Pa."

Pa's face turned pale, and I saw a muscle in Ethan's jaw jump.

"What do you mean, protect Pa?"

"Forget that, what did you mean about Caro and the girls?" my father said.

Ethan explained, and I thought my dad would stroke out.

"She'll have police protection, too. You need to fix this, yesterday, Ethan."

"I'm doing the best I can, Pa," Ethan said tiredly. "Now listen to me. The Red Barons. They like to come in strong by taking out the local sheriff first. They say it makes everybody else more willing to deal with them."

"Take him out?" I had to ask, even though I was sure I knew the answer.

"Kill him, Mickey. They're going to kill Pa unless I make a very strong case for them not to do it," Ethan said slowly, and this time there was no mistaking the pain in his face. Ethan might not think much of Pa, but he was his father, no matter the distance and difficulties that lay between them these days.

There was a pause, a beat that hammered in my head like a drum. Then I heard myself answer as if from very far away. "I'll work for you, Ethan. I already said I would, and I will. I'll work for you, and I'll stay away from Victoria. We'll find a way to protect Caro and the girls, and Pa, and we'll make sure everybody also leaves Victoria and her family alone."

"She's too good for us, anyway, Mickey," Ethan said quietly. "The farther away Victoria stays from Rhodales, the better off she'll be."

He smiled a little, and I knew he was right, but the bleakness of my future without her unspooled in my head, and I'd never wished so hard that my name wasn't Rhodale.

I didn't let any of that show on my face. "When do I start?"

CHAPTER 61
VICTORIA

"Vivi!" Buddy's voice rang out with so much enthusiasm it made me smile in spite of the decorated white cast that sheathed his leg from knee to ankle.

I hugged him, burying my face in his soft hair for a moment, and helped him out of the car and into the wheelchair while Mom and Dad climbed out of the car and stretched.

"Isn't it cool? The nurses signed it and Mom even bought me my own package of markers, so I can get everybody at school to sign! Do you think Mrs. Rhodale will sign it? I have purple. It's her favorite color, she told us."

He chattered on, and I tried to ignore the spike of pain that Mickey's mom's name caused me. I turned his chair around so he could see the newly renovated front of the house.

"We have a ramp to the porch!"

"Yes, we do, and there will be no wheelies or other stunts on it, young man," Gran said, pretending to be stern before a huge smile spread all over her face and she bent down for her share of Buddy hugs.

We got Buddy installed with the TV remote, his game system, and his books on the couch in the parlor, which was going to be his bedroom until the cast came off and he could go upstairs again, and then I followed Gran to the kitchen, where Dad and Mom were sitting down having glasses of iced tea.

"That drive feels longer every time," Dad said an uncharacteristic slump to his shoulders.

"Well, it's been a pretty horrible week," Gran said, patting his shoulder.

It struck me as if it were a new realization that she was his mother, after all, and so she had to love him, even when he was being a jerk.

Dad looked around suddenly. "Where's Melinda? I would have thought she'd be here to welcome Buddy back."

Gran and I exchanged a glance. I started to tell them, but she shook her head.

"This one is for me to do, honey."

"What is for you to do?" Mom shot a suspicious look at me, but I just shrugged. Gran *wanted* to tell it, so I didn't feel like a coward for throwing her under the bus.

"I took Melinda to rehab. It's a perfectly nice place, one of the top facilities around, and she wanted to do it, which is the first step in recovery. She won't be home for at least ninety days, and she can't talk to you on the phone or e-mail just yet, so don't even try."

Gran delivered all this in almost a belligerent tone, her shoulders squared and her chin thrust forward, but in the end none of our prepared arguments were necessary. Dad simply nodded, rubbing his forehead. His eyes were suspiciously shiny.

Mom, on the other hand, was more dramatic.

"Oh, thank God," she said, sighing. I nearly fell over.

"What? You . . . I mean, I'm glad you agree, but you were always blocking me on this," I said, bewildered.

Mom tossed her head, briefly reminding me of one of the horses. "I just can't deal with her drama right now, Victoria."

With that, she sailed out of the room, leaving me and Gran to stare at each other in disbelief.

"You know, Victoria, the universe can only revolve around one fixed point at a time, and with your mother it's always going to be her," my dad said ruefully. He drained his iced tea glass. "I'm going to go see if Buddy wants to challenge me to a game so he can demolish me in five minutes, and then I might take a nap."

After he left the room, Gran and I just sat there and stared at each other.

"Do you think they put something in the water at the hospital? Some kind of nice pill?"

Gran wagged her finger at me. "Remember, that's my son you're talking about."

Then she glanced at the doorway he'd just walked through. "I wouldn't rule it out, though."

I spent the rest of the weekend with Buddy, playing games and watching movies, fetching snacks, and helping him learn how to walk on crutches without destroying everything in the house. We had to break the news of Angel's death, and he took it very hard, but we simply told him she'd gone to horse heaven, leaving out any mention of the violent way she'd died.

Gran told my parents what had really happened, though, but whatever fury Dad felt over the situation mostly played itself out in his conversations with the sheriff's department and the insurance adjustors. At least he left me alone, and that's really all I wanted from him right now.

But every second of every minute of every day, the lack of any communication from Mickey weighed on me. I finally called the sheriff's office again, and they told me he was home safe, so on the one hand I could relax, and on the other hand I was forced to realize that he must be deliberately avoiding me.

What I couldn't figure out was why.

He *loved* me. He'd said it straight out. I kept reminding myself of this every time I felt like my heart was about to shatter into Mickey-shaped fragments. The horse I'd loved and grown up with was dead, probably because of this stupid feud, and yet Mickey couldn't even bother to call me to see if I was all right.

I kept trying to forget everything I'd heard about boys who said "I love you" to get sex and then dropped the girl like a hot potato—or damaged goods.

Damaged. *Yes*.

I was certainly damaged, but Mickey wasn't like that. I knew better. He was a good person, trapped in the unhappy expectations of Rhodale evil. I wouldn't add insult to injury by thinking the worst of him, too. I was the one who'd initiated the lovemaking, anyway. I'd still believe in him until he proved me wrong.

Even though he never called.

✶ ✶ ✶

Monday morning, when I pulled into the school parking lot, everybody was staring at me. Again. These people must not have had much in the way of lives before my family came back into town and provided almost daily entertainment. I climbed out of the truck and ran the gauntlet of curious stares and speculative whispers, almost wishing somebody would just ask me outright and get it over with.

When I got to my locker, Mickey was leaning against it. I forgot that I was angry with him and drank in the sight of his long, lean, *uninjured* body and his gorgeous, *uninjured* face.

"You're safe," I said, barely able to resist the urge to throw my arms around him right there in the hallway. "I was so worried. Why didn't you call?"

His eyes blazed with emotion, but he quickly shuttered it, so that within seconds the only clue I had that he was feeling anything at all was the muscle that jerked as he clenched his jaw shut.

Mickey looked around at the audience staring avidly at us. His upper lip lifted for a second, baring his teeth, and then he hardened his face into a contemptuous expression that shocked me because of how much it made him look like Ethan.

"I had things to do, babe. More important things than listening to you whine about a dead horse," he said loudly, as if he wanted everybody to hear him. "Maybe if you weren't such a spoiled rich princess, you might realize that the rest of us have real lives. Like all those kids your dad put in the poorhouse by firing their parents."

His words rocked me back on my heels, and pain swamped me, crushing the air from my lungs. "How—but—why?"

"Don't be pathetic, Victoria. Let's spare everybody the memory of that," he said, and the cruelty of it dug into me like that bullet had into Pete.

I couldn't think; I couldn't process this. Every instinct I had was screaming at me to run. Just *run*. Get away from this monster who was wearing Mickey's face to torture me. But I had to slow down. Think. This wasn't right.

Slowly, I shook my head. *No*. It didn't make sense. Mickey wouldn't say these things to me. Not my Mickey. Not the boy who'd touched me with so much love and caring only two days before. I opened my mouth, trying to form words, but he started laughing.

"Nothing to say? Admitting I'm right? Look, we're on opposite sides of the game, here. Rhodale and Whitfield, and never the two shall hook up, right? See ya."

"Mickey!" I caught his arm before he could leave. "What are you doing? What happened to you this weekend?"

I could feel the anguish clogging my throat, but I fought it back. I didn't understand what was happening, but there was no way I was going to break down in the middle of the hallway at school.

He yanked his arm away and laughed nastily. "Why is it always the innocent-looking ones who can't get enough of the bad boys? Sorry, babe. Just because I kissed you once doesn't mean you own me. Good thing I never got your panties off, isn't it?"

A few of the guys lurking around started laughing, elbowing each other. "Struck out, huh, Mick?"

He shrugged, but his eyes were hard. "You win some, you lose some."

"Mickey, what is going on?" I was whispering by then, afraid if I spoke too loudly I'd shake apart from the force of the pain reverberating through me.

He closed his eyes for a second, but then turned away from me and called out to a girl who'd been walking by.

"Hey, looking good. What are you up to after school?"

When she giggled and he strode off down the hall after her, my knees buckled and I fell back against my locker.

No.

What?

How could I have been so wrong about him?

Denise came running up, looking angry and concerned and so, so sorry. She'd clearly seen the whole thing.

"Help me? I have to go home," I whispered.

She nodded and helped me back out to my car, but the caustic whispers and mocking voices branded my skin like a lash all the way down the hall.

"She thought she could catch Mickey Rhodale?"

"Serves her right, after what her asshole dad did."

"Wow. He smoked her."

"Think he tapped that?"

"Nah, he even admitted he didn't. Ice princess Whitfield."

I stumbled again, but tried to cling to that small bit of comfort. Mickey had made a point to deny having sex with me, so at least that part of our relationship wouldn't be open to gossip and scrutiny and mocking speculation.

At least he'd left me with that much.

"Shut up, assholes," Denise said angrily as we walked out the door. A few people even looked ashamed of themselves and shut up, but most of them just laughed at her. Or at me.

I suddenly, viciously wished that a meteorite would fall on the school and smash it into nothingness, but I was having a hard time breathing, so I didn't say it out loud.

"He's a vile rat bastard who could never deserve you," Denise said as soon as we walked out the front door. "I hope he sleeps with some hooker and gets an STD that rots off his dick."

I stumbled and looked at her mutely as the blood rushed out of my face. He'd sleep with other girls now.

I was nothing to him.

CHAPTER 62

MICKEY

After I ripped Victoria's heart out of her chest in the middle of the fucking school hallway, I walked slowly and steadily to the gym, where I slammed my fists into the punching bag, over and over again, until my knuckles bled giant red blotches on the gray fabric of the bag.

It took Coach and three other guys to pull me away.

Then I went after *them*.

Principal Scott suspended me again, this time for a week. All the better to get going on my new drug and guns business. After all, I'd accomplished the one thing I'd come to school for today. I'd destroyed the only girl I'd ever loved, and done it so thoroughly that she'd never want anything to do with me again.

She'd be safe. From Anna Mae's plots and, especially, from Baron and his gang of pure evil.

About this one thing, Ethan was right. I didn't deserve her. I froze in the middle of starting up my bike. He hadn't said she was too good for *me*, actually. He'd said, "She's too good for *us*."

What the hell had he meant by *that*?

I decided it didn't matter, because none of it mattered anymore. I was a criminal now. I headed for home to get cleaned up. Had to look my best, in case today was the day I had to deal with any more of the criminals who had stolen my future.

But first, I was going to go see my sister. Verify for myself that she was fine and the girls were fine and she was being guarded. That was the only thing left to me now that my future had gone up in an explosion every bit as powerful as the one that had destroyed that meth trailer. I could—and *would*—take care of the people I loved.

Even if they didn't know it.

I idled the bike on the street in front of the Laundromat and fought the bile rising up in my throat at the sight of Baron's henchman—the big guy—leaning against a corner of the front wall of the building. He looked up from the knife he'd been using to trim his fingernails for just long enough to give me a one-finger salute.

I kicked the bike back into gear and took off. I had no choice but to work with Ethan. Baron hadn't been bluffing when he'd threatened my sister. I thought back to the look in his flat, dead eyes and I shuddered, ice spiking through me.

I suddenly got the feeling that Baron *never* bluffed. We were dead meat.

CHAPTER 63
VICTORIA

It took me more than an hour to make the fifteen-minute drive to my house, because I kept having to pull over when I quit remembering how to breathe. Denise had wanted to drive me, but I didn't want her to get in trouble for ditching school again just to help me.

I hoped desperately not to have to run the gauntlet of disapproving stares at home for my now world-class truancy, but I thought I might be safe. My parents had planned to be gone to a meeting in town all morning, and Buddy was at school. He'd been very excited about having everyone sign his cast.

I so very much wanted to be nine again. Nobody made casts for broken hearts.

I was in shock—shaking so hard from the pain of Mickey's terrible, terrible words that my teeth were literally chattering. I could feel myself sinking into the same black hole I'd fallen into after I watched Angel die.

How much could the human body take before it shut down? I almost wished, for the first time in my life, that I was the kind of person who could escape into alcohol, just for long enough to numb the pain, but then I thought about Melinda, and my dad, and his dad before him.

Maybe not.

After I made it to my driveway, it took almost ten long minutes for me to work up the energy and the nerve to leave the sanctuary of my truck and go into the house. I didn't even see Gran sitting on the porch until she called my name. I dropped my backpack and walked over to her on shaky legs; my will to put one foot after the other was the only thing that kept me moving forward and not succumbing to gravity's pull and slumping to the ground.

I'd thought the expression was overly melodramatic before: "a broken heart." But now that mine was, I realized it was an understatement. My heart wasn't broken at all.

Mickey had shattered it.

Gran looked a question at me, and I knew she was wondering why I was home from school barely more than an hour after I'd left home.

"Mickey," I whispered.

"Tell me," she said simply.

So I did. I had no pride left.

I told her about our dates, about our time together, although of course not about making love to Mickey—some things were not for a grandmother's ears—and about the things he'd said to me, both on Friday and today.

"How could he do that to me? How could I be such a bad judge of character?" I lifted my face to the cool breeze, wishing for a miracle—that the cool air would calm my emotions as well as my skin.

"Maybe you're not," Gran said, pushing the swing a little.

"What do you mean?"

"I met that boy, too, and I saw the way he was with you, Victoria. If he was lying to you with not just words, but even with his facial expressions and body language, then he deserves an Academy Award."

I attempted a smile that was a grisly failure, judging by the way Gran flinched, so I patted her arm instead.

"I love you for it, Gran, but you're wrong. If he cared about me even a tiny bit, he never could have destroyed me like that."

Buddy wasn't having the easiest time with his new crutches. With the resilience of youth, he'd recovered his spirits and energy after a broken leg far more easily than I would ever recover from a broken heart, but carrying his backpack and hobbling around without falling wasn't working out all that great. I was helping Mom walk him to his classroom today, but when I caught sight of Mrs. Rhodale I literally could not force myself to take one more step in her direction.

I mumbled an excuse and ran out of the school, and then I walked the two miles to Clark High just so I could avoid any of Mom's annoying and occasionally insightful questions. When I reached the school parking lot, the first thing I saw was Mickey's bike, flashing silver in the morning sun, so I turned around and walked to a secluded area of the Clark Municipal Park and sat there, unmoving, all day long.

I wasn't a coward. I'd face him the next time.

In another few days, Pete was ready to come home from the hospital, and Gran and Mrs. Kennedy and I set up his place with groceries, fresh flowers, and balloons. He lived in the biggest cottage on the ranch, and the cleaning team had been in the day before, so it was sparkling clean. I hadn't been in his place in years, since Dad had told me that Whitfields didn't "fraternize with the help," so I was surprised and touched to see that he had a picture of me and Mel as kids, both of us up on Angel's back, on his refrigerator.

We welcomed him home with much fuss and a few tears, and eventually he threw everybody out so he could "get some rest." Knowing Pete, that meant he'd spend three hours catching up on all of Gus's notes on the foaling mares.

I took a few extra minutes to clear up the plates from the welcome home cake, but when I turned to leave, Pete stopped me with a hand on my shoulder.

"I'm so sorry about Angel, honey."

I swallowed, hard. "I know. Me, too. The sheriff still doesn't know who it was or what they wanted. They didn't take anything."

"Well, you better believe we're going to have better security around here from now on."

I just nodded. Saying "too little, too late" would have hurt both of us.

"I know what happened," he said

I froze. I wasn't sure which "what" he was talking about.

"I want you to know that I don't believe Mickey had anything to do with me getting shot," he said, his face grim. "I know what it's like to be blamed for something your family does, and it's not right. I sure wouldn't have been the one to cast stones at Mickey Rhodale."

That caught my attention. He never talked about his past. "What do you mean?"

His eyes narrowed as if he were glancing back at some long-buried memory. "Nothing you and I will ever discuss. I just wanted you to know that loyalty to me shouldn't interfere with your, ah, life. I got the feeling there was something between the two of you."

I shrugged, trying to appear nonchalant, but Mickey's voice rang in my memory: "Don't be pathetic, Victoria."

"No. He . . . he decided we weren't . . . I wasn't worth his time," I said, swallowing hard to get the words past the lump in my throat.

"Well, one of you is a damn fool, and I'm not sure which," he snapped, shocking me. "I saw the way he looked at you. The way he kept up the search for Buddy even after he cracked his head on that rock. Maybe he's not what everybody thinks. He could never deserve you, that's for damn sure, but that doesn't mean he can't try to live up to becoming what you need."

"What are you talking about?" I had to clutch the countertop for support, because the planet had clearly flipped sideways. *Pete* was talking about *feelings*.

"Boy reminds me of me, that's all," he said gruffly. "Now get out of here. I'm in pain. I'm an invalid, don't you know?"

"Invalid, my butt," I said, and then I stood on tiptoes and kissed his cheek because a huge light bulb had just gone off in my head, and it had the word "epiphany" written all over it.

I ran out of the cottage and headed straight for my truck. The ravaging mass of pain inside me was taking a halting step toward hope.

I almost fought it, because hope meant the possibility of new pain, but it refused to be denied. The thing with feathers, indeed. Maybe Emily Dickinson had gotten it right in her poem all those years ago.

I texted Mickey before I started the truck.

I know why you did what you did. Meet me. Our place. 20 minutes.

So now we'd see.

CHAPTER 64

MICKEY

When Victoria's text came through, I was idling at a stop sign. I took off and threw a U-turn so hard that I nearly rolled my bike. What the *hell* was she up to now? She was going to get herself hurt, or killed, and I only knew so many ways to try to drive her away. I'd crushed her once already, and I didn't know how I'd ever find the strength to do it again.

I rode up to Lonesome Ridge as fast as I dared to go, hoping against hope that she wouldn't really be there.

Hoping against hope that she *would* be there.

When I rounded that last curve and saw her truck, my entire body breathed a sigh of relief completely against my will, as if to say, *Yes. Now the world is right again.*

Now I just had to keep her from seeing any of that on my face.

I parked the bike, threw off my helmet, and stalked over to her.

"What the fuck does it take to get rid of you?" I was deliberately crude, hoping she'd get disgusted and run far away from me, to someplace safe from Baron. Far from Ethan, Anna Mae, and all the rest of the Rhodales. Especially me.

Her face flushed a hot rose pink, but she lifted her chin and stood her ground. "Simple. Convince me you don't love me."

I stumbled to a stop and stared down at her. *Simple*.

Right.

"Well? Make me believe that you don't love me, that you're not trying to push me away to protect me from the feud and your family."

I thought of how much I wanted her, and then I forced myself to think of the cold, dead look in Baron's eyes.

"You're being pathetic again," I said, sneering down at her. I strode off, back to my bike, clenching my hands into fists in front of me to keep them from reaching for her.

"You're a coward," she called after me, and I stopped walking, but I didn't turn around.

I *was* a coward, but I wasn't afraid for myself. I was afraid for *her*. After seeing Baron's thug at Caro's place—yeah. I was glad to admit to cowardice if it kept Victoria safe.

But she didn't give up. She ran across the ground and circled me until she was facing me again. There were tears in her eyes, but she hadn't let any fall.

"You didn't say it. You *can't* say it. But if you really want me to leave you alone, forever, then it's simple enough, Mickey. Just tell me that you don't love me."

Her bottom lip was trembling, a dead giveaway that she was terrified, and I admired her even more for taking this stand. She had so much pure, shining courage that she almost blinded me, but she was afraid I would hurt her again. The cold, ruthless part of me that had grown stronger over the past week told me I could take advantage of that. Take advantage of *her*.

Keep her safe.

"I don't want anything to do with you," I said roughly. I tried to go around her, but she caught my arm.

"You're trying to protect me from your brother, I know it," she said brokenly. "We can figure this out together. You don't have to do it alone."

I shut my eyes and wished desperately for a way to make her understand.

She sighed. "Ethan—"

My self-control snapped. "It's not Ethan, okay? It's somebody so much worse than Ethan, and I can't take it if he hurts you, Victoria. Not that. Not ever."

"We can face this together—"

"No."

"Fine," she snapped, her own temper flaring. "Just do it, then. Tell me you don't love me, and I'll never bother you again."

I stood there, staring at her, for a very long time, while my brain shouted at me to say the words. Once and for all to be done with her.

Except I couldn't. My heart wouldn't let me.

"I don't know how to do that," I said slowly. "Because it's not true."

She froze, and then she leapt across the space between us and threw herself into my arms, and I kissed her until neither one of us could breathe.

CHAPTER 65

VICTORIA

"I knew it. I *knew* it," I said, holding him so tight that he couldn't let me go again. Never again.

He kissed me; hungry, desperate kisses that told me how much it had hurt him to put on that act at school.

"Don't *ever* do that to me again," I ordered him, and then I punched him in the shoulder. Hard.

"I won't. I swear it. I don't deserve for you to forgive me. I don't deserve *you*."

"That's not you talking. That's Ethan, or Anna Mae, or any of the idiots around here who judge you for being a Rhodale," I said firmly. "We deserve each other, and we can't let them tear us apart."

Mickey kissed me again, a deep, claiming kind of kiss, and I was dizzy by the time he stopped, but his smile at my dazed expression faded quickly. "If we do this—"

"We're doing this."

He nodded. "Okay. We're doing this. But there's a lot I need to tell you, and we're going to have to play by new rules."

We went to sit in the truck, and he told me about Baron.

"Mickey, no! You can't—"

"I have no choice," he said bleakly. "They'll hurt Caroline and the girls. Or they'll kill my dad, just to make a statement."

"You have to move. Take your whole family and go into witness protection or something." The thought of losing him again when I'd just found him was almost too painful to contemplate, but compared to the danger he was in? There was no choice at all.

"That only works in the movies. We don't have any information to offer. And we can't move on our own, because my parents are upside down in the mortgage since the housing market crash. Sheriffs and teachers don't make a lot of money."

He took my hand and put it on his cheek, and then closed his eyes. "I only see one way out of this, for now, and that's doing what Ethan wants. Baron and his gang of criminals can never, ever find out about you. So we have to be icy, distant, and even enemies in public."

"But only in public," I said, putting my arms around his neck. "And only until we can figure out a way to escape."

"I love you, Victoria." He looked into my heart with his achingly blue eyes. "I'm so sorry I hurt you. I couldn't think of another way to keep you safe."

I flinched a little at the remembered pain, but then I nodded. "I understand and I forgive you, but never, ever do that again. I don't think I could survive it."

"I promise."

He kissed me again. "What are we going to do now?"

I took a deep breath and finally dared to say the words that I'd been afraid to let him hear, afraid that he'd have too much power over me if he knew—afraid that the universe would play its merciless games with me if I let the secret out.

"I love you."

He kissed me and then he cupped my face in his hands and looked intently into my eyes. "Say it again," he demanded.

"I love you. I don't know how I know, or when I figured it out, or how I even understand such a huge emotion, but I love you! I love you, Mickey Rhodale, and we're going to find a way to be together."

"Tell me again. One more time," he murmured against my lips.

"I love you," I whispered.

He smiled at me, and it was like the sun breaking through the clouds on Derby morning.

"I love you, too."

He kissed me again, and I kissed him, and we kissed each other, and then the fear and anguish and relief and love we'd roller-coastered through for so long took over, and both of us needed to be closer and even closer to each other. When we made love, it was like coming home to the place I'd always dreamed of being; there was such tenderness between us that it soothed and healed the jagged, broken pieces of my heart.

Afterward, we got dressed, and then I sat wrapped in his arms on our mountain for the next couple of hours, deciding what we'd do next. Knowing that whatever we decided to do, we'd do it together. In the distance, the blue Kentucky hills stood silent sentinel, guarding and surrounding us as if reminding us that history and tradition could be built from love and family instead of violence and hatred.

"I love you, Victoria Whitfield." He took my hand and kissed my fingers, one by one.

"I love you, Mickey Rhodale."

A Rhodale and a Whitfield, together. Maybe the future didn't have to carry the weight of the past, after all. Blood might be thicker than water, but love was the most powerful magic of all.

EPILOGUE
MICKEY
Two weeks later

I looked up from my menu, wondering why nothing ever looked good when Victoria wasn't there to share it with me. But it wasn't Nora. A man I didn't recognize, wearing a dark blue suit, stood next to my table at the diner with Mr. Judson.

"Mick, this gentleman would like to have a word with you."

I nodded slowly, and the man sat down across from me.

"I won't stay, because I don't want to compromise you, but this place is quiet enough and far enough off the beaten path that we'll be okay," he said. "My partner is outside, and he'll let me know if that changes."

"Compromise me?" I suddenly had a bad feeling in my gut.

"I'm Agent Vane, from the FBI. We have reason to believe that you might know a little bit about a gang that calls itself the Red Barons, and specifically about this man."

He put a glossy eight-by-ten of Baron on the table between us.

"I'm hoping we might be able to help each other out."

I looked at the picture and then up at Agent Vane, and then, for the first time since Ethan had gotten me into this mess, I smiled.

"What exactly do you want to know?"

ACKNOWLEDGMENTS

There isn't enough paper in the world for this, so I'm going to keep it short and save trees.

First, I have to thank my amazing agent, Jim McCarthy, who is always calm when I need him to be but saves me with his wicked sense of humor the rest of the time. Thanks for being my person.

Next, a huge thanks to the unbelievably talented team at Razorbill, who believed in me and the book (the series!) all the way, even when I took crazy left turns. Ben Schrank for his vision, Laura Arnold for her amazing editorial eye, Rebecca Kilman for brilliant editorial insights and brainstorming and for saying "I love your twisty mind!" Also to Tara Fowler and Elyse Marshall for spreading the word to the world, Emily Osborne for the beautiful cover, and Erin Gallagher, Vivian Kirklin, and all of the Razorbill staff for working so very hard for me.

Also, thank you to my amazing friends. A writer's life is so isolating, and without you, I'd be huddled in the corner watching reality TV. Cindy, Marianne, Eileen, my Flamingos, all of the amazing people on my teenlitauthors group at Yahoo, and my new gang at the Indie Circle. I appreciate the encouragement and advice more than you know. I will bake you all cookies when I'm off deadline!

Thanks to my brother Jerry Holliday, who never even twitches when I call and say, "What kind of gun would a meth dealer carry?" (Because he knows guns, not drugs, I hasten to point out.)

Most of all, thank you to my family. Connor, you are a rock star (or maybe a ninja)! Thanks for the sixteen-year-old-boy perspective. Lauren, my artist, thank you for giggles and hugs and insights. Judd, thanks for love, adventure, crazy laughter, and going along with adopting all those rescue dogs. I couldn't do any of this without the three of you. (Well, maybe the dog part. But walks would be hard. I get tangled in all those leashes. . . .)